PRAISE FOR *THE ALLSPICE BATH*:

"This lovely story will have you empathize and root for Adele, a young woman caught in the cultural crosshairs of her parents' native country and their adopted land, who learns to listen closely and hear the strains of her brave new voice. "
—Shilpi Somaya Gowda, author of *The Golden Son*

"Sonia Saikaley's *The Allspice Bath* is a deeply-moving portrayal of family life and an intimate exploration of the ties that bind. From the first chapter, we are drawn into the vibrant lives of the Azar family, particularly the Azar sisters, first-generation Lebanese-Canadians who have a foot in the culture of their birth and another in that of their parents'. The result is at times a precarious balancing act, brought to life with compassion and realism through Adele, our counter-culture, free-thinking protagonist. Saikaley shows with vivid, and at times heart-breaking prose, what it takes for a young, modern woman to breakaway from tradition in pursuit of her own dreams. This book will resonate strongly with any reader who has felt torn by living between two worlds, made sacrifices to pursue a dream, or faced the hard truth that it is often the ones who love us the most that hurt us the deepest. But as Saikaley demonstrates with enviable pathos, when it comes to family, where there is love, forgiveness is always possible."
—Anita Kushwaha, author of *Side by Side*

"The title of Sonia Saikaley's coming-of-age novel, *The Allspice Bath*, beautifully expresses the dilemma faced by its gutsy main character, Adele Azar: whether to conform to the strict expectations and traditions of her Lebanese immigrant family—literally, to sink into a

bath of the spice most often used in Lebanese cooking—or to dare to rebel and live her life, her way. For Adele, there are no easy answers to the questions: who am I and who do I want to be? Growing up in Ottawa in the 1970s and 1980s as the youngest of the four daughters, she is constantly torn between whether to be a 'good Lebanese girl' or a 'real' Canadian—a struggle that begins with her mother's first words to her, 'You should've been born a boy.' Adele chafes under the limitations placed on her by her family, resents the way her sisters bow to the wills of their father, boyfriends and husbands, and secretly longs to be the daughter of a kindly Anglo-Canadian woman living next door. But she is also unable to stop herself from seeking her father's love and approval. When a medical crisis leaves young Adele 'unfit' for marriage, her father devises a surprising solution that takes the family back to the Old Country, a trip that will have repercussions on Adele's adult life. Honest, unflinching and unsentimental, the story of Adele's journey to womanhood, her self-transformation from resentful daughter to independent artist, from rejection of her family to reconciliation with them, captures the emotional complexities faced by many first-generation daughters of immigrant families."
—Terri Favro, author of *Once Upon a Time in West Toronto*

"Sonia Saikaley's *The Allspice Bath* exudes authenticity and sensibility. It is a brilliantly told tale of a turbulent father-daughter relationship set against the Lebanese immigrant experience in Canada."
—Ian Thomas Shaw, author of *Quill of the Dove*

"Caught between her Lebanese family traditions and her Canadian upbringing, Adele continuously challenges the rigorous boundaries that are drawn by her unyielding father, Youssef, and his cultural beliefs. Her journey towards independence is wrought with unexpected obstacles that only reinforce her resilience. Saikaley skillfully presents complex and passionate characters who embody the conflicting perspectives of two generations of immigrants desperately trying to find themselves as they negotiate their positions between the old country and the new one. The story exquisitely interweaves the heart-warming images of family, home, and belonging with the

inescapable sense of solitude that accompanies uprootedness and displacement. Through this unflinchingly honest novel the author presents an essential, timely, and highly misunderstood, perspective of being an Arab Canadian."
—Lamees Al Ethari, author of *From the Wounded Banks of the Tigris*

"With grace, precision, and honesty, Sonia Saikaley opens a door to reveal the inner workings of families that are both shaped and disrupted by immigration's clash of cultures."
—Dimitri Nasrallah, author of *The Bleeds* and *Niko*

"The turning point for this bildungsroman happens in Lebanon, when Saikaley balances betrayal with descriptions of olive trees, dust, and messy stone walls. To grow, to survive, Adele must rebel against her family's expectations, shifting between her two identities until she finds her way and by doing so changes her family."
—Debra Martens, *Canadian Writers Abroad*

The Allspice Bath

a novel

Sonia Saikaley

Inanna poetry & fiction series

INANNA PUBLICATIONS AND EDUCATION INC.
TORONTO, CANADA

We gratefully acknowledge the support of the Canada Council for the Arts and the Ontario Arts Council for our publishing program. We also acknowledge the financial support of the Government of Canada through the Canada Book Fund.

The Allspice Bath is a work of fiction. All the characters and situations portrayed in this book are fictitious and any resemblance to persons living or dead is purely coincidental.

Cover design: Val Fullard

Library and Archives Canada Cataloguing in Publication

Title: The allspice bath : a novel / Sonia Saikaley.
Names: Saikaley, Sonia, author.
Series: Inanna poetry & fiction series.
Description: Series statement: Inanna poetry & fiction series
Identifiers: Canadiana (print) 20190094559 | Canadiana (ebook) 20190094575 | ISBN 9781771336178
   (softcover) | ISBN 9781771336185 (epub) | ISBN 9781771336192 (Kindle) | ISBN 9781771336208 (pdf)
Classification: LCC PS8637.A4495 A75 2019 | DDC C813/.6—dc23

Printed and bound in Canada

Inanna Publications and Education Inc.
210 Founders College, York University
4700 Keele Street, Toronto, Ontario, Canada M3J 1P3
Telephone: (416) 736-5356 Fax: (416) 736-5765
Email: inanna.publications@inanna.ca   Website: www.inanna.ca

MIX
Paper from
responsible sources
FSC   FSC® C004071
www.fsc.org

For Babba, whose presence I deeply miss.

PROLOGUE: 1970

"YOU SHOULD'VE BEEN BORN A BOY," Samira Azar whispered to the baby in the small cart next to her bed. The hospital room was stark, and the shuttered windows didn't stop the cold air from coming in. Samira's body ached. She was still unable to get up and hold the child she had given birth to a few hours ago. Instead she glanced at the infant, listened to her gurgle, and watched the saliva gently sloping down her chin. She then turned her attention away from her child to the incision along her belly, hidden under the pale blue hospital gown and sterile blankets. "If you had only been a boy," Samira repeated, her voice cracking. She knew the entire community would be talking, spreading the word that she had had another girl. "Poor Youssef. Four daughters and no son to continue his family name. What a shame!"

Samira turned her head towards the wall, buried her face in her hands, and wept. Hours earlier, she had learned that she'd never have another child. The chances of providing a son to her husband were dashed when the surgeon cut out her womb, afraid the tumour he had found was cancerous. The infant opened and closed her mouth. Then imitating her mother's whimpers, she wailed, her cries filling the room and echoing down the corridor of the maternity ward. Samira dropped her hands and patted her pillowcase, searching for the tiny rod. She pressed and pressed the button until a heavy-set nurse trudged into the room, panting and out of breath.

"Yes? What do you want?"

Samira flinched as if the words had tightened the stitches on her abdomen. She wiped her face. "Take ... you take..." she said, searching her limited vocabulary.

"Come on. I haven't got all day," the nurse said, crossing her arms over her hefty chest. "Speak up."

She pointed at the baby. "Take her. I no want see anymore."

"But she's only crying because she's hungry. Don't you want to feed her?"

"No, you take away. You feed her. I can't," Samira mumbled, rolling her head to the side. She stared vacantly out the window. It was the beginning of April but the towering evergreens were still thick with snow.

The nurse shook her head and walked over to the baby, who was wrapped in a cherry blanket. A pink ribbon was tied in the child's soft brown hair. The infant continued to cry when the nurse bent down and picked her up. The nurse held the baby close to her breasts and cooed. Turning around to face the mother, she added, "I don't understand you people." She walked out, leaving Samira in the silent room.

The next morning the room was anything but quiet. Youssef Azar stood across from his wife's hospital bed. He had a small protruding belly, one that would grow to the size of a six-month pregnancy, making his daughters ask in a teasing manner, "So when are you due? When is that baby going to pop, Babba?" He was short, smaller than his wife, with deep creases in his forehead, and a receding salt-and-pepper hairline.

Youssef kept curling his thick moustache in slow motion, but after a few minutes, he placed his arms on his chest and began his rant. "*Allah*, why did you do this to me?" he cried, addressing the ceiling. By the time he lowered his eyes and stared hard at the doctor beside his wife's bed, Youssef's voice was roaring, filling the entire hospital room. "What do you mean my wife can't have any more children? She's only thirty-five. She still has a few more years."

The tall grey-haired doctor gripped the clipboard firmly in his hands, his long fingers trembling slightly as he flipped through the pages in front of him. "She had a hysterectomy. She doesn't have a uterus anymore. Because your wife was in difficult labour, we had to perform a C-section. That's when we discovered the large tumour in your wife's womb. She was bleeding so much and the mass looked cancerous, so we decided that a hysterectomy was the best option."

Youssef interrupted. "Best for whom? You or me?"

"Best for your wife," the doctor asserted.

Samira looked down at her hands; they rested on her depleted, sore belly. This delivery had been the hardest for her. For some reason, this child had become entangled in the umbilical cord making a normal vaginal birth almost impossible. They could have both died—the child from suffocation and herself from excessive bleeding. Rolling her head on her pillow, she looked at the baby sleeping quietly in the nearby cart. She had long eyelashes, something the nurses had marvelled at when they had washed all the birthing and blood from her tiny face, then lifted her up so Samira could glimpse at the small creature who had almost died before entering the world. She now studied the baby closely. Her brown hair was two-inches long, and straight, not yet curly as it would become in early childhood. Her cheeks were plump, as if she were storing nuts for the long Ottawa winter, and she was a good size, too, almost nine pounds. A pink ribbon loosely held some pieces of soft hair, making them stand up on her perfectly-shaped little head. She didn't have the compressed skull of most newborns, having escaped the birth canal. Samira's eyes moved from the child to her husband. His right hand was clenched in a fist and he was waving it in front of the doctor's long face. She was afraid that Youssef might punch the physician in the nose. They weren't in the old country. He couldn't take matters in his own hands like he could back home.

"So you're telling me that I won't have any more children? That I can't have a son?"

"That's correct. But you have four beautiful daughters." The doctor smiled at the three dark-haired girls standing silently around the baby. The oldest, Rima, gently stroked the baby's hair, without waking her new sister. She was seven. Rima's long hair was in pigtails and she wore a knee-length, blue-and-white checkered dress. A large smile was plastered on her heart-shaped face as she gazed at the baby. Beside her, Katrina stood gripping the cart. She was smaller than Rima and more serious: no smile on her face. Her large round eyes darted back and forth from the baby to her parents. Her wavy hair was pulled back in a tight ponytail and her skin seemed even paler because of the hospital walls. The second youngest, Mona, was the one least interested in the new arrival for she had to give up her own baby status to make room for her tiny sister. Her bobbed hair swung around her face while she skipped close to the door and back to the cart again, sticking out her tongue at the baby, who blinked her eyes open, waking to the sound of her father's voice.

"*Kis imak*!" Youssef shouted, throwing his arms in the air, nearly knocking the doctor's wire-rimmed glasses off his slender nose, but he pulled his hand back before he could've hurt the physician.

Stepping back, the doctor frowned. He couldn't understand why this man was acting so violently, couldn't comprehend what he was saying. If he had knowledge of Arabic, he would've known that Youssef had offended him in the most insulting way. *Kis imak*. Curse your mother's cunt. But he had no idea what words were hurled in his direction, so he said what he had felt should be said in the present situation, "Be grateful you have four children. Some people can't have any."

Youssef clenched his teeth. Then in frustration, he punched the mattress, startling his wife. She winced in pain.

The doctor touched her arm. "Are you all right, Mrs. Azar?

Do you want more pain medication?"

Samira shook her head.

"No? You're not okay?"

"No medicine. I ... I okay," she stammered.

Youssef cleared his throat. "My wife's fine. Leave her alone. You've done enough damage."

With his head bowed, the doctor quickly walked out of the room, turning back only once to see two of the small girls huddled around their mother's bed.

The entire family visited Samira and the baby again the next day. Mona, Rima, and Katrina followed their father into their mother's hospital room, trailing solemnly behind him. Samira smiled weakly while her daughters took turns kissing her on the cheeks. Then they looked at their baby sister wrapped tightly in a pink blanket, an early Easter present. Mona would have preferred a chocolate bunny.

"She's a beautiful baby," Samira said in Arabic, glancing at Youssef.

Youssef briefly stared at the infant. His thin mouth almost smiled but then he flicked his tongue over his chapped lips. "I don't care if she's beautiful. That doesn't change the fact that she's a girl." He sighed. And a smile appeared on Mona's face. This baby couldn't take Mona's place because she wasn't a boy. Seeing the smirk on Mona's face, Rima pushed her sister until she fell back against the radiator heater.

Mona began to cry and in a whiny voice she said, "Rima pushed me, Babba."

Suddenly Youssef swung around, glared at his eldest daughter then raised his right hand. "Do you want a *darbe*?"

Rima quickly grabbed onto Katrina's shoulders and stood behind her. Rima's eyes teared. She shook her head, then mumbled, "No, Babba. I'm sorry."

"Stop fighting then. Be a good daughter. Listen to your Babba like all girls should," he said, his voice softening. He dropped his hand and stared back at the baby. "Well, what do you want to call her?"

"I don't know. I guess Jamil isn't good now."

"I know," Youssef said, sighing again. "What about 'Christine'?"

"Too many Christines. Salwa?"

"Reminds me of my cousin who fled to the States with a white man. Forget that name. I don't want people to associate my daughter with that *sharmouta*." *Whore*.

Samira sighed and looked out the window. Past the thick evergreen trees was the hospital's small courtyard where benches were arranged in a semi-circle along the paved sidewalks. Wishing she could be there instead of this room with her family, Samira felt guilty and turned back to her husband. His swearing wasn't new but it still bothered her. She never swore. Now the other patient in the room, a woman with strawberry blonde hair squinted her eyes and stared at Samira then Youssef. In Arabic, Samira spoke in a whisper. "This is a respectable place, Youssef. Please don't curse." She nodded her head in the direction of the woman across from her.

Youssef turned around and glanced at the new mother, who quickly looked down at the baby in her arms. He glared at his wife again. "Don't tell me what to do, Samira. I'm the man of the family. I can damn well swear if I like to. I can do it here or any other place. Don't you dare speak back to me! Don't you remember who saved you from being alone in this country? Me," he snorted. "Remember that. I gave you a roof over your head, clothes, food, money. You couldn't even keep a job with your broken English. If it weren't for me, you would've been sent back on the next available boat. And what have you given me? Four daughters." He shook his head in disgust.

Blinking the tears from her eyes, Samira faced the window. She let her gaze fall upon her sleeping baby in the cart. A nurse suddenly walked into the room. She picked up the clipboard at the foot of Samira's bed and stared down at the chart, then at the baby. "So what's this lovely little girl's name?"

"We're still thinking about it," Youssef answered, his tone harsh.

"Well, sir, we'll need a name because your wife's being discharged tomorrow and the baby needs to be registered with the province." The nurse picked up the baby, held her in her arms. She rocked her back and forth, then handed her to Youssef. "What about Adele? Adele Azar. It has a nice ring to it, don't you agree?"

"Adele Azar," Youssef repeated over and over as he cradled his new daughter in his arms, the creases in his forehead gradually softening.

PART I: 1976-1985

CHAPTER 1

"SO WHAT'S YOUR NAME, HONEY?" a customer asked. Adele stood behind the counter beside her father. Her thick curly hair was the only thing the customer could see. Standing on her toes, she peered over the edge and glanced at the man.

"I'm Adele," she said in a quiet voice.

Youssef looked down at his youngest daughter, then patted the unruly head of curls.

"I haven't seen you here before, except when you were a wee thing. Youssef, you start working them young, eh?"

Youssef laughed. "Well, she's almost six. Back in the old country a child starts working in the fields as soon as he can walk."

"Yeah, yeah," the customer said, smiling. He looked at Adele again. "Don't believe a thing your old man says."

Adele smiled timidly at the man with grey hair who held a large cigar between his fingers. The smell of tobacco floated in her nostrils, making her rub her nose. She then hid her face in her father's hip.

"She's a little shy," Youssef said.

"That's okay. She'll grow out of it." The customer leaned over the counter and patted her head, then handed her a quarter. "A tip for the beautiful girl."

"What do you say to the nice man, Adele?" Youssef said in a humble voice.

"Thank you," she whispered, holding tightly onto the coin before slipping it into her pocket.

"So how many does this make?" the man asked, lifting the cigar to his mouth and taking a long puff.

Youssef looked confused. "What do you mean?"

"How many girls you got now? Four? You poor man! Wait until they hit puberty. Being the beauties that they are, you'll have tons of hounds at your door. You remember how young guys are, don't you?" the man chuckled. Then he looked down at Adele. "And that little one with her curly hair and large eyes, she'll drive the boys crazy. You poor man!"

Youssef frowned and gazed down at his daughter beside him. Looking up, he said, "Thanks. Have a good day." He began to wipe the counter with a rag.

"Okay, okay, I get the hint. No more talk about hounds!" the man laughed then puffed on his cigar once more, leaving a strong scent of tobacco in the air before pulling open the door and stepping outside.

Youssef folded the rag and placed it under the counter in a small drawer. Without once making contact with his daughter's large, curious eyes, he grabbed a thicker rag and led Adele to the wooden cupboards, showed her how to dust the jars of marmalade, boxes of pasta, and canned foods, and then wipe the surface clean before placing the items back in neat, perfect lines. On her knees, she followed her father's directions, wrapping her small hands around the cloth, gathering balls of dust.

You poor man! Four girls. As Adele grew up, she heard this again and again. She knew that being a girl was not a good thing but she couldn't understand why her father had wanted a son so badly. One Sunday morning, she had ventured to ask him this very question while he was tending the shop before his cousin arrived to relieve him so he could attend Sunday mass with his daughters and wife. Adele was nine. Standing in her church clothes, Adele said, "Babba?"

"Yes, Adele," Youssef answered, filling up the shelf behind the front counter with packages of cigarettes. His navy suit jacket fit tightly around his shoulders and for one second, Adele thought the seams might rip when he reached into the carton to get more packages.

"Why do people feel bad because you don't have a son?"

Youssef stopped his task and looked across at his youngest daughter. She crossed her arms over her small chest, wrinkling her lacy pink dress. Her full lips were pale against her olive complexion and her eyes were opened wide. Without answering her question, he bent down, lifted the last pack of tobacco, and placed it on the wooden shelf.

"Babba, what's wrong?" Adele asked, her voice rising slightly.

"Nothing, *babba*," he said, using the endearing term for his children which was also the way his children addressed him.

"Did you want a boy?"

Turning around, he looked at Adele. This time her eyes narrowed and her small teeth tugged on her bottom lip.

"Every man wants a son, of course. I'm no different but your mother didn't give me one."

"So," she paused, "you wanted me to be a boy?"

"What I wanted doesn't matter now, does it? I have you. I can't change that."

Adele turned and ran out the front door, slamming it hard against the yellow stucco of the grocery store, shutting her father's tiny shop out of her world.

Later, Adele pulled one of the hefty wooden double doors of the church open, holding it for her sisters, mother and father. But her Babba refused to walk through it, staying behind until she walked ahead of him. The church was crowded. Adele stared up at the domed ceiling, eyeing the colourful icons of the saints. The priest was going around the church with a censer filling the enormous room with the aroma and smoke of incense. The Azar family hurried to a pew, and filled its entire length with five females and one man.

In contrast to the priest's extravagant, golden robe, Youssef's suit looked out of style. Adele stared at Father Chafic as he made his way around the church that was the worshipping place for all of Ottawa's Orthodox Lebanese. The pews were packed with people. Adele couldn't remember another parish priest; Father Chafic had baptised her and conducted all the sermons she had attended in her short life. He was a tall and domineering man with a body as sturdy as a fisherman's. A full beard, streaked with silver in some places, covered his wide jaw. His nose was long and hooked like a bird of prey, Adele thought. She was always afraid of getting pecked when she leaned in and accepted a piece of holy bread at the end of each service.

While Father Chafic reminded her of a vulture, the women in the church made her think of movie stars because they were dressed stylishly in skirts, fancy blouses and dresses, hair held in place by clips or layers of hairspray. Gold bangles clunked on their wrists every time they made the sign of the cross, which was frequently, given the number of times Father Chafic chanted "In the name of the Father, the Son and the Holy Spirit." Make-up was thick on the women's faces, darkening their olive skin even in the glow of the huge chandelier, hanging in the centre of the domed ceiling. Adele glanced from the painted icons to the beautiful faces of the women to the priest. A few altar boys surrounded him, hands clasped together, heads bowed in prayer.

Shortly after, Father Chafic stretched his long, husky arm towards the large hampers of holy bread on the gold-embroidered cloth table by the altar. The boys hurriedly gathered the woven baskets filled with the sweet, orange-blossom flavoured *ourban*. Adele took a deep breath, letting the smell float into her small nose. She knew these loaves were offered to the church by one of the parishioners who was celebrating a baby's baptismal or remembering a loved one who now lived in Heaven. Tiny religious seals were stamped on the holy bread. She had learned from her mother what they had meant and why five large loaves should be offered to the church: the seal taken from the first loaf became Holy Communion; the second was offered to the Mother of God; the third to the angels and saints; the fourth to the living; and the fifth to the deceased. After the altar boys collected the baskets, they took their spots beside the priest as parishioners began to make their way down the green-carpeted centre aisle of the church. Before this procession, Samira touched Adele's head, patting down the loose curls. "Remember to cross yourself after you drink from the cup, *habibti*," Samira whispered, bending down to her youngest child.

"I don't want to."

Youssef heaved a sigh of impatience, then glared across at Adele. "*Ayb*. This is a holy place, remember? You mustn't disobey your father. He's watching you." He raised his index finger to the ceiling, pointed at the icon of Jesus, his arms stretching open.

"I don't want to drink that stuff. It's gross. I hate it!" Adele pouted, clasping her hands on the edge of the pew. She looked at her sisters but they only fidgeted and waited until their parents were ready to guide them down the aisle.

Samira was pleading now. "Please, *habibti*, don't be difficult. If you do it, I promise to make your favourite dish for lunch, okay?"

"Enough!" Youssef bellowed, his voice rising above the shuffling feet and whispered conversations of the others. Some people turned around to check the commotion, eager to witness an outburst that would become gossip over a cup of *ahweh*. The stares made Youssef lower his tone. "Don't bribe her, Samira. She has to learn our ways." He grasped Adele's hand and tugged on her arm until she stood before Father Chafic. She opened her mouth and swallowed the red wine filled with crumbs of holy bread and a few seconds later snatched a large piece of bread from the basket. Then she began to walk towards the altar. But before she could take another step, the chanter of the church blocked her way. "What are you doing? You're not allowed here. Go," he said, shooing her with his hands and speaking in a flat voice, beads of sweat dripping around his temples. His head was shaved, though stubs of black patches were beginning to grow. A dark cloak covered his short, heavy body.

"I just wanted to…" Adele struggled to find the right words. Her eyes scanned the room, trying to find her mother and father but they had started to make their way down the aisle, towards the front gigantic door.

"You hear me. Don't ever come this way. It's not right for a girl to be up here. You're not allowed." He didn't make eye contact.

"I'm sorry," Adele replied in a barely audible voice. The man waited for her to leave before he joined the priest and altar boys. Adele turned and glanced at him. He now smiled, standing with the men. Looking away, she saw her father, his hand on the door, ready to push it open, but then he hesitated and watched her, his head shaking. Adele opened her mouth, tried to explain to her father that she only wanted to see what was behind the altar like the altar boys. Why couldn't she go back there like them? It didn't seem fair. But instead she said nothing. Her father's accusing eyes bore into hers. Then he muttered something under his breath and ushered his daughters out into one of the last hot days of summer.

"Why can't I go behind the altar, Mama?" Adele said, now running up to her mother.

Samira looked down and sighed. "You just can't."

Just then, her father blurted, "Women don't serve behind the altar, so there is no reason for them to go there. It's just the way things are. You have to learn to accept this, Adele."

Adele clasped her mother's hand as they quickly walked

away, carrying the smell of incense and rosewater in their thick, curly hair.

At home, Adele followed her sisters upstairs and stripped off her pink dress, replacing it with her swimsuit. Her father had promised them earlier that they could head out to their neighbours' house after church to cool off in the sprinklers. With a few quick movements, Adele gathered her towel and put on her sandals then raced down the stairs behind her sisters. They all ran through the store, shouting goodbye at their father before being engulfed by the humidity of the noon hour.

Adele walked a step behind her sisters down their small street. She watched them speak to each other as if they had their own special language. They talked about clothes, music and, lately, a lot about boys. Rima was now sixteen and that's all she seemed interested in, Adele thought. Boys. Boys. Boys. Katrina seemed the least concerned with the other gender, but she still leaned in close when the sisters huddled together and giggled about one of the neighbourhood boys while he pedalled down the road, waving at the sisters. Her sisters walked close together as if one unit, connected by the same dark hair and similar strides—small shoulders slightly hunched and a bit of a bounce in their swaggers. From behind, Adele studied her sisters. They seemed to fit together. Now, walking with a bounce and rolling in her shoulders, she tried emulating them. She wanted to squeeze her body between theirs and fit in too, but instead she lagged a step behind. If she knew then that this was how things would always be for her with her sisters, she wouldn't have bothered to protest when they excluded her or tried so hard to fit in with them.

Shrugging, she quickened her pace, skipping past her sisters and unlatching the steel fence to her neighbours' house. She ran up the walkway, up onto the porch and softly knocked on the large wooden door. Behind her, she watched her sisters sitting patiently on the steps, hands folded on their laps, towels wrapped around their waists, barely covering their bony legs. In a matter of minutes, the door opened and a woman with sandy-coloured hair streaked with silver at the temples greeted Adele. Estelle Foster had lived on this block for many years. She and her husband owned the enormous house that the sisters called "The White House." It was a three-storey Victorian home with pillars positioned along the spacious veranda. Adele was enchanted by the old white house, convinced the large house itself yearned for the voices of children.

She liked the scent of pine that floated into her nostrils every time she followed Mrs. Foster inside. It was so different from her parents' home. There were piles of books in every room, even the bathroom. There was also a grand piano. Given the right amount of coaxing, which wasn't much, Mrs. Foster would pull out the bench, stretch out her legs under the piano, and play a lovely tune of Bach or Mozart, her long fingers gracefully flying over the ivory keys. Now her fingers ruffled Adele's mop of curls. "Hello, dear. I see you've come all prepared." She looked down at the young girl's pink and white-striped swimsuit. "You want to cool off in the sprinkler, don't you?"

Smiling, Adele nodded.

"Well at least you don't beat around the bush. You know what you want. That's one of the reasons I like you—you're feisty," Mrs. Foster said, throwing her head back and laughing a big belly-laugh. Mrs. Foster was different. Most of Adele's older women aunts and cousins never laughed out loud, only smiled occasionally with their painted lips pressed tight together, hiding or preventing a wide grin from overtaking their faces. Motioning for Adele to follow, Mrs. Foster said, "Let's get some brownies for you girls to munch on before playing in the water." Her slightly plump body strode toward the kitchen in a confident, happy way.

Adele followed her neighbour down the dimly-lit hallway, stealing glances into the large rooms she passed on her way to the kitchen. When she entered the pantry, she noticed Mr.

Foster sitting at the small oak table, reading a newspaper. As soon as he saw her, he folded the paper and laid it down on the table. "Hello, Adele," he said in a deep, warm voice, his smile wide. "How's one of my favourite Azar girls?"

"Good," Adele replied timidly.

He smiled again. Harold Foster was a tall, lanky man, his long legs spread wide and cramped under the kitchen table. When he leaned his elbows on the edge of the table, his tall posture was more predominant in the way he held himself up. He wore metal-wired glasses and a dark plaid shirt.

"The girls are beating the heat by running through the sprinkler. What do you think, Harold? Should we join them?" Mrs. Foster said, winking at her husband.

"Most definitely!" He pushed back his chair and rose, his towering frame in its full magnificence. "Let me grab my trunks!"

Raising her hands to her mouth, Adele giggled. "Adults aren't allowed to play."

Mr. Foster placed his hands on his hips and frowned, biting his lower lip to prevent a grin from breaking forth. "Jeez, but I was looking forward to joining you girls. It seems like such fun!"

"It is," Adele said.

"Well, can't you make an exception and let an old man like me play?" Mr. Foster loved teasing Adele.

Adele stood firm in her conviction. "But you can't. Adults can't play. Adults only work and take care of family things." She tried to remember if her parents had ever joined her and her sisters when they played together but she couldn't recall such a time.

"I see," Mr. Foster said, rubbing his chin. He went to pull the chair back so he could sit down again, but then Adele tugged at his shirt. Sighing loudly, she gave in. "It's your sprinkler so I can't say 'no'. You can play but only this one time, okay?"

He clicked his heels together and bowed to Adele. "Thank you, dear." Then he bent down and scooped Adele up in his arms. He spun her around and around. Adele laughed out loud.

With a good-humoured groan, Mrs. Foster said, "Now, Harold, put her down. You'll make her so dizzy that she won't be able to stand straight."

When he put Adele down a few minutes later, she wobbled unsteadily on her feet, holding onto the edge of the kitchen table for support. "Now, now, dear, don't worry. She's okay. See," he said, pointing at the young girl who now stood with her back straight, having regained her balance.

"Mr. Foster's right. I'm okay. Don't worry, Mrs. Foster." She felt a deep awe for Mrs. Foster. She would have liked to embrace her but she didn't. Instead, she waved at Mr. Foster, as he resumed his reading at the kitchen table and followed Mrs. Foster down the hall, who carried a tray of lemonade and brownies. Adele wished she could live inside these walls permanently rather than only on certain occasions.

By the time the sisters returned home, their mother and aunts were preparing Sunday lunch. Adele detected the scent of garlic and allspice. Adele's sisters had changed into their clothes quickly and joined their mother and aunts in the kitchen, wide-eyed and eager to learn Lebanese cooking.

"You have to always remember to use allspice. This spice is a big part of our dishes. I like to call it our 'Lebanese seasoning'. You use it in *taboulleh*, *kibbeh nayeh*, Lebanese chicken and rice. It has a wonderful aroma, doesn't it?" Samira said, dabbing a small amount of the orange-brownish spice in her palm and waving it under her daughters' noses. Adele loved her mother's cooking. She felt it was the best in the world. Adele watched her sisters sit around the green table, elbows propped on the edges, hands clasped together, and faces pinned with ear-to-ear smiles. They all sat at full attention, listening to their mother's instructions about what ingredients went in the *kibbeh nayeh*, how to chop up the parsley for the *taboulleh*, how to measure the spices without using a measuring spoon or cup.

Samira's face glowed too when she sprinkled the allspice in the chopped parsley and tomatoes of the *taboulleh*. Then she kneaded the minced raw beef, bulgar, salt, black pepper, and allspice together while dipping her hands in a bowl of iced water to prevent the mixture from sticking to her palms. She placed the *kibbeh* on a large plate and sculpted it into an oval shape, then used the back of a spoon to make little indents in the meat before scattering mint leaves and drizzling olive oil in the grooves. Minutes later, she gently held a knife around a raw onion and cut zigzags until a beautiful flower appeared. Smiling, Samira held up her creation to her daughters and they smiled just as widely as their mother; even Adele grinned, who loved how her mother seemed to be an artist when she was cooking. The prepared dishes were her mother's canvas, Adele thought as Samira centred the lotus-shaped onion in the middle of the *kibbeh nayeh*. Then she washed her hands and wiped them on her apron before she began drawing lines in the *hummus* and pouring olive oil in the swirls. Adele could tell her mother was a masterful cook.

As much as Adele loved her mother's food, and watching her mother create beautiful flowers with vegetables, she found cooking boring. Sighing, she looked around the room. Aunt Nabiha, her father's sister, was carefully scooping the seeds from the centre of a zucchini with a spoon, leaving a thin shell to be stuffed loosely with a mixture of meat, rice, cinnamon and allspice. Nabiha was a short woman with dyed auburn hair that was held up in a bun. Her tongue pushed on the inside of her cheek while she meticulously stuffed each zucchini. With her small eyes straining, Nabiha's normally pinched face was even tighter than usual. When Rima tried scooping out some of the seeds, she accidentally broke the shell, pushing the spoon through the green skin. Glaring at her, Nabiha quickly grabbed the utensil out of her hand. "You've ruined it. What a waste of food!" Adele stood by the doorway and frowned; she watched Rima swallow back the sting of tears. She wanted to tell her aunt to shut up but she knew this would be disrespectful because Aunt Nabiha was her elder and elders had to be shown the utmost respect. Nabiha must have noticed Adele's eyes narrow because she asked coldly, "What are you looking at?"

Adele stepped back and whispered, "Nothing, Auntie."

Nabiha's eyes could not hide their rage as they moved down the length of Adele's small body. Adele was still in her swimsuit. Damp from the water, it stuck to her tiny belly and sagged in the crotch area. Adele shifted nervously on her feet. She wanted to run. Being so close to the doorway leading into the living room, she could have made a quick dash. But she was frozen on the spot, only touching her bare feet to one another. Bowing her head, she looked down at the floor. Then she looked up and saw Aunt Nabiha shaking her head. "Change out of that stinky, wet swimsuit! This is a kitchen not a swimming pool." She threw her hands in the air, flicking them towards Adele. Bits of stuffing from the *koosa* flew in Adele's direction, landing on her thin legs. She bent down and wiped them off her skin. "Why can't you be more like your sisters? Get out of here and change. Hurry back. I'm going to make a cook out of you even if I have to tie you to the chair, understand?"

Adele's mouth began to quiver but she didn't dare cry in front of her aunt. Biting her lower lip, she stared across at her mother, and then at her sisters, but they lowered their heads, focusing on the food in front of them rather than Adele. She was close to tears but before any drops could fall, she turned around and headed down the hallway, then ran up the stairs two at a time. Once in her bedroom, she peeled off her bathing suit.

CHAPTER 2

"COME ON. GET UP," YOUSSEF SAID LOUDLY, poking Adele in the ribs. With the covers pulled up close to her chin, she lay in her bed. She yawned, rubbed her eyes, and looked into her father's eyes; they were wide with frustration. "You have to get ready for Arabic school. Christ, you should be used to this by now. How many times do I have to remind you to get up?" he said, throwing the covers off Adele's body. She reluctantly got out of bed and straightened her pajamas. She was now twelve. It turned out that she was not only expected to learn to cook Lebanese food, but she was also meant to speak Arabic fluently like her older sisters.

"I don't want to go," she said firmly. She hated that school, despised waking early on Saturday for that purpose. "I don't want to go anymore," she insisted, digging her bare feet into the plush brown carpet.

"Why?" Youssef asked, controlling the anger rising to his throat.

She wanted to answer because I can't stand the mean looks and comments from the other students, all of whom spoke Arabic fluently. She was an outsider even though she was Lebanese. But rather than tell the truth, she said, "I don't feel good."

"What's wrong with you?"

"My stomach. It hurts." She wrapped her skinny arms around her belly and moaned in exaggerated pain, glancing across at her father, hoping she'd convince him of her illness. But his expression didn't soften, and instead, his thick eyebrows knitted together.

"I don't believe you. Get dressed and hurry up."

"I'm not going!" she said suddenly, sitting on the edge of the bed.

"That's enough!" With one quick movement, Youssef yanked Adele up by the arms and pushed her towards the closet. She fell to the floor. He then pulled out a shirt and trousers, and threw them at her. "Now get dressed! You're going to school whether you like it or not, understand? Who knows, maybe you'll learn to speak Arabic without sounding like a complete idiot." He looked hard at his daughter. A few seconds later, he stomped across the bedroom and down the stairs.

Sullen, Adele slipped into her clothes, turning when she felt someone's hand on her shoulder. It was Katrina. "Are you all right, Adele?"

"What difference does it make? This is the way things are for us. Babba tells us what to do and we do it, isn't that right?" Angrily, she added, "Why didn't you come in earlier when Babba was yelling?" She stared up at her sister, Adele's face straining for composure.

There was silence. Katrina shook her head, looking down at her feet, "You can't beat him. There's no point in arguing with him."

"Whatever."

Katrina suddenly grabbed a pillow from the bed and playfully threw it at Adele's back.

"That's not funny."

"You have to laugh, Monkey."

Adele turned around and gave her sister a wide forced grin, then ducked as Katrina swung another pillow at her. Adele laughed, running down the stairs and out the front door to her father's awaiting car.

She did not smile, though, during the drive to the school. The big, green Chevy moved from the downtown core to the east end of the city. The streets were quiet. With her head turned toward the passenger side window, Adele stared at the houses that lined the streets her father took as he drove. Blinds were shut tight and outdoor lamps were still turned on from the previous evening, shining dully in the sunlight. Her father shook his fist at the car in front of them and cursed, "Son of a bitch, where the hell did you learn to drive? You wouldn't survive one minute on the streets of Beirut. Stupid people. They don't know how to drive." Adele looked blankly out the window once more. This twenty-minute drive was always the same. Silence punctuated with Youssef's intermittent cursing. They didn't speak with each other often and when they did, it was in angry grunts and rushed hand gestures. Adele's birthday was a day before her father's and she had often joked with her sisters that they clashed because they were born under the same astrological sign—Aries, the sign ruled by passion and sometimes aggressive action.

Within a few minutes, Youssef turned the car into the parking lot of the high school where the Arabic lessons were conducted. He dropped Adele off at the front door. She slid out of the car and said, "Thanks, Babba."

"I'll be back around noon to pick you up," he said.

"Okay. Bye," Adele mumbled, slamming the door shut. She made her way slowly up the steps to the school and walked past a crowd of dark-haired students speaking a language that was never hers.

By the time she reached the classroom, the other students were already seated. They chatted loudly. With her head bowed, Adele took her seat at the back and quietly opened her notebook. A few minutes later, the teacher hurriedly entered the room. She was tall and her shoulders stooped while she pulled out her chair and sat behind her large desk. Her black hair was swept up in a loose bun; a few strands fell around her oval face. She wore a bright fuchsia blouse under a navy jacket. Her large eyes were serious and unkind. She didn't smile while greeting the children with a quick *Marhaba*. The instructors of the classes were Lebanese-born people who had immigrated to Canada only a few years ago, and Madame Yasmine El-Sawaya fit this profile. Yet there was something endearing about her. Perhaps it was her dark, almond eyes or the way she spoke with a lyrical Arabic accent when she reminisced about the beauty and chaos of her homeland. Getting up from her seat, the teacher stood in front of the blackboard, and scribbled down some sentences. She spoke with longing and determination to get her students to appreciate their ancestry. How could a strong and beautiful voice belong to such a strict teacher? And like the other instructors, she lacked patience when explaining things that seemed simple to her but weren't so easy to some of her students. They sat before her, gripping their pencils, scribbling the Arabic words onto the lined paper of their notebooks from the back-to-the front, right-to-left. "*Yallah*, follow me. We only have a few hours together and you must learn these sentences if you're to read and write in Arabic."

Adele's own hands trembled. Madame El-Sawaya's chalk moved quickly across the blackboard; a fine white spray of dust circled her hands as she wrote. Once done, the teacher clapped her hands together and grabbed the long wooden ruler resting on the metal edge of the blackboard and hit the tip of it against the board, guiding the students through the daily drill.

"*Hal tatakallam al-'arabiya?*" she repeated, tapping the ruler. "Come on, say it louder," she insisted in Arabic. When the students failed to make the sounds correctly, Madame El-Sawaya abruptly stopped and, holding her hands up, one still clutching the ruler, cried, "Stop! That's wrong, wrong, wrong. Start over. This sentence is asking, 'Do you speak Arabic?' Do you? Obviously not if you can't even pronounce these words. *Yallah*, try again." She slapped the stick on the board again, as if the intensity of its pressure on the letters would force proper enunciation of each word. When some of the students still mispronounced the words, she shouted, "Again! Say it again until you get it right, okay?" The children shouted into the air until their voices began to crack, including Adele's. The sounds weren't found in English so Adele had a difficult time grasping Arabic. She couldn't get the back of her throat to articulate right. When she tried to pronounce the sentences, everything sounded like nonsense. She cleared her throat and tried to say the words correctly while at the same time scribbling them down again in her notebook, but she forgot to write from right-to-left and had to erase her attempts. She rubbed her forehead in frustration. Adele's tone was not as loud as the others; she was embarrassed because she didn't sound like them. To her, they all seemed to speak Arabic well.

Finally, out of frustration, Madame El-Sawaya placed the ruler on her desk. She slid into the seat behind her desk and cupped her head in her hands as if nursing a bad headache. "That's enough for today. Open your books and read."

But instead of reading, the students began to chat amongst themselves, their voices no longer cracking but laughing and joking. Adele looked at the clock on the wall. Fifteen minutes to go before the break. Turning her head, she studied her teacher. Lines were beginning to form around her dark eyes and Adele guessed she was about thirty-five. With furrows on her face and strands of grey hair sprouting between dark locks, Madame El-Sawaya had the appearance of someone not in the prime of adulthood. She pressed fingers against her cheeks and sighed, her chest expanding with weariness before she mumbled to her students to take an early recess. "Don't run, walk. Remember, you're not a herd of sheep but young people." The students rose from their seats and, ignoring the teacher's instructions, they rushed out of the classroom, heading towards the cafeteria. Madame El-Sawaya shook her head before placing it down on her desk. Adele looked sadly at her teacher then walked out of the room behind everyone else, forming her own single file line.

The cafeteria was crowded. Everyone was talking and laughing at once. Adele slowly chewed on the cookie in her hands and swallowed it down with a gulp of apple juice. Some of her classmates sat across from her at one of the long tables.

"Madame El-Sawaya is one crazy teacher and bitch too!" Zeina said in a thick Arabic accent. "I know how to speak Arabic. I was born in Lebanon. I'm a pure Leb. She doesn't have to drill it into my head."

Adele twirled the plastic cup in her hand, the remainder of the drink swirling at the bottom. "She's not a bitch. Maybe she has a lot on her mind."

"Why are you defending her, Adele? You see how she gets all mad over nothing. If you can't handle teaching, then don't teach. It's as simple as that. Anyway, what she's teaching us is for beginners like yourself, Adele," Zeina said. "How come you never learned to speak Arabic well? Do you think it's beneath you or something?"

"No, I don't think..." Adele began.

Zeina interrupted, "Just cause you were born here doesn't make you white, you know."

"I totally agree," another girl said. The others nodded their heads. In this group, Adele was the only one who was born in Canada, the only one without an accent in English. Her accent only revealed itself when she tried to speak Arabic.

"It doesn't make you better than us," Zeina continued, sitting back in her chair and staring pointedly at Adele.

"I don't think I'm better than anyone," Adele finally said.

"You're not white."

"I never said I was."

"Then learn the language. Are you a real Leb or not?" Zeina asked, her large eyes boring into Adele's own.

"Yeah," Adele answered in Arabic. "I'm Lebanese, not Canadian."

Zeina laughed. "You don't sound like a Leb. You sound like a white person trying to be ethnic."

Adele felt tears prick her eyes. She didn't know what to say next.

"Leave her alone," another girl suddenly snapped. It was Myriam, the daughter of Youssef's old friend. Her long, brown hair was pulled back in a ponytail and she wore a second-hand shirt that had once belonged to Rima, given to her when she had first arrived in Canada, which was a few months ago. But Adele had never mentioned this shirt to her or to the others in the school. She knew it would be unkind to brag about this sort of thing or to bring it to Myriam's attention. She understood it was one thing for her to wear her sister's hand-me-downs but another thing for a stranger to wear them. Myriam spoke in a soft voice and smiled sympathetically at Adele. "She sounds all right. At least she's trying."

"She still sounds like an idiot," Zeina snickered.

Adele pushed back her chair and got up.

"Where are you going?" Myriam asked.

"Going back to the classroom. Do you want to come?"

Myriam shook her head, stared at the cookie in her hands, the crumbs falling on the table. Adele looked down at the table, too, before pushing the chair in.

"Are you going to hang out with Madame El-Sawaya? I saw the way you were staring at her today. You got the hots for her or what?" Zeina said mockingly.

"That's enough, Zeina," Myriam said, staring at the loud-mouthed girl.

But Zeina ignored her. "Go run to the teacher," she said. Then added, "Freaks should stick together." Adele quickly walked away and turned back once to glance at the group of girls still sitting at the table. Before leaving the cafeteria, she heard Zeina's piercing voice add, "She's not like us."

Adele ran into the washroom and pressed her hands on the white sink while she stared at the mirror and studied her face. She looked like the other girls with her dark hair and brown eyes. Tracing her cheeks, she left a faint mark on her olive skin.

Wasn't she like them? Wasn't she Lebanese even though she was born here? Didn't she struggle with the Arabic language? Leaning closer into the mirror, she carefully examined her green-flecked eyes; they weren't as dark as her sisters'.

Other girls suddenly entered the bathroom, chatting loudly. She whirled around and quickly headed back to the classroom.

When she pulled open the door to the classroom, Madame El-Sawaya jumped. "Oh, you scared me, Adele," she said, smiling weakly.

"I'm sorry," Adele said, quickly taking her seat at the back. She opened her notebook and began to doodle on a clean page.

"Why aren't you with the other students?" Madame El-Sawaya asked, lifting a glass of water to her lips.

"I'd rather be here if that's okay."

"Sure."

Adele coloured in the three-dimensional box she had drawn on the sheet.

"I'm sorry about the way I acted earlier—getting all frustrated with the class," Madame El-Sawaya said suddenly, taking another sip from the glass before placing it down on the desk. She stared across at Adele.

"That's okay," Adele said, moving uncomfortably in her seat. She kept her eyes on the sketch in front of her.

"It's just ... it's just that things can be so difficult sometimes."

Adele stopped drawing and looked up at her teacher. Her eyes were red. "Are you all right, Madame El-Sawaya?"

"Yes. No ... I don't know. God, I'm sorry for acting like a blubbering idiot."

Adele had never seen this side of her confident teacher.

"I'm returning to Lebanon," Madame El-Sawaya said abruptly.

"When?"

"Next week."

"Oh, you'll be missed," Adele said.

"You're too nice, Adele. I know my students don't like me."

But Adele did. "I'll miss you."

"Thank you, Adele. That's really sweet."

"Why are you returning home?"

The teacher hesitated then cleared her throat. "My father's dying."

"I'm sorry," Adele said in a low voice.

"Cherish your parents, Adele. Because one day you'll turn around and they won't be there."

She looked down again. She thought about her father and his words; they were synonymous. Cherish Youssef? And his words? Where would they go? Adele wondered to herself. A few minutes later, she asked, "Will you be coming back to Ottawa?"

"No," she answered. "I'm going back home for good."

The other students began returning to the classroom, taking their respective seats. Adele's eyes were still locked onto the teacher's gaze. When she finally turned away, she noticed Zeina squeezing Myriam's shoulder. She whispered, "I told you she was weird."

Youssef touched his daughter's shoulder after she slid into the car. "School isn't that bad, is it? You survived another week," he said with satisfaction.

"Yeah," Adele mumbled, slamming the door shut.

"I won't have to pull you out of bed next Saturday because you'll be excited to come back, right?"

Adele didn't reply but stared out the window, watching a tearful Madame El-Sawaya standing in a group with some of the other teachers.

"Well, what did you learn?" Youssef asked in Arabic.

"Some sentences."

"Recite them to me."

"*Hal tata … kalleem al-'arabeeya?*"

"You're not saying it right, Adele," her father said. "Say it again. Try harder."

She repeated the words again while gazing in the car's side view mirror and watching her teacher hug her colleagues goodbye. The butchered Arabic words rolled off Adele's tongue.

When the next Saturday arrived, Adele knew she wasn't going to Arabic school or, more precisely, she knew she didn't want to ever go again. She didn't know for certain how she was going to get out of it, but she knew she couldn't go anymore. Adele got out of bed, resolving to be steady as she explained to her father why it was time for her to stop her Arabic studies.

Dressing quietly, she looked out the window. The sun had begun its ascent into the world once more, colouring the clear, pale sky a milky pink. No sounds could be heard except the soft breathing coming from Mona's mouth. Adele glanced across at her sister, cocooned under her blankets, sleeping peacefully. As soon as she was fully dressed, Adele slowly crept out of the room and made her way down the stairs. She knew her father was waiting for her in the store, ready to drive her to her lessons. Taking a deep breath, she entered the grocery store and stood across from her mother who was standing behind the counter beside Youssef.

"Remember to count the change correctly, Samira. Can you do that?"

Samira nodded her head, cupping her hands together.

Adele hated it when her father talked to her mother as if she were a child. This wasn't the first time Samira had worked in the store and in spite of her poor English language skills, she knew how to count and return change. Adele clenched her teeth.

Youssef quickly glanced at Adele. "Look who decided to get up all by herself for Arabic school. This is a miracle! For once in my life, I don't have to drag you out of bed for your studies. Allah has blessed me today with an obedient, loyal daughter!" he said, smiling. Then he stood in front of Adele, placing his hands on her shoulders.

She looked down at the floor and shifted her feet.

"Let's go," Youssef said, guiding her to the door.

"Um ... Babba," Adele stammered. "I don't think I need to go to Arabic school anymore. I can learn to speak it from you and Mama. I'm not learning much at that school anyway. Too many students and only one teacher. You and Mama can teach me. This way I'll have two teachers rather than one."

"What?" Youssef said, the smile on his face disappearing. "Listen. We're not going through this again. You're going to school whether you like it or not. The teachers are good. I can't teach you to read or write."

Adele looked up at her father's face. He looked humble and very old as he admitted his illiteracy. "I know, but you can teach me to speak Arabic. That's more important to me than writing and reading Arabic. When am I going to use those skills? I only need to learn how to speak it. You can teach me that," she changed from English to Arabic, searching her limited vocabulary. "Please, Babba. I don't want to go to that school anymore."

"That's what this is all about. You don't like the people there?"

Adele nodded. She wanted to tell him about Zeina and her bullying and was about to when Youssef barked.

"Those people are your people, Adele! Most come from Kfarmichki, our village."

"I'm not from a village. I was born here, not some village," she said, crossing her arms over her chest. "Those people aren't my people. They're yours, not mine. You're the one from a village, not me."

Youssef raised his hand. "I should slap you."

"Go ahead." Adele stood her ground. "Slap me and I'll call the cops!" She faced her mother and said, "Mama, I can't go to that school anymore. Please tell Babba. You know how hard it is to learn another language. Look at yourself; you can't speak English well." Samira's eyes suddenly filled with tears and Adele immediately regretted uttering those words.

Youssef stomped across the store and pushed Samira to the side as he took his spot behind the counter. He lifted his hands in the air. "Forget it! You don't want to go to school, then don't go. I don't care anymore. But one day you'll regret it. You think you're better than those kids but you're not."

"I don't think that," she mumbled, tightening her arms on her chest. "They tease me," she finally confessed.

"Well, I'd tease you too. You're nothing but a stupid girl who can't even speak her own language."

Biting her lower lip, she fought back the tears. "I know how to speak *my* language. I know how to speak English. Better than you!"

"Get out! Get out of my store. I can't stand the sight of you!" Youssef said, banging his fists on the counter, which made Samira jump.

Adele glanced at her mother, waiting for her to say something, but she remained silent. She simply tucked her hands in her pockets, then turned and stood at the threshold that led back to the house. Adele imagined her going into the sanctuary of her kitchen where she'd lose herself in the warm spices. With her lips pressed together and her eyes still wet, Samira frowned at Adele. "You should go to school," she whispered. Adele's eyes burned with tears now too. She suddenly hated her mother then. She knew Adele was suffering but she didn't speak up for her, nor help Youssef understand the reason behind her decision to stop school. Samira just dug her hands deeper into her pockets. Turning away from her mother, Adele ran out of the store.

CHAPTER 3

ADELE KEPT RUNNING AND AS SHE SPRINTED down the street, slowly gathering her wits, she remembered herself as a little girl playing in the snow and asking questions, fascinated by her mother's past. "Mama, tell me about Kfarmichki." Fresh snowflakes had begun to fall from the sky and Adele had tilted her head back and stuck out her tongue to taste the snow.

Samira had gazed at her daughter, her large eyes now closed as she let the snowflakes land on her tongue. "Try some, Mama," Adele had said excitedly, as if the snow were an exotic delicacy.

Samira had smiled back and shook her head. "Not for me, *habibti*. Snow," she had said, grimacing, "makes me too cold. Makes me think of returning home."

"Okay, let's go back if you like. We don't have to walk anymore," Adele said, misunderstanding.

"That's not what I meant. I meant going back to Lebanon."

"Tell me about it," Adele had repeated.

"What's to tell?" Samira had teased her, egging on the curiosity in her daughter.

"Come on, Mama. Please. Tell me about the village—the goats, the mountains, the ocean, your family there," Adele begged.

"I don't think so. It's not interesting for a city girl like yourself," Samira had replied and laughed. When she laughed her entire face lit up, as if the sun was shining through her skin.

"I'm not a city girl," Adele had pouted, tapping her right foot on the ground.

Now, she vehemently denied her connection to the village she had once begged her mother to describe in detail. She stopped running and grasped the metal spikes of the fence surrounding her neighbour's place. She stood still and watched Mrs. Foster raking the leaves on the wide lawn. There were piles of leaves everywhere. She became aware of the rich colours of autumn, taking her mind away from the argument she'd had with her father. And she fervently wished she lived in this huge house with Mrs. Foster. She glanced back and forth from the porch to her neighbour. Mr. and Mrs. Foster were childless. She could be their child, she thought biting her lower lip until she tasted blood. With the back of her hand, she wiped her mouth. Mrs. Foster would never hurt her, would never make her feel stupid. Her neighbour wouldn't call her names or yell at her for no reason. But it was pointless to wish for a new home when she already had a family and parents. Suddenly, Mrs. Foster was standing in front of her, reaching across with her gloved hand and patting her shoulder. Adele was startled out of her thoughts.

"I'm sorry, dear. I didn't mean to scare you." Mrs. Foster smiled. There was kindness in the fine lines around her large blue eyes.

And Adele let her mind imagine the possibility of having her as her mother. In the haziness of her dream, she blurted out, "Do you think I can come and live with you?"

Mrs. Foster lifted her hand from Adele's shoulder and gripped the rake. She didn't say anything though.

Adele longed for her to say "Okay, my dear. Pack your bags and head on over." Looking across at Mrs. Foster, Adele bit her lip again and prayed her wish would come true.

Mrs. Foster opened her mouth, then cleared her throat and politely asked Adele to help her with the leaves.

Adele spent the night feeling guilty. She lay in her bed and listened to the sounds of her mother's footsteps as she crept down the hallway, opening bedroom doors and peeking in at her sleeping daughters. This was a nightly ritual for Samira before she headed into the bedroom she shared with Youssef. Adele squeezed her eyes tight when she heard her doorknob turn. The floorboards groaned while Samira walked towards Mona's bed first, then came to a stop beside Adele's. Pretending to sleep, Adele lay perfectly still, keeping her eyes closed. She could feel her mother's fingertips tracing her forehead, drawing the sign of the cross on her skin. Whispering, Samira said a little prayer before slowly withdrawing her hand and tiptoeing out of the room, carefully closing the door behind her.

Adele opened her eyes and stared at the moonlit wall. She turned her head and looked at Mona curled on her side, the blankets loosely hanging over the edge of the twin bed. She sighed loudly, trying to wake her sister. Then she whispered, "Mona, wake up. I have a question. Mona."

Mona turned over on her back and mumbled, "What's wrong? Did you piss yourself?"

Adele giggled quietly. "I'm not a baby anymore. I don't do that."

"Why are you waking me up then?" she asked, sitting up and rubbing her eyes. The light of the moon shone bright on her skin.

"Do you ever wish you belonged to another family?"

Mona stopped rubbing her eyes, straightened her shoulders and stared hard at Adele. "That's a stupid question. There's nothing wrong with our family."

"But..." Adele said. "But Babba is always telling us what to do. He won't let us be like other kids. We were born here, not in Lebanon. Why should I take Arabic lessons when my English friends don't? Doesn't that make you mad? Babba's so pushy."

"Yeah, but that's just the way he is. He gives us money, takes us places, and buys us clothes if we need them. Who cares if he pushes us? Anyways, you *should* learn Arabic."

"I don't want to," Adele said, her voice cracking.

"That's your problem then, isn't it?" Mona fell back on the mattress and pulled the covers up to her neck. She said harshly, "I can't believe you want to belong to another family. What family would want a big mouth like you? You're lucky to have this one. Now shut up and let me sleep, okay?"

Silently, Adele turned on her side and stared at the window, watching the first year's snowflakes brush against the glass. She wished she hadn't opened her *big mouth* at all.

The next day the snow continued to fall in big flakes, sticking to Adele and her mother's woollen scarves and coats. They trudged along the snow-covered sidewalks towards the shopping mall. "When I was a young girl about your age, I spent a lot of time with my mother learning to cook, helping her out with housework."

"Didn't you have to go to school?" Adele asked, speaking in her broken Arabic. Samira looked down at her daughter. The green flecks in Adele's light brown eyes were more apparent in the bright light of the November day. Her eyebrows were thick, but not unbecoming. Unlike her sisters, she hadn't yet begun plucking them. But it was her open-faced smile that drew others to her, including her mother. Adele looked up and noticed her mother examining her face and she smiled back at her.

"I had to stop going to school when I was in grade three," Samira replied. "Because my parents were farmers, they needed me to help them with the farm work. They couldn't keep me or my siblings in school."

"Oh," Adele replied. She couldn't imagine not going to school.

"It wasn't that bad. I did learn how to read Arabic. I can read my language," she said proudly, raising her chin slightly.

"Tell me more," Adele prodded.

"Why are you so interested?" Samira suddenly asked.

"You're my mother. I want to know you," she said, trying to copy the relationship she had with Mrs. Foster.

"Well, when I was growing up, the homes in the village didn't have indoor plumbing so I had to lug a bucket to the river to get water for washing dishes and clothes, not to mention myself!" she said, then laughed out loud. "By the time I was thirteen, I knew how to cook almost all of the Lebanese dishes—*taboulleh*, *hummus*, grape leaves, *kibbeh nayeh*, *koosa*. My allspice dreams."

Adele asked, "What are 'allspice dreams?'"

"Well, I don't really know how to explain it but since I was a girl, I knew I wanted to be married and raise a family. I didn't have the fancy dreams city folks did. I just wanted a simple life with my husband and kids. So my friends and I came up with the term 'allspice dreams.' You know how often I use this very important spice in our dishes, well, I wanted it to reflect my dream of becoming a wife and mother—two very important roles for Lebanese women. I wanted to be a wonderful cook, whose house would be filled with this rich smell every day. My ambition was the same as all the other girls in my village: to get married, have children, and be remembered as a wonderful mother and cook. Allspice dreams. I hope one day you'll realize this dream too."

"No," Adele said too fast. "I don't want that dream. I want to be an artist!"

"But artists can get married too. And paintings can't bring joy to your life like a family can."

"I don't want to cook for a husband. I want to paint each and every day."

"Then you'll be a very lonely woman when you grow up, *habibti*. Every woman needs a husband."

"Not me," Adele insisted.

Changing the topic, Samira continued with her earlier thought, "Most Lebanese people love visiting one another and my village was no exception. There were no strangers. We'd have family gatherings almost nightly, sit outdoors, and spread colourful embroidered cloths across the tables in the yard where the olive grove surrounded us. Then the women of the village would bring out tons of plates for the *maza*, sometimes up to forty dishes! The adults would drink down the food with glasses of *arak*."

Adele interrupted her mother. "You mean the white stuff you sometimes rub with a cotton ball on my teeth when one of them is sore? It tastes like licorice."

"Yeah, you're right, *habibti*. But it does help a toothache, doesn't it?"

Adele nodded.

Samira went on, "My whole family—my uncles, aunts, cousins, and grandparents—would all scramble to speak. It was quite loud sometimes, but so much fun. If only I were a child again!"

"But then you couldn't be my mother," Adele interjected.

"No, I couldn't. And a young unmarried girl with a baby would be the worst fate. *Ayb*. I don't even know such a woman," she whispered. "Anyway, I had some good days in the village. When I wasn't cooking or helping my mother, I'd venture into the fields with my brother Ferris. He was a shepherd and sometimes he'd let me guide the sheep and goats across the mountain village. But only sometimes. I wasn't very good at it, you see. My place was in the kitchen or on the cement walkway in front of my parents' stone house, kneading dough into circular pieces of pita bread."

"How come you don't make it here? How come we only buy it?" Adele asked.

"It's too difficult to make in Canada, much easier to buy from a store. Who has time, *habibti*? Don't ask such stupid questions."

"I'm sorry, Mama," she said, casting her eyes on the ground and remembering that Mona said the same thing to her last night.

Samira noticed that Adele's eyes were tearing up. "I'm sorry. It wasn't a stupid question. Do you want to hear more?"

"Yes," she mumbled. Adele was used to being called "'stupid" by her father but when her mother said it, she felt something inside her shrivel up.

Samira cleared her throat. "Your Uncle Ferris once dared me to beat him up to top of the mountain. Whoever reached the top first wouldn't have to help our Sito wash her feet. Thinking that I could beat Ferris, I accepted his offer. But I should've known better. He lived in the fields, spent most of his time there and around the mountains. I should've known better," she said, shaking her head.

"So you lost the bet? You had to clean your Sito's feet?" Adele asked, laughing, having forgotten her mother's cruel comment a few minutes ago.

"Yup. But it wasn't too bad. My Sito was a wonderful, strong Lebanese woman. She raised eight kids and helped with the fieldwork, gathering the olives, making goat cheese, and selling it in the marketplaces of Baalbeck and Zahlé. She was amazing. And she had a good sense of humour. Always joking. She made all of us laugh like when she'd belly-dance with a bottle balanced on top of her head. When I knew her, she was already quite old. Her skin all puckered, reminding me of withering olives. Everything about her was ancient except her laughter. You know how warm the *kaaks* I make during the Easter holiday are."

Adele smiled and nodded, remembering the rosewater taste of her mother's Easter sweet bread.

"That's how warm and rich her laughter was." Samira stopped and made the sign of the cross. "May God rest her soul. You know, she used to tell me to always be happy. She'd say 'Laugh a lot and be happy. Life's too short to be unhappy.'" Samira gazed down at the sidewalk, now almost completely covered with snow. Adele stared at the furrows around her mother's tired eyes. She imagined hearing her great-grandmother's voice echoing across continents, over the Mediterranean Sea into the Atlantic. The memories were so vivid in her mother's stories that Adele felt she had been a part of them.

She touched her mother's arm and said, "Be happy like your Sito said. Remember?"

"I know, *habibti*, but sometimes it's hard to remember," she sighed, taking a long breath.

Adele dropped her hand to run to the front entrance of the shopping centre. She pulled open the door for her mother, then followed her into the mall. "Thank you, Adele," Samira said, patting her daughter's head, which was now uncovered. Adele began to tie the scarf around her waist; her hands moved fast, looping it into a knot. And her curly hair was a tangled mess. The sunlight made the reddish-brown of her hair more visible. But when they were indoors, it looked almost as dark as her sisters'. Touching her head, Adele turned to her mother and exclaimed, "Look, I'm Medusa!" She shook her head frantically, making herself dizzy, and letting the curls whirl around her face.

Samira covered her eyes with her hands and teased, "Oh no! I don't want to be a statue!"

"You're my mother," she said, looking serious. "I can't turn you into stone." Then she laughed loudly. Samira smiled, took her hand, and they strolled hand in hand through the large mall.

Adele watched her mother trace a silk scarf on a rack, her long fingers moving across it, touching the fine pattern of interlinked lines of green, red, and white. Her mother stared so hard at the colours that Adele thought they reminded Samira of the Lebanese flag. Samira's eyes began to tear up. Her breathing became shallow.

Adele stood beside her mother, fidgeting. She wasn't much of a shopper, disliking the hurriedness and crowdedness of the shopping mall. But she knew her mother liked this place filled with bargains, greasy food, and lots of action.

While Samira stared dreamily into space, holding the scarf in her hands, the sales clerk across the store rummaged through another rack, glancing up every few minutes at Adele and her mother. He was tall and thin, almost to the point of emaciation. Adele watched the way he stared at them. His tiny eyes narrowed. The man suddenly stepped closer to them, watching Samira's dark hands move over the scarf. Her tongue licked her painted lips as she leaned into the thick hair near Adele's ear. "What do you think, *habibti*?" she asked. "Do you like the scarf? Should I buy it?"

Adele nodded her head but her eyes didn't leave the clerk's face while he made his way closer to them. He was frowning openly now.

"Maybe next time, Adele. I don't think your father would be pleased if I bought the scarf. You know how he hates it when I spend money," she said in Arabic, sadly putting the scarf back on the rack. "Let's go." She motioned to Adele and was about to lead her out of the store when the thin man blocked her way. Samira abruptly stopped, nearly walking into the sales clerk. She hadn't noticed him there, hovering. "Sorry," she said, trying to move to the side and pass him. He moved his body with hers as if they were dancing. When he grabbed her by the arm, she let out a gasp of surprise. Her eyes grew wide as he pulled her back to the cash register, which was in the middle of the store. "Excuse me," he said coldly. "You forgot something."

With her brows pressed together, she frowned. She had no idea what this man was talking about. Looking across at Adele for guidance, who stood a few feet from her, she asked in Arabic, "What does he want?"

Adele bit her lower lip. She didn't understand why this man was picking on her mother. She had only *looked* at the scarf. Her face grew hot. Then she shook her head and replied quietly, "I don't know, Mama."

The man gripped Samira's arm tighter, his bony fingers digging into her coat. "Speak English. This is Canada, not whatever country you come from. In Canada, we speak English."

"She wants to know—" Adele began.

But the man interrupted, "I'm speaking with your grandmother, not you."

"She's my mother," she said, correcting the man.

"Oh," he paused. "Well, she no speak English?" he said, taunting. "How long you been in this country, girl?"

"My whole life," Adele answered, now standing beside her mother.

"I wasn't speaking to you. I was addressing your mother."

"Why did you call her 'girl' then?" Adele asked.

The man didn't reply but instead stared into Samira's eyes, which made her shy away uncomfortably; Samira was not used to strange men looking at her so closely. The clerk squeezed Samira's arm so tightly that she cried out in pain.

"What matter? What I do wrong?" she said, her voice shaking. Her lower lip trembled as she spoke in broken English. Adele's cheeks turned red while her mother attempted to speak with the man. "What I do wrong? Why you hurt me? I only look at scarf. Only look, no steal. Only look, only look," she repeated, tears filming her eyes.

"Why you no speak English?" he said, laughing. He finally let go of her arm. "You want to know 'what you do wrong?' You stole the scarf. I saw you stuff it into your purse," he said, motioning to the leather purse strapped over Samira's shoulder.

"That's a lie!" Adele shouted.

But this didn't stop the man from suddenly pulling the purse off from Samira's body.

"No, no," Samira said, struggling with the man who managed to grab her purse out of her hands. He unzipped it and emptied the contents onto the counter where the cash register was. A lipstick tube, change purse, pack of Kleenex, gum and a sanitary napkin tumbled out. Adele looked away from her mother's things.

"I no steal. Only look," Samira insisted. "Scarf not here, no scarf. See," she said, pointing to the items on the counter. "I no steal!" she yelled, the tears now streaming down her cheeks.

Adele stared back at the front entrance of the store. People were beginning to gawk at the commotion ensuing in the shop. Some stared directly at them and others fumbled with their bags, pretending not to see Samira's tear-stained face, her coat sleeve dragging across her eyes. Quickly turning away, Adele stared back at her mother and the sales clerk.

"Listen, girl, I swear I saw you stuff the scarf in your purse. Maybe it's under your coat. Open up," he said, grasping the collar of Samira's coat. He tried to pull it open but Adele suddenly pushed his hands away from her mother and let out a cry. At this moment, another man walked into the store. He wore a white shirt and tie and had a nametag pinned to his shirt with the store's name printed in bold letters. He smiled at Samira and patted Adele's head.

"Hello, Ma'am," the man with the tag said. He had a trimmed grey beard and a wide-open smile. But he stopped smiling when he saw the contents from Samira's purse. "What's going on here, Steve?" he said to the sales clerk.

Steve hesitated, then said, "This lady was shoplifting. I saw her with my own eyes."

"What did she steal?" he asked, now rubbing his right hand along his beard, trying to spot the item among Samira's things. The clerk began to shift nervously through the things as if trying to find the stolen item. "Answer me, Steve."

"Um … I'm sure it's here."

"What did she steal?" the grey-bearded man repeated, his voice now stern.

"My mother didn't steal anything. My mother's not a thief. He's a liar!" Adele said, her voice rising and her finger pointing at the clerk. Her hand trembled, as if she'd eaten too many Christmas cookies.

Steve blurted out, "It was a scarf. She stole a scarf."

"Well, I don't see a scarf in this pile."

"Dirty Arab thinks she can come into our store and steal from us."

"This isn't your store, Steve. You only work here, under me. You're not the owner, understand?"

Steve lowered his eyes and nodded. "But we're not in the Middle East. We have laws here and one of those laws is 'not stealing'. I was only protecting your store, Mr. Brooks," he murmured. "Damn dirty Arabs think they can do as they please."

Mr. Brooks suddenly interjected, "That's enough." He looked across at Samira, who was wiping her face with a crumpled Kleenex. "I don't see a scarf here, so obviously you didn't steal it. I'm so sorry, Ma'am, for the misunderstanding," he said, carefully placing the items into Samira's purse. He handed it back to her. "I'm very sorry."

Samira shook her head. "I only look. I no steal."

"I told you my mom isn't a thief," Adele said quietly now.

Mr. Brooks nodded his head in agreement. "I know." He turned to the sales clerk and said coolly, his lips pressed together, "This customer deserves an apology."

"Sorry," the clerk muttered.

Grumbling something under his breath, Mr. Brooks turned away from his employee in disgust and lightly touched Samira's shoulder. "My sincere apologies, Ma'am." He then walked to the scarf rack and sifted through it, pulling out a few and holding them up to Samira. "Which one would you like? It's on the house." The green, red, and white one she had been admiring was amongst the bunch.

Adele opened her mouth and was about to answer for her mother when Samira dragged her away from the man, rushing toward the exit. Adele nearly tripped on her own woollen scarf, which was sliding down her hips. "Mama, the man wants to give you the scarf for free. Take it," Adele said with a wide grin. She thought her mother didn't understand the man's offer.

Samira glared back at the store, the two men standing across from one another, their voices rising in a heated argument, the scarves swinging in the owner's hands. Samira's eyes began to fill with tears again.

"Mama, the man wanted to give you the scarf, the one you liked," she repeated, tugging on her mother's coat.

"Hush, *habibti*, I don't want the scarf anymore," she said in a whisper, wiping her eyes quickly. "Let's go back home, okay?"

Adele followed her mother's lead. Samira wrapped her woollen scarf around her head and they hurried out the mall and down the street. Samira looked down at Adele and, her voice unsteady, said. "Promise me you won't tell your Babba about this, okay?"

Adele wanted to ask her why, but the desperate look in her mother's eyes silenced her; she just nodded. While they walked, Samira shook her head in disgust. As snowflakes landed in the open space between her neck and collarbone, Adele wished she had spat in that clerk's face! Instead she had only listened to her mother stumble over words in a language not her own.

When they returned to house, Adele walked inside and tripped on her mother's boots by the front door. Samira didn't look back at her daughter as she raced up the stairs. After Adele regained her balance, she sat on the steps and pulled off her own boots. Head tilted back, she heard the door to her parents' bedroom slam. Once she hung up her coat, she ran up the stairs and grabbed onto the banister while she swung her body around the corner. Then she stopped, frozen by her mother's cries. Adele tiptoed to the door, the floorboards creaking under her weight. She pressed her ear against the door, fingering the knob, unsure of whether to intrude on her mother. After a while, she slowly opened the door. She peeked into the bedroom, spotted her mother on the edge of the bed, in front of the mahogany dresser with the large vanity mirror, the one Mona often used when fixing her hair. But her mother wasn't brushing her hair. She was sitting with her elbows on her knees, leaning into the mirror and scrubbing her face with her hands. Adele wondered why her mother was rubbing her face without a facecloth. What was she trying to remove? Her make-up?

Samira chanted something over and over. Adele craned her neck to hear but she couldn't make the words out at first. She leaned in closer, opening the door a little more. Her mother still didn't know she was there. And suddenly the words became clear. "Dirty Arab, you dirty Arab!" Samira chanted again and again in a melancholic tone.

Samira fell back on the bed, crawled to the middle of the mattress, turned to her side and hugged her knees to her chest, the low sobs still shuddering through her. Adele stepped back and pulled the door shut again, crept away from the bedroom and carefully tiptoed down the stairs. Through the window next to the front door, her eyes followed the snowflakes drifting across the front steps. She leaned in close to examine her reflection in the glass, and stroked her cheeks. She examined her fingertips. There was no dirt on them. Why had the man called her and her mother "dirty Arab?" She was only twelve and didn't understand why the man had called them "dirty." They weren't dirty. But after hearing the man's cruel words, she knew some people saw them differently. Through her own reflection, she watched the falling snow carpet their front lawn.

CHAPTER 4

THE SNOW FELL LIGHTLY. Adele looked at the trees her father had planted in the front yard for herself and her sisters. Four trees for four daughters, she remembered hearing her father say to countless customers over the years. He had spoken these words with a hint of pride even though Adele knew he had longed for a son. She guessed the trees helped ease the bitterness. Nature could do that. She thought of the trees now, saw the crocuses that had recently emerged, dusted with snowflakes, most likely the last before spring, as she made her way down the street. And she wondered if her father could ever love her the way she imagined he would have loved a son.

Within a few minutes, she stood in her junior high school yard and waved at her friends in the distance. Her curly hair bounced as she walked towards them and joined them on a bench. "Hi, Adele," said Melissa, Adele's friend since kindergarten. Adele still longed to trade her dark unruly hair for the silkiness of Melissa's long, straight blonde hair. "Can you come to my party tonight? My parents won't be home because they have dinner plans, so it'll be just me and my friends. We can probably sneak in some of the boys after my parents are gone," Melissa said, her blue eyes shining brightly as she smiled.

"Some of the boys?" Adele teased, raising her right eyebrow. "You mean Todd?"

Melissa shifted her legs on the platform and smiled more widely. "Yeah, but we can invite others too. Like Ben."

Adele grinned when she heard Ben's name. He was a blond, blue-eyed boy who was new to their school and Adele had a crush on him since the beginning of the year when he chose the desk next to hers and smiled at her with those big, blue eyes. Sometimes she imagined taking his hand and guiding him around the side of the school, gently pushing him against the red-bricked wall and kissing him softly on the lips while his fingers touched her cheeks and felt the heat coming from her skin. As she thought of Ben, her stomach began to flutter. She suddenly felt flushed.

"So, can you make it?" Melissa asked, waking Adele from her fantasy.

"Probably not. You know how my father is," Adele replied, her voice dropping.

"But I'm turning thirteen! I want my best friend to be with me," Melissa said and got up from the bench. She stood in front of Adele and added, "Tell him that. Say it's Melissa's thirteenth birthday and she really wants me to be there. He should understand this. This is a big birthday. I'm becoming a teenager! Why do you think my parents are allowing me to have this party without them in the house? If you want, don't tell them my parents won't be there."

Adele turned from Melissa's downcast face and glanced at her other friends. Tracy and Erin were blonde like Melissa. They were still sitting on the bench, swinging their legs as they too chatted.

"My father wouldn't let me go either way," Adele finally confessed.

"He's so old-fashioned," Melissa groaned.

"I know," Adele agreed. "He thinks I'm some village girl."

"With the goats and donkeys!" Melissa laughed, then Tracy and Erin joined her.

Adele smiled weakly but made no comment. She wanted to explain that those animals were a part of her heritage, a part of her parents' homeland, but she couldn't find the words to do it. Instead she stared down at the ground and shuffled her feet.

"Your father is annoying sometimes. I don't know how you live with him. I would be so embarrassed to have him as a dad," Melissa said.

"He doesn't even look like other dads," Tracy piped up, "with that big, curling moustache. You should try to get him to shave it off, Adele."

Still looking down, Adele lowered her voice again, "I can't get him to do that."

"That's too bad," Melissa answered. "If you had parents like mine, you'd be able to go to my party."

"Well, I don't," Adele said. Her friends knew nothing about her and her culture. Her parents didn't own expensive cars or have university degrees. They didn't read or write English. They couldn't possibly understand the importance of turning thirteen. For them, it was just another number. It didn't guarantee more freedom. She suddenly felt very sorry for herself. Why didn't she have parents who could read and write in English? Why was she born to Samira and Youssef and not to parents like Melissa's? "I'm Lebanese," Adele said, louder than she had intended. "My parents are the way they are because we're Lebanese."

None of her friends replied for a long, awkward moment. Then Melissa finally laughed, reaching her hand out to Adele and squeezing her arm. "But you're like us. You were born in Ottawa, right?"

Adele nodded, sniffling now and wiping her nose with the bottom of her sleeve.

"Didn't you learn anything in Mrs. Johnson's class? That makes you Canadian, not Lebanese."

Adele nodded again and when the bell rang, she followed her friends out of the yard, into the school.

When she walked back home later that day the snow on the crocuses from earlier in the day had melted and the purple flowers were wide open under the sun that now shone, turning the sky a dark shade of orange as dusk began to fall. Adele unzipped her coat, letting her body feel the warmth of the sun. Spring was almost here, she thought, deeply breathing the damp scent that comes when winter melts away and spring arrives again. Kneeling, she touched the purple petals, careful not to break them off the plant and as she rose again, her eyes fell on the layered black hair of a teenaged girl sitting in a red Trans-Am a block away from Adele's house. Her hair was just like Rima's. Was it her? Then Adele spotted a boy, leaning into the girl's face and kissing her. There was no way that Rima could be allowing that, Adele thought, but when the girl turned her face slightly, Adele gasped. It was her sister. She quickly stepped back and hid behind a maple tree, pressing her hands in the rough bark while she peered at her sister and the teenaged boy in the red Trans-Am. From what she could see, he had blond hair and a square-jaw. He definitely wasn't Lebanese. Without budging from her spot, she prayed Rima would pull herself away from this boy and get out of the automobile before their father saw her. After a few minutes of kissing, Rima finally got out and waved at the boy before he sped down the street. Hurrying, Adele came out from behind the tree and ran up the sidewalk to join her sister. She hooked her arm into Rima's, chanting, "Rima and blond boy sitting in a tree, k-i-s-s-i-n-g."

Rima jumped. "Shit, you scared me, Adele!" she exclaimed.

"First comes love, then comes marriage then comes Rima pushing a baby carriage!" Adele teased.

Rima stopped and pushed Adele away from her. "Shut up! Don't tell Babba about this."

"Who is he? Your boyfriend?" Adele crooned.

"None of your damn business."

"You know Babba won't let you date him."

"I don't care what he thinks."

"Then why didn't you let him drop you off at home, eh?"

"Shut up, Adele! You better keep your mouth shut or I'll shut it for you," Rima said, raising a clenched fist towards Adele's face.

Adele stepped back. "I'm only teasing."

"Well, I'm not. I'll break every bone in your body if you open your big mouth, understand?" she said fiercely.

Adele noticed the tension around her sister's mouth and realized she wasn't kidding. "I'm sorry," she finally answered. "I won't say anything to Babba."

"You better not." She then grabbed Adele's face and squeezed it between her palms. "I'm sorry, too, Monkey but you have to understand that Babba won't like Mitchell."

"Because he's white?"

"Because he's not Lebanese." She dropped her hands and walked ahead of Adele in the direction of the store.

Adele silently followed her sister inside. Youssef was behind the counter as usual. He looked at them and smiled. "*Marhaba*, my girls. How was school?"

"Good," the sisters replied simultaneously before heading up the stairs to the house.

The next evening, the front door slammed so loudly that Adele dropped the sketchpad on her lap to the floor. She leapt off her bed and ran towards the hallway. She peered over the banister to see her father stomping up the stairs as if the house were on fire and he was trying to save her and her sisters from the raging blaze. But there was no fire. The only thing blazing was his face; his nostrils were wide with each breath he took as he ascended the staircase.

Adele quickly retreated back to her room, where she picked up the pad and pretended to draw. She didn't notice her father's glare as he walked past her room and headed into Rima's bedroom, where she was listening to her Rex Smith album, the blond heartthrob's sexy voice crooning under the crack of the closed door. In a matter of minutes, his voice was shattered when Youssef dragged the needle across the record.

"What are you doing?" Rima shouted.

"Don't raise your voice to me, you *sharmouta*!" Adele heard her father yell. She then walked out into the hallway and watched her father push Rima back on the bed, where she held her knees to her chest.

"My friend Joseph saw you last night with some blond boy at the theatres. I thought you were going to the movies with a friend."

"I was," Rima answered quietly.

"A boyfriend?"

"No, he's just a friend."

"Friends don't kiss. Joseph said you were kissing that boy as if he were your husband."

"I wasn't kissing him. We were only watching the movie together, nothing else."

"Don't lie to me, Rima. I swear if you lie to me again I'll slap you so hard that you'll never disobey me."

Rima didn't move. But Adele did, making the floorboards creak. Youssef turned around and glared at her before turning to face Rima again. "How could you disgrace me like that, Rima? How could you? The whole Lebanese community is talking about you, saying *bidt* Youssef is a whore."

"I love Mitchell. He's good to me."

Youssef raised his hand and slapped Rima across the face; her head snapped back. He clutched Rima by the shoulders but Adele lunged at him and pulled his arms away from her. He grunted and pushed Adele backwards, so that she fell hard on the floor. She got up quickly, rubbing her buttocks.

"You're forbidden to see this *enklese* boy again, understand?" Youssef didn't wait for a reply and stormed out of Rima's room and down the stairs.

"No, I don't understand," Rima said, rubbing her red cheek. Adele stood in front of the record player, lifting the needle and dropping it on the vinyl until she found a salvageable song;

Rex Smith lamented his heartbreak out of the speakers into Rima's small room.

Adele didn't hear about Mitchell again until a few weeks later. "I don't care what Babba thinks. I love him and I don't care what he says," Rima shouted, running down the stairs with Katrina following behind. Rima was now eighteen and her parents were pressuring her to date a Lebanese man named Ziad. Adele sat on Rima's bed and listened to the rising voices of her two older sisters.

"You knew you were going to get caught eventually," Katrina said from the bottom of the stairs. "Anyway, it's better to marry a Lebanese man...."

"So Babba feels better? What about me?" Rima said, her voice cracking.

Adele felt her eyes tear up. But she wiped them quickly when she noticed Mona staring at her. Mona leaned in close and put her arm around Adele. "Don't cry, Monkey."

Adele turned and stared blankly at the wall. She could no longer hear her sisters' bickering. Dark clouds had turned the bedroom walls into shadow puppets of Adele's and Mona's figures. When a gust of wind blew, the maple tree outside Rima's bedroom window hit the pane. It was a cool night in May. Light rain wept on the roof. Adele sat on the bed and hugged her knees to her chest. She stared out the window at the swaying branches, then suddenly heard the heavy footsteps of someone running up the stairs. She turned her head and spotted Rima walking down the hallway again, gripping onto a small suitcase. Shortly after, Katrina followed her down the hall, her breathing rapid and her face flushed. Adele watched Rima throw the bag on the mattress of her bed. Quickly, she unzipped it while Katrina sat next to Mona and Adele on the bed, staring at Rima's small hands as they pulled clothing out of the drawers and then stuffed it into the bag, making the bed shake. Adele sat quietly, watching her sister sway to and fro from suitcase to drawers, her hips swinging back and forth. Rima was a great belly dancer with her beautiful hips and small belly. The way her wavy hair tumbled past her shoulders, but not too far down her back, made Adele think of all the times she watched her sister dance at a *hafli* at the church hall. Always smiling.

But Rima didn't smile now. Face strained with worry, she continued to fill the small suitcase with her clothes. Rima suddenly stopped packing, and frowning, put her hands on her hips. Adele saw Rima looking across at her reflection, lifting her hands to her cheeks as if feeling the heat coming off of them. Rima's face was flushed and hot. Adele imagined Rima's palms were damp, too, as she pulled her fingers through her dishevelled hair. Rima blinked a few times, holding back the tears that Adele could see were pricking at her eyelids, then she stared down at the carpeted floor.

"What are you doing, Rima?" Adele suddenly asked, something she knew by the way Mona and Katrina stared back at her, their eyebrows arched in question, that her sisters were yearning to ask too. Rima didn't answer. She shook her head and grabbed a handful of underwear from the open drawer and shoved them on top of the other clothes in the suitcase. Adele realized that Rima was hurrying because her mother had whispered to her a few hours ago, "I have to go, *habibti*. Your father and I are visiting Aunt Nabiha in the east end. But we won't be too long." Samira had reached out and patted Adele's arm then left. Adele sat on the edge of the bed, not believing what she was seeing. Her sister was actually leaving.

"What are you doing, Rima?" Adele repeated, straightening her back. The mattress shifted under her weight.

"I don't know. To be perfectly honest, I don't know what the fuck I'm doing, Adele," Rima said, sighing once more. She pulled at the hair near her temples. "Oh, shit," she said, "What the hell am I doing? The only thing I know is that I love Mitchell and I want to be with *him*, not Ziad."

"Tell Babba that then."

"Yeah, right. Have you forgotten who our father is, Adele?"

"Stand up to him for once in your life," Adele said suddenly.

"Like you always do. Where does that get you? In your bedroom crying like a suck. You don't understand anything. You're just a kid."

"No, I'm not. I'm almost a teenager," Adele protested, crossing her arms over her chest and remembering Melissa's declaration about turning thirteen.

"Well, you don't know shit," Rima said, sitting on the bed now. She squeezed her body next to her sisters then lay down with her hands behind her head, her short legs barely touching the footboard. Adele looked at her sisters, their shoulders slightly hunched and furrows forming along their foreheads, covered by the loose strands of dark hair that fell into their eyes, forcing them to push the strands back behind their ears.

"Where are you going?" Katrina finally said, her voice barely audible. She was the soft-spoken one in the family, the one who never argued back. Her manners matched her physical features. Gentle face, kind eyes, bony shoulders, a frame so tiny that Adele's own pubescent body was already larger than hers. Katrina stared into Rima's eyes.

But Rima looked away. Adele realized her sister knew that her choice to leave would affect not only herself but her sisters, too. They would have to deal with Youssef's wrath. Adele knew it too. Rima got up from the bed and began to pace back and forth, the floorboards creaking. "I don't know where I'm going, Katrina. Somewhere. Anywhere but here. I want to be with Mitchell."

"Just tell Mama and Babba this," Katrina said, "tell them you love Mitchell." She hesitated as if their father were in the room with them, staring disapprovingly at her for speaking up. It didn't matter that Youssef wasn't there. "Speak with Mama and Babba before you run off."

"What good will that do? You heard Babba. He said he'd kill

me if he saw me with that 'white' boy again. He won't listen,"
Rima said, slumping back down on the bed again. Adele was
still sitting quietly on the edge of the mattress, dangling her
thin legs over the edge.

"Big fucking deal if you can't see Mitchell again," Mona
bellowed even though she was a few feet away from Rima.
"So, you can't date him anymore. You'll find another boyfriend
and this time a Lebanese one. You can always date Ziad like
Babba wants. He's an okay guy. Who cares if he's not the
greatest looking guy in the world? He's a few years older, big
deal. You can learn to love him. Anyway, you can't just run
away," Mona said, brushing her fingers through her long hair
while staring at her reflection in the mirror. Adele smirked
at her sister's vanity. Even in times of crisis, her appearance
was everything to her. Mona puckered her lips as if kissing an
imaginary person; herself, Adele thought.

Adele laughed out loud. "You're gorgeous, Mona!"

Mona glared back at her. She reached over and poked Adele.
"I know. You don't have to tell me." Then she flipped her
straight hair back over her shoulders in an exaggerated way.

Rima broke in. "I love Mitchell! I don't want to date anyone
else. Ziad is thirty years old anyway. An old man for god's
sake!" She glared fiercely at Mona, her heart-shaped face
tightening. "A few years older, my ass! More than a decade!"

"Don't get all pissed off with me, Rima," Mona barked back.
"I'm only trying to help. Why are you in love with a white man
anyway? There are plenty of good Lebanese men."

"Fuck you, Mona. You don't understand shit," Rima said,
still pacing. Suddenly there was a loud creaking in the house.
"Oh shit, they're back! Christ, Babba and Mama are back!"
Rima lifted the bag by the handle and was ready to make a
quick dash when she realized no one else was in the house; it
was just settling. The sisters remained still. Adele only heard
silence.

"False alarm," Adele said, sighing. "They're not home, yet."

Rima took a long breath and let go of the suitcase, falling back onto the mattress. "I don't have any other choice but to leave. I can't stop dating Mitchell...I don't want to..." she paused then leaning forward, placed her head in her hands and began to sob.

Katrina reached over, tears brimming in her eyes too, and patted Rima's back.

"You'll find someone else to love. It's not the end of the world if you can't see Mitchell anymore," Mona insisted.

"Like Ziad, right?"

"Yeah, he has money. He can buy you whatever you want. He's not that bad," Mona said.

Rima wiped the tears from her face and turned to Mona. She hissed, "Money's not everything." She pushed Katrina's warm hand away. Katrina looked down at the floor, and brought her hands back on her lap, clasping them together. "You don't know anything about love. I'm in love with Mitchell, not Ziad. He's so hairy and rough. Imagine kissing and fucking..."

Katrina's pale face pinched up and she frowned at her sister's language. But Adele noticed that she didn't lecture Rima this time. Katrina stared down at her hands, the bones protruding under the thin skin. Adele had expected Katrina to start her usual lecture of how foul language had no place in a Lebanese girl's vocabulary. But she said nothing.

Adele suddenly teased, "Hey, you're in the presence of a minor, remember, Rima? No mention of S-E-X."

"Oh, wow, she's not only cute but she can spell, too!" Rima said, smiling. The tensions slightly shifted and Adele turned to Katrina again who was now grinning.

"You could always put a bag over his head when you're in bed together," Mona said, fingering her hair. She looped a long strand in her right hand and looked down; not one split end was visible.

"You mean a body bag?" Rima laughed.

"Well," Mona paused, letting go of her hair. "One with an

opening right here." She pointed to her crotch and formed her hands in a large circle, the tips of her long fingers barely touching.

"He won't need that big of an opening. We're talking about Ziad, remember?" Rima said.

"How would you know, eh?" Mona asked, arching her left eyebrow. "You've seen it?" She looked serious. "You've seen his..." she paused. "You know..."

Rima laughed. "Yeah, I have dated him a few times and I've even touched it!"

"With your mouth or hands?" Adele suddenly interjected, smiling to herself. She loved shocking her sisters; they thought she was so naïve.

Rima playfully nudged Adele on the shoulders. "Listen to you! I was only joking about seeing Ziad's penis. The mouth or hands? My God, Adele, what are they teaching you in school these days?" She was grinning.

Katrina shook her head disapprovingly.

"I should go," Rima murmured. Her shoulders tensed as stared hard at the suitcase.

"Where will you go?" Katrina asked.

"I don't know," she said, looking at each of them in turn. "I'm not supposed to be thinking about marrying some old Lebanese guy just because Babba wants me to. Fuck, I'm only eighteen! I'm not even out of high school yet. Really, does this make any sense? What a fucked up family! What kind of parents encourage their daughters to date old men? Fucked up ones, that's the kind."

Adele silently nodded in agreement.

Katrina rolled her eyes.

"Don't look at me that way, Katrina! You know I'm right."

"Calm down," Katrina said. "That's the way things are..."

"Stop it! Stop saying that. Now you sound like Mama. We're in Canada, not some fucking village in the Middle East," Rima screamed, grabbing the suitcase from her bed. At the same time,

Katrina placed her hands on the top of Rima's and tried to pull the bag from her hold. The two sisters struggled, neither one refusing to let go of the suitcase. Rima suddenly pushed Katrina; she stumbled back, finally letting go of the handle.

Adele suddenly got up and ran toward Rima. She didn't want her to leave so she hugged Rima hard. Rima squirmed in Adele's grip, dropping the suitcase on the floor. "You can't go, Rima. We need you. Stay with us. Please," Adele pleaded.

Rima stopped squirming. Adele's warmth spread into hers. But then Adele saw a mixture of sadness and determination in Rima's eyes and she knew she was determined to leave. She realized, too, that things wouldn't change. Rima pushed away, but Adele refused to let her go. She grabbed onto Adele's right arm and twisted it; suddenly she had Adele pushed up against the wall. "You're hurting me," Adele cried.

"Stop it!" Mona said, jumping up from the bed. "Let her go, Rima! You're going to break her arm. Stop it!" But Rima held tight, refusing to let Adele go. Mona shoved Rima away from Adele. Tears were spilling down Adele's face once more.

"Stop crying!" Rima wailed. She punched the wall, just inches away from Adele's face, cried out wildly and then grabbed her own hand, examining the scraped knuckles. "I'm sorry, Adele," Rima whispered. "I didn't mean ... I'm sorry."

"You're such a bitch!" Mona said, coming to Adele's defence. "You're just as bad as Babba."

"Don't you dare compare me to him, Mona!"

But Mona didn't stop there. "You think you're so tough. Well, you're not! You're a coward, a chicken shit! Go," Mona said, flinging her right arm in the air. "Go. Leave us. We're the ones who'll have to deal with Babba. Take your fucking suitcase and run. Run, chicken shit, run," she taunted her sister. "Leave us to deal with your mess. Just go, Rima," she said, almost pleading.

"What are we supposed to tell him?" Adele asked in a small voice.

"You don't have to tell him anything," Rima whispered, staring across at Adele. But Adele avoided her sister's eyes and wiped her face with the sleeve of her shirt.

"What fucking world do you live in? '*You don't have to tell him anything.*' Yeah, right. Are you crazy?" Mona growled.

"I don't have time for this," Rima said, pushing past her sisters. "You guys don't understand. You have a lot of growing up to do."

"And look at yourself? You're running away! That's so mature. I admire you," Mona said. Pressing her hands against her chest, she said, "I aspire to be like you, dear Rima. Oh great, mature one!"

"Shut up, Mona! You don't know shit. You haven't even kissed a guy yet. Fifteen and never been kissed or felt up or anything," Rima said defensively.

"Well, at least I'm not a *sharmouta*."

"I'm not a slut. I'm still a virgin, you know. Just because I've experimented a bit doesn't make me a slut." Rima lunged at Mona and pushed her back on the bed. Jumping on top of her, Rima grabbed a fistful of Mona's hair. Mona yelled as they rolled together on the bed. Katrina jumped off the bed as their arms swung wildly at each other.

"Stop it! Stop it!" Adele shouted by the doorway.

Just as quickly as she had attacked her, Rima let Mona go and sat up on the edge of the bed. Then she got up fast, wrapped her fingers around the handle of the suitcase and lifted the bag as she walked out of the bedroom. "I have no other choice."

Adele waited until she heard her sister tiptoeing downstairs. She ran out of the bedroom and peered over the banister. Rima opened the front door and walked out. Adele screamed Rima's name but she didn't turn back.

CHAPTER 5

THE TV BLARED IN THE FAMILY ROOM while the three sisters watched an episode of *Happy Days*. Their eyes were pasted on the television screen, following the action between the Fonz and Richie Cunningham.

"But Fonzie, don't you want to meet your father? You haven't seen him in years," Richie said, sitting across from the Fonz in the apartment above the Cunninghams' garage. He sat up on the sofa and leaned towards the Fonz who stood with his thumbs gripping the front pockets of his jeans. The leather jacket was half-unzipped, revealing a white undershirt. Pacing back and forth, the Fonz finally said, "The old man deserted me when I was just a kid. My Ma had to support me herself. He didn't even say bye to me when he took off and left. How can I meet a man like that? I ain't got an old man."

Richie sat back and sighed. "Everyone has a father, Fonzie. It's whether you want to forgive him, that's the real question."

Adele looked away from the TV. She sat beside Mona on the sofa across from Katrina. She glanced at her sisters, the glow of the screen on their skin made their flesh turn bluish-green. If only they had a friend like Richie to help them with their problems, she thought. A commercial came on and Adele turned to look out the window, checking for her father's green Chevy. She knew he didn't like having the TV on too loudly. The streets were deserted on this Sunday evening. Although their house was located in the downtown core, the loud noise from the cars on the main avenue didn't travel down their small, quiet street. As Adele stared out the window, her eyes fixed on the apartment building across from their home. The sisters referred to it as "the castle" because that's what it looked like. Adele was startled when she spotted her parents' silhouettes; they were walking towards the front door. "They're back," Adele said out loud.

Katrina's body was stretched out on the large sofa, her arms behind her head but when she heard Adele, she sat up quickly, straightened her shirt and clutched the remote control, lowering the volume of the TV.

"Hey," Mona protested. "I can't hear the show anymore."

"Shh," Katrina said, holding a finger to her lips. "Didn't you hear Adele? Mama and Babba are back."

The sisters sat on the couch with their hands folded on their laps. Their faces paled as they listened to the sound of the key slipping into the lock. Within a few minutes, their father walked into the house, their mother trailing behind him. Youssef switched on the light in the hallway and shouted, "We're back. How many times do I have to tell you girls to turn on some lights so it doesn't look like the house is empty?"

"Sorry, Babba. We forgot," Katrina replied from the family room.

"We've got very forgetful daughters, Samira," he said to his wife, closing the door behind her.

"No, they're young, that's all," Samira said in Arabic, removing her overcoat. Adele leaned her elbows on her knees and listened more closely.

"No excuse. When I was their age, I was already working and helping my parents with the land. I never forget anything," he said, tapping his head with his fingers. "I have a memory like an elephant's."

Samira smiled. "Things are different here, Youssef."

"Why do you always defend them?"

"I'm not defending..."

He interrupted. "If only I had a son, then I wouldn't worry so much. He'd remember to turn on the lights," Youssef said, leaning into the doorway of the family room. He turned back to his wife. "Stop defending them, okay?"

Adele sat back and breathed deeply, watching the shadows of her parents. She saw her mother grab a hanger from the closet and place her coat there. Then she heard her father say, "Are you listening to me?"

"Yes," Samira replied.

"There's no excuse for stupidity. Katrina's old enough to know better. Instead, she's stupid," he muttered in a low voice. Adele looked across at her second-oldest sister. She knew Katrina heard her father's mumbled words by the way her sister dropped her head and gazed at the floor. With her hands, she wiped her eyes before the tears had a chance to wet her cheeks. Their father had always called Katrina "stupid." It was his preferred nickname for his second daughter. Adele watched Katrina roll her shoulders inward until she was curled on the sofa, her knees pinned against her chest, her eyes still fixed on the floor.

"She's not stupid!" Adele shouted back at Youssef, defending her sister. The light from the doorway made her father's shadow flash on the wall.

His shoulders tensed. "Listen to her," he said to Samira. "That damn young one is always talking back. I should've whipped her like her sisters when they were younger to teach her some discipline and respect but, no!" he said, throwing his hands up. "Damn school teaches her to threaten me with the cops if I slap her. What do the government and school have to do with raising children, especially ones as defiant as Adele?" Youssef's footsteps pounded the stairs leading down into the TV room. With his hands on his hips, he looked at his three daughters who now sat upright on the sofs. "Where's the converter?" he bellowed.

"Here, Babba," Katrina replied, handing him the remote

control. He grabbed it from her and nudged Mona on the shoulders. "Go sit beside Katrina." Mona got up and obediently sat next to her sister on the other couch. With her father next to her, Adele frowned and moved to the opposite corner of the sofa.

Youssef aimed the converter at the television set and flipped the channel to wrestling. Two bulky men in skin-tight shorts and undershirts struggled together in the ring, pushing each other against the flimsy, flexible ropes. Their bodies crashed down on each other while the crowd clapped and cheered at the barbaric display.

"This is so fake," Adele said suddenly. She sat up on the sofa, straightening her small back. Mona and Katrina glared at her to keep her mouth shut, but she ignored them. "It's so fake."

Youssef immediately defended his favourite show. "No, it isn't. It's real. It's a sport." He sat back on the sofa.

Adele continued. "Everyone knows it's fake. Even a kid like me. It's fake and boring."

"Look at that man, look at the pain on his face. That's not fake," Youssef said, pointing at the set where one of the wrestler's face was crunched up in pain, clutching his right arm after the other wrestler twisted it behind his back.

"Fake. It's called 'acting,' Babba. Everyone knows wrestling is fake," Adele insisted. "Let's watch something else."

"This is my TV. I pay for the cable. We watch what I want, understand?"

"No, I don't understand," Adele persisted, her reedy voice rising in anger.

"Shut up, Adele!" Katrina finally said. "Listen to Babba."

"Why should I?"

Youssef turned from the TV and glared at Adele, his dark eyes narrowing, his thin lips pressing together. "Because I'm your father. I brought you into this world. I support you, feed you..."

"Mama feeds us, not you. You don't even know how to cook."

His face tightened even more and his thick eyebrows arched inward.

"Let it go, Adele," Mona whispered from across the room. "Just let it go." Adele stared blankly at her, then she turned to face her father again, defiant.

"I'm the one who pays for the food, not your mother," Youssef shouted, splattering spit on Adele's forehead and pounding his fist against his chest.

She wiped her forehead quickly. "Money isn't everything."

"What do you know? You're just a stupid kid. You'll never amount to anything. You'll be lucky if you find a good husband. Nobody wants a stupid girl and ugly too!" He stared hard at her as these words tore from his mouth.

"You're a bastard," Adele blurted out.

Youssef raised his hand and slapped her across the face. Katrina and Mona jumped but didn't look across at Adele as she rubbed her cheek.

"I hate you! If you hit me again, I'm calling the police on you, understand?" she said, trying to control the tremor in her voice.

"You're no good for nothing. No one could ever love you because you're so ugly."

Adele looked down at her hands, kneading her knuckles together. She felt the tears gathering but refused to cry. Youssef continued, "Only a dummy would think wrestling was fake. Can't you see right, even with your four eyes?" Adele pushed her glasses up her nose. Katrina and Mona lowered their heads while Adele took the brunt of their father's abuse. Without blinking, Adele stared intently at the television and let her father's words enter her eardrums, worming their way into the lobes of her brain, her heart. She glanced across at her sisters, who didn't raise their heads to meet her gaze. They stared silently at the floor.

Suddenly, Youssef stopped talking. He looked around the room. "Where's Rima?"

No one answered him.

"I told her to stay home with you. Is she in her room?"

"I don't know," Katrina answered. "I think so."

Youssef stood slowly, casting one more glance of disgust at Adele, and left the family room. The three girls looked at each other as the stairs creaked under his weight. Now he was walking down the hallway. Adele imagined him standing in the doorway to Rima's bedroom, his small lips puckering in anger at finding it empty. A minute later, he came racing downstairs again. Back in the family room, he looked hard at Katrina. "Where is your sister?"

"She's not upstairs?" Katrina asked, pretending her best to sound surprised.

"No. Where the hell is she?" he asked louder. Samira came into the family room, her face complicated with worry.

"What's wrong?" she asked.

"Rima's not home."

"Maybe she went out with a friend." She spoke in Arabic. Samira sat down on the sofa next to Adele. She smoothed her daughter's hair.

"Where is she?" Youssef repeated.

"She's gone." Katrina spat the words out.

"Where?"

"I don't know."

Youssef balled his right hand into a fist, slapped it into his left palm, more than once, as if he were warming up for a baseball game. "Where the fuck did she go?" he cursed. Then he quickly calmed down, and asked, "Did she go out with Ziad?"

"No. She doesn't like Ziad."

"Doesn't like Ziad? Why? 'Cause he's a good Lebanese man?" he shouted.

"She doesn't like him because she loves Mitchell," Katrina said.

"I told her to stop dating that boy!" Youssef threw his hands up in the air and shouted, "Son of a bitch! She better not be with that bastard. Where the hell did she go? She ran away with him!" He stomped across the room and said, "What are people going to think?"

"Why are you so concerned about what other people think?" Mona asked.

"*Ayb*," he said nervously, the consequences of Rima's actions flooding in on him in an unstoppable tide. He ignored Mona's comment. "*Ayb*. How could she disgrace us like this? Wait until everyone finds out that she's run away. This isn't good."

"Well," Samira said, "we need to find her. Maybe we can find her before anyone else finds out about this."

"Of course, they'll find out! Especially if she refuses to go out with Ziad because of this *enklese* boy. Ziad wants to marry her. What am I supposed to tell him and his aunt and uncle if she refuses? *Ayb*," he said again, his voice trembling. He turned to Katrina. "Where is she?"

"I don't know."

He stood in front of her and grabbed her by the shoulders. "Where the fuck is she?"

"Honest, Babba, I don't know. I tried to stop her," Katrina said, her body shaking in her father's grip. "I don't know where she is."

"Did she go with that boy?"

"I don't know," she mumbled.

Youssef grunted in disgust then let Katrina go. He sat on the sofa and cupped his head in his hands. His daughters and wife sat silently in the blue glow of the TV, too afraid to turn the channel or shut the television off. Adele twisted away from her father's face and stared at the television set. Two wrestlers were at it again, pounding each other on the floor of the ring. The taller of the two—a man with wild blond hair pulled back in a ponytail—suddenly grabbed the shorter wrestler, flung him over his shoulders, then slammed the man's muscular body on his knee. The man winced and lay on the floor, groaning. Adele glanced over at her father. Youssef's face was as severe as the small wrestler's face, all tight and wrinkled. She studied the way her father sat, hanging his head in his hands. What was the big deal? she wondered. So Rima was dating a white man. It wasn't the end of the world, she thought, shifting on the sofa. What was the big deal? She turned to the television set again and took a long breath as the short wrestler regained control, smashing the other man into the elastic rope, now making them both fall onto the mat like objects flung from a sling-shot. Adele slumped back into the sofa once more and wished she were anywhere but here. She stared vacantly at the wrestlers pounding each other senseless. Maybe Babba was right, she thought. Maybe it was real.

The next morning, Adele sat at the kitchen table while her mother hurriedly moved from the stove to the phone, wiping her hands on her white apron before lifting the receiver. Mona, Katrina, and Youssef had left the house shortly after they had all awoke to continue the search for Rima, which had gone on most of the evening. Sleepy-eyed, Adele had watched her older sisters quietly dress before joining their father in the awaiting car. Adele was to stay behind in case Rima or Mitchell called. She wondered if Mitchell and Rima had indeed run off together. Did they elope in Niagara Falls? She had heard of a chapel there that performed quick weddings for cheap. She imagined Rima standing next to her blond boyfriend, the rushing falls a romantic backdrop as they exchanged their vows. Her imagination turned to the phone as it rang loudly. She was about to pick it up when Samira pushed her back in her seat and headed for the phone instead.

"Hello," Samira answered. "Who's this? Rima?"

Adele sat up, pressing her elbows on the table. "Where are you, Rima?" Samira asked in an anguished voice. She switched into Arabic. "What are you doing at Norah's grandparents' house?" Adele listened intently, cupping her face in her hands. Norah was Rima's best friend. Rima had known her since kindergarten. The Azar sisters had visited her grandparents'

farmhouse on several occasions, sometimes sleeping over if
Youssef was feeling generous. Adele closed her eyes, could see
the steeple-like roof and the red shutters while she imagined
Rima talking on the phone in the living room where Haida
masks hung above the fireplace. But Adele suddenly awoke
from her reveries to hear soft whimpers from her mother's
throat. "Please don't cry," Adele whispered across the room.
Samira's eyes met hers then looked at the cradle of the phone
again. "Why did you leave?" Samira asked.

Adele guessed there was no answer on the other end because
silence echoed in the kitchen. Finally, her mother said, "You
know your father won't allow you to date him. He wants you
to marry a Lebanese man, not an *enklese*. There's nothing
wrong with Ziad. Why don't you want to date him? He's a
good man and he can support you. He's a lawyer. What does
this other boy do for a living? He's just a student. How can
he take care of you? Come home. We can talk about this
some more at home. Maybe your father will change his mind
about Mitchell. We'll talk at home about this. Your father's
out looking for you now with Katrina and Mona but they'll
be back soon. Come home, *habibti*," Samira pleaded. "No,
he won't be angry. He's just worried about you, that is all. He
wants you back home."

Adele wondered if Rima would obey their mother. But then
she heard her mother say in broken English, "You good girl,
Rima. You do right thing. We talk with your Babba, okay?
Bye, bye, *habibti*."

Adele sighed, then watched her mother open the oven door,
bend down and sprinkle the simmering food with allspice, the
orange-brownish spice melting into chicken skin and shaven
potatoes.

That afternoon, Adele sat in the backseat of her father's green
Chevy. She watched her father lean forward and stare out the
window of the car while Katrina stood on the front porch of

Norah's grandparents' farmhouse. Within a few minutes, Rima emerged from the house with the suitcase she had hurriedly packed the other day in her hands. Katrina and Rima walked slowly down the stone pathway to Youssef's car. Adele couldn't take her eyes away from Rima's eyes. They were swollen and red. Only when her father opened the door, did she stop staring and look at Youssef as he slid out of the car and walked to the back where he opened the trunk.

"Hello, Babba," Rima said, smiling weakly. Adele looked at Mona beside her but Mona didn't meet her gaze, only dug her heels into the floor of the car.

Youssef didn't reply. He grabbed the suitcase out of Rima's hands and lifted it into the trunk. Slamming the trunk shut, he walked back to the driver's side, formed his lips into a tiny smile before waving goodbye to Norah's grandparents. He then slid into the car once more. Rima slipped into the passenger's side while Katrina squeezed into the backseat with Adele and Mona. They drove home in silence.

"What were you thinking disobeying my orders to stop seeing that *enklese* boy? Why were you acting like a crazy girl? Running away!" Youssef screamed, tapping his finger against his temple. He stood by the counter in the kitchen, near the fridge while his daughters sat at the table and his wife stood in front of the stove. The smell of spiced chicken and potatoes in the oven floated in the air. "Were you even thinking? Running away for God's sake! How stupid can you be? You know how people talk. What if someone saw you with the suitcase?"

"Maybe they'd think she was going on vacation," Adele said, laughing. Youssef turned around and glared at her.

"You keep your big mouth shut!"

"Jeez, I was only joking," Adele whispered, leaning close to Mona.

Mona shoved her aside. "What's wrong with you?" she hissed while their father barked.

"What you do not only affects you but your entire family, Rima. You should know this by now. You're Lebanese! Everyone talks. You disgraced us with your thoughtless behaviour. Your Aunt Nabiha knows the whole story and you know how she talks."

"Then why did you tell her?" Adele said innocently.

Youssef slammed his fists on the oak counter. Adele jumped. "Didn't I tell you to shut up?"

"Yes, Babba." She bit her lower lip.

Mona hit her on the arm. "Shut up, Monkey!"

"Okay," Adele mumbled. "You don't have to yell at me too."

Youssef started in on Rima again. "You're taking my good name and dragging it through the mud."

"I'm sorry, Babba," Rima cried, sitting at the kitchen table.

"You have to stop dating this boy. You should date Ziad because he'll marry you. The *enklese* boy is only after one thing. Ziad won't take advantage of you," Youssef insisted. "If you don't show any interest in Ziad, people will talk. They'll know that you love another man and they'll call you a *sharmouta*."

"No they won't," Adele spoke up again.

Youssef turned from Rima and glowered at Adele. He drew his lips together. "Shut your fucking mouth, Monkey. Mind your own business. You know why they call you Monkey? It's because you look like one!"

"And you're an ape. A stupid ape!" Adele shot back.

Youssef stomped across the kitchen, stopped in front of her and raised his arm. Samira said nothing, glancing at Adele then quietly taking the chicken out of the oven and letting the pan cool on the stovetop.

Adele startled then said, "Hit me, Babba. I swear if you do, I'm calling the cops."

Instead, Youssef slapped his hand against his thigh. He grunted then faced Rima and continued his tirade. "You have to break-up with that *enklese* boy and marry Ziad," he said. And as he spoke, he looked from daughter to daughter and somehow he realized he was outnumbered. Adele could sense this too, by the way her father hesitated, then added, "Ziad can give you a good life. What's more important than that, Rima?"

"Love, Babba," Adele answered again. "Love is more important." Rima glanced up from the floor across at Adele and faintly smiled. "She loves Mitchell," Adele added.

Youssef looked at Adele, his voice rising in anger once more. "How many times do I have to tell you to shut up?"

Adele wanted to stick her tongue out at her father but she didn't. She just glared back at him.

"Babba, Adele is right," Rima finally said. "I don't love Ziad. I love Mitchell."

Adele lifted up her legs and sat cross-legged on the kitchen chair. Mona and Katrina looked at her, their faces strained with worry. Youssef also looked at Adele, the way her large eyes scrunched and glared at him. "I don't know how I ever produced such a defiant child. You're always fighting with me. How the hell did I have a child like you?" Then he turned to look at Rima. "You'll start dating Ziad again and forget about this Mitchell guy. You'll see. Everything will be all right. But I'll never forget this, Rima. This running away. You've disgraced your Mama and me. Hopefully, Ziad will still want you after fooling around with that *enklese*. You made yourself out to be a whore."

Rima began to cry. Youssef walked out of the kitchen with Samira following him. Adele placed her left hand on top of Rima's right one. "Babba's a bastard."

Rima nodded, sniffling at the same time.

"You're not a whore," Adele insisted. "Don't listen to him. He called me an ugly monkey and that's not true," she said, flipping back her curly hair and smiling. "I'm too beautiful to be a monkey." Rima laughed out loud. Adele smiled, too, happy to hear her sister's laughter.

Then Rima stared across at Mona and Katrina, their faces pale. "You guys look like you've seen a corpse."

"Well, we thought you'd be one," Mona said.

And, rather than cry, Rima laughed. Her sisters joined her and they laughed until tears ran down their faces.

Four weeks later, Adele sat in the living room and watched Ziad slip a large diamond ring on Rima's finger. Her entire family, along with Ziad's uncle and aunt, were gathered in the Azar house to witness this engagement. Ziad was thirty years old but looked younger than his years with his thick black hair. He wore an open-collared dress shirt and a large crucifix on a gold chain. Following her sisters' lead, Adele leaned in close and gave him a kiss on each cheek. His dark skin was clean-shaven with the exception of a thick moustache above his full lips. And his eyelashes were just as long as Adele's and her sisters'. His deep-set eyes sat under a bush of black brows that were positioned close together and over a large, hooked nose. Adele hated the feel of his moustache on her face and afterwards, she rubbed her cheeks to erase the itchiness from the coarse hairs. He then grabbed her thin wrist and pulled her to his lap. His breath smelled like tobacco. "Hey, Adele, you can be one of the bridesmaids," he smirked. He pointed at her flat chest. "But we'll have to get oranges to go into your bra, so you'll match your sisters." She hated him that instant. Pulling away, she straightened her shirt and sat beside her mother, who got up and walked into the kitchen. "I'm only kidding, Monkey."

"Don't call me that," Adele said, moving away from Ziad. "That's a family nickname."

"And Ziad is now family," Youssef said, grinning widely.

Adele wondered why Rima was letting this man into their family. What about Mitchell? But Ziad had charmed Rima with flowers and jewellery, all the things she loved. She learned the story of his life. How he came to Canada ten years ago, went to university to obtain a Canadian law degree, and built his law practice with nothing but the brain in his head and a small loan from his uncle. He found a good clientele through the large Lebanese community. If you needed a lawyer, he was the man to go to. Rima had even overlooked her initial disgust about his unsightly hairiness. Now his ape-like hand rested possessively on Rima's arm, making sure she didn't get away. It suddenly occurred to Adele that Rima was indeed marrying a man exactly like their father, only younger. Adele kept quiet, pretending that she hadn't noticed Ziad's resemblance to her father by focusing on the maple trees outside the living room window.

Samira returned to the living room and served the others red wine then she gave Adele a glass of juice. Adele tried to smile as everyone raised their glasses and made a toast to Ziad and Rima, but she couldn't. She ground her teeth as she concentrated on the large diamond ring adorning her sister's short finger. She pulled her eyes away from the ring and settled them once again on the maple trees outside.

CHAPTER 6

ADELE RAN DOWN THE STAIRS TO GET HER BIKE. She was now fourteen. Once in the grocery store, she rolled the bike past Katrina, who was reading a magazine. "Where are you off to?" Katrina asked, looking up.

"Just a bike ride," Adele replied, looking across at her sister. Katrina's pale face was bright in the nectar glow of the morning sun. Unlike her sisters, Katrina had unusually white skin; she didn't look Lebanese. She was just as pretty as Mona and Rima but there was one difference: she was modest. Katrina suddenly stared at Adele and exclaimed, "Don't stay out all day like you usually do. Remember we have the *hafli* for Rima and Ziad tonight."

"How can I forget?" Adele answered, making a face at the mention of her future brother-in-law's name. "It's not even ten o'clock yet and everyone's in the kitchen making noise. I just need to get away for a little while."

"Okay. Tonight's important, Adele. It's the party before the big day."

She smiled sarcastically. "I'm so excited. Rima is marrying a wonderful man." She stuck her finger in her mouth and pretended to gag.

Katrina frowned and warned, "Be nice."

"I'm always nice. It's Ziad you should be warning because he's the one who's always opening his big mouth, not me," Adele insisted. "But I promise to be nicer to Ziad even though he's a chauvinist. You hear the way he speaks." She coughed before she started to imitate Ziad with his thick Arabic accent. "When I marry your sister Rima, I expect her to bring me a glass of water if I want one. Even if I'm standing by the fridge, and can lean over and pull out the pitcher of water, pour a glass for myself, I expect Rima to do this for me. You see, she's my wife. This is what a wife does for her husband. She must honour me. And obey me like the wedding vows say. And being the pig that I am, I can slap her ass while she's reaching into the fridge," Adele said, lifting her hands from the handlebars of her bike, slapping them together.

Katrina covered her mouth to stifle her laughter.

Adele continued. "Rima is very lucky to marry a man like me. I can't cook. I don't know how to clean. I don't know how to find my way to the laundry room. You see, the only difference between her and my mother is that she has the honour of having sex with me and carrying my children, which will be boys because unlike your father, I make baby boys. After all, I'm a macho man and the man wears the pants in the house, even if they're dirty from not knowing how to turn on the washing machine!"

Katrina began to laugh again. "Stop it, Adele. Babba might hear you."

"Yeah, and I really care what Babba thinks. You should know me better."

"That's why I'm warning you, Adele. Get out of here," she said, playfully. "Go for your ride. See you later, Monkey."

As soon as the bike was out of the store, Adele hopped on it and pedalled down the streets of her neighbourhood, feeling the coolness of the morning before the humidity of this July day would fill her lungs.

With the wind in her hair, Adele cruised along streets lined with houses built over a century ago. The sun rose behind a cluster of grey clouds. The only noise Adele could hear was the rubber tires of her bike on the pavement. She gazed at the red-brick homes. She loved the old houses for their porches and shuttered windows, the wooden steps that creaked when she stepped on them while delivering groceries to the older residents. Her parents' home was modern, built in the late seventies. It stood out amongst the historical houses of the neighbourhood. Not only were they the only immigrants in the area, Adele thought, but their home was an outcast too!

She took a deep breath then suddenly swerved to the side as one of her pant legs got caught on the chain of her bike. In an attempt to free herself, she pulled her body up from the seat. At the same time, she tried to shake her pant leg free, but abruptly crashed down on the bar of her bike. "Oh, God," she groaned, guiding herself and the bike to the curb. The pain between her legs shot through her body. She clenched her teeth, trying to hold back the tears. Standing by the sidewalk, she bent down and tugged her trousers from the chain. The material tore as she pulled her pant leg but she didn't care, she was in too much agony. She lifted her leg over the bar and pressed her thighs together, which helped alleviate the sharp pains pulsating in her pubic area. She limped unsteadily while she gripped the handlebars of her bike and rolled it down the street back home.

"How was your bike ride?" Katrina asked, standing behind the counter, fumbling with a package of gum.

Adele looked at her sister briefly then stared down at her body. Her pants were torn and grease-stained from the chain.

"Did you have a nice ride?" Katrina asked again.

"Yeah," Adele lied, looking across at her sister. She then quickly carried the bike into the backroom, leaving Katrina to gaze out the window of the store again with the white noise of the cooler humming in the background.

In the bathroom, Adele unzipped her pants and pulled them off. She threw them on the floor, then slipped off her underwear and spotted the bloodstains. Her hands shook while she turned on the faucet to the sink and held her underwear under the lukewarm water. Grabbing the bar of soap, she moved it across her stained panties until the blood was sucked down the drain. She wrung her underwear tightly and bent down on the floor, opening the cupboard of the sink, and hanging her wet underpants on the steel pipes of plumbing. Quickly, she picked up her torn trousers and scurried across the hallway into her bedroom, then closed the door softly behind her.

She rummaged through her dresser, found a clean pair of underwear and slipped them on. Afterwards, she fell back on her bed and stared up at the white-specked ceiling. The ache between her legs made it feel like the bones inside her were shattered. She suddenly wondered, too, if she was still a virgin. She knew the bleeding wasn't from her period because it wasn't that time of the month. She remembered reading somewhere that when the hymen broke, there was blood and this bleeding meant the loss of one's virginity. Had the bike accident made her lose her virginity? She turned on her side and started to cry, then squeezed her arms around herself to make herself stop. She had to be brave. She promised herself not to tell her sisters about the accident. And definitely not her mother. Their mother and father mustn't know.

"Adele!" Youssef shouted from the bottom of the stairs. As Adele came fully awake, she still felt the dampness between her legs, the stickiness that usually accompanied her menstrual cycle. She stood up, lifting the band of her underwear and cautiously peering down; dark stains had formed on the cotton briefs. Oh no, she thought, I've lost my virginity again! If only she could confide in one of her sisters, but she knew they wouldn't understand. Her father yelled once more. "Adele!" Hurrying out of her bedroom, she dashed towards the linen closet, grabbed a sanitary napkin and ran back to her room, placing the pad on another pair of underwear. She then opened the closet and pulled out her jeans.

"Adele! Where the hell are you?" Youssef barked again as if his voice had a volume dial.

She quickly slipped on her pants then heard her father's heavy footsteps creak on the floorboard. He now stood outside her door. She jumped under the comforter of her bed before her father entered the room. He crossed the bedroom and threw the covers off her body. "Get up," he said. "I need you to deliver some groceries to Mrs. Foster. Katrina can't do it because she needs to come in and help your sisters and mother with Rima's party. Christ, get up," he said, poking her in the ribs.

"I can't go," Adele said, not up to delivering groceries after her accident. Her vagina still ached.

"Why? Are you sick?" he sighed deeply. Then glanced at Adele who clutched her stomach and moaned. Suddenly concerned, he asked, "What hurts?"

"My stomach," she answered hesitantly, sitting back on the bed. "It hurts. I think I have the flu."

"You don't look ill to me."

Looking down at her bare feet, Adele dug her toes into the thick carpet. "I can't go. I feel like I'm going to throw up."

Youssef rested his hand on her forehead. No fever. "You feel fine," he said, letting his hand drop to his side. "You're just faking it. Go get the box in the store and deliver it."

"Really, Babba," Adele persisted. "I don't feel well."

"Look, Adele, I'm tired of this bullshit. I know you don't like working in the store but you have to learn."

"I'm not lying. You've got to believe me, Babba," she said in an anguished voice.

"Stop it!" Youssef shouted, his hands slashing in the air.

She suddenly fell silent, casting her eyes on the floor again.

"I'm so tired of this bullshit." He looked around the room. His eyes stared at the bookshelf then he stood in front of it and fingered the spines of the books. Grabbing one, he threw it at Adele. She raised her arms to protect herself but the book hit her in the chin. "You and your damn books. That's all you care about. There are more important things in the world than books, you know. Work is more important than useless books, so you're doing as I tell you. Get the box and deliver it to the customer. You know, if you didn't read so much, you'd have perfect eyesight like your sisters. You've ruined your eyes with your reading."

Adele leaned her elbows on her knees and rested her head in her hands. Her back shook as she cried. "Books are useless crap," Youssef snarled.

"No, they're not," Adele mumbled. "What would you know anyway?"

Youssef stood by the doorway and asked, "What did you say?"

"Nothing, Babba."

"Even with your reading and writing, I'm still smarter than you any day."

"Yeah and that's why you're a grocer," Adele said sarcastically, getting up from the bed and wiping her face. She immediately regretted her words.

Youssef cleared his throat and spoke in a low voice, "The box is in the store on the counter. Mrs. Foster's waiting for the groceries." He sounded hurt.

"Okay," she replied quietly, leaving the room. Her father followed her and stood at the top of the staircase as she ran down the steps. At the bottom of the stairs, she turned to look at him. His shoulders drooped. His face was crumpled. Adele heard him sigh. She turned and ran into the store.

When Adele rested the box of groceries against the fence to open the latch leading to the Fosters' house, she saw weeds. The small garden used to be filled with vegetables, but the stalks were all dead now. It had only been a year since Mr. Foster's death and Mrs. Foster was still coping with the grief and memories that were now her only companions. It had been a few weeks since she had visited Mrs. Foster. Lately, Mona had been delivering the groceries. After Mr. Foster's death, Estelle barely ventured outside of the house with the exception of the front porch where she would sit on the swing chair and gaze out into the street in a vacant way. Her deep-set blue eyes lacked the glimmer they had had when her husband was alive. She used to walk in a purposeful way, but now Mrs. Foster hobbled down the hallway with her shoulders hunched, her stride slow and unsteady. She unlatched the screen door and held it open. Adele carried the box down the long, dim hallway. Once in the kitchen, she began to unpack the groceries and place them in their respective spots. She knew this kitchen as if it were her own. After she was done arranging the items, she turned and looked at her elderly neighbour who sat down heavily on one of the wooden chairs at the kitchen table.

"Thank you, dear," Mrs. Foster said. She pulled out a small change purse from the pocket of her loose dress and pushed some money across the table for the groceries.

"How are you doing, Mrs. Foster?" Adele asked, slipping the money into her pocket.

"Some good days," she said, lifting her hands in the air, "and some bad days. To be completely honest, dear, there are more bad than good. Pull out a chair and sit with me for a bit. Are you in a hurry, dear?" Mrs. Foster asked, motioning to a chair.

"No, I have time. The party for Rima isn't for another few hours. My parents said that you couldn't make it. That's too bad. It would've been nice to have you there," she said, pulling out a chair next to her neighbour and smiling.

"I know but I can't...." Mrs. Foster paused and then sighed.

"I understand," Adele said quickly, rubbing her hands together. A black and white photograph of Mr. Foster, wearing a golf shirt and a grin on his face, was held up with a magnet on the fridge door across from the kitchen table. The horn-rimmed glasses were large on his long face but from the comfortable way he posed, hands in his pockets and shoulders relaxed, Adele knew the photographer had been his wife. Mrs. Foster suddenly reached over and placed her hands over Adele's.

"You have long fingers. The sign of an artist...."

"Maybe," Adele answered, blushing, turning her eyes away from the photograph to look at Mrs. Foster. "I love the art classes I'm taking in school."

"Good for you," Mrs. Foster said. "My Harold had long fingers, too, but of course yours are so very pretty."

"Thank you," Adele whispered as she gently squeezed Mrs. Foster's hands.

A small grin appeared on Mrs. Foster's face. At the same time, she lightly tugged on one of Adele's spiral curls. "And these curls! I always wanted your curly hair," she said, laughing.

"If we could only trade."

Mrs. Foster winked and smiled. "If only...."

Adele continued, "I have always wanted straight hair like the rest of the kids in my class."

"Hmm ... people always want what they don't have. But you know what? There are folks who pay a lot of money to get those beautiful curls."

"You're right," Adele laughed. "I guess I'm lucky then."

"You bet! Lucky and pretty. I used to be pretty," Mrs. Foster said, touching her grey hair. Adele noticed how badly it needed to be washed. There were dark shadows under her eyes and the skin on her face was puckered and dry.

"Would you like me to wash your hair, Mrs. Foster? Help you bathe?" Adele quickly asked, hoping her neighbour wouldn't take offense.

"Are you sure you have time? I know how busy young people are these days."

"I have all the time in the world for you. Anyway, remember all those times I barged in on you and begged you to turn on the sprinkler so my sisters and I could run through it on your front lawn?"

"It was my pleasure, dear," she answered, smiling. She got up from her chair, held up her finger and said, "Hold on a moment. I found something the other day when I was going through old photo albums. Just one second." She walked into the living room.

While she waited in the kitchen, Adele focused her gaze on the stainless steel utensils that hung on an antique holder, then turned her head towards the pale walls which were stained with grease and dust. How had things fallen apart so quickly after the demise of Mr. Foster? Adele remembered a time when everything in this beautiful house was spotless and clean.

Mrs. Foster walked back into the kitchen with an old photograph in her hands. She passed it to Adele who snorted with laughter when she saw it. "My sisters and I were quite the bunch with our cute swimsuits!"

In the photo, the Azar sisters stood on the lawn in exaggerated poses with a spray of water hitting their already soaked hair and bodies. Adele's tiny belly protruded from her swimsuit while Rima held her up in her arms. Katrina and Mona stood beside them, grinning widely.

"You girls were like my own children," Mrs. Foster said, resting her hand on Adele's shoulder. Adele looked up at her and smiled. She wanted to tell her that she was like the mother she never had but Adele knew this was cruel because she had a mother. She wanted to confide in Mrs. Foster about the accident on her bike. If anyone would understand, it would be her. But Adele was too ashamed. Her face paled as she thought about the blood and pain.

"What's the matter, dear?" Mrs. Foster asked, noticing the change in her face.

"Nothing," Adele answered. She got up from her seat and changed the subject. "Well, let's see if I have any talent as a hairdresser."

In the bathroom, Adele undid Mrs. Foster's dress and slipped it off, then helped her out of her undergarments. Adele filled the tub with warm water while Mrs. Foster stood watching her, her hands on her hips, her skin exposed with all its wrinkles and brown spots, so different from Adele's own mother who always pulled her robe tightly around her body when leaving the privacy of a bath. Mrs. Foster grasped a fold of flesh from her belly; it shook in her unsteady hands. "Look at this. See what age does to you? I once had smooth skin like yours. Now I'm as wrinkled as a prune. Ah, don't get old, Adele," she joked. "But that's impossible to do, right?"

Adele nodded and smiled, kneeling on the floor and testing the water with her fingers. Then Mrs. Foster turned to look at her reflection in the mirror, the steam from the bath already fogging up the glass. Her shoulders drooped and her breasts sagged close to her waist; they were lined with fine purplish-blue veins. "But, I must confess I look pretty damn good for an old lady, don't you agree?" she said, arching her left eyebrow. The old woman preened in front of the mirror.

Adele looked away for a second. She wasn't sure what to say in response.

Mrs. Foster turned from her reflection. She had a look of deep concern on her face as her eyes stared at Adele. "Don't be ashamed of your body, dear. This is the only one we can be truly intimate with, really. One day, you'll find someone and fall in love and so on. But he won't know you like you'll know yourself. It's your body. Get to know it. Have fun!"

Adele chuckled but her cheeks turned red.

"Don't be embarrassed, dear." Then Mrs. Foster cleared her throat and reached into the medicine cabinet for a small container. At first, Adele thought it was some sort of medication but it was actually a glass bottle filled with allspice, the same spice that Adele's mother used for cooking. Mrs. Foster freely sprinkled some in the water and explained that she had heard about the healing properties of allspice. Somewhat sceptical, Adele pursed her lips in a tight line but then she softened her gaze and let the older woman fill the tub with this strong spice. Before slipping into the tub, Mrs. Foster bent down and kissed Adele on the forehead. "You're a good person. So sweet. You are so kind to humour an old woman!"

Adele's eyes began to tear. Maybe she could confide her injury to Mrs. Foster. She wiped her eyes quickly with the back of her hand and watched her neighbour as she submerged her body in the water. They sat silently before the rippling of the water from the movement of Mrs. Foster's body and Adele's hands, slapping a bar of soap across a facecloth, echoed in the humid air. Adele scrubbed the older woman's back with the cloth, gently moving it over the folds of loose flesh. She then massaged Mrs. Foster's scalp and lathered the shampoo until her head was covered with suds. Adele scooped some water into a silver canister and slowly poured it over Mrs. Foster's head, rinsing off the shampoo. At the same time, Mrs. Foster rubbed her eyes.

"I'm sorry," Adele said. She brushed the wet strands of hair away from Mrs. Foster's face. "I got shampoo in your eyes." Her blue eyes were red and puffy. And she took deep breaths as if struggling for air.

With trepidation, Adele stroked the woman's forehead like her mother did whenever she was ill. "Are you okay?"

Mrs. Foster took a second to calm down before she answered. "I miss him so much, dear," she whispered as she gripped onto the edge of the bathtub with her hands. Then she leaned her head on the side of the tub while Adele lowered hers. She felt like slipping out of the bathroom door, the emotions were so raw, so open. She was unfamiliar with grief. "I miss him so much. I miss Harold." Mrs. Foster's body began to shake with sobs. Adele patted Mrs. Foster's wet hand and blinked back tears. After a few minutes, Mrs. Foster raised her hand and rested it on Adele's face; it felt hot against her cheek but Adele didn't move back. "Thank you, dear. I really appreciate your help."

Adele smiled and said, "No problem, Mrs. Foster. Would you like to get out now?"

Mrs. Foster nodded. Getting up from her knees, Adele grabbed a towel and held it open for her neighbour. This time she didn't look away as Mrs. Foster stood up, her flesh glistening from the bath, her nakedness open. Adele then helped Mrs. Foster out of the bathtub, wrapping her carefully with the soft bath sheet.

A few hours later, Adele closed her eyes to the image of Mrs. Foster weeping in the bathtub but then opened them when she heard someone tiptoeing into her bedroom. She saw her mother slip a flower-print dress on her bed then exit discretely out the room. Samira had bought this dress for Adele to wear to Rima's party. As she slipped into the dress, the memory of her elderly neighbour's grief entered her mind again. She looked down at her hands as if they were still wet with soap. Her whole body began to shake and she started to cry with the memory of her neighbour's sorrow and her own, remembering the pain she felt from the accident on her bicycle. She cried harder. Wiping her eyes with the back of her hands, she stared out the window and followed the sun as it fell behind a grey-stoned apartment building in the distance.

After a while, she turned away from the sunset and gazed at her reflection in the mirror. The dress hung loosely from her body, one size too large for her thin frame. She lifted her hands and traced the open-collar of the dress, fingering the gold necklace she wore with a pendant of the Madonna and a turquoise stone used for protection against the evil eye. She jumped slightly when she noticed Rima standing by the doorway. "You scared me," Adele said.

"Sorry, Monkey," Rima said, looking cheerful. She came and stood behind her sister, ruffling Adele's curly hair. "You look great, kiddo. Maybe you'll find a boyfriend at this party. You never know."

"I'm not interested in finding a boyfriend." Adele preferred drawing and reading her books to thinking about boys.

"Not now but one day, that's all you'll be thinking about. Boys, boys, and more boys," Rima said, sitting on the edge of the bed.

"Whatever." Adele sat on the bed next to her sister. She looked into her beautiful face, which was covered with make-up. Adele didn't like it. Her sister didn't need much makeup. Rima's complexion was perfect, without a single blemish. She had recently cut her long wavy hair and now wore it in layers. The white jumpsuit she wore accentuated her skin, making her look very tanned, even though Rima avoided suntanning at all costs, because she was afraid of wrinkles.

"Are you happy, Rima?" Adele suddenly asked. "Is this what you really want?"

"What do you mean, Monkey?" Rima said, staring at her hands. The long tips of her fingernails were painted white.

"Are you sure you want to marry Ziad?"

"What kind of question is that?" Rima said. She moved away from Adele and sat at the foot of the bed.

"It's just that he's so much like Babba."

"You don't know him," Rima answered harshly. "You're just a kid. What the hell would you know anyway?"

"I'm not a kid. I'm fourteen years old. I'm a teenager," Adele insisted.

Rima glared at her. "Don't start pouting."

"Why would you marry someone like Babba?"

"Ziad's not like Babba."

"Sure he is. I see the way he treats you. He thinks because he's a man that he can treat you like a nobody. Don't you want more? Don't you want to go to college or university? You're only nineteen."

"I'm not into studying like you. I want to have children. I want to be a mother and a wife."

"A slave is more like it."

"Shut up, Adele. Why can't you be happy for me? At least I'll get out of here, away from Babba."

"You think?" Adele said. "Escaping from one hell hole to climb into another."

"Ziad's not like Babba," Rima repeated. "He's gentler, more loving."

Adele sighed. "I hope you're right."

"I'm right. Believe me. I know Ziad and he wouldn't hurt a fly," she said, smiling at Adele again. "Be happy for me. I'm getting married tomorrow. I'm leaving this 'hell hole' as you put it." She nudged Adele's shoulders with her own. "Don't worry about me, Monkey. I'll be all right."

Adele lifted her eyebrows. Rima smiled at her.

CHAPTER 7

A DELE'S JOB WAS TO ANSWER THE FRONT DOOR. "*Marha-ba*. Hello," Adele said, greeting the guests with a kiss on each cheek and then guiding them into the living room. There the guests admired the large cherry oak table visible in the dining room that was covered with a gold, hand-embroidered cloth. Several dishes were spread out on the table—garlicky *hummus* garnished with paprika, oil, and parsley; *taboulleh* atop fresh lettuce leaves; *fattoush* filled with bite-size pieces of pita bread; and *fatayers* of meat, potato, and spinach, and triangular pieces of cheese bread. Her mother's allspice dreams. The strong herbal aroma of Lebanon's rich foods filled the entire house. Decorated china and silverware sparkled under the chandelier of the dining room. On a smaller table in the corner of the room, bottles of soft drinks, uncorked red and white wines, and licorice-flavoured clear *arak* were lined up between glasses and napkins.

In the kitchen, crowded with Adele's older female relatives, Adele watched her mother glide from plate to plate, making last-minute adjustments, and her hands sprinkling various dishes with chopped parsley. Adele stood by the doorway, watching her mother orchestrate the chick pea or eggplant dishes as if she were a conductor and the musicians were plates heaped with lemon juice, garlic cloves, and crushed dry mint. "*Habibti*, come here for a second," Samira said, looking away from the plate of *baba ghanouj* sitting on the oak counter.

Pushing through the crowd in the kitchen, Adele brushed against the older women with their perfume-scented bodies. Now standing in the middle of the room, surrounded by the women of her culture, the kind of women she was supposed to emulate, Adele suddenly blushed, her cheeks getting warmer as she listened to the haunting voice of Fairuz, one of Lebanon's famous female singers, floating out of the tape deck. Adele looked at her shoes. The patent leather was still shiny and new, and the shoes glistened against the grey-greenish colour of the floor. As Adele stood beside her mother, she looked at the women around her, women with sturdy bodies and faces, lathered nightly with Oil of Olay. Their colourful dresses fit snugly, hugging their large bellies and breasts, bodies that had been vessels for the children they had brought into the world. These women were proud of their professions as child bearers, mothers, wives, cooks, cleaners, seamstresses, and so on. They lived for their children and husbands, Adele thought, gazing at their weary faces covered with foundation and eye shadow. Like Rima's makeup, she thought. Adele fidgeted uncomfortably in the dress her mother had bought her, pulling the collar of the dress so it rested more evenly on her upper body. Unlike her sisters, she had never been comfortable in dresses and skirts. She preferred wearing trousers to skirts any day. And she had begged her mother to buy her a pair of dress pants and shirt to wear to the party. But Samira had insisted that a young woman should dress like a young woman in a pretty, flowery dress and patent leather pumps, and wear makeup too. Being the youngest in her family, Adele had become the queen of hand-me downs. And because her sisters loved girly things, she ended up having to wear skirts she hated, lacy or frilly blouses, and form-fitting Capri pants with flowers embroidered at the bottom. Every now and then, she would use her Christmas or birthday money to buy T-shirts, lumberjack shirts, blue jeans, and khaki pants. But Samira would only let her wear these items occasionally, insisting she put on her sisters' used but more appropriate clothing. Adele looked across at her mother. Adele's cheeks were still flushed when her mother rested her hand against her face. "Are you feeling okay?" Samira asked, looking concerned.

Adele nodded without opening her mouth. She thought she was going to throw up any minute. She always felt ill at these family gatherings, too many people, too much talking and criticizing. She would have preferred to be on one of her solitary walks when she stayed outside for as long as possible.

"You don't look good," Samira said, staring into her daughter's bloodshot eyes. She rubbed Adele's forehead, felt for a fever. "You don't look good," she repeated.

Thanks for the compliment, Adele wanted to say, but she didn't. Gently pushing her mother's hand from her face, Adele said, "No, I'm fine, Mama."

"Maybe you're coming down with something. Your eyes are as red as tomatoes."

"Maybe I'm becoming one," Adele suddenly laughed while she raised her left eyebrow. "Maybe under this flesh, I'm really a juicy tomato. Care to sprinkle some salt on me?"

Adele's aunt turned away from her task and stared across at her niece. Aunt Nabiha squinted her mouth into a tight line. "You silly," she said in her accented English. "You talk dumb. You a tomato!" She shook her head disapprovingly.

Samira whipped around to face her sister-in-law. "She's not dumb," she said in Arabic, glaring at Nabiha. "Adele's very smart. One day she'll become something. You wait and see."

Aunt Nabiha waved her hands in the air, the gold bangles clattering against one another. "We'll see what becomes of your daughter, Samira," she sneered. "Youssef tells me she talks back all the time. She's not like my daughters, Odette and Josephine. They're good girls. Very outgoing and smart. They help their father in the restaurant all of the time. They're only sixteen and eighteen and already know what hard work is. Youssef tells me that Adele's scared of working in the store.

She's like a mouse, all shy and stupid, and speaks in a quiet voice when serving customers."

Adele tightened her fists, let them hang close to her sides. She wasn't scared of working in the store. She had done her share of packing shelves, serving customers, and delivering groceries. But when she had the chance, she wandered around the neighbourhood or rode her bike along the pathway of the Rideau Canal. She didn't want to end up a shopkeeper like her father. She had other dreams.

"That's not true," Samira said, defending her youngest daughter. "She works in the store."

"Not the way Youssef would like her to," Nabiha barked back. The other women briefly eyed the bickering women then continued with their tasks.

Rather than continue this fight, Samira quickly pushed the dish of *baba ghanouj* into Adele's hands. "*Habibti*, take this into the dining room. Place it next to the *hummus*, okay?"

Adele nodded and walked out of the kitchen. She looked down at the mashed pulp of eggplant, welcoming the scent of garlic and lemon that drifted into her nostrils. She placed the plate in the right spot then turned and looked in the direction of the kitchen once more. Her mother was staring out at her, a shadow of darkness in her beautiful eyes. She quickly wiped them with her apron, then continued preparing more food. Adele pressed her hands onto the dining room table letting her eyes run across the various dishes that had been arranged on the table.

When some guests made their way into the dining area, she looked up. The doorbell rang again and she quietly moved past the guests sitting in the living room, her shoulders hunched, the dress slightly falling off them. She straightened the collar, cleared her throat and greeted the new guests with the traditional kiss on each cheek and a forced "*Marhaba*." In the living room, she found a spot in the corner and sat down on one of the foldout chairs her father had bought for the party.

She held her hands in her lap and let her eyes wander over the people who sat around her. They all had dark hair and accents. And they bellowed over the music that played out of the stereo system. They spoke of their families, bragged about their kids, reminisced about the old country. Adele listened to the bits of conversation and tried to piece them together. "My daughter Anessy is getting married in a few months but the *hafli* before the wedding day won't be crowded and tight like this one. My house is very big. We have a living room that's three times this size."

"Did you hear about Tony's daughter? She got herself pregnant and that's why she's getting married so quickly. Imagine that! A Lebanese girl having sex before marriage. If that were my daughter, I would've taken the strap to her. *Ayb!* Well, at least Kasim's son is marrying her. She should've resisted him. She should've remained clean until the wedding night."

"I just renovated my family home in Lebanon. It's like a castle now. No old stone house for my family. They live like kings. We've got indoor plumbing, a garage for our Mercedes, a large grove in the front yard with fig trees. Mmm, I love those figs! Canada knows nothing about good food. The figs here aren't as good as the ones back home and especially the ones on my property."

Adele listened and smiled to herself. These were her people, she thought, the people she loved and loathed. They all spoke at once, clamouring to be heard. The house pulsated with Arabic music and the language Adele struggled with every day. She glanced over at one of her young cousins, talking busily across from her with some of her uncles. Jamil was only eight but he spoke Arabic as if he had just come to Canada, which wasn't the case. Like Adele, he had been born in Ottawa. But the Arabic words rolled off his tongue easily. Outside the window, the streetlights had turned the maple trees into shadowy figures. She could see more people making their way up the front steps. She got up quickly and pulled open the door before the doorbell rang, kissing the new visitors before ushering them inside. From the corner of her eye, she saw her father making his way down the staircase. She turned around and looked up at him dressed in his best suit, the navy one that hugged his round belly. It was out of style. His salt and pepper hair was slicked away from his wide forehead. She felt sorry for him in his old-fashioned suit. Adele smiled up at him; a sudden surge of love for Youssef went through her. "You look good, Babba," she said, smiling. He slowly, self-consciously raised his hand. For one moment, she thought he was going to touch her face, but instead his eyes met hers briefly, then moved past her. He smiled at all the guests, his hand already stretching out to the visitors. She stepped back and stood in the frame of the doorway.

CHAPTER 8

"HEY, YOUSSEF, MR. BIG SHOT!" Uncle Fadi shouted from one of the sofas, his dark face clean-shaven. Deep dimples were engraved in his robust cheeks. Bushy eyebrows covered large brown eyes that seemed to illuminate when he spoke, no matter whether the topic was sombre or light. He was a tall, burly man who laughed easily and often. He wasn't really Adele's uncle but she had called him that since she was a little girl. She addressed most of the older guests in the room as "uncle" or "aunt" as a sign of respect. She smiled when she heard Fadi's voice again, teasing her father. Youssef grinned back and slapped his hand into Fadi's. Why can't Babba look at me that way? she wondered.

Leaning against the wall, she let her hands rest behind her back while she watched her uncle's face transform the way she wished her father's face would when he looked at her. "Hey, big shot!" Fadi owned a sports bar where her father sometimes took Adele and her sisters for lunch. There, she liked to sit at one of the booths and sip on a vanilla milkshake, studying all the football paraphernalia her uncle had collected over the years. Helmets and jerseys of NFL teams were hammered above the bar and adjacent walls. A TV set always played the football games. Adele had listened to the men at the other tables, and the cooks who filtered in and out of the kitchen to watch the game, shout over the fumbling of the ball or a failed touchdown. She and her sisters ate their grilled cheese sandwiches and sipped their milkshakes surrounded by men. They were often the only females in the restaurant.

Now she stared at her uncle and wished her father could be more like him. Uncle Fadi always called her "honey," not *habibti*. She knew he said this to her sisters, too, but she didn't care; it still made her feel special. He caught her staring at him now and, winked. Adele grinned back. The next thing she knew, Fadi grabbed onto her hand and her father's, linking them together. Adele stood between the two men while they formed a line that other guests began to join. Someone turned the music up. Fadi took the position of leader and twirled a string of worry beads, *masbaha*, while the rest of the dancers kept up the slow, then fast rhythm of moving around the living room in a circle. Adele looked down at her father's feet stomping on the hardwood floor. Then there was jumping and everyone lifted their left leg in perfect unison and kicked into the air; they shouted too. She remembered her father explaining the meaning of this traditional folk dance of community often performed at weddings and other joyous occasions such as this one—Rima's *hafli*. Youssef had said that *dabke* meant the "stomping of the feet." The *dabke* leader was like a tree, with arms in the air, as Fadi continued to dance, proud and upright like a trunk. The dancers' feet pounded the ground— in this case the Azar household's hardwood—to show their connection to the land. Beads of sweat slid down Fadi's face and over his dimples. Adele followed her father's feet, trying to keep up with the quickening rhythm. Someone turned up the music and the crowd went around in a circle faster and faster, kicking their feet in the air, shouting and cheering at the same time. Adele smiled weakly as her uncle pulled her along the line. But she wasn't very fast or good at the *dabke*.

"*Yallah*," Youssef said, perspiration gathering at his temples. "Keep up with the pace," he mumbled.

Frowning, Adele struggled to keep up. The people around her flipped their heads back and shouted out in Arabic while they jumped up and down, following Fadi's lead, the string of beads flying above his head as if a lasso. Adele's palms became slick between her uncle's and father's grips. She lost the rhythm half way through the song. Her patent leather shoes slid on the floor as she tapped them and lifted her left leg. Fadi tightly held onto her hand and tried to guide her but he was so involved in the music that he hurried his pace, making her run beside him rather than stomp. Tripping over her feet, she looked up at the people at the other end of the line. Their faces glistened with sweat as they laughed out loud and stomped their feet.

Frustrated by the whole thing, Adele dropped her father's hand then pulled herself free from Fadi's. "Hey, honey," Fadi said, now slowing his pace, "Where are you going? Don't stop dancing. Come on. You'll get back on track, there's nothing to it."

Adele shook her head and withdrew from the crowd. She stood by the entrance towards the store, almost tempted to sneak down the stairs into the quiet solitude of the storage room. But she stood there and stared at everyone as they danced, their hands clasped together, their bodies jumping as they moved around in the circle, smiling across at each other.

Rima came pounding down the stairs, interrupting Adele's thoughts. Her wavy black hair was held in place with hairspray and its scent travelled down the staircase with her. Before the crowd could spot her, she grabbed onto Adele's shoulders and hid behind her. "Hey, Monkey! They didn't see me running down the stairs," she said, looking past Adele's body at the dancing crowd. "Next thing you know, they'll be forcing me to belly dance!" Rima grinned widely at her sister, no longer upset about the argument they'd had earlier. That was Rima, not one to hold grudges.

"You know you're going to have to belly dance," Adele said, smiling. "It's tradition." Like her sister, she knew belly-dancing was as much a part of a traditional Lebanese wedding as the exchange of vows and the wearing of gold crowns in the church service if you were Orthodox. "And what are you so afraid of? You're a great belly dancer."

"Yeah, but I'm nervous as hell," she said, holding out her right hand in front of Adele's face. "I'm already shaking so much. I might end up jiggling one of my boobs right out of my jumpsuit!"

Adele laughed. "What an embarrassment!" She deepened her voice, mimicking her father. "*Ayb!*" She then spoke in her regular tone. "Babba will have a heart attack right on the spot!"

"You think?" Rima asked, raising her left eyebrow and laughing. Suddenly, Fadi stopped swinging the beads and interrupted the dancing, having noticed Rima standing by the doorway with Adele. In his loud, bellowing voice, he shouted, "Rima, honey, come and dance with us." He waved his large hands in the air for her to join the crowd but she hesitated and stood behind Adele's small body. She held onto her shoulders so tightly that the already large flower-print dress slid off Adele even more.

Adele whispered to her sister. "If you keep pulling on my dress, my boobs, not yours, will pop out for everyone to see."

"Who are you kidding, Monkey? You're flat as a board!"

Rima and Adele laughed. By this time, the crowd was staring at the two sisters, the oldest and youngest of Youssef Azar's daughters. Youssef suddenly turned around and also studied his two daughters. "*Yallah.* Hurry up," he hissed in a low voice to Rima. And at the look of disgust in his eyes, the two sisters stepped apart, Rima joining the crowd while the other stepped back into the doorway again.

Now Fadi picked up the handheld drum and began to pound it slowly. The men in the crowd walked over to Rima and lifted her into the air, placing her on their shoulders. They walked around the room with her as if she were an Arabian princess. And in a way, she was. Virginal and pure. Adele watched the way the men bounced Rima on their shoulders in rhythm to the music. She clung onto their shoulders, her long fingers gripping their dress shirts. Fadi hit the instrument harder and faster while the music from the stereo continued to play. At this point, Ziad joined in. The crowd shouted and cheered for the groom, who smiled. He was dressed in a silk burgundy shirt with a black tie Rima had bought for him and dark dress pants. The men let Rima slide down, placing her beside her future husband. Ziad leaned into her body and planted a quick kiss on her mouth. The crowd clapped their hands at this public display of affection. Rima blushed as much as Ziad, who looked nervous. Then the women in the crowd touched Rima on the shoulders, pushing her to start belly dancing in front of Ziad. She hesitated until Aunt Nabiha took her arm and led her into the centre of the living room where the older woman began to shake her hips in rhythm to the Middle Eastern music that now played loudly on the stereo. Imitating Aunt Nabiha, Rima timidly moved her curvaceous hips while Ziad's wide eyes followed. Her entire belly jiggled as well as her curved thighs. Rima lifted her arms up to the ceiling and moved her body in rhythm to her aunt's. When she moved forward, Aunt Nabiha arched her body back and vice versa. People gathered around the two women, clapping their hands in tune to the music. Except for Adele. She remained by the doorway, her hands pressing into her hips.

Someone pushed Ziad into the centre of the room where he slowly moved his body awkwardly beside Rima's. Then a silk scarf was passed into Rima's hands. She dropped it around Ziad's neck and slid it over his shoulders and down his chest. He stretched out his arms and began to roll his belly, following the flow of the scarf. Rima made more sensuous movements of the hips and abdomen before Samira pushed through the crowd toward the stereo and lowered the volume, interrupting the mock seduction. Samira announced in Arabic, "Dinner is served. Welcome everyone."

Adele sat beside an older male relative on one of the foldout chairs around the dining room table. "You should speak Arabic fluently," he said, scooping up a small portion of *taboulleh* into a tiny piece of lettuce leaf. Across from them sat some of her older aunts, ones who had been in Canada longer than Adele had been alive, but spoke not one of word of English. This didn't stop them from criticizing the generation that spoke English fluently. They were the old women who clucked like hens, hatching proverbial eggs of gossip, cracking shells and spilling yolks of the supposed "wrongdoings" in the community. With their heads held high, they sat with their backs pressed against the velvet-cushion seats of dining room chairs while the rest of the guests sat on the foldout ones. Several people were sitting around the buffet dinner that had been lavishly spread out on the dining room table and others filtered into the adjacent living room with platefuls of food and glasses of wine or soft drinks. Adele was uncomfortably seated beside the man named Nadim. In spite of being in the middle of July, Nadim wore a large wool sweater that reeked of his body odour. She politely shifted over so she was a little closer to the doorway leading into the living room. She moved the chair without anybody noticing, in particular the old battleaxes across the way from her. She smiled at them but they just stared at her as if their faces were granite. She turned back to Nadim.

"Speak to me in Arabic," he demanded with his mouth full. His teeth were brown and rotten from years of neglect. Adele's own parents had their decayed teeth removed when they came to Canada. They had started to wear dentures in their mid-twenties. Nadim still had his real teeth; Adele tried not to stare at them. She had also noticed that his mouth was lopsided as if he had suffered from a stroke, something she dared not ask. Most Lebanese people didn't speak of their physical or psychological problems, so she privately wondered what had made his lip curl to one side when he opened his mouth and lectured her. And the scar above his right eyebrow— brown and deep—also made her wonder what had happened. Had he been a soldier in the old country? Or had his father beaten him for disobedience? From the corner of her eye, she watched the way the scar twitched when the old man spoke. Like her own father, the man had a receding hairline but with thick wavy hair on the sides of his head, pressed down by the small plastic comb he most likely kept in the back pocket of his baggy green pants. Youssef had often enough pulled out a black comb from his pocket and ran it through his hair when visitors unexpectedly dropped by the house or when a gust of wind had blown what remaining hair he had out of place. Adele smiled at the thought. She knew where Mona had gotten her vanity. "*Yallah*, speak in Arabic with me," Nadim said again, still talking with food in his mouth.

Adele looked away from his mouth once more. "I understand Arabic, but I don't speak it very well. I used to when I was younger but then I lost it."

"You should try harder," he insisted. "How will you speak with your Lebanese husband?"

"Maybe I won't marry a Lebanese man."

"Not marry a Lebanese man!" he exclaimed, and hit his leg with his hand. The dish on his lap nearly tumbled to the floor. Other guests stared curiously as the man caught the plate and demanded, "What man you marry then?"

Knowing very well what the man's reaction would be, Adele said, "Chinese."

"Chinaman!" he slapped his palm against his forehead.

"Chinese, not 'chinaman,'" Adele corrected. "What's wrong with marrying someone outside our race?"

"*Ayb*," he said. "You lose your heritage. That's what's wrong. You become lost and become nothing but a person without roots. Worse, your children won't know who they are."

Well, she wasn't a product of an interracial marriage, but she didn't know who she was either. She glanced at the faces surrounding her, wrinkles of disapproval engraved in the foreheads of the whispering old women, the people in the kitchen. This was her tribe. Wasn't it? She blinked down at the plate on her lap. The lemon juice from the *taboulleh* had flowed into the *hummus*, between the stuffed grape leaves and *kibbeh nayeh*, making everything on her dish soggy. The carefully cut piece of pita bread shook in her left hand. Her stomach no longer growled with hunger. She licked her lips, which had suddenly become dry.

"Why don't you speak Arabic fluently?" he repeated.

"I'm trying," she muttered.

"You sound like the gypsies who used to live in our village. Perhaps you're a descendant of them and not the Azar family," he said, mockingly.

"And what's wrong with being a gypsy?" Adele shot back. Her face reddened when she realized that those around them were now staring at her.

Nadim patted her shoulder and leaned closer, flooding her nose with the smell of garlic. "Calm down. This is a joyous occasion. Your sister is getting married tomorrow, remember?"

Adele nodded. She threw the half-eaten piece of pita bread onto her dish, then got up and gathered the guests' empty plates as they handed them to her.

"Ziad is a good *Lebanese* man," Nadim emphasized.

Bowing her head, she carried the dirty dishes down the hall. Friends and family carried glasses of *arak* and wine in their hands from the dining area into the living room. Feet once again began pounding on the hardwood floor. The deep beat of Arabic song reverberated off the cream-coloured walls as guests lined up and danced the *dabke* once more. Adele looked back at them but continued towards the kitchen. At the sink, she rolled up her sleeves and curled her small, round shoulders into her body, closed her eyes tight so the tears wouldn't slip out. But rather than wash the dishes, she pulled her sleeves back down and walked out of the kitchen, past the guests who were immersed in the dancing and music. By the doorway, she turned and studied her sisters: Rima, Katrina, and Mona were leaning into each other's bodies, laughing and belly dancing in the middle of the room while a group of people surrounded them, clapping. Everything seemed a blur; the energy of her people seemed to make her dwindle into herself until she could no longer breathe. She lowered her eyes and took deep breaths until she was able to look up at her sisters again. They spun around with wide smiles, beads of sweat sliding down their temples. Adele turned away from her sisters' radiant faces and ran down the front steps of the house.

Arabic music echoed in her ears. Before unlatching the fence to Mrs. Foster's yard, Adele turned to face the yellow grocery store and adjoining house. With its green roof and *Coca-Cola* sign jutting out from the stucco, her father's business looked picturesque, almost peaceful.

She slowly pulled open the gate and walked up the pathway leading to the white front porch. It was almost nine o'clock at night and she didn't want to disturb Mrs. Foster. She sat quietly on the swing-chair without making it rock too much. She listened to the crickets in the grass and the sound of music coming from her parents' home. Leaning back against the cushion of the chair, her shoulders finally relaxed. Only now, sitting on her neighbour's porch did she feel comfortable, though she knew that running away from the party proved she was an outsider—the Lebanese girl who was an impostor, a fake. Suddenly, the screen door to Mrs. Foster's house swung open. Adele jumped up and stumbled away, steadying herself against the brick exterior of the house.

"Oh, it's you, Adele," Mrs. Foster said, clenching a broom in her hands. The brush was up and pointed away from her body in anticipation of swatting the intruder. She slowly lowered the broom and rested it against the door. "Why aren't you at your sister's party, dear?" Mrs. Foster asked.

"Um, I ... I just," Adele stammered, then stared down at her patent leather shoes. She touched one foot to the other and crossed her arms in front of her chest. "I needed a break," she confessed.

"Oh, I see," Mrs. Foster said, lowering her body onto the old and rusty swing-chair that squeaked as she made it swing by pushing her feet away from the ground.

Adele didn't look directly in her neighbour's eyes; instead she angled her face to the moon.

"Parties can sometimes be overwhelming, can't they? I would much rather curl up with a good book than chat nonsense with complete strangers who are only being polite for the sake of appearances," Mrs. Foster said, looking up at the moon too. Adele quickly glanced into her neighbour's eyes. They were so blue. Adele's own eyes were bloodshot from crying earlier.

"I'm not a social butterfly. I could never flutter from one group to another." Mrs. Foster pressed her back into the chair. "Harold was the outgoing one in our relationship."

"But you don't seem shy at all," Adele said, moving closer to her neighbour, now leaning against one of the pillars that faced the chair.

"It's all an act, dear," she whispered, then laughed softly.

"Sometimes I feel like I'm acting too."

"What do you mean?"

"I feel like..." she stopped, looked down at the wooden panels of the porch. They were cracking in some places.

"It's okay, Adele."

"I feel like I don't belong with my family, like I'm not a part of them. Sometimes I wish you were my mother. I feel different when I'm with you. You make me feel good about myself. My father ... it's just," she paused and wet her lips with a quick flick of her tongue. Adele watched Mrs. Foster from the pillar, waiting for her to stop her, but she didn't. "My father sometimes says mean things to me. I ... I sometimes wish I could run away. I thought I could handle the words but..."

"Adele..."

"I'm sorry, Mrs. Foster. I'm sorry...." Her voice was shaking.

Stretching out her hands, Mrs. Foster said, "Come here, my dear."

Adele shuffled across the porch and grasped onto Mrs. Foster's hands then fell to her knees in front of her and laid her head on her neighbour's lap, her shoulders jerking up and down as the tears flowed. The old woman patted the girl's head, the sound of Adele's muffled cries joining the music coming from her parents' house.

CHAPTER 9

WHEN ADELE RETURNED HOME, she looked around the store and house and felt a sudden hatred for her father's property. What took place on Mrs. Foster's porch rushed to her mind. How had it gotten to the point where she had to sob on her neighbour's lap? Why did she let this house and her tyrannical father control her? For a few minutes she stood with her arms folded and stared hard at the place her father had built after she was born. Her eyes darted back and forth from the grocery store to the attached red-bricked house. The stucco of the shop was beginning to crack. The outer coat of paint had also lost its lustre; it was no longer a bright golden hue but a washed-out yellow. Adele tilted her neck and gazed up at the sign with her father's name captured in green letters. A few minutes later, she trudged up the steps, and past empty paper cups left by some of the guests. Standing at the door's threshold, she noticed that the visitors had dwindled down to a few stragglers, listening to the latest gossip or snacking on her mother's *baklawa* or *ma'moul*, icing sugar dusting the corners of their mouths. Her eyes scanned the hallway and adjacent rooms. The entwined pink, purple, and white streamers that they had strung up earlier that day were now cascading down the doorways and cream-coloured walls. She stepped inside. The house smelled strongly of *ahweh* and tobacco. She took a deep breath before joining her sisters in the living room where they were surrounded by a small group of young men. She tucked herself next to Mona on the beige sofa. Mona straightened her slender shoulders, turned and whispered in Adele's ear. "Where have you been? People were wondering."

Adele rolled her eyes and shifted away from Mona, making the springs of the couch creak.

"Thank God Babba was too busy to notice. You shouldn't have run off. What's wrong with you?" Mona questioned.

Adele thought again about what had happened on Mrs. Foster's porch, how she had cried, showing her weakness, and she knew Mrs. Foster would never judge her but this didn't stop her from regretting what happened. She looked around the room at the people she despised and loved at the same time.

"Aren't you going to answer me?" Mona asked, leaning closer. Adele peered at the tiny hairs above her sister's painted lips. There were clumps of mascara on her long-lashed, large eyes. "Answer me," her sister insisted. Mona's face was heavily powdered with makeup, and now the foundation and blush were oily and patchy. The nostrils of her sister's aquiline nose flared when she spoke. Unlike her own shoulder-length dark brown curls, Mona's jet-black hair was long and straight. Most of the time, she flipped it back in a seductive manner, but at this moment she sat still and scowled at Adele. She spoke in a low, serious voice, so the men across from them couldn't make out the conversation. Although, they couldn't have heard anything the sisters said, their own voices growing louder as each tried to gain control of the conversation. "You shouldn't have left. This party was really important for Rima. What kind of sister are you? Jeez, running away! You're not some *enklese*. Family sticks together, no matter what."

Adele felt a lump in her throat but she refused to cry. She had cried enough, the tears soaking Mrs. Foster's cotton nightgown. She bit her lip to prevent another flood. Not here, she silently thought in her mind. Not in front of them.

Frowning irritably, Mona said sharply, "Babba's right about you." She then turned to face Rima and Katrina, quietly listening to Mona lecturing their baby sister. Raising her eyes, Adele, too, looked at them and a faint smile appeared on her mouth. But they didn't return her gesture; they sat expressionless. Adele rose to her feet and bid them a quick goodnight before ascending the staircase.

When everybody else was gone, the Azar family slept. The sky thundered and rain thrashed against the steel sign of Youssef's grocery store, making it sway back and forth and clang against the wall. Adele couldn't sleep. She fidgeted in her bed until she finally sat up. She listened to the sign. It made her think of the shrieks of lambs being slaughtered in her parents' village, a sound Youssef had described over and over in his stories of Lebanon. But they weren't in the old country anymore. She had never been there but she thought she knew how it felt.

Outside the streetlights flickered against the green-coloured letters of Youssef's name while the wind continued to thrash against the sign. It was as old as the store itself, a fossil in an area slowly succumbing to the temptations of superstores and shopping malls. Yet Youssef was still famous in this neighbourhood; Youssef's Grocery was a household name.

But it wasn't the noise from the sign or the rain that made Adele sit up in her bed. It was her injury. Her pubic area still hurt. Quietly, she got up and stood by the window with her hands on her hips. Turning, she slowly crept out of her room, glancing at her sleeping sister Mona before slipping into the hallway and tiptoeing into the bathroom. She closed the door softly behind her. Then she knelt on the floor and opened the cupboard under the sink. She reached and pulled out her underwear that was now dry. The bloodstains had disappeared.

She began to cry. She was no longer clean and she thought no Lebanese man would want her because she had been broken and Youssef and Samira had told her and her sisters many times that all Lebanese men wanted their potential wives to be virgins. How would she explain to her husband the lack of blood when he entered her body on their wedding night? Would he still want her to be his wife, would he kick her out of his bed and house, giving her no choice but to return to Youssef and his disapproval? *Ayb, ayb, ayb*, she imagined her father fiercely shouting. *You've dragged my good name through the mud!* What would happen to her then? She remembered Mona's words: *Babba's right about you.* Her face grew hot and she thought, damn you for taking Babba's side. She rubbed her face and wept again. Her heart was throbbing so violently that her ribs ached. She could tell no one what happened. She had wanted to tell Mrs. Foster about the accident on her bicycle but instead she cried on the old woman's lap without revealing her secret. She got up and looked hard at herself in the mirror. The skin under her eyes was swollen and her curls were messy. She brushed her hands over her cheeks, wiping away stray tears.

She opened the door and walked down the stairs, past the living room and down another flight of steps into the basement. She flipped on the light switch. As a young child, she had been terrified of this basement even though it was fully furnished. This was where she and her sisters played and watched television when Youssef had taken over the family room upstairs, clutching onto the converter and refusing to let the girls watch their shows.

Walking into the laundry room, she cursed and threw her dirty underwear into the basket with the other clothes, then returned to the TV room and flung herself on the couch. She was no longer afraid of the basement. Years ago, she had thought the devil lived there, something that had entered her mind after having watched *The Amityville Horror* with her sisters. They warned her to go upstairs when watching the movie, but she wouldn't listen to them. She was eight years old and she wanted to do what her older sisters were doing. And she had nightmares for weeks afterward and wouldn't come down to the basement for almost two months. Instead, she had to sit through hours of wrestling with her father. Laughing out loud at that memory, she was unexpectedly comforted by the sound of her own voice. She turned and stared at the bar lined with bottles of red and white wines. There was no devil down here. Just Youssef, sometimes, entertaining his relatives with his dinner parties. Adele turned away from the bar and examined the wood panelling on the walls. The walls were covered with pictures of movie stars, men her sisters had admired. A large painting of a village house and an old woman carrying a bucket of water across a rickety wooden bridge hung on the wall across from her. Her parents bought this work of art because it reminded them of the village they had abandoned for Canada. She knew her parents wanted her to be a young woman carrying water, a village girl. They expected her to be a virgin and stay at home until her future husband came to rescue her. But Adele had lost her virginity to her bike! She laughed again, now that the absurdity of it filled her thoughts. "Jesus Christ," she said out loud. "I may have broken my hymen, but I'm still a virgin. I haven't been with a man yet." She slapped her hand against her forehead and stretched her legs back on the sofa. Closing her eyes, she smiled at herself and let the night enfold her as she drifted off to sleep.

The following week, after days of rain, the sun made itself visible in the sky. Now the brilliant light filled Adele's bedroom while she sat on her bed with a sketchpad on her lap. The sunshine warmed her hands. Between her thumb and forefinger, she held a pencil and moved it over the bumpy, mulberry stationery as she glanced up and down from the paper to the weeping willow in the distance; its drooping branches touched the earth as if thanking the soil for allowing its roots to spread. Suddenly, she heard the front door open. The sound of footsteps entered the house and shuffled across the hardwood floor. She raised her head in the direction of the hallway. Within a few minutes, a clamour of voices travelled up the stairs and into her bedroom.

Adele immediately recognized her eldest sister's light-hearted tone, but then she also heard her brother-in-law's deep Arabic accent, drowning out Rima's greeting. Adele got up from her bed then went downstairs to greet her sister.

"Hi, Rima. Welcome back!" she said, jubilantly.

"Hello, Monkey," Rima replied softly. They embraced. And behind her sister, Adele saw Ziad, his hand on the small of his wife's back.

"*Marhaba* Ziad. *Kif Haalak?*" Adele mumbled, freeing herself from Rima's hold.

"Good, good," Ziad answered. The smell of aftershave flooded Adele's nostrils when she leaned in and gave her brother-in-law two quick kisses on the cheeks. Then Adele looked at his large hand as he squeezed her sister's arm and guided Rima into the living room. Adele followed behind. Her family, and Ziad's mother, Mrs. Jaber, were gathered there. Mrs. Jaber was staying with Ziad and Rima and returning to Lebanon in a few days. Adele sat down between Mona and Katrina, but her eyes scrutinized Ziad and the way he took a seat on the sofa as if he owned the place and owned Rima, his broad shoulders pressing into the beige couch, his long legs spreading wide, touching Rima's, his hand clasped her left thigh. The rich smell of Arabic coffee hovered in the humid July air. After a few seconds, Adele turned and studied Mona and Katrina. They both wore skirts of varying lengths. Mona's miniskirt fit tightly on her slim body while Katrina's long flowing skirt made her look bigger than she actually was. Their faces were coated daily with makeup and today was no exception. Foundation covered their skin and pink and purple eye shadow smeared their eyelids. Things were changing. Her sisters were with Lebanese boys and socializing with more Lebanese than English friends.

Adele glanced at her own body. Her developing chest was small and her appearance was tomboyish. She sported jeans and a red polo shirt, falling over the waistband of her trousers.

Her face was free from makeup. She was still always arguing with her father. She was still the defiant daughter.

Adele focused her gaze on Ziad's mother, a woman whose face was as rigid as steel and just as cold, Adele presumed. The woman's eyebrows furrowed on her round face. Mrs. Jaber stared hard at Rima, who smiled too easily and too frequently. Mrs. Jaber sat upright on the sofa and tucked the loose strands of silver hair that had escaped from the tight silk scarf wrapped around her head behind her ears. The grey dress Samira had given her fit snugly around her belly and the seams looked as if they were about to come undone. Snug as a bug, Adele rhymed in her mind, but she looks more like a scorpion! Adele knew Mrs. Jaber had preferred her son to marry a Lebanese-born woman rather than a Canadian one just by the disapproving frown on her face.

Youssef's voice startled them all. "How was your honeymoon in Niagara Falls?" he asked in booming Arabic.

"Beautiful," Ziad replied.

"It rained here the entire week while you were away," Adele interjected, as if suggesting the sombre weather had something to do with her sister's union to Ziad.

"Well, it was absolutely gorgeous where we were," he said firmly.

Adele glanced from her father to her brother-in-law. Youssef was short and Ziad was tall. Youssef was pale and Ziad was dark. Youssef was balding and Ziad had thick hair. But their voices both sounded harsh. Youssef butted in, "I remember taking the girls there when they were young. It was nice, although the drive was hard because the girls ended up getting sick. We had to stop at so many gas stations to use the washroom."

"Perhaps they needed to freshen up their makeup or fix their hair all under the disguise of illness," Ziad sneered. "You know how women are."

Youssef grinned and nodded his head with agreement.

Samira said nothing, sitting quietly next to him.

"I know, I know. You don't have to tell me." Youssef lifted his hands in the air and waved them around. "I'm surrounded by females. I have my own little harem!" He threw his head back and laughed, then continued. "But they were really ill. And at that time they didn't wear makeup."

"On our drive there, Rima made me stop at every exit so she could freshen up," Ziad said, pretending to flip back his short-cropped hair.

Rima playfully hit her husband's shoulder. "That's not true."

Adele watched the way Mrs. Jaber stared at Rima without cracking a smile, even though Rima looked directly at her and gave her a warm smile.

"You can't travel with girls without them always wanting to take 'beauty breaks,'" Ziad continued, raising his fingers in quotation marks.

"Nothing's wrong with a little refreshing. Beauty is important," Mona said seriously.

"Looks are everything to you, aren't they, Mona?" Adele asked, turning away from Mrs. Jaber's glower.

"What else is there? The first thing people see is your face."

"I have to agree with Mona," Ziad said. There was a slight leer on his face. Adele knew he loved being encircled by women even if they were only his sisters-in-law. With his right hand, he subtly groped his crotch. Adele looked in disgust as his cigarette-stained fingers rubbed the material of his trousers. Then, he brought his hand up and stroked the gold chain around his neck; his open-collared shirt exposed soft curls of chest hair.

He thinks he's so hot, Adele thought before speaking. "You would. But what about one's mind, one's compassion?"

"Not as important," he replied. "First impressions aren't formed by one's mind. The face, as Mona said, is everything and...." He rested his elbows on his knees and bent forward. He whispered, sneaking a quick look at Youssef and his mother, making sure they couldn't hear him, "it certainly helps if that pretty face is on top of a gorgeous body." He sat back on the sofa and winked at Adele.

Adele snapped, "You're such a chauvinist."

"And what are you? Don't tell me." He gave an audible sigh. "A feminist."

"Yeah, I believe in equal rights." She turned her head and stared at her father. He gave her a disapproving look, then she stared at her mother. Adele wished Samira would somehow agree with her or at least think it was all right that one of her daughters was non-traditional. But how could Samira possibly understand feminism? "If that makes me a feminist, well, then I'm a feminist." From the corner of her eye, she saw Mrs. Jaber sit up straight at the mention of this word. A term, Adele guessed, she had heard in Beirut when visiting some relatives. A feminist, a woman who demanded equal rights, who expected her husband to share in the household chores and the care of children. A feminist had no place in Mrs. Jaber's family, Adele thought.

The old woman squinted at her daughter-in-law and asked in Arabic, "Are you such a woman?"

"No, no," Rima answered quickly. "I'm very traditional."

"Good."

"Yes, Mama. Rima's not like that. She knows her place," Ziad replied.

Rima cleared her throat. "Ziad is right. I'm not a feminist and, to be perfectly honest, I don't get the whole feminist thing. I'm a woman and I was raised to take care of my husband, my family. I see nothing wrong with this. Lebanese women know the true meaning of home and family. Don't worry, Mother-in-law," Rima said, speaking in Arabic. "I'll be a good wife."

Mrs. Jaber pursed her lips. "*Enshallah.*" God willing.

Adele was unable to speak. She couldn't believe the words coming out of Rima's mouth. She glanced across at Mona and Katrina but they ignored her and looked blankly at Ziad's mother.

Ziad declared, "I wouldn't marry a feminist. Feminists don't like men. Aren't they all lesbians?" he laughed out loud.

Adele shook her head with annoyance. "That's bullshit," she mumbled.

"What did you say?" Youssef said, glaring at her.

Bullshit, Adele mouthed. Youssef clenched his jaw. But Adele knew her father better than he thought she knew him. There was no way in hell he'd raise his voice or hurl words of insult in the presence of a guest. So she silently pronounced the word again until her father sat on his hands, his feet slowly tapping the floor. She watched the way his tongue clucked against the inside of his cheek as if he were willing it to calm down before he let it loose in a room with a very traditional Lebanese woman, who would report such an outburst upon her arrival back to the village.

Mrs. Jaber turned to Youssef and asked, "What's a lesbian?"

Youssef stopped shaking and uncovered his hands, resting them on his knees.

Before he could reply, Adele smirked, "I think Ziad should answer that question, not Babba." Youssef shot her a scornful look. And at the same time, Ziad shifted uncomfortably on the sofa.

Blinking in confusion, Mrs. Jaber pushed the question. "What's a lesbian?"

"A woman who likes another woman as if she were a man," Youssef explained.

She looked down at her hands and folded them on her lap. "*Ayb*."

"Exactly, Mama, that's *ayb*," Ziad agreed.

Youssef asked, "Why are we talking about this?"

"Ziad brought it up," Adele replied. Ziad glared across at her. "Maybe he should explain his obsession with lesbians. Is it one of his fantasies?"

"Be quiet, Adele," Rima said, immediately coming to her husband's defence.

Adele was silent for a moment then lifting her hands, she went on. "Whatever. He's the one who started it."

Then, changing the topic completely Mrs. Jaber suddenly asked in Arabic, "Did you use the sheet as I instructed?"

Adele looked at her sisters with surprise at the mention of the dreaded wedding sheet, the virgin detector. But they avoided her probing gaze, lowering their eyes. Did Rima actually use one on her wedding night? Getting up from the sofa, Ziad walked into the other room where their suitcases were situated. Everyone was silent; the sound of the suitcase zipper was like a roar. Adele looked at Rima whose cheeks began to turn a sallow shade; it looked as if she were about to vomit. Adele slightly rose from the sofa, wanting to sit next to her eldest sister but at that moment, Ziad stepped back into the living room, holding the white linen in his hands. She sat back down and watched Ziad grasp the edges of the blanket and throw it in the air so as to spread it out. Seizing it between his fingers, he let his mother examine it. Mrs. Jaber tightly clutched the sheet, pulled it close to her face and traced the dried stains as if making sure they were droplets of blood and not cranberry sauce or paint. She moved closer to the cloth and Adele thought she might lick the spots. Adele gaped at the white sheet with her sister's blood on it.

Finally letting go of the cloth, Mrs. Jaber looked across at Rima and for the first time, a large smile spread on her round face. She got up from the sofa, then cupped Rima's head in her hands and kissed her on the cheeks before pulling her into her arms and embracing her. "You good girl," she said. "You good girl." Adele's eyes opened wide in disbelief at the woman's sudden warm reception.

Rima patted her mother-in-law's heavy back and fixed her eyes on Adele, but then turned away and looked at her parents. Youssef and Samira sat there with enormous grins on their proud faces. Adele didn't look at them. She knew if she did, she would lose her temper. Flushed with embarrassment, Adele stared past her feet and watched a tiny black ant disappear between the cracks of the hardwood floor.

The next day, a calm smile lifted Samira's mouth as she carefully folded Rima's wedding sheet by halves, patting the creases from the friction of the newlyweds' lovemaking. Wide-eyed, Adele watched the way her mother's hands glided over the cloth, slow and gentle. Samira's fingers were long and her knuckles were big. Adele's own hands were lighter, less work-worn, but they were Samira's hands, prominent bones, smooth skin.

The crimson smears on the white cloth made Adele cringe. She hated this old world tradition, this "virgin detector," hated the fact that her sister Rima had allowed her husband to place the sheet on the hotel bed while he made love to her for the first time. And now, in this quiet room, safe, she thought of her bicycle accident. Yesterday, with Ziad and her family, she hadn't let the bloodstained sheet bring back the excruciating memory of her hymen being torn from her fall on her bicycle. What would she do if she married a Lebanese man, lay in bed with a sheet under her body and not one drop of blood into it? She closed her eyes, wishing she could erase the bike accident from her memory forever and heal her broken hymen. She wanted to be clean again. But it was too late to mend damage already done. As a Lebanese girl, she had failed in one of the most important lessons her parents had drilled into her and her sisters' brains—protect your virginity at all costs.

Adele remembered a time when her sister Katrina had been shaking after coming out of the examination room at their family doctor's office. Katrina had sat on the empty chair between Mona and Adele. Mona had leaned close to Katrina's pale face and had whispered, "What's wrong?" Adele had quietly sat in the waiting room, too, for her yearly check-up.

Katrina had spoken in a low voice. "She had to examine me down there." She pointed to her crotch.

Mona's face had whitened, then she had exclaimed, "You let her *examine* you."

"No, no," she had answered quickly. "Not like that. She only looked at the outside part. Remember the burning I was telling you about?"

Mona had nodded her head.

"Well, it's nothing. Just a yeast infection."

"Good thing you didn't let her inside. Babba would've skinned you alive if you let her do that."

"I know, Mona. I'm not *stupid*," Katrina had murmured. Adele had silently flipped through a magazine, patiently waiting for her turn.

Adele heard her father's voice: *When you visit the doctor, don't ever let her touch you down there.* Even if she was going to the doctor for an earache, he cautioned this at every appointment.

Samira finished folding the white sheet into a tidy square, then placed it in a plastic bag.

"Rima's a good girl," Samira said, smiling widely, before walking out the room, leaving Adele with the feeling that she would never say that about her. Adele quietly sat on the bed and listened to the hinges of the linen closet door squeak loudly, then the soft steps of her mother approaching her bedroom once more. Samira leaned against the door and smiled at Adele. She began to sing an old Arabic lullaby, one she had sung to Adele when she was a baby. "My *habibti*, drift to sleep. I will give you doves if you sleep. My pretty one, drift to sleep. I will give you the world in your dreams. My *habibti*, close your eyes and sleep." Samira came in and sat next to Adele.

"Mama," Adele whispered. "Why are you keeping Rima's soiled sheet?"

"*Habibti*, it's not a soiled sheet. It's so much more important, sacred. A part of our culture," Samira explained, her hands playing with Adele's ringlets. She spoke in Arabic.

"But why is it important?" Adele persisted.

"It just is. It's part of being a Lebanese woman. A Lebanese man wants to marry a clean girl like Rima and you."

"What if she isn't a virgin?" Adele asked, struggling to speak in Arabic. When she spoke with her mother, Arabic and English collided. And sometimes Adele would give up out of frustration. She asked her mother why she never learned English, but Samira routinely asked why didn't she make more of an effort with Arabic. Before kindergarten, it had been Adele's mother tongue. Suddenly, she buried her head on her mother's lap, tracing the pattern of flowers on Samira's dress with her fingertips.

Samira shifted slightly from her daughter's warm touch and replied, "If a woman isn't a virgin, her husband won't respect her. He'll think less of her."

"Were you a virgin when you married Babba?"

"Of course!" Samira said, shocked. "Of course."

"Then why is he mean to you?"

Samira stopped stroking Adele's head and stared out the window. A deep crimson sun swiftly moved through the clouds, throwing light on Samira's dark skin. She pushed Adele from her lap. With one quick movement, Adele sat up and gazed at her mother's face; it was sad and resigned. "I'm sorry, Mama," she said, squeezing her mother's arm.

Samira got up from the bed, straightening her summer dress. She pulled a tissue out from one of the pockets and wiped her eyes. Standing by the doorway now, she cleared her throat and said, "You ask too many questions. Be silent and obedient. This is our culture. This is the way things are for us."

"I don't like it," Adele protested.

Samira shrugged her shoulders. "Nobody cares whether you like it or not. I know we live in Canada, but remember who you are, Adele. You're not one of them..." Samira said, pointing her finger in the direction of the window, the neighbourhood. She patted her chest. "You're like me. You're Lebanese."

"But I'm Canadian too. I was born here."

"By citizenship only, not by blood," Samira whispered fiercely. "Don't ever forget that."

PART II: 1988

CHAPTER 10

WITH TWO RESTFUL WEEKS AWAY from the routine of high school, Adele lay in bed, admiring the sunlight that filtered through the enormous window. It was a chilly December day. Snowflakes tumbled through the blue sky. Yet the coolness was overshadowed by the spectacular sunrise pouring into her bedroom, one she had finally claimed as her own after Mona married two years ago. All three sisters were married now, living their own lives with husbands and children or babies on the way. They had all married Lebanese men, and had children within a year or two of their wedding vows. Rolling over on her stomach, hugging her pillow, she turned her head to the window and watched the sunrise, appreciating how it rose with the promise of new things; countless sketches of it were in her drawing pads. She threw the covers off her body and felt a sharp ache moving along her pelvis but then it faded quickly as she got out of bed, pulled up her pajamas, and headed into the bathroom.

The cold ceramic tiles under her bare feet made her shiver. She came close to the mirror and studied her face, which had a combined look of kindness and seriousness. But now her eyelids were swollen and she looked pale. She slipped off her pajamas, threw them on the floor, and glided open the glass door to the bathtub. Slowly, she closed the sliding door and turned on the shower. For a few minutes, she stood under the warm spray, letting its steam envelope her before she grabbed a bar of soap and trailed it over her skin. Her eyes followed her thin frame: the firm breasts, the slight curve of her hips, and the muscles in her thighs. She had always been slender, had been able to eat whatever she wanted without gaining extra pounds. Lately though, she had noticed a small protrusion developing in her belly. Her fingers felt something hard in the space reserved for her future children. Returning the bar of soap to its holder, she pressed her right hand into her stomach to check the unusual bulge that made her flat abdomen stick out. With the tips of her fingers, she probed the lump; it was the size of an orange. She grabbed the soap again and began to lather her body once more, a mixture of water and soapsuds flowing down her legs. But suddenly, the soap slipped from her grip and as she bent down to retrieve it, she fell to her knees because of a razor-sharp pain in her pelvic area. Her kneecaps thudded against the bathtub. She clutched her belly while droplets pounded on her head, making her curls heavy. Slowly, she seized the edge of the tub, her fingers slipping until she got a firmer hold. She lifted herself up, sharp pains pulsating in the right side of her abdomen and lower back. On limp legs, she stood up and turned off the faucet, then slid open the shower door and stumbled out of the tub. "Oh God," she moaned, reaching for her towel. She wrapped it around herself then sat down on the toilet seat, doubled over in agony. Beads of blood trickled down her thighs.

A half-hour later, the blood was still gushing, ruining her nightclothes and bedding. But Adele couldn't bring herself to get up and head into the bathroom again. This was her third accident, the most severe in her menstrual cycle yet it wasn't the time of month for it. She had earlier changed her sheets and pajamas, and all she could do now was lie motionless because any movement caused severe pains in her right side. But lying still was also becoming unbearable. Sharp, intense cramps moved in the depths of her womb as if she were in labour. Open-mouthed, she took deep breaths to lessen the throbbing.

She closed her eyes but she couldn't fall asleep. She suddenly heard Samira speaking with Youssef in the living room, their voices travelling up the hallway, arguing over what Samira would make for dinner. She closed her eyes tighter and tried to tune them out. After a few minutes, she slowly hoisted herself out of bed, pressing her hands on the drenched mattress. Her top was soaked with sweat; it clung to her body. Escaping the confines of the damp, bloodied sheets, she stumbled across her bedroom.

In the bathroom, she stripped off the bottom of her pajamas, taking along her undergarment. Then she slipped on clean underwear and fastened two large sanitary napkins on top of one another. She was unable to straighten her body; she stood bent over, close to the mirror. Suddenly, she fell to her knees in front of the toilet. She lifted the lid and vomited into the bowl. A few minutes later, she rested her forehead on the cold rim, and at the same time, her right arm reached up and flushed the contents down, water spattering her burning face. Tears streamed down her cheeks now. "What's wrong with me?" she cried, wiping her eyes with the back of her hands. She got up from the floor and stood at the sink, turned the tap on full. Her arms felt heavy as she lifted them and splashed water on her face. Then she squatted down again, drawing her knees to her chest.

An hour must have passed before Adele tilted her head, peered down at her crotch, and noticed the bleeding had ceased. She pulled on her pajama pants again, even though the back was covered with dried bloodstains. There was a loud knock on the door. "Open the door. What's the matter? Are you okay?" Samira asked at the other end, her muffled voice coming through the wood. "Answer me, Adele!" she shouted.

A few minutes later, Adele got up from her knees. Unsteadily on her feet, she unlocked the door, pulled it open. Samira stood before her, frowning. Adele stared at the floor rather than face her mother's concerned gaze. Quickly, Samira touched her daughter's forehead, rubbing her large hand against the hot flesh. "You're burning up. What's wrong?"

"I don't know, Mama," Adele answered, squeezing her tummy.

Samira looked down at Adele's abdomen, then pushed her arms away from it. Adele struggled with her mother, afraid of her sudden grasp. "Let me see." She raised the top of Adele's pajamas with her one hand and pulled at the waistband with the other. Then she traced the mound on Adele's belly, making her cry out when she dug her fingers into it. She looked into Adele's eyes, bloodshot from the pain and earlier tears. "What have you been doing? Have you been with a boy?"

"What?" Adele said, exasperated.

"Have you done something with a boy?"

"Mama!"

"No Mama! Your belly is as swollen as a melon! Answer me," Samira demanded.

Adele suddenly pushed her mother's hand away, squeezing past her heavyset body. She walked back into her bedroom, then lay on the edge of the bed, where the blood hadn't consumed the sheets.

Her mother followed her. She eyed the crimson-stained bedding. Swiftly, she threw off the covers, making Adele tumble to the floor. "What's all this? Why are you bleeding so much?"

"I'm sick, Mama," Adele finally said, struggling to sit up. "I need to go to the hospital. I'm in a lot of pain."

Samira turned, reached down and helped Adele back on the bed. She pushed the dirty sheets to the side, then sat next to her, brushing the hair away from her tear-stained face. "*Habibti*, what's wrong?" she asked again, softening her tone.

"My stomach hurts. I need to go to the hospital."

Samira nodded and stood. Adele listened to her mother's footsteps echoing down the hallway, then the stairs. Leaning forward, she rested her elbows on her knees and held her head in her hands, breathing deeply. The soreness throbbed in her gut again. By the time her mother returned, she was bent over in pain. This time Samira stood behind Youssef while he stared at Adele; her face was crumpled. He directed his gaze to the bloodied bed sheets then to Adele's swollen belly, which she was now grasping, her fingers massaging her exposed flesh. She fell back on the mattress.

"You know I'm busy in the store. I had to close it now just to come and see you. What's wrong with you?" Youssef said, his tone on the verge of breaking.

"I don't know, Babba." She gave an audible sigh. "I've been through this with Mama. Please take me to the hospital." She rubbed her stomach more fiercely as if this would make the pain stop. Then she turned to her side, embracing her knees, peering at her mother, opening and closing her mouth, silently pleading for her help. But Samira wouldn't look at her.

Abruptly, Youssef rolled her on her back. He squinted at her; his eyes darted back and forth from her face to her swollen belly. "What have you been doing?"

"Oh, God, not this again!" Adele groaned. "I haven't done anything. I'm a virgin for God's sake!" she said, shouting.

"Don't raise your voice to me!" Youssef said angrily. "Show me some respect. I'm your father."

Adele pushed her father's hands away from her and sat up in spite of the pain. Before she spoke again, she took a deep breath, calming herself. "I'm sick, Babba. People get sick. It happens. Please take me to the hospital."

Youssef paced the room. The floorboards exhaled noisily under his shoes. "I don't know. Wait until tomorrow when your doctor's office is open. You can't be in that much pain."

Adele opened her mouth in disbelief. Her voice rose unsteadily; she was shaking. "If you won't take me today, I'll take a taxi."

"Yeah, so you can disgrace us if the cabbie turns out to be Lebanese."

"Christ, if it'll make you feel better, I'll tell him I'm Chinese, okay?" Adele rose from her bed, walked across her room, pulled open the closet and rummaged through her clothes. She then unbuttoned her pajamas, slipped them off and put on a pair of jeans and striped turtleneck. The floorboards moved again while Youssef swung his hands in the air as if swatting a bunch of mosquitoes.

"No respect!" Youssef yelled at Samira. "Look at her!" He pointed at Adele as she zipped up her pants. "Showing her naked body to her father!" He turned away from Samira and stood behind Adele. "I didn't raise you to be a *sharmouta*."

"I know, Babba," Adele said, finally turning around. She said in a quiet voice, "You raised me to feel shitty about myself." She looked hard at her father now, tried to find an ounce of compassion in his greenish-brown eyes. But he let his gaze drop to the floor before she could find it. She cleared her throat. "Have you forgotten, Babba? Well, I haven't. Yes, I'm a virgin and I'm a whore at the same time. I'm pregnant, didn't you know? See that blood on the sheets," she said, pointing to the double bed. "That's from the miscarriage I'm having right at this moment. Yeah, that's right. I've lost the baby. A virgin and pregnant! But it happened once before. It can happen again." Before she knew it, Youssef raised his hand and struck her in the face. Her head snapped back from the blow. Falling to the floor, she curled herself over her knees and began to sob.

Finally intervening, Samira lightly touched Youssef's arm. "Take her to the hospital, Youssef. I'll watch the store. You know I can't take her. If only I knew how to drive, but you thought I didn't need to learn," Samira sighed. "She needs a doctor. You'll have to take her."

After a momentary silence, Youssef lifted Adele up, his hands digging into her sides. "Okay," he mumbled under his breath.

Adele didn't struggle this time with her father. She let him guide her out of the bedroom, down the stairs where he slid on her winter coat then buttoned it up for her as if she were a young child again. He grasped her arm while he led her outside.

The dwindling light of the sunset filled the hospital's emergency room; red and violet streamed through the waiting area, which was packed with people clasping their bellies or heads. It smelled of vomit and stringent disinfectants, a smell that only faded briefly with the opening of the sliding doors, bringing forth another ill person and a gust of frigid wind. Adele peered over her father's shoulders and stared at the people who were either sitting on the plastic chairs or lying on their sides while a TV set blasted in the background. She faced the nurse at the front desk. Her greyish-blond hair was pulled back in a ponytail, some strands were falling loosely around her long face. Her eyes looked tired, glancing every few seconds over at the increasing number of sick people in the waiting room. She asked in an exhausted voice, "What's your daughter's name, sir?"

Youssef held up Adele in his arms as she moaned in pain. "Adele Azar."

In spite of her weary expression, the nurse looked at the form then smiled kindly at Adele, who was frantically gripping her belly and moaning. "Do you want to sit, dear?"

Adele mustered a faint smile. "No, it hurts too much when I sit." The sound of her shallow breathing surprised her.

"How old are you?"

"Eighteen."

The nurse scribbled this information on the green registration form. She glanced up at Adele over her reading glasses, which were positioned on the tip of her narrow nose. "Have you had this pain before?"

"No. It started a few hours ago. It began in my lower back then moved to the right side of my belly." Adele explained, gliding her right hand from her back to the front of her abdomen.

The nurse glanced at Adele's body. "How long has your belly been distended?"

"Distended?"

"Swollen, dear."

"Oh, about a month or two. I just thought I was gaining weight," she laughed weakly.

The woman smiled. "Is there any chance that you're pregnant?"

At this point, Youssef piped up even though this had crossed his mind earlier when he had interrogated Adele with the insensitivity of an ogre. "What kind of fucking question is that? She's not a slut. She's eighteen for God's sake! And not to mention unmarried! In our culture, a woman doesn't have sex until she's married."

"We have to ask, Mr. Azar. This is Canada. Premarital sex is common among teenagers here."

"Not for my teenage daughter," he answered coldly.

The nurse reworded her question. "Are you sexually active or have you been?"

Youssef smacked his hand against his forehead. "For fuck sakes! The answer is no. I didn't raise my daughter to be a whore." Adele looked at her father. She drew her brows together and sighed aloud. She clenched her teeth.

"Please, Mr. Azar, I need your daughter to answer. If you continue to use foul language, I will have to call security."

Relaxing the muscles around her mouth, Adele now touched her father's arm in a comforting way. "It's all right, Babba." She looked at him, his winter coat hanging open and revealing a round belly under an old sweater, his pants drooping on his slender thighs. In the modernized, sanitized hospital, Youssef seemed out of place. Adele was suddenly conscious of the heavy frame of black curls around her dark-eyed face. She and her sisters joked about being "off the boat" but it wasn't funny now, as she looked down at the unravelling threads of her second-hand coat. Like her father, she too seemed to have walked out of another time, an old world. She turned to the nurse and said in a low voice, her face reddening, "I'm still a virgin."

"Okay then." The nurse jotted something down on the file

before getting up from behind the desk. "Can you walk or should I get a wheelchair?"

"I can walk."

"Please follow me." Youssef and Adele followed the nurse down a dim-lit corridor and inside one of the examination rooms. The nurse pulled out a robe from one of the cabinets. She handed it to Adele. "Please change into this gown and a doctor will be with you shortly." The nurse faced Youssef. "You may want to wait in the hallway."

For the first time since they had arrived at the hospital, Youssef obeyed the nurse's instructions. He walked out of the room, his right hand tracing the curling moustache above his thin lips. Adele then slipped off her clothes and put on the blue gown; it sent shivers down her spine. The room was unpleasantly cold. In a matter of minutes, there was a knock on the door. A young female doctor with sand-coloured hair walked in with Youssef trailing behind her. She wore a mid-length white jacket over her powder blue sweater and grey skirt. Her thin lips were covered with frosted pink lipstick. She looked barely a few years older than Adele with her tall, slender body and heart-shaped face. The doctor turned and stared at Youssef curiously.

Adele explained. "He's my father."

"Oh, yes." She extended her right hand out to him, then Adele. "Hello, I'm Dr. Shoemaker. Nice to meet you." Then she looked down at the chart in her hands. "So, you've been experiencing abdominal pain?"

"Yes."

"How are your periods?"

Adele lowered her eyes, stared at the floor, ashamed she had to answer such personal questions in front of her father but she couldn't ask him to leave the room. Her cheeks burned. "Heavy. They've always been heavy."

"How are you feeling now?" Dr. Shoemaker asked, standing close beside Adele.

Adele looked shyly into the young doctor's blue eyes; they looked dull, almost void of any emotion. She was only performing a task. The coldness made Adele twist away. But then she raised her eyes and answered the question. "I'm in a lot of pain. It hurts with movement."

"Could you please lie back? I want to examine your abdomen." Adele lay down on the table.

The physician pulled up Adele's gown, exposing her swollen stomach; she pressed her fingers against the mound of soft flesh. "Well, I certainly can feel a large mass. But I'll need to do a pelvic exam to be certain. Have you had one done before?"

"No," Adele replied.

Youssef suddenly said, "She's a virgin. You can't do one. You'll break her and then no decent Lebanese man will want to marry her."

Adele sat up, cupping her head in her hands; she rubbed her cheeks in frustration.

Dr. Shoemaker looked at her then Youssef. "It's the only way I can determine whether there is something inside her uterus, Mr. Azar." She exhaled deeply. "If you like, I will only use one finger and try to be as gentle as possible. This is a very routine procedure."

"One finger or two. Won't make a difference. You'll still open her."

Dr. Shoemaker frowned. "I'm afraid I don't understand. Open her?"

"Break my hymen," Adele mumbled, now folding her arms on her chest. She took a long breath before staring blankly at her father, wishing she could disappear from this entire conversation, but then she bent over as another bout of pain surged through her abdomen down her pelvis. After the throbbing subsided, she looked up at the ceiling and remembered the long-ago accident with her bicycle, how she thought she had lost her virginity back then. But she didn't dare bring this up to the doctor with Youssef in the room. She cringed at the memory. She'd been too ashamed to tell anyone about her injury. Pushing this recollection out of her mind, she'd forgotten the soreness she had felt when her hymen tore and blood trickled on her cotton briefs. How strange, she thought, that the mind buried pain like a flower bulb; it could grow again. She pressed her hands on the plastic cushion of the examination table and glanced at the young physician who stared back at her, the fine lines around her eyes softening, then straining when she turned away and addressed Adele's father.

"A pelvic exam won't mean she's not a virgin anymore. It's just a medical procedure…" she paused for one moment, tugging on her lower lip, "like taking blood. Do you really believe breaking her hymen in this way is the same thing as sexual intercourse?"

"Yes, yes," he said, nodding vigorously.

"Well, I don't know what else to say. I assure you that a pelvic exam is not the same thing as losing one's virginity."

"Will she bleed from this examination?"

Adele stared off into the distance. The room was suddenly becoming smaller. Her hands clenched the cushion; she wanted to break the lining, slip inside it and lose herself in the foam. Her eyes darted between her father, the doctor, and the closed window. Snowflakes were trapped in the screen, making a kaleidoscope of a wintry scene in the grey-black meshing of the panel. She imagined being one of those tiny flakes, melting into nothing but a spot of water.

Dr. Shoemaker cleared her throat and said, "Probably."

"Then no pelvic." Youssef smacked his hands together, the sound echoing in the sterile small room, which was dull apart from a vinyl chair, a wooden stool for the doctor to sit on, and a countertop covered with a few glass jars stuffed with packages of gauze, tongue compressors, and bandages. There were no pictures. The most predominant thing in the room was the brown-cushioned examination table with its oven mitten-covered stirrups. Adele knew she would have to slide her feet into those, spread her legs and let the young physician examine her insides. Her stomach began to flutter at the thought of this. She looked at her father and knew he wouldn't agree to such a thing but rationally she knew this was her only option. Youssef insisted once more, "No exam."

"Babba, please..." Adele whispered, tears filming her eyes.

He ignored her and continued, staring directly at the doctor. "I'm not risking my daughter's chances at marrying a Lebanese man."

Dr. Shoemaker scoffed. "You'd rather she suffer with pain? What if the mass is cancerous?"

"It's in God's hands then, isn't it?" Youssef replied, his voice gruff.

Adele looked away from her father as he turned towards her. She steadied her gaze on the doctor. She wondered what this woman thought about them. Primitive. They must have looked primitive—a strict, immigrant family—to this white woman in her long, wool skirt and V-neck sweater.

Youssef muttered, turning away from Adele's downcast look, "It's in God's hands." He stared hard at the doctor, his bushy eyebrows furrowing.

"No, sir," Dr. Shoemaker corrected, "it's in your hands."

"Nobody is taking my daughter's virginity but her future husband!" he shouted. He stood beside Adele. Tightly gripping her arms, he tried to lift her up but she refused to budge, enclosing her fingers around the metal edges; she desperately held onto the steel frame. "*Yallah*, get up."

"I'm doing it, Babba," she said, controlling the tremor of her tone.

Youssef leaned close to her face and raised his voice in a despairing wail. "What? Come on! You can't have this procedure. You won't be a virgin anymore. No Lebanese man will want you if you're not clean. Think about your future." He pushed some loose curls away from her face then bent down, kissing her on the forehead, his moustache grazing her, his moist mouth feeling cool on her fevered skin. He whispered, addressing her warmly, "You don't want to do this. Don't listen to the doctor. She doesn't understand our culture. Listen to me. Please don't do this, *babba*." He stroked her cheeks. His touch was so tender. This was the first time in years that he'd caressed her in this manner, soft and gentle. She could remember her father holding her in his arms when she was a young girl and how she'd rest her face in the nape of his neck and breathe in his fragrance, a familiar mixture of cologne and sweat. "Please listen to me. You can't do this," he begged. She felt sad for him.

Fighting back the tears, she sighed deeply. "I have to, Babba." She looked across at the doctor who stood by the door, shifting nervously on her feet, almost ready to leave if the emotions became too raw. But then she observed Dr. Shoemaker inching closer to her. Adele tipped her head in the doctor's direction. "I'm ready." But deep down, she knew she wasn't. Her heart pounded at the thought of the physician's fingers tearing open her vagina.

"Are you sure?" Dr. Shoemaker said, now standing at the foot of the table.

Adele nodded. And at the same time, she felt her father's gentle hold, releasing itself from her face. He stood with his mouth open. She expected him to argue but he didn't. He didn't challenge her, only stared at her one more time, his eyes resigned, before turning around and blindly reaching for the handle, pulling open the door and slamming it behind him. She fell back on the table. Lifting her head, she watched the doctor fit a pair of latex gloves over her hands.

"Are you sure we can't do another test? You know, like an ultrasound or something?" Adele asked, slipping off her underwear. She neatly folded and hid them under her other clothes on the chair across the room before hoisting herself on the table again.

The doctor shook her head. "This is the only way. I need to examine you internally, then we'll do an ultrasound." She sat on the wooden stool by the foot of the table. Then adjusted the lamp so it would be positioned between Adele's legs once she opened them for the procedure. Dr. Shoemaker's shoulder-length hair fell around her face while she leaned over, moving the lamp closer to the stirrups.

Adele sat on the table with her hands under her bottom; she swung her legs over the edge, nervously shaking. Straining her neck, she turned and looked at the young doctor preparing for the pelvic examination, pushing the oven mittens deeper on the stirrups then twisting the latex gloves between her fingers so they fit snugly.

Dr. Shoemaker suddenly patted the spot near the end of the table. "I'll need you to slide down here and place your feet in the stirrups."

When Adele didn't respond, the doctor got up from her seat and gently pushed her back, coaxing her to lie down. "Don't be nervous. This is very routine. Every woman has to do it, so you should get used to it." She let out a small laugh. "It's part of being female, unfortunately. Come on. Slide down and place your feet in these things," she said, pointing to the foot supports. "It'll only take a few minutes and I promise to be gentle." She sat back on the stool and turned on the lamp while Adele slid down and did as she was told. Suddenly, the doctor stood up. "On second thought, it'll be easier if I just stand." She said this out loud but Adele thought it wasn't intended for her. At the same time, Dr. Shoemaker pulled Adele's legs further apart. The latex made a swishing sound against her bare thigh. "Can you move a little closer?" Adele slowly moved so her buttocks were at the edge of the table. "Much better." The doctor then opened a tube of lubrication and squirted some on her fingers while her elbow continued to hold Adele's legs away from each other.

Adele tried to distract herself by thinking about all the good things in her life: her neighbour Mrs. Foster, her sisters, her friends, the two weeks of Christmas vacation that awaited her, her nieces and nephews who adored her and followed her everywhere, saying she was the coolest aunt ever. She smiled while these thoughts inundated her mind but the sudden piercing in her vagina jolted her out of her pleasant memories. Flinching in pain, she tried to move back but the doctor had a firm grip on her knees. "You're hurting me," she winced.

"It'll be less painful if you try to relax. Your stomach muscles are so tense. Just breathe," she said, almost angrily, and levered her elbow against Adele's quivering thigh.

Adele took a deep breath and tried to do as she was instructed but it didn't stop the pain. She fidgeted.

"Stay still. I just can't," the doctor paused, "I can't get a good feel of your uterus."

By this time, Adele's entire lower body was shaking. She closed her legs somewhat only to have the doctor push them apart again, this time quite roughly.

"Stop moving! I'm almost done. Just let me finish." Strands of hair dropped over her eyes; she blew them away from her face. When she thrusted her fingers deeper into Adele's vagina, Adele cried out. Then, as though finally satisfied, the doctor pulled her fingers out. She pulled the blue gown over Adele's knees, which were still spread apart. She walked back to the other side of the room where she snapped off the bloodied gloves and discarded them in a canister.

By now Adele was shivering violently, trembling to the point that she had to clasp the metal edge of the table to steady her body. Her insides felt torn. She raised her head, looking dazed. She stared at the doctor while she scribbled something on the clipboard in front of her. Adele inhaled and exhaled, slowly, quietly. She sat up with difficulty. Dr. Shoemaker suddenly turned around and smiled at her. "You were very brave. You can get dressed now and I'll get one of the technicians to do an ultrasound on you. Okay?" Walking over, she patted Adele's arm before marching out the room with her white jacket flapping away from her grey skirt.

Once alone, Adele closed her legs and buried her face in her hands. She now understood what it felt like to be violated.

CHAPTER 11

A DELE WINCED AS ANOTHER DOCTOR pressed the rod hard into her swollen belly. She closed her eyes to the monitor across from her, didn't want to see the tumour growing in her womb. A few minutes later, he stopped probing and put the stick back beside the ultrasound machine. He turned to the technician. "She has a large mass and it'll have to be taken out. And she has several cysts generally associated with endometriosis. That explains all her pain. She doesn't have any kids?" The doctor didn't make eye contact with Adele.

"No," the technician replied. "She's just eighteen and unmarried."

"Unfortunately, these things happen." He finally faced Adele who lay still on the table, the gel chilly on her skin. Pushing his glasses up his nose, he said in a monotone voice, "You'll need a hysterectomy. The tumour is the size of a grapefruit. It has taken over most of your uterus, which is usually the size of a pear. Yours is abnormally large because of the mass, and the shape suggests it may be cancerous, so it's best to remove the whole womb. You won't be able to have children, though." Tall and stooping, he still didn't make eye contact with her even though she tried to meet his gaze. "Your options are limited. A lot of women have hysterectomies. Very routine and safe. Nothing to worry about. If I were in your position, I'd be thankful to get rid of the pain and heavy bleeding. One advantage is that you'll never have another menstrual cycle."

She wanted to scream, *But I can't have any children if I don't have a period!*

Instead her quiet, serious gaze flitted from the doctor's face to the woman technician's. The technician gave her a small smile and added, "Just think of all the money you'll save too. You'll never have to buy another box of tampons or pads." Adele nodded politely as rage swarmed in her stomach. She backed down, glancing at the picture on the monitor.

"We'll make a follow-up appointment for you at the Obstetrics and Gynecology department so they can meet with you for a pre-op," the doctor said. He scribbled something on a pad then handed the sheet to Adele. "For the time being, here's a prescription to help with the pain. Use a heating pad to relieve the discomfort. Unfortunately, we don't have any beds available at the moment so I'm sending you home, but if you feel you are getting worse, come back to the emergency right away."

After, Adele was left alone in the dark with the image of her womb. She raised herself off the examination table and wiped the remaining gel from her belly with a towel the ultrasound technician handed her before leaving. The black and white glare of the screen, showing the incomprehensible photograph of her womb, cast an eerie glow in the dark space. Suddenly the technician whipped back in to turn on the light then handed Adele some painkillers and a cup filled with lukewarm water. Adele swallowed two pills with some difficulty then placed the cup on a side table while she dressed, keeping her head down the entire time while the technician cleaned the ultrasound rod before she finally left the room.

Alone once more, Adele crossed the room, and peered through the sliver of the drawn curtains. A half-crescent moon shimmered in the distant sky. Hours had passed since she had first entered the hospital. But the pain in her abdomen hadn't subsided; her pelvis throbbed. For a while, she stood in front of the window and stared into the vast sky. How unthinkable that her young body couldn't carry a baby. She had always wanted children, but today she learned she wouldn't have any. A wave of panic engulfed her and she sank into a chair. Her arms tightened around her chest. Her relatives had often said that a woman who couldn't bear children was only half a woman. The purpose of a Lebanese woman's life was to marry, bear children, raise them and take care of a husband, they had concluded at many family gatherings. Half a woman. Adele looked down at her body. She wasn't broken. She had all her limbs, all the parts that encompassed being female. Though numb at this moment, she could still move, walk, dance. She wasn't broken. She looked perfectly normal, only pale and worn from this entire ordeal. She pressed her arms closer to her chest, wanting to suffocate the pain shooting up from her belly to her throat. Something shrivelled within her when she replayed her relatives' words. She closed her eyes. Five minutes later, she opened them and made her way out of the room and into the foyer. As she walked down the hallway, she spotted her father standing by the entranceway, his hands stuck in his pockets, his greyish-black hair ruffled.

A shadow overtook his face when he saw her. He didn't smile or wave; he stood with his eyes narrowed, his lips pressed together. He didn't open his mouth and greet her as she limped past the sliding doors and stood in front of him. Adele's eyes darted between her father's severe face and the darkness outside. Removing his hands from his pockets, Youssef led her outside into the brisk air towards the parking lot. Silence engulfed them while Adele followed her father, trying to keep up with his fast pace though the pain in her belly prevented her from doing so. She stared through tears at the back of his old coat.

Youssef slung his coat over the back of the couch in the living room.

"So what's wrong?" Samira asked almost immediately when Adele walked into the house, trailing behind her father. Samira had closed the store a few hours earlier. Adele's stride was unsteady. Her shoulders slouched.

Her father pushed past her mother, nearly making Samira fall down. Adele was too weak to argue and stand up to him for acting roughly with her mother. Instead, she sat on the stairs leading to the upstairs bent over in agony, the painkillers she was given at the hospital fading. She peered up at her father, but he didn't look at her while he tramped across the room. He flung himself hard on the sofa, making its springs creak like an old house. He didn't look at her once. Rising from the steps, Adele unbuttoned her coat, hung it up in the closet by the front door then sat back on the stairs, her arms wrapped around her stomach.

Samira looked at her then turned to Youssef, raising her eyebrows in question. But he didn't answer her. Then she knelt in front of her daughter, resting her hands on Adele's knees. "What did the doctor say?" she asked in Arabic. Her voice was quiet, almost a whisper.

"I can't have children," Adele said in an equally inaudible tone. She opened her mouth, closed it, then opened it again, afraid that more words would make her cry.

Samira got up from the floor and stared across at Youssef again. "What does she mean?" Sadness overtook her. Her voice broke.

"What are you? Fucking deaf? You heard her," he snapped.

Adele looked up at her mother's face; it had turned as red as a poppy. She wanted to defend her, shout back at her father but she couldn't. She felt depleted, completely empty. The tears began to stream down her face. Finally, she let the deep-throated sobs fill her entire body. Her shoulders rose up and down.

"But why? Why can't she have children?" Samira almost shrieked, horrified with this possibility.

"She's defective. Her female part isn't good. It needs to be taken out. That's why she's in so much pain."

"But..." Samira paused, her gaze flitting between Youssef and Adele. "She can't have children?"

"Are you fucking dumb?" Youssef shouted. "Why can't you understand? It's not complicated. She's defective. Not a whole woman."

"How will she get married now?" Samira asked in a loud voice. Another low sob escaped Adele but her mother paid no attention. Samira was still looking to Youssef for an answer.

"No man would want her anyway," Youssef muttered. He finally raised his head and looked across at Adele, his deep-set eyes glaring in disappointment. "She let the doctor break her. She's no longer a virgin."

Samira raised her hands to her mouth and said in an exasperated voice, "Oh, Adele. Why did you do that? Why did you let the doctor touch you down there?"

Adele dragged a sleeve across her eyes. She took in a deep breath and stopped crying. After a few moments, she replied, "I had no other choice, Mama. I'm in so much pain. I had to find out what's wrong with me."

"But couldn't the doctor do something else?" Samira folded her arms across her chest. Her eyes darkened.

"No, the doctor said..."

Samira sighed. "What doctors want to do, they do."

"What are you saying, Samira? You think it's all right that Adele let the doctor touch her down there?" Youssef said.

"No, I don't think it's right but I know how some doctors can be. You remember when they removed my womb. Don't you remember that, Youssef? They didn't give me a choice."

Youssef interrupted, raising his index finger. "No, wait. This is different."

"No, it isn't," Samira said. Adele glanced at her mother and lifted her mouth in a small smile. For once, Samira was standing up for her.

"Canadian doctors don't understand our culture, our ways," Youssef grunted. "You're not clean now, Adele," he added harshly. "What good Lebanese man will marry you if you're not a virgin?"

"That's old-fashioned thinking. Thinking from the village. We don't live in a village, Babba. This is Canada not Lebanon. Nobody cares if you're a virgin or not."

Suddenly, Youssef lifted his arms above his head then flung them back and forth, grasping onto his temples. He began to shout. Adele jumped. "Allah, why did you give me such a stupid daughter? Nobody cares if you're virgin! Lebanese men care. You think they want a dirty woman to be their wife, to bear their children? Do you think they want that?" He cast his eyes at Adele.

Adele whispered, "I can't have children, remember? I won't be able to give them any."

And at this comment, Youssef stopped and stood silently. He glared across at Samira. Then as if remembering her place, Samira roughly rubbed Adele's face, wiping the tears and asked, "How could you let the doctor touch you? Wasn't I a good mother? Didn't I teach you to remain clean until marriage? Your sisters listened to me. Why are you so stubborn? How could you disobey me, your Babba?" She turned and looked at Youssef again, who sat with his hands dangling between his open legs. Then she faced Adele again. "How could you?" she said, her voice dropping.

"I had no other choice, Mama." She felt her mother's hands slipping away from her cheeks. Through the tears, she looked at her mother as she joined Youssef on the sofa.

"I don't know you at all," Samira said, sitting next to Youssef, shaking her head.

Adele rose from the steps. She stared at her mother. "You're just figuring that out?" Then she stumbled up the stairs.

A week later, Adele had a hysterectomy. When Adele awoke from the surgery, she lifted the covers off from her body and stared hard at the large white gauze on her abdomen. She had a scar in the exact same spot as her mother. Now they were inseparable. Samira stood beside Adele's hospital bed and gazed at Adele's belly. Adele could hear tears catch in her mother's throat. Samira gently stared at her and whispered, "You'll be all right, *habibti*. We'll get through this together." After all, Samira couldn't bear any more children and Adele would never have any of her own, would never know the joy and chaos of carrying a child in her belly. Now more than ever, Adele was a second-class citizen. She turned her eyes from her stomach and fixed her gaze on the snow that fell from the sky. Tomorrow was Christmas day. The gift of barrenness was hers. She watched the snow as the wind blew it around in a playful way while the evergreen trees caught the snowflakes in their needles.

"I'm sorry this happened to you, *habibti*," Samira murmured. Then she tenderly kissed Adele on the forehead and sat in the chair next to Youssef. Adele lifted her head and looked across at her father. The hospital room looked bare with only two chairs and another bed, which was empty, fresh linen perfectly tucked under the corners of the mattress. There was a vase of flowers on the bedside table and Adele could smell their scent. Yellow roses were her favourite. They looked beautiful in this sterile space. She turned from the silky petals and stared at her parents. They were now both slumped on the chairs opposite her bed, eyes dull and worry lines engraving their skin. Their frowns made Adele think of all the times she had failed as the good Lebanese daughter. And now all of a sudden she felt relief that she no longer had to follow tradition. In the past week, she had done the unthinkable: she had allowed a doctor to break her hymen, then a surgeon to take out her womanhood. She looked away from her parents and directed her gaze to her sisters. They stood quietly in the room. Their faces were withdrawn, the colour drained from their cheeks. Rima hadn't even broken into a smile, something she was known to do in the most sombre of situations. She was always smiling and talking. But she remained silent now. Words seemed pointless at this time, Adele thought, sighing. Her sisters were all married and had children of their own. They married young and had children right away. What could they possibly say at this moment to make things better?

The next morning, Adele opened her eyes to the sound of her father's voice in her hospital room, but she quickly squeezed them shut and pretended to sleep. She heard her father say in a muffled tone, speaking Arabic, "You can't ever mention this operation to anyone. This is our secret. If an outsider finds out about her problem, then no one will marry her. Make sure you tell your husbands to keep their big mouths shut too. There's no need for anyone to know about this. It's *ayb*, disgraceful, a virgin having this type of surgery. But this is what Allah wanted, so be it." Adele heard the sound of palms rubbing together. She then shifted her legs. "Shh," Youssef said, "she's waking up. Remember what I said, not a word, you understand? Not a damn word."

Adele opened her eyes. She stared at her parents and sisters, her gaze fluttering between them.

"Good morning, *habibti*," Samira said, rising from her seat. She stood next to Adele's bed and bent down to plant a kiss on her forehead but Adele turned her head the other way.

"Don't touch me. Don't ever touch me!" she hissed under her breath, now clenching her fists. Her arms rested straight by her sides.

"Adele, please don't be mad," Samira said, tears filming her eyes.

"Come on, Monkey," Rima coaxed, now standing beside the bed. She put her arm around Samira's waist. "Don't be like that. We know you're going through a hard time but things will get better. We're family. We'll get through this together."

Adele pursed her lips. "Yeah, that's coming from someone who has children." Her vision blurred with tears and her voice cracked, "I've disgraced the family like Babba said." She looked at her sisters, then at her mother. They all turned and faced Youssef who sat in the chair with his eyes directed at the window. "I heard every damn word. I can't have children, but I'm not deaf!" Adele twisted her head towards the wall. The room was suddenly quiet. Her mother and Rima pulled away and Adele continued to stare hard at the white wall. After a few minutes, all she could hear were the dwindling footsteps of her family on the linoleum floor. She closed her eyes again and tried to fall asleep.

A few hours later, Adele awoke to the sound of a baby crying. She blinked her eyes before she realized that a new patient had been placed in the room with her. Adele glanced at the woman, guiding the infant in her arms to her chest. Her gown was opened wide, revealing her breasts and the baby, his dark head slightly bobbing back and forth. Small gulping noises filled the room. Adele couldn't help but stare at the woman and her newborn. When the baby grasped at his mother's breasts, Adele studied the young woman gazing tenderly down at her child as if they were the only two people in the room.

The new mother looked up and smiled. Adele tried to meet her eyes but she couldn't. She quickly looked down at her body. Loathing it, she squirmed under the covers. The other woman frowned, then smiled again as she stared down at her son. Adele moved her legs, ran her hands over the bed sheets, frantically searched for the rod to call the nurse. Once she found it, she pressed the button over and over until a nurse came running into the room. The nurse was a middle-aged woman with short brown hair, bangs slicked away from her weary face. She was new, someone Adele had not seen before during her stay in the hospital. "Are you all right?" she asked in a hoarse voice. She stood beside Adele's bed, rested her hand on her arm. Adele didn't respond but lifted her chin in the direction of the mother and child. The nurse shook her head, not understanding. "What's the matter, dear?"

Adele remained silent, a vacant look on her face. Walking to the foot of the bed, the nurse picked up the clipboard that listed Adele's condition. She gently put the clipboard back, letting it dangle from its chain. Then she quickly grabbed the curtain, slid it around the steel rod until Adele was enclosed like a caterpillar in its cocoon. The nurse stood beside Adele's bed, touched her arm again and asked, "Is that better?"

Adele nodded her head and then closed her eyes before the tears slipped out.

A few hours later, she felt someone gently tugging at the waistband of her pajamas. It was a young nurse, who exposed Adele's belly and removed the bloody gauze covering it. Adele stared at the foot of her bed while the nurse's fingers brushed against her stomach, efficiently replacing the soiled bandage with a fresh one. She briefly looked up at the nurse's face; she had the youthful look of someone barely past the age of twenty-five with her red hair pulled back in a ponytail and her face free from make-up. When her eyes met Adele's gaze, her pale lips widened into a grin but Adele quickly twisted away. But the nurse continued to beam as she said, "It's a beautiful day today. I hate winter but when the sun's shining, it's almost bearable. Don't you think?"

"Yeah," Adele mumbled. She clenched her fists and stared at the wall while the nurse finished tending to the incision. The nurse's fingers gently pressed clear tape over the gauze. After she was done, she patted Adele's hand and said, "Everything will be okay. You know that, right?"

She pulled her hand away and faced the nurse. She squinted angrily. What the hell did this woman know? She wasn't the one suffering, wasn't the barren one, the defective woman but more importantly, Adele thought, she wasn't the Lebanese woman who had failed miserably. She looked hard at the nurse's red hair and freckled skin. She inhabited the white world, not ancient scriptures and Corinthian columns. Adele said nothing.

The nurse smiled sympathetically, gathering her supplies and placing them in a bag. She walked to the door and stood in the threshold, looking back at Adele. "Take care. Remember the pain is only temporary. It'll go away. You'll see. Everything will work out."

"Thank you," Adele said reluctantly, thinking, *you have no idea.*

After five days, Adele was sent home to continue recuperating. It was better to be in her sunny bedroom, under her own comforter, but her belly still throbbed from the centre of her pelvis to the right side of her ribs in a steady, dull beat. Over the past few weeks, her skin had turned pale but the sun tinted it now as if she had a faint tan, only she hadn't vacationed somewhere warm, hadn't left the confines of her bedroom since her discharge from the hospital. The sunlight grew bright. Adele lifted her hands again to protect her eyes. After the surgery, she had insisted the curtains be closed. She didn't want the sun to touch her, warm her "defective" body. But on this particular day, she wanted to feel connected to the outside world so she had allowed her mother to open the curtains. She imagined her womb floating in a jar of formaldehyde under the glaring lights of a sterile lab. She imagined the doctor's gloved hands holding the diseased uterus; its grapefruit-sized tumour sliding out with one quick slice from the thin blade held between the physician's fingers. Golden-orange rays flickered on the walls, and on her withdrawn face. A squirrel was perched on the branch of a tree with its claws holding a crumb of bread to its mouth, nibbling at a speedy rate. Adele smiled. She hadn't smiled since she had learned that she'd never be able to carry a child of her own. Suddenly, she turned away from the window and lifted the covers off her body. She stared at her belly then listened to the cars driving down the street of her neighbourhood, the wheels treading on snow-covered pavement. The maple trees stood naked in the cold, their branches swaying in the mid-morning wind, the heavy, wet snow bending them like weeping willows. She pulled the covers up over her stomach once more. She looked out the window and thought again of the nurse's naïve promise.

The nurse was wrong. Everything did not work out. Adele slid into a deep depression, refusing to get out of bed, not even sitting up until her mother forced her to. "Come on," Samira said, bending down and wrapping her arms around Adele's upper body. She lifted her and pulled her out of the bed, then slung Adele's arm over her shoulders. Samira dragged her to the bathroom. There, she stripped off Adele's pajamas and placed her on the toilet seat while she squeezed a warm, wet cloth over the sink. She bent slightly to wipe Adele's body, moving the wash cloth down her neck, around her collarbone, then between her breasts. Adele rested her back against the cold tank of the toilet, tilted her head and stared up at the ceiling. For one brief moment she lowered her head and looked at her mother's hands as they glided the cloth over her naked protruding hipbones. She looked down at her emaciated body, barely able to raise her arms to wipe the tears that now poured out of her mother's eyes, down her sunken cheeks.

Though the daily bath was routine, the tears were new. On other occasions, there had been muscles straining in her mother's neck, around her mouth when she asked Adele if she was still in pain, whether her gentle sponge baths were too much to endure. Pretending they didn't hurt, Adele had let her mother continue the regime. But this morning, Adele began to shake uncontrollably until her mother gripped her by the shoulders, steadying her. After a while, the quivering stopped and Samira began the task of cleaning the incision. Adele rolled her head to the side but her eyes caught glimpses of the sutures on the lower part of her abdomen. The once smooth, taut skin was now blemished, imperfect. Samira's dark eyes flitted over the carefully stitched flesh. A redness encompassed Samira's cheeks and Adele could tell that her mother suddenly felt at fault for her predicament. On most of these mornings, when her mother bathed her, Adele had avoided her mother's eyes, but now she met her gaze. Pity and disappointment shone there, like the time Adele had refused to continue going to the Arabic school.

She had failed in so many ways at being the good Lebanese daughter. She wasn't like other Lebanese girls.

Her mother's fingers traced the scar as if memorizing its length, its contrasting colour on Adele's olive skin, the meaning it held in seven inches of space. Adele flinched, pressing her spine on the toilet tank. Her mother continued to whimper. She suddenly said, "May I ask you something, Mama?" Eyes still pasted on the ceiling.

"What is it, *habibti*?" Samira replied softly, clearing her throat.

"Do you think I'm half a woman, that I'm worthless?" she asked, swallowing hard.

Samira shook her head and opened her mouth, but no words came out. She then fell forward, rested her forehead on Adele's shoulders. A warm, wet sensation slid down Adele's chest, back. Adele lifted her right arm with difficulty and patted her mother's head. "It's okay, Mama," she whispered over and over.

From the corner of her eye, Adele watched her mother stand up straight and drop her hands into the basin. She squeezed the cloth, turning the water pink. Adele noticed the way her mother's arched, finely-sculpted eyebrows came together, how they put pressure on her eyelids, how sad she looked with her hands submerged in the dirty water. Adele quickly wrapped a towel around her body. She shivered while the steam of the bath transformed into drops of condensation, sliding down the mauve walls.

When she returned to her bed, the walls of her bedroom were still bright with the sun. Her mother tucked her in, pulling the covers close to her neck. Samira sat on the edge of the mattress and uncapped a small plastic bottle. She lifted the container and dabbed a few drops of liquid on her fingertips, then she dropped them on Adele's forehead. A few years ago when visiting a large outdoor Cathedral on the outskirts of Montreal, and being a devout believer in God, Samira had filled this tiny container with holy water. Adele looked at the bottle and remembered her mother's journey up the steep steps. Despite her bad knees, Samira had trudged up the cobblestone leading to the alcove where a statue of the Virgin Mary was surrounded by a fountain of sparkling water. Once on top, Samira had leaned back against the grey slabs of concrete, regaining her breath before entering the shrine. It was rumoured that the water from this holy place could heal those with ailments. Adele had stood at the bottom, watching her mother as she rested at the entranceway. Adele had wished she had joined her mother instead of watching her bend alone, scooping the blessed water in the bottle. Getting up from her knees, Samira had wiped her dress, tightened the lid on the container, and stuffed it in her purse. Before leaving, she stood once more at the threshold and stared at the statue of the Virgin Mary.

Now Adele studied her mother's unsmiling face while she anointed Adele's forehead with the holy water she had collected from Montreal. Adele thought her mother looked old; the skin around her eyes was swollen and her cheeks were beginning to droop. She felt her mother's fingers drawing the sign of the cross on her forehead. Normally, she would've pushed her mother's hand away while performing such religious rituals, but this time she lay still and let her mother's faith rub into her flesh. What harm could it do? she thought. She closed her eyes and allowed her mother to anoint her. The infertility had killed something inside her. Maybe this "holy water" would awaken her as Jesus had done for Jarius' daughter. Adele stirred from her mother's warm breath on her cheek, then she felt her lips on her face, softly kissing her. The mattress suddenly shifted and Adele heard the creaking of the floor. She fell into a deep sleep.

When she awoke, she heard the approaching footsteps of

someone, making his or her way up the stairs and into her bedroom. Adele lifted her head from the pillow and glanced at Mona slowly walking across the room, balancing a tray laden with soup and crackers. She carefully placed the tray on the nightstand next to Adele's bed. Then, she put her arms around Adele's upper body and helped her sit up. Adele struggled with her sister, refusing to cooperate. "Stop fighting me, Adele," Mona insisted, blowing strands of long, black hair from her eyes. "You need to sit up and eat." After a few moments, Adele succumbed to her sister's ministrations and let her arrange the pillows behind her back. Sitting on the edge of the bed, Mona held the bowl in her left hand, and then stirred the spoon in the soup with her right hand before lifting it to Adele's mouth. Adele rested her head against the wall, turning her face away from her sister. She refused to open her mouth.

"Come on, Monkey," Mona coaxed, playfully nudging Adele's thigh. "I'm *not* that bad of a cook." She held the spoon in the air.

"Fuck off!" Adele retaliated, bowing her head so her chin touched her chest while Mona moved the spoon towards her mouth.

Mona persisted. "Come on. Please, pretty please. Do you want me to beg?"

"Leave me alone! I don't want to eat."

"You have to. How are you going to get well if you don't eat?"

"Who wants to get well? I'm defective, remember?" Adele raised her eyes and stared directly into her sister's tear-filmed eyes.

She quickly looked down at the bowl in her hand. "Babba didn't mean what he said."

"Yeah, right."

She looked up at Adele once more, the lines around her eyes softening. "You have to forgive him. He's from the old country. He doesn't know any better. He has that old country mentality.

He wasn't born and raised here like us." She held the spoon against Adele's closed lips again. Still refusing to cooperate, the broth slid down her chin. Mona sighed and gave up. She put the bowl back on the tray and grabbed a napkin to wipe Adele's face. She then held her hands, gave them a squeeze and smiled. "Do you remember the time I gave you a fat lip?"

Adele turned her head from her sister.

"I will always remember that fight," Mona laughed softly. "I think it was the last physical fight we had. Remember?"

Adele kept her eyes cast down.

"I remember you wouldn't leave me alone. You were always following me, always trying to invade my space. I was sixteen and I didn't want my little sister tagging along with me and then one day you overhead my conversation with Hassan. Do you remember him?"

Adele said nothing.

"Anyway, I was secretly dating him because I knew Babba would never approve of our relationship. He wasn't Christian, wasn't Orthodox. He wasn't even Lebanese."

"He was Iranian," Adele finally said.

"Yeah, that's right. Good memory. Well, when I heard your breathing on the other end of the phone, I freaked out, afraid of my secret getting out. You know how Babba was."

"Was?"

"Is, is," Mona corrected, laughing again. "After I hung up the phone, I chased you around the house until I caught you. You were shouting 'I'm gonna tell Babba on you!' Luckily, he was in the store working so he didn't hear you and Mama was outside. I then pinned you on the floor...."

"You were always a better fighter than me."

"I was also bigger, older. I shouldn't have let my quick temper get the best of me." She continued. "I pinned you on the floor between my legs. You struggled to get free. Then you grabbed my hair and pulled really hard."

"Yeah, I remember that," Adele said, tugging on her lower

lip, trying not to break into a smile.

"You know how I am with my hair."

"Who are you kidding? Your entire appearance. You can be so superficial, Mona," Adele quipped.

Tossing her long, straight hair over her shoulder, Mona replied, "I can't help it that I got all the good looks in the family." Adele stared at her sister's high cheek-boned face that was perfectly covered with makeup, not one blemish visible. She was beautiful, Adele thought. Adele knew that Mona's exotic features and thin body, dressed in miniskirts and form-fitting blouses, attracted the attention of many men. When they walked down the street together, it was always Mona who got the leers and whistles. Adele was too conservative with her blazer and trousers, glasses that made her look like the serious and studious bookworm that she was.

Mona continued with her story. "After you pulled my hair, I slapped you across the face but you moved your head..." she hesitated, touching the gold bangle on her right wrist. "I ended up hitting you in the mouth with my bangle. I felt so bad when you started to cry. But I really thought you were faking it. You can sometimes be so dramatic, you know."

Adele smiled. "That's my privilege being the youngest in the family. I'm allowed to be a whiner."

"Yeah, whatever," Mona said, flicking her hand. "You ended up running into the bathroom and slamming the door shut. When you didn't come out, I began to worry. I knocked on the door but you wouldn't open it. You can be so stubborn."

"It's the Aries in me," Adele explained.

"That explains why you and Babba always clash. Two rams in one family, always butting heads. Anyway, you finally opened the door and I saw your mouth. Your upper lip was as swollen as a balloon."

"And you were really worried about getting in trouble for hurting me."

"Yeah, you're the baby after all."

"I'm not a baby anymore," Adele interjected.

"I hate to be the bearer of bad news, Monkey, but you'll always be the 'baby' no matter how old you are. When you're fifty, you'll still be the baby."

"Really?" she said, sarcastically. "And you'll always be the wicked sister who abused her helpless little sister," she said in a taunting tone. Then the sisters began to laugh.

When they stopped, Mona softly brushed the hair away from Adele's face. "It's good to see you smile again."

Adele asked in a low voice. "Do you think Babba is right?"

"What do you mean?"

"That a Lebanese man will never marry me?"

"I don't know. There must be some that are more liberal than the ones we know. Anyway, who needs a Lebanese man, there are plenty of good Canadian men."

"What will Babba say?"

"Do you really care what he thinks?"

"You all did. You all married Lebanese men."

"That's us, Adele. We're different from you, you know that. You've always felt that way. You're the smart one."

"I'm not that smart."

"And modest. My dear, dear Monkey, you know what?"

"What?"

"I love you."

"I love you too." Mona lightly rested her hands on Adele's, then she picked up the bowl of soup and guided the spoon into Adele's open, willing mouth.

The next morning, Adele awoke with a sense of calm. She stretched her arms over her head and turned to look at her desk. A small, flat package wrapped in gold paper sat in the middle of it. Slowly, she raised herself and moved her legs over the edge of the bed. She looked down at her body, lifted up her pajamas, and let her fingers trace the cotton bandage. After covering her belly again, she carefully pushed herself up, hands pressed deep into the mattress. She held onto the edge of the bed and dresser for support as she made her way to the desk. Holding the gift in her hands, she read the small card attached to it: *For Adele, whose beautiful spirit inspires me. Love, Mona.* Adele smiled. She slowly unwrapped the gift. It was a burgundy journal filled with mulberry paper. Pulling the drawer open, she grabbed a pencil and took slow steps back to her bed.

She sat up as she opened the journal, her fingers rubbing against the bumpy texture. Resting her back against the pillows, she looked out the window, taking quick glances up and down, as she began to sketch the clouds and sun in the immense sky. In the quiet of that morning and after her postoperative care, when others were at school or work, she let lines as tender as berries drip onto the paper. After a while, she let the journal drop beside her. Out the window, the heavy snow had slowed down to flyaway snowflakes. The questions in her mind were like the snow, swirling around. Would her future lover be sympathetic to her inability to conceive? Would her first time be similar to the experience of a woman with a womb or would it be as hollow as she felt at this moment? She was only eighteen, hadn't yet experienced that intense first love, nor lovemaking. She didn't know if a potential lover would still desire her—a woman without the organ that sustained life.

Suddenly exhausted by the weight of these thoughts, she slid down the pillows, buried her body under the covers and fell deeply asleep.

CHAPTER 12

THE SMELL OF PAINT FILLED HER NOSTRILS as she stood in front of the easel set up in her bedroom. With a paintbrush in her right hand, Adele left strong strokes on the canvas, browns and greys mixing together, blue as clear as an aquamarine stone. After a few moments, she smiled to herself, happy she had finished her latest project, one that depicted her ancestry in the ruins of Baalbeck and mountains of her parents' homeland. When she painted, she forgot her father's voice, the way he had said she was "defective." Though she was still angry, she thought how good it was to be interested in something again. She put the brush down and sat on the edge of her bed, her face radiant.

It was the middle of June and the end of her senior year. Soon she'd learn whether she had gotten accepted into university. She had selected three schools: two in her hometown and one in another city. She knew what her parents would think of her going away to school: *A good Lebanese daughter would never consider leaving her parents until she had a marriage license.* But Adele had decided to apply to the University of Toronto anyway.

She suddenly heard the familiar squeak of the mailbox. She ran down the stairs, grabbed the banister, and swung her body over to the front door where she unlocked it quickly. Hand in the mailbox, she sifted through a packet of letters until she found the one she was looking for. The return address had the emblem of the University of Toronto. She stepped back, took a breath, holding the envelope up and studying the bold letters of her name as she walked into the dining room. She left the other mail on the table, and gripped hers tightly with both hands as she bounded up the stairs to her room.

Back in the safety of her bedroom, she sat at her desk and slit the envelope carefully. Her hands shook while she pulled the contents out and placed them on the desk. Unfolding a thin white sheet, she read it out loud:

> *Dear Ms. Azar,*
>
> *Congratulations on your admission to the University of Toronto. As Dean, it is my great pleasure to welcome you to the Faculty of Arts and Science. We are pleased to admit you as a full-time student to the Honours Bachelor of Science with Major in Psychology program for the fall session.*
>
> *Enclosed you will find additional information about your offer of admission.*

Adele traced the words on the stationery; this was her escape. She folded the letter, got up from the chair, and dressed quickly. Then she stuffed the offer into her pocket and walked out of her bedroom, down the stairs, tracing the banister as if the guidance she needed was engraved in the nicks and worn grooves of the old oak.

Adele left the house and walked swiftly to Mrs. Foster's home. As she walked, she wondered what it would be like to live on her own in Toronto. She wondered, too, if she'd have the courage to leave. She stood still and studied the house where she wished she'd grown up. The grass was unkempt. Dandelions sprouted between patches of earth and brownish-green blades. She closed her eyes and in her memory, she saw the former house in its splendour: a flourishing lawn and garden,

Mr. and Mrs. Foster on the swing-chair, holding hands and watching her and her sisters race through the sprinkler. And though she wanted to leave this neighbourhood, she knew that she'd miss it and this house in particular. Opening her eyes, she walked up the steps of the porch. The swing-chair was gone and the veranda looked bare except for a few sparrows pecking at the birdseed Mrs. Foster must have left for them. As Adele approached the front door, her footsteps echoed on the wooden boards, making the tiny birds flutter their wings hesitantly, unsure of whether to take flight. Adele made their choice easy by tiptoeing the remainder of the way, leaving the birds to feast on the seeds. Once she reached the doorway, she pressed the doorbell and waited for Mrs. Foster. Within a few minutes, she stood before Adele with her hands in her apron pockets and a weak smile on her mouth. Adele looked down at the cracked beams. It hurt to stare into her neighbour's face, which had become sallow over the last month. Her kidneys were failing and her memory too. Mrs. Foster would soon be in a nursing home.

"Hello, dear," Mrs. Foster said, holding the screen door open for Adele. The tiny smile on the old woman's lips was warm and inviting, but sad at the same time. Her blue eyes lacked the vivaciousness they had once held. She had lost weight and her face was gaunt, defeated. Adele quickly turned away when Mrs. Foster's gaze connected with hers.

"Don't feel sorry for me, dear. Everything must come to an end ... especially for an old lady like me," Mrs. Foster said, her smile weak.

Adele could feel tears burning her eyes as she looked at her friend again. She loved Mrs. Foster. "You're not that old," Adele teased. "Aren't you just twenty-one plus the taxes?"

Mrs. Foster laughed weakly, then started to cough. Adele quickly patted her back. "Are you all right?"

Mrs. Foster nodded and cleared her throat. "I'm just laughing at your joke, my dear. Very funny." She rested her hand on

Adele's shoulder. The older woman gently squeezed. "You're too thin. You need some flesh on these bones."

"I know, I know," Adele replied light-heartedly. "Speak to my metabolism. I do eat, sometimes too much."

"Well, your mother is a great cook. Her *taboulleh* is the best. You're very lucky to have her."

Adele said nothing.

"And..." she added, "she's lucky to have you, too."

Adele smiled, then followed Mrs. Foster into the living room and sat on the lone sofa with mahogany arms carved in the shape of hearts. The sofa was a little corny but definitely well-suited for the Fosters, who had been high school sweethearts. Sitting here in the sunlight, Adele saw the advanced state of Mrs. Foster's illness. A multi-coloured scarf was wrapped around her head, strands of fragile hair falling around her face. A large skirt hung loosely on a body that had once been robust and sturdy. Now bones jutted through the cotton blouse, faintly showing withered breasts held in an oversized, laced brassiere. Adele's mother wore the same kind of bra but it barely contained Samira's overflowing bosom. Mrs. Foster scratched at her irritated skin. "No matter how much body lotion I use, I can't stop the itchiness," she said, looking into Adele's eyes.

Cardboard boxes were stacked in neat piles. This room had once been alive with antiques of the past—a bookshelf that held old classics as well as Mr. Foster's law books, a grandfather clock that chimed on the hour, a grand piano that Mrs. Foster gracefully played, producing music as sweet as the candied carrots she used to make for the Azar girls. But now there was only an old musty couch, a coffee table, cardboard boxes, and two unlikely friends.

Mrs. Foster reached over and took Adele's hands in her own. They sat quietly together, but the clawing of a squirrel at the base of the living room window interrupted the silence.

"Damn squirrels," Mrs. Foster cursed, releasing Adele's

hands. She lifted her own in the air and batted in the direction of the furry creature. "I won't miss those rodents! They were always eating from my vegetable garden! You know, I tried everything to keep them away but they always came back for more. I even left nuts outside for them, but they always went for the tomatoes and zucchini."

"Obviously, they know vegetables are good for them."

"True," Mrs. Foster nodded, then added, "but stay away from my tomatoes!" The black-eyed creature scurried away almost as if it had heard Mrs. Foster's scolding tone.

Adele stood up slowly, reached into her pocket and pulled out her acceptance letter. "I have some good news," she said, handing the note to her friend.

Mrs. Foster lifted her glasses from the coffee table and adjusted them on the tip of her nose. She unfolded the letter and read the contents. "I'm so happy for you, dear," she exclaimed. "This is wonderful news! Well done." The old woman embraced her and added jubilantly, "Congratulations! Your parents must be so proud of you."

Adele pursed her lips, then said, "I haven't told them yet."

"You must," Mrs. Foster encouraged. "Being accepted to university is a wonderful milestone in a young person's life. And you're the first person in your family to go, aren't you? What an accomplishment!"

"But the school isn't here."

"So? They'll bend the old world rules, don't you think?"

Adele was on the verge of tears. "I don't know."

"You won't know until you ask, my dear," Mrs. Foster insisted, putting her arm around Adele once more. "Maybe they'll surprise you."

"You're right, Mrs. Foster. This is a good thing for me and parents only want the best for their kids, right?"

"Exactly. My dear, bless you for being so positive after all you've been through," the older woman gently squeezed Adele's arm before leaning in and giving her another hug. Deeply breathing in Mrs. Foster's jasmine scent, Adele knew what it felt to be loved.

Youssef sat in the living room when Adele announced her good news. She tried to decipher her father's face. A look of pride was nowhere to be found. He kept silent as he listened to her.

"I got accepted to the University of Toronto. It's a great school and some of my friends are going there, so I won't be alone. There are some Lebanese people there too," Adele added with a smile, thinking this fact would encourage her parents to accept her decision.

Samira's eyes were fixed on the floor. Adele stared at her mother willing her to look up and say "Good for you. Congratulations." Instead, she kept her eyes down and didn't speak.

Youssef, on the other hand, opened his mouth and grunted, "No daughter of mine is going away to school. No marriage, no leaving my house. You got two choices: stay in Ottawa for school or get married, then do as you please." Youssef slapped his hands together, rubbing his palms to symbolize the finality of his decision.

"But Babba…" Adele started, exasperated. Her face lost its smile. She leaned forward and spoke with her hands, waving them frantically in the air. "But Babba…"

Youssef interrupted. "No 'but Babba.' You've always been the pig-headed one in this family."

Adele scoffed. "Me? You're the one as stubborn as a mule. We're not in the old country, Babba. Times are changing. Women are allowed to be independent, to move out of the house without being married."

"Enough," Youssef said, lifting his hand. He pointed his finger at Adele. "You're not some *enklese* girl. You follow tradition, not some Canadian rule where kids are supposed to move out on their own. You're Lebanese, not white, remember? And you're my daughter. No daughter of mine is becoming some … some…" he sputtered as he searched for the right word.

"What do you call those girls always demanding equal rights, the ones always on the news causing problems?"

"A feminist," Adele mumbled, sitting back on the couch. She clutched the letter in her hands and it wrinkled in her fist. "No daughter of mine is a feminist. A feminist got no place in my family, understand?" he said, glaring at her. He slammed his hand back on the arm of the sofa. "Like I said, you got two choices: go to school here or get married and see if your husband agrees to move to Toronto. End of story."

Adele looked across at her mother for support but Samira's eyes focused on her hands in her lap. With one quick, angry movement, Adele rose from the sofa and held the letter up in front of her father's face. She then tore it apart, throwing bits of paper at him as if a squall had blown into his cheeks. "Are you happy, Babba? You won."

Adele observed a change of colour in her father's face but she didn't care. Let him have another outburst, she thought. Adele turned to her mother again. Their eyes met for a moment, but then Samira lowered her head again. She remained silent.

Heaving a deep sigh, Adele rested her hand on the banister before making a quick dash up the stairs.

Two weeks later, Adele received a letter of acceptance from the University of Ottawa. Reluctantly, sadly, she checked the acceptance box, signed the form and stuffed it in the return envelope. Depression overwhelmed her while she walked into the grocery store and stood in front of her father. He was wiping the counter with a wet rag, leaving perfect straight lines across the wooden surface. The light from the early dusk reflected inside the store, touching Youssef; his face had multiplied in wrinkles over the past few years. His eyes were sunken and less luminescent, almost sad. Adele couldn't help but feel pity for her father. This store was his livelihood. Keeping a shop was the only thing he had learned to do and business was dwindling with the introduction of superstores. Standing before her father, Adele held up the envelope. "I'm staying here, Babba," she said, biting her lower lip and trying to stop the tremor in her voice.

"You're doing the right thing, Adele," Youssef said. Having inherited her mother's oval face and pensive look, she looked nothing like her father. His eyes opened wide and softened simultaneously as he gazed at her. "You look beautiful."

Adele looked away. Her father had never complimented her before. She wondered what was happening. What had come over him? They stood face to face. Adele watched her father stretch out his hand and press his palm into her cheek. She looked up at her father. There were tears in his eyes.

The days passed and the month of June came to an end. Fireworks exploded in the dark clouds. Beams shooting skyward then collapsing downward as partygoers watched in awe at the colourful display. When it was all over, the national anthem pounded out of loud speakers on Parliament Hill. Another Canada Day was over. People began to disperse. Adele's face disappeared amidst the crowd but then she was reunited with her family who were making their way back home where Samira and Youssef awaited them. The four sisters now joined the ranks of three brothers-in-law, Ziad, George, and Marcel, and a tiny chorus of nieces and nephews singing *Happy Birthday* in Arabic. Adele was absorbed in her thoughts while her sisters and their families hurried back to the home they had all once lived in together. She was the only single daughter. Years earlier, her sisters had all managed to leave and become independent women, obtaining this freedom acceptably, through marriage. But Adele couldn't even pursue her education in another city! She laughed in spite of herself. Rima and Katrina turned and looked at her. Her thick hair was pulled back and held in place with a red bandana though ringlets spilled out, coming to rest around her neck. Mona had tried to convince Adele to remove the bandana, but she refused. "Why are you dressing as if you're from the old country? Aren't you a self-hating Leb?"

Adele pushed her sister's groping hands and tightened the bandana. "Mind your own business. I don't tell you how to dress."

"No one has to tell me how to dress. I have great style," Mona had said, touching her hair, now cut in a bob. She wore a miniskirt, revealing her thin legs and perfect hips, things she had managed to retain in spite of the birth of her son and daughter.

Adele glanced from one sister to another. Rima, who had once always smiled now frowned and fretted with her three children, pushing hair out of their eyes, adjusting collars of shirts, wiping drool from the youngest child's mouth. Adele studied the way Rima's forearms jiggled with the extra weight she had gained since her pregnancies. Ziad had remained the same since their nuptials, cocky and arrogant as ever. His open-collared shirt revealed the gold chain and crucifix he always wore. The only new features were the grey hairs sprouting on his chest and head. Married life had been good to him, Adele thought.

"Danny, stop at the sidewalk. Danny! Don't cross the street by yourself," Rima said harshly. "Stay on the sidewalk, okay?"

Adele turned back to look at her sister. Her beautiful face was pale and her long hair was brittle, pulled back in the ponytail she always wore these days.

Ziad suddenly laughed, nudging George, Katrina's husband. "Look at her!" The two men stared at a young woman walking by, her buttocks barely contained in her cut-off shorts. The young woman smiled and winked at Ziad. "*Habibi*, I'll be thinking of you tonight!" he said, stroking his crotch. Slinging his arms around George and Marcel, he said in a whisper, "Wouldn't you love to get a piece of her? She's probably wild in bed. Rima's so old-fashioned. She only likes to do it one way and that's all. Sometimes I can't even bother with her. I have no desire to be with her."

Adele was about to scold him but when she saw Rima's red face, she kept quiet. This wasn't the first time Ziad had openly belittled his wife. Adele couldn't help herself. "You know, Ziad, there are pills out there for impotence. You should seriously consider visiting your doctor."

Coldly, Ziad replied, "I don't need pills. I need a sexier wife, that's all."

"You're an asshole!" Adele snapped.

Ignoring this comment, Ziad said, in a mocking tone, "The girls of this country think just because they're born here makes them superior to us men." He lightly slapped Marcel's back. But Mona's husband remained silent.

At that moment, Rima extended her arm and rested it on Adele's shoulders. Her right hand squeezed Adele's forearm. She held her back while the others went ahead, Ziad still guffawing. "Stop arguing with Ziad. He's my husband, not yours," Rima said angrily. Adele sighed and watched her sister join her husband, hooking her arm into his.

In a few minutes, they were back at Youssef and Samira's house. The members of the family climbed up the stairs, moving inside while Adele stayed back and sat on the steps, glancing at her parents' small front yard. She looked at the grapevine her father had constructed with panels of wood, hooking veins along the sides. The plentiful grape leaves fluttered in the warm summer wind. Tiny purplish-red grapes had started to grow; the leaves were edible when Samira stuffed them with rice and meat and made *maza* for her family. A bit of the old country existed in this small plot of land, Adele thought. The neighbouring homes had lawn ornaments and flowers adorning the well-trimmed grass. But her parents had brought Lebanon with them by planting this grapevine. Engrossed in her thoughts, she jumped when Youssef called out her name. "Adele," Youssef said quietly, holding open the screen door.

She turned to face her father. "Yes, Babba?" she asked with a smile.

Youssef glanced at her, addressing her in a soft tone. "Adele..." She realized her acceptance to the local university must have affected him profoundly because he said, "*Habibi,*" Sweetheart. "Come inside. I have some good news."

Adele got up from the steps, wiped the back of her skirt and walked towards her father. She bent down slightly as her father's arm pushed the screen door wider allowing her more room to pass. She slid past him and once inside, Youssef rested his hands on her shoulders and led her into the living room where her mother, sisters and brothers-in-law were seated. The strong scent of *ahweh* filled her nostrils. She turned her head towards the basement entrance and heard the voices of her nieces and nephews playing in the room she had once played in as a child. She then sat down on the sofa beside her father, his hand resting on her left knee.

Surrounded by her family, she smiled and said, "So what's the good news?" She looked across at her brothers-in-law chewing on pistachios and sipping steaming Arabic coffee. She glanced between her sisters and mother. Their faces gleamed with delight. Adele knew they had already been told the secret. "Come on," Adele pleaded, "tell me."

"Patience, *babba,*" Youssef said, now gently squeezing her knee. He leaned over towards the tray in front of him and lifted the small copper pot, then poured the black liquid into a tiny cup. He handed it to Adele. Shocked, Adele tried to hide her surprise at her father's sudden kindness. In all her years, she had never seen him serve anyone and least of all herself. She bit her lower lip to prevent a large grin from taking over her face. She sat back and lifted the cup to her mouth, taking tiny sips of the bitter coffee.

Then she smiled, placed the saucer on the tray and sat with her hands under her thighs. She straightened her back, faced her father and gave him her full attention.

"As we all know, Adele just got accepted to a university here in *Ottawa*," he emphasized.

Adele smiled faintly and looked across at the other family members. They nodded their heads.

Her father continued, patting his chest. "She has made her Mama and me very proud."

Adele tried not to stare at her father too hard.

"And as a symbol of our pride, I have decided to take my girls and wife on a trip."

The brothers-in-law sat up and shouted, teasingly, "What about us?"

"Someone's got to watch the kids and take care of the store," Youssef muttered, laughing.

Adele smiled again. Everyone was speaking loudly, happily.

"Where are you taking us, Babba?" Mona asked, resting her arm on the back of the couch and combing her fingers through her husband's short hair.

"Rome? Paris? Egypt? Disney World?" the sisters teased, each taking turns at guessing the destination.

"No." Youssef shook his head, the smile pasted on his face. "All wrong. I'm taking you to the best country in the world."

"Canada? But we already live here," Rima said, feigning disappointment.

"No, no, the other best," Youssef said, nodding his head vigorously. "Lebanon."

Adele and her sisters clapped their hands and started talking at the same time, eyes glistening. Samira smiled too, lifting her hands to her mouth then slapping them against her thighs, also excited by the happy atmosphere.

"Adele has never been to Lebanon like her sisters, so I thought this would be the perfect gift. She made the right choice to stay in Ottawa for school," Youssef said.

Adele leaned over and quickly kissed her father on the cheeks. "Thank you, Babba. It's a wonderful gift." As she leaned forward, she noticed the coffee pot was nearly empty.

She rose, picked up the copper container and walked into the kitchen.

Samira rose, too, and followed her. She took Adele aside in a corner of the kitchen. "Are you happy, *habibti*?" she asked eagerly.

She nodded. For once in her life, she felt content and loved.

But from where she stood, she couldn't see the smiles tensing on her sisters' faces, couldn't see Youssef lean forward with his elbows on his knees nor hear his whispered words.

PART III: 1988

CHAPTER 13

THE OLD SILVER MERCEDES SWERVED through the streets of Beirut, scarcely missing the cars on the opposite side of the road. It was a stifling July day. The sun pounded through the windshield, heating the crowded vehicle and its passengers: Adele, her sisters, and their parents. The driver was her cousin Rafic. His short curly hair was gelled back. The beginning of a goatee encased his full lips. Studying his face, Adele thought this must be the boy her father had always yearned for. Rafic looked very much like Youssef, only he had a darker complexion. Adele sat between the two men. "Thank you, nephew, for picking us up from the airport," Youssef said, the smile on her father's face one she had never seen before.

"No problem, Uncle," Rafic answered.

Sweat rolled down Adele's neck to her belly. A mild breeze swept the sand from the adjacent beach and entered the open windows of the Mercedes. She blinked, wiped the dust from her eyes, then looked out at the blue Mediterranean bordering the road. She stared at the bare-chested men and the women with brightly coloured sarongs wrapped around their hips, dangling earrings brushing against their suntanned cheeks, strolling along the shore. She clenched her jaw when she felt her father reach over her shoulders to touch her cousin.

"So, how's my boy? Or should I say 'man'? You've grown so much. I remember you when you were only this tall," Youssef said, holding up his other hand in the air. "Now, you're a grown man!" He lowered his hand and placed it back on his thigh, the smile on his face still radiating.

Rafic beamed and replied, "Well, Uncle, I'm twenty-four now and soon to be a father!" Rafic's wife was expecting their first child.

Adele kneaded her hands on her lap, pressing her knuckles together. She turned to look at her father. His deep eyes widened when he spoke with Rafic. "You've made me so proud, Rafic," Youssef said, his normally stern face relaxed and happy. "I hope you have a son to carry on the Azar name."

"*Enshallah*," Rafic replied, glancing at Adele and smiling.

But she turned away from him and stared at her sisters and mother through the rear-view mirror. Their eyes were pasted to the windows and on the shimmering waves of water.

Youssef breathed deeply. "The name dies with me in my immediate family because I don't have sons, but I hope and pray you have a handful of handsome boys."

Adele pretended not to hear, but her father went on.

"Having a boy is so important. Girls are okay, but sons are crucial to maintaining our bloodline."

Rafic nodded politely, turning down a narrow street and swerving to avoid another vehicle that almost crashed into them. "*Kis imak!*" Rafic cursed. Adele's body plunged forward. Her father gripped her and asked her if she were all right. She nodded, pressing herself into the tattered cushions of the front seat.

Two hours later, Rafic parked the car in front of a restaurant in Zahlé, a red-roofed town near the eastern foothills of Mount Sannine. Everyone quickly slid out and stretched their legs and arms. The riverside café was a flat red brick building with wide windows and a large patio filled with plastic tables and chairs. Adele stepped into the shade of a tree and immediately felt cooler.

Rafic now stood beside her and pointed, "Cousin, you see that river?"

She nodded.

"That's the Bardouni River. It flows out of Mount Sannine, down through Zahlé. Very beautiful."

"Yes, it is," she agreed, smiling.

Youssef walked towards them and genially slapped Rafic's back. "Okay, enough with the tour guide. Let's eat." He then led Rafic into the restaurant, leaving Adele standing alone outside.

Adele stood open-mouthed, stung by the interruption, until Mona grabbed her by the arm and dragged her inside. The air smelled like the spices that Samira cooked with back home. "Come on, Monkey. Don't get jealous. Babba hasn't seen Rafic in ages. It's only natural for him to feel affection for him."

"Yeah, but what about us? Why doesn't Babba act all happy when he's with us?" Adele asked.

"We're too close to him. We haven't been absent long enough to let his heart grow fonder." Mona poked Adele in the ribs and tried to get her to smile.

"You mean Babba has a heart?" Adele said sarcastically.

"Yeah," Mona said, tapping Adele's stomach, "but it's hard to see because of his potbelly!"

The sisters laughed before joining the others on the patio and pulling out the plastic chairs from under the simple, white table. Adele sat down, briefly closed her eyes, and listened to the rushing cascade of the river.

After *maza* was served, Adele watched a man in baggy trousers with a fez on his head as he stood at their table and poured steaming *ahweh* into everyone's cups. His curling moustache reminded her of her father. This place was so different from back home, she thought, where waiters and waitresses were always rushing to serve impatient customers and almost pushing them out the door to make room for others. This café was peaceful with the trees and water surrounding it.

She watched her father, who was in deep conversation with Rafic. In the glow of the diminishing sun, the lines around

Youssef's deep-set eyes had softened. Suddenly Adele sat up, leaned her elbows on the table and looked closely at her father—there was a widening grin on his face again! Sighing, she fell back in the chair and stared again at the man in the baggy trousers; he had moved to another table and provided the diners with a hookah. These customers were middle-aged men. They wore frayed sweaters over stained white shirts in spite of the evening heat. Some of them held turquoise worry beads in their dark hands, rolling each stone to the next, while others passed the hookah between them, taking short puffs on the pipe and drawing out a line of apple-scented smoke. A haze of tobacco clouded the patio. Adele covered her mouth as she coughed. Her sisters sat tensely in their chairs, listening to the conversation between Youssef and Rafic. Even Samira sat quietly with her head in her hands. She frowned when Youssef patted Rafic's back and proclaimed, "You're like the son Samira didn't give me. I'm so proud of you."

"Thank you, Uncle," he said, smiling timidly. He glanced across at Adele and her sisters, then lowered his eyes and stared at the small cup in his hands.

Adele looked away too, the colour in her face disappearing like the sun behind the cliffs of the Bardouni river.

It was after midnight when they arrived in her parents' village. In Kfarmichki many of the lights of the stone houses were on and several people were gathered on balconies and flat roofs, playing cards and drinking *ahweh* or *arak*, empty plates of *maza* pushed aside. The houses they passed on their way to her father's childhood home didn't stand out from each other. They were small grey-stoned dwellings with diminutive windows and red roofs. Yet they seemed to accommodate a lot of people; dozens of men and women lounged in plastic chairs outside, slapping cards on a table.

The car coated these homes with orange dust as they drove by, even though Rafic had slowed the Mercedes down when he entered the village, easing it through the narrow dirt roads. By the time they reached Youssef's home, the dust had lifted into the surrounding hills and olive trees. Samira, Rima, Katrina, and Mona jumped out of the Mercedes along with Rafic. Adele nudged her father on the arm; he had fallen asleep. Youssef woke with a start. He blinked a few times, frowning in confusion. She wasn't sure whether to say, *you're home.* Was this still his home? she wondered. He stumbled out of the car, Adele following. Light from the homes around them filled the surrounding darkness. He rubbed his eyes, then stared out into the yard where fig and olive trees abounded and a donkey lay asleep. The animal's sudden snort made Adele jump. Youssef lightly touched her shoulder. "Don't be afraid of the donkey. It won't kick ... as long as you don't argue back with it like you do with your Babba!" He burst into laughter.

She didn't smile.

"Let's call a truce, okay?" he said suddenly, holding out his hand. "No arguments while we're here."

She stretched out her hand and firmly shook her father's, their palms sticking together. She smiled and then helped her cousin carry their luggage up the steps; she slowly walked inside her father's childhood home.

The smell of old musty walls floated into Adele's nose. She dragged the suitcases inside, following her sisters and parents as they too carried their bags and headed down the hallway, but Adele stopped in the living room, which was crowded with four couches, a table and a couple of chairs. Deep violet and red vases engraved with gold flowers were set between the sofas.

A man emerged from the dark hallway into the softly-lit room. "*Marhaba*, Adele," he said. "I'm your Uncle Issa." He had striking similarities to her father: a receding hairline, though his hair was still black rather than grey, and a round belly. Adele's frame towered over his as he leaned in and embraced her.

She patted his back while he held her tight in his arms. His smell— the scent of earth and sweat—filled her nostrils but she didn't move away or let go. Her uncle came to life, a man she had only known in old black and white photographs, while he hugged her. She glanced at her father who stood a few feet away, his face blank. Youssef sat down on a torn brown sofa and looked around, not letting his gaze meet hers. She wondered if he felt envious. After the long embrace, Adele let go of her uncle and looked into his eyes, which were as sunken as Youssef's, but not so lined; his skin was tanned from fieldwork.

"Uncle Issa, it's so good to finally meet you. You're as handsome as I imagined," she teased, then quickly glanced at her father, who finally looked up.

"*Shukran*, Adele," Issa said, grinning.

"What did you expect, Adele? He takes after his older handsome brother," Youssef said, throwing his head back in laughter.

This was the first time she had seen her father so carefree and happy. She laughed, too, and slapped her forehead. "Of course, Babba, how could I forget?"

Smiling, Issa took the bags from Adele's hands and followed Rafic into the adjacent room where Adele and her sisters would sleep during their visit. She could hear her mother and sisters chatting in the kitchen with her Aunt Frida. Then she followed her uncle and cousin into the living room and sat on the sofa beside her father, her eyes exploring the walls covered with photographs, a pendant of the Lebanese flag, and pictures of Jesus. Adele rose from the couch and stood in front of one of the old photographs, glancing from the portrait back to her father.

Youssef was also taking in the room. "The house still looks the same. It's exactly as how I remember it. Not much has changed," he said in low voice. Adele moved closer to the photograph. Three children sat on the back of a donkey; a woman and a man stood at either end of the animal. She stretched her neck to get a better look at the middle-aged man in the photo, presumably the father of the small clan. He certainly resembled Youssef. This was Jido Salim, her grandfather, Adele guessed. His lips were chapped and pursed in a tight line and furrows were engraved deeply on his sunburnt face. He had dark circles under his small eyes and deep wrinkles in his forehead. Adele looked at the woman whose hands rested protectively on the eldest child's back. She had a slight hunch and Adele wondered if Sito, her grandmother, had had to fetch water from the well and river with a carrying pole over her shoulders, hoisting buckets on either end of the wooden stick. She had heard various stories over the years about Youssef's mother, how she struggled raising the children and, at the same time, took care of the fieldwork alongside her husband. Adele remembered photos of her paternal grandmother, taken when she was old, her skin leathery by years of working in the sun. She was poor, always dressed in ragged clothes, and her toothless mouth hung half-open.

But in the photo on the wall, her grandmother was still a younger woman, still strong. Adele examined the children positioned on the back of the donkey. Mostly though, she stared at the oldest of the three, her father. He had a serious, almost sad expression. He wasn't looking into the camera, but at Jido Salim, his Babba, who stood at the front of the donkey holding the rope, and Adele recognized his look and all its longing. Jido Salim, she realized now, looked angry. She thought how that very anger had influenced so much of her own life and she was thankful when her uncle rested his hand on her shoulder.

"So, Youssef tells me you're the smart one in the family," Issa said, dropping his arm and heading towards Youssef where he sank into the couch next to him, making the springs squeak loudly.

Adele's jaw dropped at her uncle's comment. *The smart one in the family.* She glanced at her father, waiting for a rebuttal or a denial. But Youssef only smiled proudly, pressing his back into the sofa and patting his brother's knee.

"She wants to be a doctor," Youssef said.

"A psychologist," Adele corrected. She really wanted to be an artist but her father wouldn't allow her to follow that road. She sighed and turned her attention back to her uncle and father.

"What's that?" Issa asked, his thick eyebrows knitted together.

Adele explained, speaking in her broken Arabic. "Um ... it's a doctor who studies the mind." She tapped her finger against her head, then continued. "Say you feel sad and you don't know why, you'd go to see a psychologist and talk about your life, family, problems. You talk and talk until you have a better understanding of yourself."

Issa shifted on the couch and faced Youssef. "*Ayb*. You're letting your daughter do this? Talk with crazy people?"

"They charge about a hundred dollars an hour. Good money," Youssef said.

"Even so. Why not be a regular doctor and fix broken bones, take care of colds ... now that's a respectable career, not some 'doctor' who speaks with crazy people," Issa said. "Anyway, family problems should stay in the family. It's *ayb* to discuss such matters with strangers." He stopped, leaned close to Youssef's ear and whispered, "I thought you said she was the smart one."

Adele puckered her forehead; she heard every word. She turned away from her father and uncle and looked hard at the old donkey in the photograph. She would be, she vowed, as stubborn as that animal.

Lying in an unfamiliar bed that night, cramped between Mona and Katrina, Adele struggled to sleep, and failed. For a while she watched Rima in the small, metal cot across from the bed and listened to the soft breaths that escaped from her sisters' mouths. She slowly raised her body with her forearms, then slid herself to the foot of the bed, taking the crumpled sheets with her. Once she was up, she covered her sisters, and tip-toed down the dark hallway and into the living room. She sat on the edge of the window. Staring into the horizon, she watched the shadows of the olive trees against the mountains as if moving' with them in a mysterious dance under the blu-ish-white moonlight. She felt homesick; her stomach churned. She missed her friends, her bicycle, and mostly Mrs. Foster. She looked at the full moon, fearing that during this visit her neighbour would pass away. Before she could stop herself, she had begun to cry. Her shoulders shook until she felt the weight of someone's hands on them, squeezing her tight and steadying her whimpering body.

"What's wrong?" Youssef whispered, leaning close to her ear.

"Nothing, Babba," Adele lied, wiping her eyes.

He stepped back, his hands still on her shoulders. "Why are you crying then?"

"I miss Mrs...." she caught herself, "I miss home."

He dropped his arms to his sides. "You'll be back soon enough and then I'll be homesick."

Youssef's face appeared grey in the moonlit room. She wiped her eyes. "It must've been hard for you to leave Lebanon. Do you ever want to move back, make a life here, Babba?" she asked gently.

He snickered, slapping his right hand against his thigh. "With the goats and donkeys! That's a life."

"If that would've made you happy, yes."

"You don't understand, Adele. You talk too much and never listen."

She sat up straight. "I'm listening now, Babba. I want to understand you."

Youssef turned around and pointed at the photograph on the wall, the one with the donkey and children. "Your Jido wasn't the easiest man to live with."

Neither are you, she thought.

"I had to leave to a start a new life for myself."

Too loudly, she replied, "Like I wanted to do when I got accepted to the University of Toronto?"

"No, this is different," Youssef said, shaking his head and stepping away from her.

"How so?"

"A daughter must stay with her parents until she's married, but a boy can leave if he likes. It's just the way things are."

"It's so unfair!"

"Boys don't have to worry about certain things."

"What things?" she asked, the nerves around her mouth tensing.

"Female things."

"Like what?" she pushed, interested in hearing what her father thought about these concerns. Their whispering voices filled the small living room. The moonlight softened the usual rigidity of her father's face. She mustered a small smile, reached out to touch her father's arm then, unsure, let her hand drop in her lap.

"If I have to tell you what they are, then you're as dumb as that donkey!" he snapped, pointing to the animal in the front yard tied to the wooden fence.

Adele turned away from him.

"Boys have certain privileges, that's all. If you had been a boy, I would've let you go to school outside of Ottawa but you were born a girl."

Adele said nothing. What could she say to that? Youssef remained quiet too, then he walked out of the house and stood in the yard beside the donkey. His shoulders were slightly bent as he reached down and stroked the donkey's folded ears. Adele stared at her father's shadow as it blended into the night. She shrank back against the wall of the window frame.

She woke to the cry of a rooster. She lay with a stiff neck on the Persian rug in the living room then sat up quickly and rubbed her eyes, adjusting them to the morning light that filled the stone house. Adele got up from the floor and stretched her arms above her head, releasing the kinks from her restless sleep. She stepped quietly across the floor, attracted to the light in the kitchen. Standing in the shadow of the doorway, she listened to the whispers of her father and uncle. How similar they sounded, she thought, their voices both harsh and deep.

"It's all been arranged, Youssef. No need to worry about anything. They're very happy. Everyone knows about their son. They didn't want people to know but it's a village. Gossip travels. What can you expect?" Adele peered over the edge and saw Uncle Issa raising his hands in the air then slamming them on the kitchen table. "Everyone feels bad, of course. But at least now the boy has a chance of leaving this place, making money, and sending it back home to his family. He's a good boy, too. Don't worry about anything. Everything will work out, you'll see," Issa reassured.

"*Enshallah*," Youssef sighed.

Adele's fingers traced the rough, uneven wood of the doorway, pressing her head against the wall, and leaning closer to hear them better. She wondered what her father and uncle were discussing. A son for Youssef to take back to Canada? The son he always wanted? Her forehead furrowed.

"Everything will work out," Issa repeated.

"Good, good," Youssef said, more confident. Adele watched her father's small hand clasp Uncle Issa's. "It's all settled then. When will we meet him?"

"Today."

She stepped lightly back into the hallway when she heard the scraping of chairs on the kitchen floor. She scurried down the corridor and opened the door to the bedroom where her sisters lay asleep. As she closed the door behind her, another rooster in the yard began to crow. The high-pitched cry didn't wake her sleeping sisters.

A stone wall, messily constructed, and countless olive trees surrounded Youssef's childhood home. While crossing the yard, Adele recalled her father's stories of how he had built this wall. She placed the last dishes of *maza* on the beige cloth-covered table before taking her seat. A flower design had been carefully embroidered into the beige tablecloth. It was a shame that the plates had to cover the pattern, she thought, as she touched one of the intricately crafted flowers with her fingertips. Her father's voice brought her back to the conversation.

"I used to tend the trees until the olives were ready to be harvested and shipped to cousins in Canada. I'd help my mother and father make the olive oil, too. Now Uncle Issa does this for his Canadian brother," Youssef said, his voice cracking.

"You Canadian, not Lebanese?" Issa laughed. "You've forgotten who you are?"

"No, no," Youssef said quickly, his eyes squinting in the afternoon light. "I'll always be Lebanese. And..." he added, "my children are too. I raised them to be good Lebanese daughters."

Adele noticed her uncle staring at her, then felt her father's eyes on her face, too.

"I won't argue that point, Youssef. You're a good father," Issa said.

Adele cleared her throat and her sisters immediately turned to look at her, silently pleading her not to rebut their uncle's last statement. Fortunately, she concentrated on the young man who stood quietly at the entrance of the gate with his hands in the pockets of his light brown tweed blazer. He was tall and lean with black wavy hair, falling to his chin, not cut short in the style that most men of their culture wore. He seemed to be in his mid-twenties. His jaw was square and covered with stubble. He was handsome in a dishevelled sort of way but it was his bluish-green eyes that made Adele turn away from the conversation and look across at him.

"*Marhaba,*" he said, moving closer to the table. He stretched out his right hand and shook Issa's hand, then Youssef's. He nodded at the women around the table and smiled timidly.

"*Marhaba*, Elias," Issa said, pulling an empty chair out for the young man. "Sit down and join us."

"Elias, this is my niece Adele and her sisters." Issa didn't bother to introduce the others by name. Elias sat back in the chair beside Adele and rested his hands on the arms of it.

"Do you speak Arabic?" Elias asked, turning to face Adele. She nodded. "Not very good, but I'm getting better."

"Well, Adele, I can teach you." His cheeks turned pink as he said that and Adele couldn't help but smile at the young man's nervousness. There was something sweet about it. There was also something intriguing in the way Elias leaned close to her face and whispered in his accented English, "I'm very happy to meet you."

"Likewise," Adele answered. Now it was her turn to blush.

The next day, she sat in front of the house with her sketchpad on her lap, drawing the mountains in the distance, and she looked up and spotted Elias standing a few feet away from her. "Hello, Adele," he said. Nodding at the empty chair across from her, he asked gently, "May I join you?"

"Sure," Adele answered, placing the notebook on the plastic table.

Elias pulled the book closer to him and looked down at the picture. "You're a very talented artist. How long have you been drawing?"

"Since I was a child."

"Maybe one day, you can draw a portrait of me?" Elias smiled shyly. "And I can say, *I knew her when*."

Adele laughed. "Well, I don't know if I'll ever become a famous artist or anything, but it's one of my dreams."

"I had a dream once too." There was a sadness in his voice.

"Do you want to talk about it?"

He shook his head and said, "Maybe another time."

Adele didn't push, moving the pencil between her fingers. "I think you can have more than one dream in lifetime. I think when one dies another can blossom."

"I like that."

"Do you have other dreams?"

"Not at this moment but I always wanted to be a model for a beautiful woman."

Adele could feel her cheeks growing hot, which made her drop the pencil in her hand. It landed on the ground. As she bent down to pick it up, Elias's head bumped into hers. He, too, was attempting to pick up the pencil.

"Sorry," they said simultaneously then smiled at each other. Elias had the pencil and he handed it to her with an exaggerated flourish of his arm. "Well, how about starting that sketch of me?" He got up quickly and posed, flexing his muscles in a macho way. "What do you think?"

"I'll call it the 'Essence of a Lebanese man!'" Adele laughed again.

"Unfortunately, the picture will be fake because I'm so very different from that machismo," Elias said, sitting back down.

"So you're not your typical male Leb?"

"No, I'm your typical bookworm. If I had the choice between bulging biceps or a set of books, I'd take the books any day."

"I love books too."

"Have you heard of Kahlil Gibran?"

"He's one of my favourite writers."

"Mine too." There was a silence as Elias stared into Adele's eyes, which made her quickly look away.

Elias cleared his throat. "Here, please," he said, handing her the sketchpad.

And Adele began to draw his face.

A few days later, Adele slipped a package into Elias's hands while they sat in the front yard of her uncle's house. It was a warm afternoon and the smell of garlic and allspice filtered out the windows and open doors, along with the loud voices of Adele's family members as they swallowed their meals down with small glasses of *arak*. Seeing Elias coming up the walkway, Adele had rushed outside to greet him and present him with a gift.

Her eyes followed his finger as he slowly unwrapped the rectangular parcel, revealing a drawing of Elias's square-jaw and full lips, Adele watched the young man's expression, how it seemed shy at first then radiant when he uncovered the picture she had captured of him with her strong lines and shading. "It's beautiful, Adele," he said, smiling. "I'll always cherish it. *Shukran*."

"You're welcome, Elias. I'm glad you like it."

"I love it." Elias leaned in and kissed her on the cheeks. She leaned back against the doorframe, and motioned for him to come inside. "Let's have lunch," she said.

Over a plate of stuffed grape leaves and homemade yoghurt, Adele looked across at Elias. He sat between her father and uncle, turning his head to and fro, trying to keep up with the conversation going on at the table. "But Youssef, I don't want to leave my country. I've told you many times that Canada can never be my home."

"But what's here for you? Nothing."

"Nothing?" Issa asked. "There's my family, the figs, the olives, the goats..."

"Fuck the goats! Look at this fool," Youssef said to Elias while pointing at Issa. "He wants to stay in a country filled with uncertainty because of the goats! Now is that crazy or just plain stupidity?"

Elias didn't reply, only stared across at Adele with his eyes wide.

Adele smiled and tried to change the subject, "You know, Uncle, Canada has a lot of great things too."

"Like what? Snow and bloody cold temperatures."

"Yes, but there are other things, too, like great health insurance, good jobs...."

"I'm healthy as an ox. I don't need health insurance when I've got a good heart and bones. This comes from hard farm work, not some job where you sit on your behind all day, serving customers like your Babba," Issa said, smiling and staring mockingly at Youssef.

"*Ya sharmout!* I work just as hard as you and more so. You can finish whenever you want but I stay open until ten every night. Now who's the hard worker?" Youssef said with a mischievous grin.

"Okay, okay, you win but I'm not leaving my country, brother. This is my home. I'm Lebanese, not Canadian."

Youssef grunted then scooped up some *laban,* pouring the yoghurt over the cigar-shaped grape leafs and stuffing one into his mouth. And Adele was glad that her father was silent for once.

When lunch was finally over, she and Elias headed outdoors. "Your father is a really funny character."

"Yeah," Adele mumbled though she really wanted to say, when he's not being a bastard, but she kept her opinion to herself, following Elias down the dirt road towards the river. Once there, they sat at the edge of the riverbed.

Elias lay down on the grass, placed his hands behind his head and gazed up into the sky. It was a clear blue, peaceful in spite the ever-present chaos that was going on in Beirut, the possible bombs, the shelling and gun smoke, the unrest, and threat of another war.

"It's so quiet out here," Adele said. "It's almost surreal. All we see at home on the news is a broken country, but if they showed the villages then we'd get a totally different perspective."

"News is always where the action is. Peace and quiet do not make good stories."

"I suppose. Have you ever been to Canada, Elias?"

"No. But I would like to go one day, perhaps live there

permanently. I know I would miss my family though. And I would hate the cold."

"You'd get used to it."

"I don't know," he said. "Would you ever consider leaving Canada, moving to another country?"

"You know, I never thought about that. It would be exciting to live abroad but my father would never allow it," she said in a quiet voice.

"I'm sorry. That was a stupid question. Being a Lebanese girl, you're expected to get married then move out with your husband, not on your own. I thought perhaps this rule didn't apply to a Canadian-born woman." He sat up cross-legged.

"My father's very traditional."

"And you're not?"

"Is it that obvious?"

"A little." Elias moved closer to her so their knees were touching. Without thinking, Adele rested her hand on his thigh, rubbed the material of his jeans. Getting up quickly, Elias wiped the dirt from his pants and said, "I better head back home. Would you like to go out tomorrow?"

"Sounds good," Adele said, now standing.

"I want to take you to the town of Baalbeck. We can bring your sisters too."

"If that's what you want."

"Okay, then it's a date." Elias turned and waved as he sauntered off.

The next day, Adele strolled beside Elias, the tips of their fingers finding each other as he showed the Azar sisters the ancient ruins of Baalbeck. Elias and Adele walked along a path of dry orange sand lined with whitish-grey rocks. The air was hot and smelled of dust. Gigantic ruins towered around them, pillars of extraordinary height and width, making it seem unimaginable that ancient crews were able to construct them without the aid of modern technology. But there they stood, only somewhat battered by many centuries, wars, thrashing storms, and the burning sun. Adele had to shield her eyes with her hands as she tilted her head back and gazed at the vast ruins. Lichen found its way in some of the grooves, darkening the stone. Sunlight poured through open holes between the cracked surfaces. Elias pulled her forward, eager to show his favourite structure. As they walked together, her eyes stared ahead at her sisters' backs and every now and then one of them would turn and smile at her. She felt like a young teenager who had developed her first crush. She glanced at Elias and thought how handsome he looked amongst the ancient ruins. With his dark features and broad shoulders, he could pass as a Roman soldier.

He let his arms swing so his fingers continually found their way to Adele's hand. She had wanted to reach over and hold his hand, but that would have been too presumptuous, almost risky, because she barely knew this man by her side. Instead, she linked arms with him and let him describe the towering temples that surrounded them. She liked feeling him beside her. Elias turned his head and smiled as he looked down at their entwined arms. "Adele, see that temple," he said, pointing to the six Corinthian columns jutting into the blue skyline. She liked the way he said her name, the way it rolled off his tongue. His voice was warm and deep. "That's the Temple of Jupiter." Adele was mesmerized by the vast structure. Then he gestured toward a circular monument a short distance away. "And that's the Temple of Venus." He guided Adele past a gate and up stone steps leading to the Temple of Bacchus. Breathing deeply, he stood still and said, smiling, "This is my favourite."

Adele tilted her head back and admired the gigantic building surrounded by several pillars. He rested his hand on the wall of the temple and explained, "Some poppies and grapes were carved in the stone back in the days of the young god named Baalbeck. Several worshippers brought wine and food to honour the god. It's very beautiful." He ran his fingertips along the markings then reached over and guided Adele's hand over the carvings, pressing his palm on her knuckles. She suddenly felt a warmth in her belly and before she knew it she leaned into Elias's face and kissed him on the mouth. He froze and jerked back, digging his hands into his pockets. Clearing his throat, he said, "Let's join your sisters."

She looked down at the ground, twisting the toe of her ankle boot into the dry orange earth. "Okay," she mumbled, sprinting ahead. Her sisters stood between the Corinthian columns, calling out to her to join them and complete a photograph. She hurried, not once turning to face Elias. He trailed behind her like a helpless pup.

"I'm sorry," Elias said, holding a small cup of *ahweh* in his large hands. They sat on the terrace of his parents' house while his family settled in the living room, the sound of the television set filtering into the evening air. His long fingers were wrapped around the saucer as he turned it before him, glancing up from it every few seconds and into Adele's probing eyes.

"What happened back in Baalbeck? Didn't you want me to kiss you?" she asked, not letting his eyes go. She glanced back at his family; they continued to watch the show, ignoring them.

"Yes ... no ... I don't know. It's happening so fast. I thought this is what I wanted, especially since this is what my parents want. I want to be a good son...a good husband but...I don't know." He paused, put the cup down on the small plastic table between them and rubbed his forehead in frustration. The voices of his family began to drift out to the terrace. He got up and slightly closed the door leading to the terrace, then sat back down across from Adele. "Jeez, this should be easy."

The part about being a good child reminded her of all the things she had done to please her parents. She could understand his desire but the rest was making her squint and frown. "Husband? What are you talking about?" she finally asked, confused.

"Your father thought we'd make a good match given our circumstances…"

She held up a hand. "Wait a minute. What did you say? My father thought what?"

"Sort of like an arranged marriage but not in the traditional sense … what other option do I have? Since my accident, I haven't been able to … you know…" he stuttered. Elias moved his hands as if he could describe what he needed to say in sign language. Only Adele didn't understand; she stared at him dumbfounded.

"You're not making sense, Elias. What circumstances? What accident?"

He rested his elbows on the edge of the table then cupped his chin in his hands. "I thought your father explained everything to you and this is the reason you came to Lebanon. I thought this is what you wanted."

Speechless, she shook her head.

"Is this the first time you've heard of our arrangement?"

She nodded.

"Oh Christ," Elias whispered. "I am sorry. I thought your father would have told you." He leaned in closer to Adele and spoke in a low voice so his parents couldn't hear them. Adele followed Elias's eyes as they stared worriedly back at his family. They were still enthralled with the Arabic dancing on the TV. He turned back to her. "Let me start from the beginning."

"About two years ago, I was in a serious car accident. A bomb exploded while I was driving on the streets of Beirut. So many people were hurt; it was horrible. So many children hurt, so many women … a bomb doesn't discriminate. People were running all over the place with gashes and burns on their skin. I shouldn't have taken my eyes off the road, but I couldn't look away from the fear on people's faces and by the time I saw the car racing towards me, I didn't have a chance to brake or swerve. When my parents saw me in the hospital, they thought I was going to die but I didn't. I pulled through.

Sometimes I think it might have been better if Allah hadn't spared my life. When days are bad, I think this way. The impact of the collision forced a metal plate between my legs...." After a long pause, he continued. "My testicles were severed. I was only twenty-two. A young man! I had a steady girlfriend and we had dreams of moving to France, where I would become a professor of Arabic literature and she'd be a journalist. But when she learned of my situation, she refused to see me again. She said it was too hard for her to face me, to know that I'd never be able to make her a mother."

Adele took hold of his hand.

"When I recovered from my injuries, I learned the extent of my problem. I learned that I wouldn't be able to function completely as a man. And, well, our parents thought we'd make a good match. You can't have children. I can't have children. It's logical, right?" He shook his head. "I kept telling them that it wouldn't be fair to you. You could at least still have a healthy ... um, sex life while I can't ... I said it wouldn't be fair. Didn't anyone tell you this?"

She shook her head. After Elias finished talking, he slumped back in his chair and Adele rose from hers. Elias reached out to take her hand but she pushed him away and walked past his family, mumbling a hasty goodnight. She stumbled down the stone steps, pressing her hands into the walls, trying to balance herself. Her mind would not be still. She heard Elias's words over and over again until she reached the dirt road and found she was light-headed. A short distance away, she looked up at Elias, who was still on the terrace, collapsed in the chair and resting his forehead on the table. He looked at her once more before dropping his head to his arms. She rushed down the dimly-lit road to her father's old home. "Fuck! I can't believe this bullshit," she cursed and, at the same time, kicked at stones on the unpaved street.

CHAPTER 14

WHEN SHE REACHED THE LANEWAY of the old stone house, the living room emanated a blue glow. The moving light of the TV caught the audience in its toxic spell. Adele stood outside and watched the belly dancers on the screen animate her father's face. His hands clapped in rhythm to the Arabic music. She stood quietly and watched her family gathered around the TV, snacking on pistachios and drinking *arak* or coffee. She stepped closer to the door, and clasped the brass knob, her fingers shaking from the anger she felt. She lifted her shoulders, held her head high. Heart racing, she slowly turned the knob. She was so sick of them controlling her, telling her what to do and how to do it. Damn them. She was going to let them know that her life was hers, not theirs. Suddenly, she dropped her hand and stepped back. Rather than confront her family, she turned and sprinted in the opposite direction.

She went to the edge of the village and sank down to her knees on the riverbank, pressing her hands onto her thighs while she calmed the quick pounding in her chest. After a few minutes, her breathing returned to normal. Then she sat cross-legged and watched the light from the moon reflected on the surface of the sea-green water. Adele let her eyes travel over the low mountains surrounding her parents' village. The entire landscape was a study of peaks, olive trees, and ridges. Even the dirt road had turns and bumps. She wanted to yell, throw her voice into the mountains. But she remained quiet

and replayed Elias's story in her mind. Then she lay back on
the riverbank, her knees bent, her hands tucked behind her
head. She breathed the river-scent, which reminded her of the
smell of wet leaves after a downpour. She pulled her hand from
underneath her thick hair, put it to her chest and felt her heart
thumping. How could her sisters deceive her? she wondered.
Then she thought of Elias, of how his own pain was much like
hers. Should she marry him? Bring him to Canada? After a
while, she sat up, rubbed her cold arms, and listened to insects
chirping in the fields. She rose and walked slowly back to her
uncle's residence.

Back in the stone house, the television set was off, its blue
glow replaced by the dim hallway light. She opened the front
door and crept over the floorboards towards the bedrooms.
Undressing in the moonlit room, she glanced at her sleeping
sisters. Their faces were soft and relaxed, eyes closed, strands
of black hair grazing their foreheads, their lips slightly part-
ed. How dare they condemn her to a life with a man who
was neutered, who couldn't make love to her? she thought,
breathing heavily. Fine, she couldn't have children but there
was nothing wrong with her sexual organs for pleasure. She
stared hard at her sisters and tried to fathom the logic behind
their deceit. She was young and a virgin, but she longed for
sexual experiences and now her family wanted to deny this
birthright to her. She needed to sleep. This anger exhausted
her, made her legs numb and weak. She crawled into bed
next to Mona. As soon as she slipped under the covers, she
gave in to the night.

A few hours later, she opened her eyes. It was still dark and
when she glanced at the clock on the dresser, she saw that it
was only three in the morning. She turned over and tried to
fall asleep on her stomach, tightly gripping the pillow, but she
couldn't get back to sleep. Her mind returned to Elias's story,
the truth connected to it, the betrayal. How could her sisters

do this to her? she thought, sitting up now. And her mother? She looked at her sisters and felt pained by what they had done. They had colluded and plotted with her father to marry her to someone who could not even fuck her. She couldn't imagine doing something like this to them, but somewhere deep inside she hoped her suspicions were wrong. The silver of the moon streaked the pale walls. Adele lifted her right hand and she began to make hand puppets, something she used to do as a child when she awoke late in the night. She didn't find it comforting as it had been when she was a child. She fell back on the mattress and closed her eyes tight, hoping this would force her into a deep sleep.

The next morning, she roused herself awake, the sheets drenched with sweat. Sunlight poured through the large window. Mona suddenly shoved her out of the bed. "Christ, did you wet yourself or something? You're all sweaty, Adele."

"Sorry," Adele mumbled, loosening herself from the damp blankets. She wiped her brow and stared down at the perspiration on her palm before dragging her hand across the sleeve of her pajamas. "I'm not used to the bed," she lied, knowing the real reason was her fury.

Mona sat up and nudged Katrina. Katrina rubbed her eyes and looked across at Adele stripping off her nightclothes and standing naked before them.

"Put on some clothes before someone walks in and sees you. Haven't you any shame? You're always parading around as if you're the only one in the room. This isn't even our house," Katrina whispered.

"Save it for your Bible study group." Adele turned away from her sisters and stood in front of the window. She gazed at the mountains. They looked ordinary, dull in the morning light.

"Katrina's right. Put on some clothes." Mona got out of the bed and rummaged through a drawer. She pulled out a pair of pants and a blouse, and passed them to Adele.

Adele grudgingly slipped them on and, at the same time, sneered at her sisters. "You're fucking prudes!"

"What's come over you? You're not a child anymore. Show some respect," Mona hissed.

Adele shrieked, "Show some respect! I'm so tired of always doing what others tell me to do and like you said, 'I'm not a child anymore,' so I should be able to do what I want. If I want to stand in a bedroom completely naked, then I can. Who the fuck is going to come in? Speaking of respect, a respectful person would knock before entering a room but given our fucked-up family, they'd just rush in. Now that's respect!"

Katrina twirled her finger around her temple and glanced across at Mona. She made a face.

Adele answered, "Yeah, I'm crazy. Totally, fucked up!"

"You said it, not us," Mona snickered.

At this point, Rima walked into the room.

Adele quickly said, "See? She just barged in. Did you hear a knock? I certainly didn't."

Puzzled, Rima stared at Adele. "What's all the yelling about?"

Mona shrugged her shoulders. "Just Monkey having one of her outbursts. You know how her temper is...she pissed herself in the bed..." she began to laugh, then Katrina and Rima joined in.

"Fuck off, Mona!" Adele snapped.

"Jeez, I'm only joking. Take a pill. No, maybe you shouldn't. You're acting like someone on drugs."

"Leave me alone," Adele said in a low voice. She then sat on a wooden chair covered with a colourful knitted blanket. Her fingers traced the pattern of the wool as her eyes stared blankly at the wall. Her sisters glanced at each other. There was a moment of silence before Adele spoke again. "You're all traitors!" she hissed. "Elias told me everything!" Her voice began to crack. She glared at them, and one by one they looked away from her. She was certain then that they had been part of the plan.

"We tried to stop Babba," Mona suddenly confessed.

Adele said nothing.

"Don't be mad, Monkey. Babba was only trying to help," Rima added, resting her hand on Adele's shoulder, but Adele pushed it away and got up. She walked towards the door. Rima continued. "He wants you to have a chance at marriage with a Lebanese man. Elias is a good guy. He's cute, smart and..."

"Impotent," Adele spat out.

"Sex isn't everything," Katrina said.

"Anyway," Mona added, "you can do plenty of other things. Intercourse isn't all that great. Women have better orgasms with oral sex."

Adele folded her arms on her chest and sighed in exasperation. "I can't believe what you're suggesting. Would you've settled for a marriage without intercourse? Answer me!" she snapped.

There was a brief moment of silence then Mona finally said, "No."

"Why do you want me to marry Elias then?"

The sisters said nothing.

"You're all fucking hypocrites!"

"But if you marry Elias, you'll never have to worry about not being able to provide him with a child of his own. You'll never feel guilty about not giving him that precious son or feel less worthy because you only gave him girls like Mama. You'll be happier. Think yourself blessed in that respect," Katrina interjected.

Adele's shoulders stiffened. "Yes, you're so right. I should feel blessed."

"That's the right attitude," Rima said cheerfully.

Adele bit her lower lip and looked at her sisters. They were all sitting on the bed, the mattress sagging under their weight. "I should feel blessed..." she started and paused, then spat out, "...to have traitors as sisters!"

She stormed out of the room and slammed the door behind

her, making it vibrate as if in the aftershocks of an earthquake.

Standing in the front yard, Adele heard Rima's voice floating through the living room window. She tiptoed closer to the house and leaned against the windowsill, making sure she was out of her father's vision. "Adele knows everything, Babba," Rima said.

"How? Did you tell her?" Youssef said, his voice rising in anger. Adele imagined her father furiously curling his moustache. "I told you not to say anything!" he yelled.

"I didn't," Rima croaked. "She found out on her own."

"Impossible. Someone must have told her." Adele peeked over the ledge and watched her father as he paced the room, pressing his right palm into his forehead. "What did she have to say?"

"Not much." Rima quickly looked out the window and spied Adele's curly hair as she ducked out of the way. Then Adele peeked over the ledge again and glanced from her father to the donkey in the yard; it was munching on weeds and also beginning to bray. She shooed it to be quiet but the animal went on.

"Well, things might be okay. Perhaps she'll see that I'm right about this whole thing. She'll realize that I'm right. Just wait and...." Youssef broke off and looked away from Rima, drawn to the braying. Giving up, Adele stood defiantly in front of the window now. She regarded her father sternly. He smiled at her. She stood up straight, hoping she looked as tough as she was trying to feel.

Later, Adele sat between her sisters on the large sofa in the cramped living room of Uncle Issa's home, surrounded by other members of her family, including Elias and his parents.

"It's the perfect solution to both our children's..." Youssef trailed off and glanced across at Adele, "...unfortunate situations." She didn't meet his eyes, just turned and stared vacantly out the window. Several village children were playing on the road, throwing a ball back and forth; the midday sun hanging over the mountains lightened their dark hair. Youssef cleared his throat, then continued, now facing Elias's parents. "Their choices are limited when it comes to having a husband or wife. We all know that no other Lebanese families would accept a daughter- or son-in-law who couldn't perform all the necessities of marriage. They want grandchildren, full-blooded ones, not adopted. They want their children to marry healthy people. So, as I said before, Adele and Elias are a perfect match."

"A perfect match," Adele mumbled. "Because we can't have children." She cast a look of disgust at her father. Youssef looked at Elias's parents. He fingered his thick, curling moustache. Adele watched him. He nervously tapped his right foot on the floor, which made his entire body shake.

After a few seconds, he forced himself to be still, and said, "It wasn't their choice, I suppose. Allah chose this fate for them but it doesn't have to be all bad. Adele..." Youssef leaned forward and rested his hand on her arm. "...Elias can make you happy. He's educated and polite. He has a good heart. A gentleman. Give it a chance."

"No, Babba," Adele answered quickly, pushing his hand away from her. She sat up and looked at Elias sitting beside his parents on the other couch in the room. Elias smiled unevenly and rubbed his hands together nervously. Strands of hair were brushed behind his ears and the stubble she had seen on his cheeks when they had first met was now a beard. The tweed jacket fit him snugly as did his jeans. She thought she might be able to love him, but would it be enough? Could this love replace physical desire? Her eyes dropped down to his crotch then quickly she glanced away.

"Listen to your Babba," Samira said quietly, sitting on a chair beside Youssef. She had her hands folded on her lap. She wore a black dress, and a grey shawl was draped over her shoulders. Her curly hair was pulled away from her suntanned face.

Adele looked scornfully at her mother and repeated, "No. Not this time, Mama. I won't listen to him this time."

Samira sighed loudly. "You're being stub..."

Youssef interrupted, "Well, I don't know what to say." Samira leaned back into the chair. Her father went on. "You're being difficult as usual. This is a good thing. Why can't you see that? Be reasonable for once in your life. You can be married to a Lebanese man, keep your heritage intact." Youssef smiled, then frowned. "We've come all this way and whether you like it or not, you're marrying Elias," he said determinedly, smacking his hands together. "No more arguments, understand?"

Adele looked from her sisters to her mother, but not one of them met her gaze. She sat up and lifted her right hand in the air while she spoke. "No, you can't make me do it. I'm not a baby anymore, Babba. I'm eighteen and an adult. You have no right to my life anymore, *understand?*" she said angrily. She rose from the sofa and looked out the window once more. The village children were now racing down the road, orange dust chasing them.

Youssef suddenly leaped up and grabbed onto her wrist, wrapping his hand around her. "Don't turn your back on me! I'm your father!" he shouted, tightening his grip.

The others lowered their eyes.

"Let me go!" Adele cried out, struggling to loosen herself.

Elias got up quickly and clasped his hand over Youssef's, attempting to pull it away from Adele's wrist. "Uncle, let her go," he said in a quiet, unsteady voice. A few seconds later, Youssef obeyed, letting his hand fall to his side.

Adele rubbed her wrist.

"She's going through with this wedding even if I have to drag her by the hair to the altar," Youssef muttered.

"I'm not getting married!" Adele insisted, firmly digging her feet in the Persian rug.

Youssef raised his arms in the air. He lurched his head back and looked up at the ceiling, slapping his hands hard against his forehead. He shouted in Arabic, "Allah, why did you curse me with such a disobedient daughter? Why? What did I do to deserve this?" Finally, he sank down on the chair and hung his head.

Adele crossed her arms over her chest. Elias walked towards her and put his hands on her shoulders. He leaned into her ear. "Adele," he whispered. "Let me handle this. Trust me. Everything will be all right." His large eyes were filled with tears. For some reason, Adele nodded, silently agreeing to his proposition.

Elias turned around and faced Youssef. He stood before him, then crouched in front of him, resting his hands on Youssef's knees. "Uncle," he began, "you know what's best. We'll agree to the marriage." He looked back at Adele. She hovered at the end of the sofa and felt everyone's eyes fix on her quivering face. What on earth was Elias doing?

The following morning, Adele left her uncle's house early and wandered around the village. Of course she would not marry Elias. It was out of the question, she thought as she walked. The sun had begun its ascent into the world again, streaks of soft mandarin and deep red coloured the clouds. She longed to sketch and paint and not think about anything else. When she reached Elias's home, she looked around the courtyard and noticed that the previous night's glasses and ashtrays were still sitting on the table. Playing cards were also scattered all over the finely embroidered tablecloth. She walked across the yard, then stood at the door and knocked. She could hear Elias whisper, "I'll be out in a minute." She listened to his hurried footsteps as he made his way to the door. She put her hands in her pockets and stared at the orange sand at her feet; a thin layer of dust covered her black ankle boots. Kneeling, she gathered a pebble in her right hand and began to sketch in the sand the mountain in the distance, glancing up and down until she heard Elias's voice behind her.

Eyeing her curiously, Elias asked, "What are you doing? Playing in the dirt?" A wide smile spread across his handsome, rugged face. He had shaved his beard and the width of his square jaw was now more apparent.

Dropping the stone, Adele brushed the dust off her finger-tips and looked up at him. He smiled at her again. She was amazed by his ability to remain content in spite of the pain he had endured, both physically and emotionally. He smiled even though he'd never be able to have intercourse. Adele dropped her head and stared at her belly, the hollowness of it. As she stood up to greet him, sharp aches ran along her stomach. It had been seven months since her operation but the phantom pains still throbbed, reminding her of her absent womb. A deep sigh escaped from her. Then she suddenly felt Elias place his hands on her arms and with gentleness, he lifted her to her feet. She stood before him and inhaled his scent: the smell of soap and fresh laundered clothes. "Come on," he said, motioning with his head. "Let's go for a walk."

A half-hour later, they were standing at the entrance of a cave. From where they stood, the red roofs of the stone houses in the village looked like miniature figurines on a board game. The area around the cave was secluded, encased by olive trees. The river she had lain down beside after learning of her family's betrayal trickled lazily next to the narrow dirt road lined with weeds that sprouted sporadically along the cracked pathway towards the cave. The sound of crashing waterfalls echoed in the distance. Elias turned to Adele and stretched his arm out, She accepted his hand in hers and when she looked into his eyes, Adele felt her face turn crimson. She hastily turned away from him and looked down at the rocks that led inside the gaping mouth of the open mountain. She hesitated and stepped back.

"Don't be scared," Elias said warmly. "I won't let you fall."

With that assurance, Adele followed him into the cave. He pulled out a small flashlight from the back pocket of his jeans and the light that emanated led the way as they walked deeper inside. A spray of spring water splattered on their faces and the coolness felt good on Adele's cheeks. She could smell the freshness of the springs and feel a cool breeze blowing from the entrance through the cramped area. She couldn't believe how happy she was in the presence of such natural beauty and a man she suddenly cared about. Elias led her to a flat stone embankment where he lifted her hand to his mouth and kissed it.

She pulled away and murmured, "What are you doing?"

He dropped his arm to his side, then sat cross-legged on the stone. "I'm sorry but I couldn't help it."

She sat down beside him and stared at him for a long time. "It's okay," she said. "You're my fiancé, after all." They burst into laughter, their voices echoing off the rocky walls.

A few minutes later, Elias said, "Speaking about our wedding...." He laughed again. "I have the perfect plan. Let's pretend we eloped. No one will ever suspect we were never married. I'll be able to leave my past and start fresh somewhere else and you'll be able to return to Canada, a supposedly married woman! You can run away and no one will know otherwise. They'll think you're with me. They'll never suspect we aren't married. It's perfect. You'll get your freedom in the 'proper way' and I'll escape the pity the villagers feel for me..." He stopped abruptly, then looked intensely at Adele and continued. "It's not easy having everyone know that you can't have sex with a woman."

Elias's words stirred her own grief. She took his hand in hers and squeezed it. "Are you sure you want to go through with this, Elias? It's a big sacrifice for you. You'll be leaving the only home you've ever known."

He raised his eyebrows and looked directly into Adele's tear-filled eyes. "I want to reinvent myself. Go somewhere where no one knows about my accident. Who knows? Maybe I'll even meet a woman who can love me despite my problem. But mostly, like yourself, it's my ticket to freedom."

She smiled weakly and nodded. She understood completely.

That evening, she played along with his plan. Preparations began for their forthcoming wedding. Relatives baked several pastries, chopped bushels of parsley, crushed chickpeas, mixed garlic cloves, kneaded dough into pita bread, carefully placing several dishes of *maza* in various refrigerators. Unlike her sisters' gigantic weddings, it was to be a simple celebration. Pretending she was exhausted and needed her sleep for the big day, Adele excused herself to the guest room and undressed slowly. She planned to meet Elias in the early morning hours before the rooster at her uncle's house had a chance to awaken the entire household. She lay in bed quietly until she fell asleep.

A few hours later, she opened her eyes, lifted her arm and stared at her wristwatch, waiting for three o'clock. She listened to the soft breaths escaping from her sisters' mouths. She had only fifteen minutes to go and she dared not close her eyes again, worried she would fall into a deep sleep and miss Elias. She crept out of the bed, slipped off her pajamas, and hastily dressed. She tiptoed across the room and opened the door slowly. She turned to look at her sisters, their bodies curled under thin sheets. In the moonlit room, she could make out their figures: Mona's long, thin legs, Katrina's rounded breasts, and Rima's curved hips. She remained at the doorway for a while. Then she looked down at her watch. It was time to go. She glanced at her sisters once more time and repressed the urge to whisper a farewell. With her lips clamped together tightly, she slipped out of the bedroom, down the hallway, and out the house.

The early morning was cold. Adele stood shivering by the side of the road where she had agreed to meet Elias. The darkness of the early hours had not yet vanished. She heard rustling in the fields and she jumped as a lone goat ambled out of the bushes and came up to her. She laughed at herself for being startled by the creature. Then her laughter stopped and her heart began to pound until her breathing had gotten so loud that she didn't hear Elias coming. He put his hand on her shoulder and she jumped again.

"Sorry," he said. "I didn't mean to frighten you."

She turned to face him. He looked pale in the dark, as if he had been the one frightened, not Adele.

"Ready?"

She nodded. Crossing the field, they silently walked to Elias's car. Adele swallowed and nervously entered the tan Mercedes. She watched as Elias slid into the driver's side. His hands trembled as he clutched the steering wheel.

Before letting him start the ignition, Adele rested her hand on Elias's arm. He looked down at her fingers, then into her face. Silence prevailed. Bending her head toward him, she finally said, "*Shukran.*" Thank you.

He smiled and nodded, then directed his eyes to the road.

The car sped on its way. Still somewhat uncertain about her decision to leave her family, Adele huddled next to the passenger door, staring out into the darkness.

As they approached Beirut, the sun began to rise, spreading yellowish-orange streaks through the dark blue skies. Adele yawned and peered out the car window. The dirt roads they had travelled on through the villages and small towns, stopping at various checkpoints, had now manifested into paved streets and sidewalks, lined with several fast-food chains and fashion boutiques. Neon signs flickered off with the approaching daylight. Adele sat up and gazed at the sea, the waves crashing against the rocky shore that curved around the city. The shoreline was no longer the lush green of the riverbed in the village, but man-made slabs of concrete holding the sea back. They drove on. Adele leaned her back to the door so she could face Elias. He was fully awake despite the two-hour drive it had taken them to reach Beirut; he hadn't taken a break, except for the time it took them to show identification papers to the military troops at the roadblocks. Adele reached across and stroked his handsome face, his stubble tickling her palm and, for a brief moment, he glanced at her, his full lips breaking into a smile.

She dropped her hand onto her lap and cleared her throat. "We should take a break. You've been driving for hours. Let's get some breakfast."

Elias arched his eyebrow and Adele noticed a small scar on his dark eyelid. She lifted her hand again and traced the brown line. "A remnant of my accident," he said. "My body tells that story over and over. Sometimes I forget, or try to, but my body reminds me again and again. That's my *hayat*, my life, I suppose. Scars and memories of my experience constantly remind me of things I'd rather forget..." He stopped suddenly, then changed the subject. "What about breakfast? Do you want to eat at McDonald's? This is what Americans eat, no?"

Adele laughed, resting her head on the car seat. She rolled her face to the side, looked at Elias. "But *habibi*, you have it all wrong. I'm not American. I'm Canadian."

"American, Canadian, what's the difference? Aren't they the same?" he grinned mischievously.

She laughed again. "Depends on whom you ask."

"True, true. So, it's McDonald's? Or would you prefer a Lebanese breakfast of warm *zahter* fresh from a stone oven or *labaneh* and *zeitoun* rolled up in homemade pita bread with a cup of *ahweh*?"

"I don't care much for coffee," she said, pretending to be difficult.

"Okay, okay, *habibti*, a cool glass of *halib* for you. Sounds good?" Elias said, smiling.

"You're paying, right?"

"You're the American, remember? You have all the money."

Adele raised her head from the seat. Gazing into Elias's eyes, she snorted and said, "Canadian."

"Ah, Canadian."

"Since you've been driving, I'll treat you this time. It's the least I can do. Us 'Americans' are rich, after all."

They burst into laughter once more as the vehicle sped along the busy morning streets.

Elias turned the car into a small alley, barely wide enough for two vehicles. He parked the old Mercedes around the corner. Adele stepped out of the passenger's side and followed Elias through the cobblestone street, and down a flight of stairs that led to the entrance of a small café. When Elias pulled the door open, the smell of sumac and thyme enveloped Adele along with the warmth of a large stone oven that was radiating heat at the far end of the establishment. Six small tables covered with flower-print tablecloths filled the room. A water pipe was positioned behind the cramped counter where an old man sat on a wooden stool, his eyes half-closed. He looked to be in his mid-eighties; his cheeks drooped and deep wrinkles lined his forehead. Beyond him, two windows were open wide, allowing a gentle breeze to enter the softly-lit, tiny restaurant that was empty but for the old man and one other customer. The old man was dressed in what appeared to be a woman's polo shirt and baggy trousers common to older Middle Eastern men. He greeted them with a broken smile and a large space between his two front teeth flashed when he opened his mouth. "*Marhaba*. It's a beautiful morning," he said, wiping his hands on the grease-stained apron around his protruding belly.

"It sure is," Adele answered in Arabic.

"You're not from here. I can tell by your accent."

She smiled timidly; she was surprised the old man could tell immediately that she had an accent. She spoke hesitantly and now wondered in the warm heat of the café how she had lost this language that had been her first as she looked at her reflection in the mirrored walls behind the cash register. Her curly hair dropped over her shoulders and her face was unusually pale compared to Elias's and the old man's equally dark complexion. Yet, unmistakably, she looked like them.

"Come on," Elias said, waking her from her thoughts. He placed his hand on the small of her back. She didn't move away and let his hand ease into her spine. He guided her to one of the small tables, pulled out a chair for her to sit on, and then dropped his hand to his side. Immediately, she missed its warmth. She sat down and she sighed loudly as she followed Elias's movements, his long legs striding elegantly across the restaurant back to the old man, who handed him a plate filled with *zahter* and two cups of steaming *ahweh*.

When Elias returned, she smiled up at him. He stood beside the table and began to serve her as if she were his guest. The aroma of the flat bread powdered with dried thyme, sumac, and sesame seeds caressed her nose. As he placed the dish and coffee cups down, he smiled then smacked his large hand on his forehead. "Oh, I forgot! You're not a coffee drinker. Back in one moment with your *halib*."

Affection filled her heart for this thoughtful man. She touched his wrist and said, "It's okay, Elias. Sit down. You've done so much for me already. Sit and share this wonderful meal with me."

"Our last breakfast?" he said, slipping onto the chair opposite her.

"I suppose. But does that mean there will be a resurrection of sorts?"

A smile lifted his mouth. "Most definitely. Resurrected from family obligations..."

"And guilt," Adele added quietly. They ate in silence until the old man came to their table and placed a round bowl of *zeitouns* in front of them, the oil glistening on the green olives.

"These come from tree in yard at home," he said in broken English. He also handed them a basket of pita bread. "I make bread too. Well, not right. Wife make bread," he said, kneading his knuckles on the tabletop. "She make on ground. Hard on knees. She yell every time she do bread. Allah, she say, why you curse me to be woman?"

Adele raised her eyebrows and frowned. She didn't like this last comment because it seemed that being born a woman was indeed a curse, the worst possible fate. She looked away from the old man and out the window. A few feet away a young man dressed in military garbs with a finely-trimmed beard and crew-cut was standing with a rifle flung over his left shoulder. His slender body bent forward as he questioned people in their cars. She imagined his voice resonant with forced authority. He looked boyish. She guessed he was only a few years older than herself. Twenty-two at the most. Adele sensed the old man's eyes on her. She turned her attention back to him.

"I say something bad? You mad?"

Adele asked quietly, "Why does your wife think it's a curse to be a woman?"

"Life not easy for woman. They cook, clean, take care of child, husband. They work hard and for what?" He slapped his hands together. "Nothing. No respect, only grief. A woman lose lots. Husband boss, child make body fat then break it in birth. Not easy to be woman, that why curse. Man have easy life."

She stared at the man. There was neither coldness nor meanness in his eyes. He wiped his hands on his apron and smiled.

"Now eat. Enough about man, woman. Can't live with woman. Can't live with no woman, right? This American phrase?"

She nodded and popped an olive in her mouth.

CHAPTER 15

As THEY RETURNED TO THE CAR, a sudden rumbling and tremor under their feet caused Adele to stumble awkwardly into Elias's shoulder. Adele caught herself from falling, but she was alarmed. "What's happening?" she mumbled. Elias didn't reply. Instead, he grabbed Adele's arm and pulled her into the safety of his body, hurriedly leading her into the entranceway of another shop, past several toppled over vendor stalls, figs crushed, cloth torn, and gold bangles bent in the chaos of people running. Adele watched a vendor kneel and stuff precious stones into the deep pockets of his apron as he hurled Arabic curse words that assaulted Adele's ears. But it was the wailing from the injured people that made her shake uncontrollably. Elias held her close so the smell of his skin permeated her nostrils—a mixture of sweat and soap.

Adele asked again, "What's happening?"

"A street bomb."

His answer silenced her. She twisted her head that he had clasped to his chest and stared at the burning building across from them. Through black patches of smoke, she could see bodies sprawled in the corner, limbs dismembered, and shattered windows all over the asphalt. Everything was in an uproar. She began to shake more violently. There was a distinct and sharp stench and she realized it was the smell of blood. She closed her eyes for a moment then opened them to Elias placing the warmth of his hand against her face. "Don't worry. I'll get us out of here." She swallowed and watched the fire dying down with the tide of water spurting from the emergency crews' hoses, embers burning on the streets. She had never experienced any of the violence in the Middle East firsthand, though she had witnessed it many times on Canadian broadcasts, and read about it over and over in the world information section of newspapers.

The noon sun rose above the haze and cries. She suddenly became aware of how hot it was. Beads of sweat trickled down her ribcage. The intense sunlight made her raise her hands to her eyes, protecting her pupils from the brightness.

Some distance away, she saw a woman on her knees clutching a child. The boy jerked a few times, then remained still in his mother's arms. Blood was on the woman's hands and on her son's face. She pulled him tight to her chest, her wails drowning out the sirens. Adele hated the light that now hit these victims. She saw the torn look on the woman's face— her eyelids swollen, cheeks disfigured by shards of flying glass—and Adele cried out at the stranger's grief, and her loss. She turned away, stepped back from the noise, the sun. Burying her face in Elias's hard chest, she felt him stroking her head as she wept.

They hurried down several streets, away from the burning debris and rubble. Thick dust swirled in the air. Adele let go of Elias's hand, rubbed her eyes, then reached for him again, afraid of losing him in the rush of people, bumping their shoulders against hers, breaking her free from Elias's hold. She searched for his fingers as if not reconnecting would be the end of her existence. She needed him and this frightened her because she had never had this feeling of complete reliance on another person, had actually felt suffocated when her family depended on her for handling everyday things. She held onto his hand tighter and liked the way his fingers entwined with hers. All of a sudden, she felt a longing for the person she was supposed to marry, one as broken as herself.

She squeezed Elias's hand then felt sick and stopped him. The taste of vomit surged through her throat. She had to stop running. Bent over, she felt Elias's fingers pull back her hair while she threw up at the side of the road. He stood in front of her and reached out to wipe her cheeks with a handkerchief. Then he took her face tenderly in his hands and at this moment her eyes filled with tears because she felt what it was like to be loved. Yet a feeling of sadness overwhelmed her when she looked around and realized they had stopped running, not because of her sudden illness, but because they had reached their destination. And worry filled her mind as she thought about her family and the danger taking place in the country. Could she leave them? "Elias, maybe I shouldn't go? What if my family is hurt by a bomb?" she asked, her eyes opened wide in concern.

"No, things are fine in Kfarmichki. Your family will be safe." With that reassurance, Adele stepped through the sliding doors of the Beirut International Airport.

Adele sat in the departure lounge with her clothes sticking to her, making the worn leather seat squeak. She nervously tapped her left foot on the tiled floor. Elias rested his hand on her knee to calm her. After a while, she stopped shaking and placed her hand on top of Elias's. She looked down at their joined hands, perfectly still, resting on her knee. Though they were surrounded by several people, saying goodbyes, talking about what journey awaited them, flipping through agendas, scribbling down addresses and phone numbers, she felt as if they were the only two people in the busy airport. She didn't hear the voice on the intercom announcing flights nor the sirens outside, a reminder of the crumbling capital and chaos they had just fled. If it weren't for Elias, she'd probably be awakening to the sound of her family preparing for her wedding day. The loud voices would have drowned out the rooster crowing, the donkeys braying. Realistically, she knew her family would be waking up to the note she had left them. Elias had written it in Arabic, stating their decision to elope and to move to another country. She knew her sisters would be heartbroken at her sudden departure. At this moment, she breathed deeply and wondered whether she really should leave. Suddenly she viewed everything around her with sadness and confusion. She felt an urge to return to the village and go on with her life no matter how difficult it had been for her. Casting a glance at Elias, she said in a quavering voice, "Maybe I shouldn't go."

His eyes opened in astonishment; he was taken aback. As though he couldn't believe what he was hearing, he stared at Adele.

She braided her fingers with his, raised his hand up and shook it, breaking the stillness they had shared a brief moment ago. "Elias, did you hear me?"

He silently stared at her face.

Lowering her eyes, she let go of his hand and whispered, "Don't look at me like that."

He gave a nervous laugh then said in a low voice, "You must go. Why would you want to stay? You've told me everything about your father, your lack of freedom, the way you feel you're living only half a life. This is your opportunity to break free and now you're scared! Why are you so afraid?"

His comments hurt her because they were so honest. And she remembered how Rima had tried to escape years ago too but had returned because she was too afraid to disobey their father and bring shame to the family. Now Elias forced her to realize that she, too, was a terrified girl, like Rima had been, who said things but when it came to action, she couldn't follow through. She whispered resentfully, "No, no. I'm not afraid."

Elias said softly, "My words have angered you."

She took a deep breath. "No. You're right. I'm scared. I don't know if I'll be able to survive on my own. I've never done it before and, well, I'm scared shitless."

"What's this? Sheetless?"

"No, no," Adele laughed in spite of herself. "Shit, not sheet."

"Oh. You mean feces." He patted her leg and assured her with a warm grin, "You'll be fine."

"How about yourself?"

"Don't worry about me," he said. "I'll manage somehow, especially now that I've left behind the gossip and pity. Pity is a terrible feeling."

"What do you mean?"

"Pity is also contempt. I know people pity me and I hate it. So I can't have an erection. It's not the end of the world."

She lowered her gaze so he wouldn't detect signs of sympathy in them. Silence prevailed for a few moments then she said, "Where will you go?"

"England. I always wanted to see the Queen."

She smiled. "Are you serious?"

"Not really. But I got you to smile." He playfully nudged his shoulders with hers.

A few minutes later, a voice on the intercom announced Adele's flight. She rose from her seat, her heart pounding. Elias got up too. She pressed her hand into his cheek. The prospect of never seeing him again saddened her more than she expected. She embraced him so tightly that it was almost painful. Her breasts were crushed against him for a long moment, but then seemed to ache for him when he pulled away. "Thank you, Elias," she said, almost crying. "You'll never know how much you've given me."

He smiled shyly, stepped back, and waved goodbye.

When she handed her ticket to the clerk, Adele glanced at Elias now standing alone, leaning against the railing, his head bowed and his hands clasped together as if in prayer. She turned and faced the clerk again.

And when she boarded the airplane, her earlier fear evaporated and she experienced a feeling of great excitement.

It was a little after midnight when she arrived back to Ottawa. She emerged from the taxi and walked up the steps of her parents' house. As she fumbled to put the key in the lock, she started to sweat. Had she really left Lebanon, her family? When she pushed open the door, the darkness enveloped her. There were no shouting voices, no heated arguments, no sobs, no scents of her mother's cooking. Just silence. It was as if her family had never existed in this two-storey house. Nothing was visible except the moonlight that slipped through the lace curtains of the living room. Flipping on the light switch, she brought the house back to life. Her eyes glanced at the mahogany coffee table at the centre of the room, photographs decorating it. She crept across the hardwood floor to the table, knelt down and picked up one of the framed photographs, her fingers tracing the faces under the glass. The Azar sisters stood on the Fosters' driveway in front of the green wooden fence that separated their father's grocery store from the old white house. Now she looked at another photo of herself and her sisters. The young girls in knitted ponchos with wide grins on their faces. They were surrounded by piles of autumn leaves. In this photograph, she saw the young child she had once been. She wore the yellow and white poncho her Sito had knitted for her before she had returned to Lebanon, hating the winters in Canada and missing her bachelor shepherd son. Inhaling deeply, Adele remembered the smell of rosewater embedded in the yarn and how it floated up her small nose, making her reach up and pull at the collar, the tiny strings with balls at the ends hitting her chest. She couldn't remember her grandmother. But she had heard the story of when she had stayed in Canada, how she had fed and bathed Adele because her mother was too ill to do so after her hysterectomy, and how she had cried at the airport when her grandmother had decided to return to Lebanon. According to Samira, weeks after her grandmother's departure, Adele had been inconsolable. But Adele regretfully couldn't remember crying out 'Mama!' to her grandmother as she boarded a plane back to Lebanon.

Now, in the softly-lit room, she remembered the scent of the handmade poncho. Her grandmother had died when Adele was in grade ten so she never had the opportunity to meet her again but Adele's Sito still lived in her memories and in the ring she wore, one given to her by her grandmother. Adele looked at it on her finger now. Three tiny ruby stones ran along the raised top that also had a sketch of lines engraved on the sides. It had an antique appeal, not trendy like the more common silver stone rings. It was as if the soul of her grandmother shone in the rubies. After a while, she raised her head, rose from her knees and headed upstairs.

The next morning, she woke up late, alone. Usually she rose early but last night she couldn't sleep, jolting awake every few hours from the settling of the house. She dreamt her father had found out about her running away and had burned all her belongings starting with the paintings she had created in her high school art classes. Her hand went to her mouth as she stood watching the flames engulf the oil and watercolour paintings, shrivelling the self-portraits she had spent countless hours sketching, then painting for her final year project. Afterwards, he threw in her clothes. She glanced across at her father; his face was rigid while he discarded every item that bespoke her history. He was erasing her existence, leaving no trace of her. Burying her face in her hands, she wept until the orange-red flames swallowed her too.

Now rubbing her weary eyes, she got out of bed, brushed her teeth and showered. She felt lonely suddenly standing in the bathtub with warm water falling on her head. She began to cry as the realization of what she had done pounded her in the gut. Wasn't this what she always wanted? Why was she crying? For a while, she let the fear inside her come out in the weakness that surged in her shivering legs, but the soothing warmth from the water released the anxiety in her skin. A few minutes later, she turned off the shower, wiped her face with her towel, and quickly dried her body. She had a lot to do. Numbers to call, arrangements to make. She was free now and freedom required action.

CHAPTER 16

S HE HURRIED DOWN THE STREET towards a local printing shop. The fluorescent sign of the store flashed in the overcast morning. The air had the damp quality of condensation as if raindrops were hovering in the grey clouds, ready to fall to the earth and splatter passersby without mercy. No one had rain gear: umbrellas or hooded coats. These people would be drenched like Adele. Her thick hair would become fuzzy, forcing her to pat it down. But she reached the shop before the sky opened and spewed out a morning summer shower.

From her knapsack, she took out a brown envelope that contained her résumé. "Good morning," Adele said, smiling at the clerk who looked no older than Adele. Her blonde hair was pulled back with a wide headband and the mascara on her short lashes was thick. When she blinked, a few lashes stuck together and she had to blink in a fast succession to loosen them from the over-applied make-up.

"Hello," she answered, neither friendly nor unkind. "How may I help you?"

"Can I get twenty copies of this please?" Adele handed the woman her sheet.

"Sure. It'll be about ten minutes."

"Okay. Thank you." Adele turned around and looked out the large window. The rain now came down hard, pelting the asphalt and cars. Windshield wipers flapped ferociously while pedestrians sought shelter in doorways; their clothes sticking to their skin as if they were another layer of epidermis. Adele sighed, glad she was inside. Her thoughts suddenly turned to her family in Lebanon. Were they arguing over her, frantically calling other relatives and maybe even the local police to find out where she and Elias had vanished? She also thought of Elias, how he unselfishly helped her in spite of the consequences he'd have to face when his parents realized his place in this escape. *What on earth were you thinking helping this crazy girl?* she imagined Elias's parents yelling. But deep inside, she knew leaving her family was the bravest thing she had ever done. It broke all cultural laws but how liberating it felt to gaze out this large window knowing her eyes would not fall upon her father's stern look of disappointment and shame.

So enthralled in her thoughts, she didn't hear the photocopier stop or the clerk's voice saying "Excuse me, miss. Your copies are done," until the clerk raised her adolescent pitch and repeated herself.

Adele swiftly turned and apologized.

"No problem," the clerk said as Adele paid her, then stuffed the envelope back into her bag and headed outside, the rain spiralling down her curly hair.

When she walked inside the house, her hair and cheeks were wet. Fortunately, her knapsack had protected her résumés. She quickly pulled them out and laid them on the dining room table, her experiences open to whoever happened to walk in, but the house was quiet. She glanced at the papers, dark ink on a white background, words she had carefully chosen to display her work ethic, strong and bold: *well-organized, punctual, hardworking* and she couldn't believe she was finally taking some steps to leave her parents' home. But when she moved out of the eating area and stood in the hall, a sadness gripped her. She was struck by a family portrait hanging on the wall, one taken before her birth. Her sisters sat on a long brown couch between their parents. They were wearing party dresses and white knee socks, their hair pulled back with barrettes. Youssef wore a grey suit and necktie, while Samira's dress, a pretty pastel colour, was carefully draped just over her knees. Faint smiles appeared on her sisters' small faces. Adele stared at the picture for a long time and worried this would be one of the last times she'd gaze at this family portrait, the last time she'd stand in this hallway. She glanced at her wristwatch. It was a little after eleven in the morning. Her body began to shake and her breathing became rapid. Even in her father's absence, this house made her feel weak and small.

The phone began to ring all of the sudden. Adele walked towards it and before picking up the receiver, she took a deep breath. "Hello?" she said.

"You *bint a kalb*!" Youssef shouted.

There was brief moment of silence before Adele replied. "That's nice! Calling me a daughter of a dog. May I ask you a question, Babba?" She didn't bother to wait for him to reply. "Are you the dog or Mama?" She wanted to laugh at her clever comeback but she didn't.

"Shut up and listen! You've disgraced me yet again. When will you learn that what you do affects your entire family? People don't think of you as an individual. They think of you as *bint* Youssef. *Bint* Youssef! Now who looks bad? Me. How dare you drag my good name through the mud! You didn't think we'd find out that you ran away. You didn't think Elias would come back home and let everyone know what you did. How stupid can you be? Did you really think that Elias would leave Lebanon? The boy doesn't have a penny to his name. Of course, he was going to return home to his parents. Everyone is talking and calling you a *sharmouta*, a stupid for giving up her chance to be married to a Lebanese man ... everyone in the community knows you're defective, a half fucking woman who will never be able to give a son to her husband or even a girl. Useless. You should've died six months ago because when the doctors took out your womb, they took out your brain too!"

Adele swallowed hard. "Are you finished, Babba?" she asked weakly.

"We'll talk some more when we get home. We should be back on Thursday," he said. "Don't you dare think of leaving, Adele. You have no money. How are you going to survive on your own? We'll talk about this more when we return home."

Adele detected a crack in his voice but it could have been the static of long-distance lines. Just as she was about to hang up, she heard her father say, "Your sisters want to say hello," but the receiver was already back in the cradle.

In three days, she'd be shackled again, persecuted and crucified. She wondered whether she'd be resurrected. Whether she'd wander the earth for forty days in splendour and glory, knowing her spirit would live for an eternity even though her body was dead. Or would her body live and her spirit die? She knew if she stayed under her father's roof this would be her fate.

By the afternoon the skies decided to stop their melancholic downpour. Adele took this opportunity to head out again and this time she wore dress pants and a tailored shirt, hoping to impress a potential employer. She wished she had the nerve to head to Toronto directly from Beirut, but she had no contacts in Toronto nor a firm plan of going to university there. She also had no money as her father had stated, so first thing she needed to do was find a job and save for her escape to Toronto.

Now she marched down the street. The pavement glistened with stray raindrops. She made her way from one place of business to another with the usual, "We're not hiring at this time, but we'll take your résumé and keep it on file." When she heard this, she smiled politely but couldn't stop her eyes from staring at their wastepaper basket.

When she felt her shoulders droop and her legs weaken, she headed toward a bench and sat down. She looked around, hoping a sign would appear to her. She believed in fate, destiny. Maybe something would tell her what to do. The street was wide open, not one car drove by. Across the way was a tiny red-brick building that housed a small bookstore and what looked like an apartment above it. Adele hadn't noticed this shop before. She got up from the bench and walked across the street. There were several books in the showcase window and a few posters advertising local writers' events. As soon as she walked inside the shop, the smell of lavender enveloped her yet it wasn't overwhelming; it reminded her of the lilacs along the Rideau Canal.

A middle-aged woman with red hair greeted her. "Hello."

"Hello," Adele answered. Her eyes scanned the store, which was quaint with some potted plants interspersed between books neatly displayed on a round table and the wooden shelves. The faint scent of old wood combined with the lavender. The sound of a stream, its current softly flowing, poured through speakers situated atop one of the bookshelves. Adele felt as if she were standing in the middle of a forest and the woman behind the counter appeared to fit in perfectly with her red hair dropping past her shoulders, her loose-fitting blouse and beaded belt dangling around her waist. Adele asked, "Are you hiring?"

"Do you have a résumé, my dear?"

These last two words brought Adele back to her childhood and to Mrs. Foster. It was moments like these that made her long to hear her friend and neighbour's voice one more time and see her bright face. Her friendship had awakened the possibility of more for Adele, that she could become the one thing she truly wanted most in life—to be an artist. With this simple term of endearment, this middle-aged woman reminded her of that hope again.

"Yes." Adele handed her a copy of her experience.

The woman looked down at it, then cursed, "Damn…"

Adele was surprised. She knew she didn't have a lot of experience but she didn't think her résumé would elicit such a reaction.

The woman placed the sheet down on the counter, then reached under it and pulled out a small brown case. "I keep forgetting that I need these things now," she said, laughing. "The progress of age, my dear." Adjusting the tortoise glasses on her narrow nose, she held up Adele's résumé and smiled. "I see you have some retail experience. Youssef's Grocery. Isn't that that wonderful little yellow store?"

Adele nodded.

"The owner is quite a character, always joking and smiling."

"That's my father," she said, trying to sound enthusiastic.

"Hmm ... interesting." There was a moment of silence as the woman read the résumé. She looked up and asked, "Are you a reader, Adele?"

"Yes, I love books," Adele said, smiling.

"What have you read lately?"

"Letters to a Young Poet."

"Ah, you like the classics."

"I also like contemporary books. I'll read almost anything." She continued to smile.

"What are your ambitions? I see you're a recent high school graduate. Are you planning to attend university?"

"Well, I've been accepted at the University of Ottawa, but I'm planning to apply to the University of Toronto," she stopped, not adding the word "again" then continued. "There's a program there I really want to take and hopefully I'll be accepted for the winter session."

"And what program is that?"

"Fine Arts."

"An artiste!" The woman laughed out loudly. "I thought you were an artist." She reached across and held Adele's right hand, stretching out her long fingers. "You have the hands of an artist." Her touch was warm and gentle but Adele still blushed until the woman finally let go.

Adele cleared her throat. "I'm a hard worker too."

"I can only pay minimum wage but the benefits are that

you'll have all the free reading material you want and you'll be one of the first people to hold a new book in your hands. Does this sound appealing to you?"

"Yes, very much so."

"Well, let me think about it and I'll call you in the next while. Out of curiosity, when can you start?"

"Right away." The sooner the better but she didn't say this out loud. She shook the woman's hand. "Thank you for your time, Ms...?" Adele realized that she didn't yet get the woman's name.

"Oh, my apologies, dear. I'm Bertha Freudenberg."

"Thank you, Ms. Freudenberg."

"Call me Bertha."

"Okay. I look forward to hearing from you, Bertha." Adele left the store but turned around one more time to see Bertha waving and smiling at her. She waved then walked down the street, cars now zooming past her.

Bertha Freudenberg telephoned the next day. "Are you still interested in working at my bookstore?" she asked after Adele had greeted her.

"Of course. Thank you very much for this opportunity," Adele replied enthusiastically.

"There's one condition though."

Adele hesitated briefly. "Yes?"

"Well, I have a friend who owns a local art school and I explained to her that considering where you're going to work and how lousy the pay is, that you might like to take some art classes," she stopped and laughed. "She offered the lessons for free. How does this all sound to you, my dear?"

"Oh, it sounds great. I don't know what to say. This is very generous and thoughtful of you, Ms. Freudenberg."

Bertha interrupted. "Call me Bertha."

"Oh, Bertha. I'm so very grateful. Thank you so much." Adele's voice cracked.

"So I'll see you tomorrow at ten in the morning."

"Thanks again, Bertha. I really appreciate this."

"You're welcome, dear. See you tomorrow."

After hanging up the phone, Adele dashed to her bedroom, flopped down on her mattress, and grinned. Things were slowly happening. She got her first "real" job all on her own and would be taking art classes. She thought she had done pretty well for herself considering her father thought she didn't have a brain. She cradled the pillow in her arms and imagined the life she had always wanted, could almost see it in the bumpy surface of the white ceiling above her, her paintbrush creating stories in brilliant shades. In two days her father would return and she would explain her need to move to Toronto and pursue her dream of becoming an artist. She promised herself not to let him dissuade her this time around and she knew that it would take all the courage she had to do so.

The two days passed quickly. When the alarm rang out with a song from the radio, Adele threw off the covers from her body and sat up, somewhat dazed. The past few days were a blur. She had started a new job and registered for the fall session at the art school; now her family was scheduled to return today. Finally, she got out of bed and walked into the bathroom. She stripped off her pajamas and climbed into the shower, letting the water awaken her tired body before heading to the bookstore.

A few hours later, she returned home, somewhat worried about what awaited her. As soon as she opened the front door, the scent of her mother's cooking engulfed her. She was amazed at how her mother could enter the house even after an overseas flight and jetlag, head into the kitchen, chop up parsley, grind some beef, stuff the grape leaves and prepare a feast of allspice dreams. Where did she find the energy and creativity? Nothing seemed to stop her, not even the unpacked suitcases, the clothes to be changed into, the greetings of welcome, and so forth. Now Adele entered the house and expected to be bombarded with words of insult and perhaps a raised hand but there was no such welcome, only a few strained smiles and a quick look from her father who disappeared upstairs, walking past Adele with a weary face. Adele was about to say "hello" but Mona motioned for her not to, then returned to unzipping the suitcase in front of her and pulling out a package of dried fruit. She passed it into Adele's hands. "Here, I got you some figs and dates. I know how much you like them."

"Thank you," Adele said, then asked, "How was your flight?"

"Okay, given the circumstances. What did you expect? Babba and Mama to be happy that they had to cut our trip short because of you," Rima answered, unzipping her bag and pulling out some bundles filled with the black grinds of *zahter* and white powdered *kishk*. She walked into the kitchen and Adele followed, not asking any more questions. When she saw her mother, Adele leaned in and tried to kiss her on the cheeks but Samira turned the other way and spoke to Rima who handed the packages to her. "No, *habibti*, take some for Ziad and the kids. I know he loves this stuff."

"No, it's okay, Mama. Keep it for Babba and Adele."

"Nonsense. Get me a container from the cupboard. What time are Ziad and the kids coming over tonight?"

"They'll be here in about an hour, Mama," Rima said. She passed another package into Samira's hands.

"No, no, *habibti*. Too much. Keep for yourself. Anyway, I don't need much, only some for your father. Adele only thinks about herself so she might as well cook for herself," Samira said, taking the tupperware from Rima's hand and pouring some of the Middle Eastern powder and spices into it.

"That's not fair," Adele finally said, unable to remain silent. "I'm the one who should be angry. You arranged a marriage for me to a man who can't even fuck me!"

Samira stomped over to her and slapped her hard across the face. Adele's head snapped back. "You have a dirty mouth! You're not like your sisters at all."

"I learned to swear like dear Babba. And stop comparing me to my sisters. I'm sick of it!" Adele yelled. She became aware of heavy footsteps pounding down the stairs, then the hallway, and then kitchen, until the sound stopped completely and her father stood in front of her, his skin darkened from his stay in Lebanon. Deep creases throbbed in his forehead as he frowned, and pursing his lips, spit out. "You're no longer welcome in my home." Grabbing Adele's arm, he pulled her out of the kitchen and into the hallway leading to the front door. "Get out!"

Dumbfounded, Adele looked at her sisters. Rima stood quietly while Katrina and Mona did the same. Adele was glad their husbands and children hadn't yet arrived to take them home. Out of the corner of her eye, Adele watched her mother dart around the kitchen doorway and yank onto Youssef's shirt. Adele couldn't believe what was happening. Samira clutched onto Youssef's shoulders until he finally let go of Adele. She stumbled into the living and fell back on the couch, her head in her hands.

"Stop it, Youssef! Stop! She's still our daughter. She made a mistake. Let's forget about what happened in Lebanon and move on. Anyway, it's a blessing in disguise that she didn't marry Elias. He has nothing, absolutely nothing. How was he going to support Adele? She would have had to support him for the rest of her life. Remember how hard it was for us when we first arrived in Canada? Why burden Adele with a husband like that. She's more Canadian than Lebanese. I don't know how I managed to raise her like that but I did. We did." Samira stopped talking and wiped the tears from her eyes with her apron.

Adele lifted her head and a surge of love pulsated in her body for her mother.

Youssef grunted something under his breath then stomped into the kitchen while Samira moved closer to Adele and brushed loose curls away from her face.

"Where's my food, Samira? Where's dinner?" Youssef shouted.

"In the oven, of course." Samira leaned into Adele and whispered, "Where does he expect it to be? In my ass? Just back and he's already hungry," Samira sneered.

"That's Babba," Rima said, nudging Adele's shoulders.

"Yeah," Adele mumbled.

"Come on. Help us unpack the food and gifts we got," Rima said, joining Katrina and Mona, back on their knees and unravelling packages of spices and jewels of the Middle East.

It was now mid-October and the experience Adele had encountered in the mountain village of her parents' ancestral home seemed a distant memory, like the pain of grief. The body healed and the mind seemed to forget or perhaps it was simply so filled with everyday things that it couldn't possibly contain every heartache and every loss. Adele had moved on. She still worked in the bookstore and took her art classes.

One morning, she heard the caws of the crows. It was nine in the morning. She wiped her hands on her faded jeans, leaving trails of paint on the worn denim, and stared out the enormous studio window of her art school. Suddenly her eyes fell upon the canvas in front of her. She had painted a picture of her father's yellow grocery store and their adjoining house, including the grapevine structure in the front yard, showing her parents' attachment to their homeland. If the house hadn't been so modern, any viewer would have thought this small corner store was situated in the Middle East. The colours were bold and rich. For a few minutes, she stood in front of the painting, taking deep breaths. At this moment, she hated the childhood she had experienced under her father's roof and she also hated herself for feeling so weak.

The back door to the studio suddenly opened. Adele startled, dropping the paintbrush in her hand, yellow paint splattering on the tiled floor. The art instructor quickly picked up the brush and handed it back to Adele, who rested it on the table next to the easel, then knelt down and wiped the paint from the floor with a rag. The instructor spoke in a soft voice. "Sorry, Adele. I didn't mean to frighten you."

"It's okay, Cheryl," Adele answered politely, now standing up.

Cheryl was one of the new instructors and was in her mid-thirties. She was completing a Ph.D. in Fine Arts and worked at the school to pay her tuition fees.

"What a great painting! I really like what you've done with the structure of the store." She raised her right hand, which was covered with an intricate henna design, and pointed very close to the canvas, following the lines of the store's exterior with her finger. Cheryl was a newlywed and had married an Indian man named Tariq. "The stucco looks so real. Great job. You've come a long way, Adele."

"I still have a lot to learn though. My technique could be better and the shadows are not so good yet."

"Art's not a sprint. And you've improved a great deal. Don't be so hard on yourself, kiddo."

She wanted to ask Cheryl how she was supposed to live with her father's harsh words consuming her thoughts. Instead, she nodded politely but silently ignored Cheryl's words and blended the colours on her palette, trying to mix the perfect shade of lemon.

"Keep up the good work," Cheryl said, patting Adele on the arm, then whirling out of the room.

Adele picked up her brush and inched closer to the canvas, acutely aware of the smell of the oils as she worked on the sign to her father's store; Youssef's name became forever embedded in her painting. She was surprised how deeply she loved her father's store.

After her hours in the art studio, Adele walked around the

downtown core until she came upon a post office. She quickly pulled out a brown envelope and looked down at it for a long time, checking the address more than once, making sure it was going to the right place; it contained her second application to the University of Toronto. Before dropping it into the mailbox, she looked down at it one more time and closed her eyes tight, as if praying. Then she slid the envelope in the slot.

She quickened her pace. A cool wind blew through her coat, raising goosebumps along her forearms. Shaking, she tightened the collar of her coat and walked even faster. But the autumn air wasn't the only thing responsible for her shivers. Her nerves were producing so much adrenaline that they were forcing her into the flight or fight response. She knew it was time to approach her parents and let them know she was ready to venture on her own.

As soon as she entered her father's store, she raised her chest and pulled her shoulders back trying to look as tough as she hoped: a responsible, capable adult who could function on her own in her own apartment, cook her own meals, clean her own place, do her own laundry and grocery shopping. But as she stood in front of her father, her body went limp, her shoulders drooped, and her chest curled in. Her father was behind the counter, slightly stooped over, his hands resting on his thighs, his chin tilted into his chest.

"Hello, Babba," Adele said quietly.

Youssef quickly got up and wiped his mouth with the back of his hand. "Hi Adele. I didn't hear you come in. Already finished your classes?" There was something different in his expression, Adele thought. His face was pinched up in pain and his cheeks were white, almost ghostly, and his lips were dry and chapped.

A sudden stench wafted in the air and Adele knew why her father had been bent down. Youssef took the wastebasket from under the counter and was about to head out the store to the garbage cans outside.

"Let me take it, Babba."

"No, you stay in the store until I come back."

"You're not feeling well. Let me help you." Adele tried to grab the canister from her father's hands but he pushed her away, nearly making her trip against the shelves of potato chips.

"No, I'm all right. Just a little flu bug. Nothing serious."

Adele stood at the counter and stared at her father walking around the building. He disappeared for a few minutes then returned with the basket now empty and clean; the smell of vomit was replaced with the scent of rainwater, probably from the bucket her father kept outside beside the trashcans.

"So did you have a good day, Adele? Are you enjoying the art classes?"

"Very much. How are you feeling, Babba?"

"I'm fine," he said abruptly, then his tone softened. "But business is slow, as usual. I think I may have to close the shop soon."

Adele frowned, sad at this prospect.

"Don't worry. It's probably time for me to retire anyway. I'm old now."

"You're not that old, Babba."

"My bones disagree with you, *babba*," Youssef sighed. Adele had noticed her father's appearance had become haggard over the past months, his skin was beginning to gravitate downwards, his hair was now almost completely grey. And she was surprised, too, by the way he hardly argued anymore with her or her mother.

"We're all getting older, including me. I'm almost nineteen— an adult now."

"A baby to me and your Mama. The youngest in the family. You know, Adele, your Mama was right. Elias wasn't for you. You deserve better."

Adele's mouth opened. Where was this coming from? And why now? Now when she had the courage to leave her parents.

"Babba?"

"What is it?" Youssef's tongue flicked over his dry lips. He reached into the cooler for a bottle of water and Adele couldn't help but look away when his hands began to shake as he uncapped the bottle and held its rim against his mouth.

"I've applied to the University of Toronto again..."

Youssef interrupted. "What for? You can go to the University of Ottawa. I don't know why you decided not to go when you were accepted. When you get married, then you and your husband can move to Toronto if that's what you really want to do. But now, your home is with me and your Mama. You can go to a university here." Youssef began to cough and retch, and suddenly he was on his knees again in front of the wastebasket. Walking around the counter, Adele quickly patted her father's back until he was done. She handed him some water and watched him as he tilted his head and swallowed a few drops, most of them sliding down his chin.

He stood up again. "You can't move out." His eyes were red and Adele couldn't tell whether it was from the vomiting or whether he was really sad at the prospect of her leaving. "You can't," he repeated, his voice cracking. Staring down at the floor, he shifted from one foot to the other.

"Okay, Babba, okay. Don't worry. Why don't you go inside and rest. I'll work in the store."

Youssef smiled weakly. He walked past her and stood at the doorway leading to their home for a few minutes before he disappeared. The only thing Adele could hear was the hum of the cooler and Youssef's footsteps shuffling up the wooden steps.

There were times in her childhood when she'd hide under the dining room table, her tiny hands clasped together. She'd pray her father's footsteps would fade further away from her hiding place, pray that his voice would become as sweet as the syrupy layers of her mother's baklava, and that Youssef would suddenly become animated with love instead of anger.

She was only a child but she knew her father could be gentler, especially when he'd reminisce about his homeland.

Youssef was a talented storyteller even if he only had a grade four education. Tucked on the couch next to her father's body, resting her head on his round belly, Adele would listen intently to the stories of his youth, stories filled with hardship, betrayal, and hope.

"I was a shepherd in the old country and one day the herd just took off in all sorts of directions. By the time I had managed to find them, half of them had disappeared, scattered along the countryside. When I returned home, my father, your Jido Salim, whipped me until I was black and blue."

Adele had squinted her eyes and tried not to cry.

Youssef had looked down at Adele, his expression sad, then quickly stared vacantly across the room while he continued his story. "Well, I let him beat me. I actually hoped he'd kill me in the process so I wouldn't have to endure my life with him anymore but then my Mama came running out of the house, screaming until the heavens shook. She covered me with her own body and took the final blows for me. And it was then that I swore I'd leave forever and never return. That's when I decided to board a ship with my cousin Abdullah and come to Canada. I begged Mama to come with me but she refused, saying her home was with my Babba not some cold, foreign country named Canada. So I left with Abdullah..."

"Uncle Abdullah?" Adele asked.

"That's right. I left with your Uncle Abdullah and one suit-case carefully packed with dried figs, *zahter*, pita bread, and second-hand clothes from my Canadian cousins. I had two hundred dollars to my name and the bruises on my face. When I arrived in Canada, I longed to return home, to return even to my old man. The first few months were so difficult for me. I didn't speak a word of English, didn't know where I was going or what I was doing. Where would I make my living? I couldn't be a goatherd or shepherd. At least in Lebanon, I could handle the beatings. It had become a part of my daily routine. But Abdullah forced me to stay. We got jobs in a restaurant owned by a Lebanese couple. They gave us room and board in exchange for working in the restaurant. I started to learn to speak the language with the help of some generous customers. They gave me tips, not only money, but also words. *Thank you. Have a good day. How are you? We're having beautiful weather, don't you agree?* So I learned a little bit every day. But I still missed my Mama, her cooking, her gentle smile. I also missed the mountains and I know this will sound totally ridiculous, I even missed the damn sheep! I yearned for my homeland. Canada was so different from my birthplace," he said, his eyes trailing to the window.

"Why was Jido Salim mean to you?" Adele asked quietly.

"I don't know, *babba*."

Bit by bit, story by story, her father weaved his history into hers, entwining it into her mind.

Now as she stood in her father's store, these memories crowded her mind. Why hadn't Youssef showed this kind side more often when she was growing up? For the next few hours, she dusted shelves, rearranged packages and cans, and served a few customers before the moonlight shone inside and urged her to lock the door and close the lights, leaving her memories in the dark alongside the boxed goods.

Dark turned to light and the next day, Adele stood in the dining room where she had set up her easel beside the enormous window. Her fingers were stained with acrylic paint but this didn't stop her from continuing to work on her current project. She had decided to paint an old family photograph of her paternal grandparents. Jido Salim and Sito Najwa were walking hand-in-hand across a field in their village. Sito Najwa had a handkerchief tied around her head and she wore an old brown skirt and loose-fitting grey sweater. Adele thought she could detect flour between the folds of her long skirt.

Jido Salim wore traditional Middle-Eastern style pants, the crotch hanging baggily between his thin legs. His jacket was torn near the flaps. Their hands were connected, palms subtly touching, fingers not quite fully clasped together. Nonetheless, they were unmistakably holding hands. Adele had been drawn to this old snapshot because of this intimacy; it suggested a love connection in spite of the harsh lines around Jido Salim's mouth and eyes. They must have been in love at one point, Adele thought, and maybe still were when this photograph had been snapped. They were both in their late-sixties when the photograph had been taken. Now Adele wondered if it was possible to still love a man who could make you cry with a movement of his head. While she thought about this, she let her right hand guide the paintbrush to the canvas and tried to finish the dusty earth her grandparents tread upon. As she was about to capture the colours of the earth, Samira called out to her from the kitchen. "Adele, put that paintbrush down and come here for a minute."

Frustrated, Adele grunted. "What, Mama? I'm busy." She didn't take her eyes off the canvas, didn't stop her long, even strokes.

"I'm making *sheik el mihshe*. I want you to learn how to make this dish."

"Mama, I'm working now."

"You're just painting. That's not real work. Put the brush down and come here now. Your sisters all know how to make stuffed eggplants and now it's your turn to learn. No Lebanese man wants a wife who can't cook," Samira said, her voice sounding excited and harsh at the same time. "Come on, *habibti*, come let me teach you," she said gently now.

Adele slammed the paintbrush down on the table next to the easel, walked over to the kitchen sink and rinsed her hands. She didn't say a word as she stood across from her mother and watched her remove the skin from several eggplants. Her mother's method of teaching cooking was to watch and learn; it was not hands-on for Adele or anyone else for that matter. "I've already started the filling. See, it's made up of beef, onions, pine nuts, salt, cinnamon, pepper, and allspice. Remember, allspice…"

"Is a very important spice for Lebanese dishes. I know, Mama. You've told me a hundred times over," Adele said more curtly than she intended. It was also the spice Mrs. Foster had told her could soothe skin while in the bath. But Adele didn't share this with her mother.

Samira didn't speak. She began to stuff the eggplants with the meat filling, then poured tomato juice carefully over them. Within minutes, she had prepared the tray and had placed it in the oven without one further word of explanation for Adele. Wiping her hands on her apron, she finally said, "I won't always be around to cook for you. You should learn."

"I know how to cook," Adele said.

"What? Hamburgers, French fries, steak, western sandwiches … all Canadian dishes. What about your Lebanese heritage? You don't even know how to make *hummus*! Our neighbours know how to make it and they're not even Lebanese!" Samira stomped back to the kitchen table and pulled out a chair where she sat and glared across at Adele. "So what if I've explained to you before how important allspice is? Would it hurt you to listen again?" Samira took the end of her apron and rubbed it across her eyes.

"I'm sorry, Mama." Adele reached towards her mother's hand, but Samira pulled it into her lap. "I don't want to be a great cook like you. I have other dreams."

"What are your dreams? I want to better understand you, Adele."

"They don't include allspice, that's for sure."

"Then what? What's your dream? To paint? How are you going to make a living like that?"

"I don't know but I want to try."

"And all I want from you is to try to cook some of your

ancestral dishes. Am I asking for too much?"

Adele got up, pushed her chair under the table, and walked back to the easel. She picked up her paintbrush and moved it in tiny, swift circular motions, creating some stones in the earth beneath her grandparents' worn shoes.

After that, Adele did most of her painting at one of the studios in the art school. There were several instances where she had tried to explain her passion for painting to her parents but in each attempt, they simply couldn't understand why someone would spend countless hours working away at something that wouldn't make money. What was the purpose of all this drawing and painting? They couldn't understand why she would vanish for a few hours, embrace her own solitude as if it were a lover, spend a glorious afternoon, sun shining bright, in the confines of her room. They couldn't understood why anyone would deliberately choose to be alone rather than learn how to cook, marry, and raise a family. That's what all good Lebanese girls wanted, they concluded over late-night conversations in their bed. Adele would often sit up in her bed and listen to her parents' hushed voices as they worried about the fate of their youngest child. A woman couldn't survive without a man, they both whispered. Why didn't she want to join the groups at the Orthodox Church, a place where she'd find a respectable Lebanese man who'd become her future husband? But she refused every time her parents suggested she join. After a while, Adele gave up explaining that she didn't want that life, that she wanted to paint and become an artist, perhaps spend some time abroad, studying art in a villa in Tuscany or a chalet in Provence, and if she met a man that would be great, but if she didn't that wouldn't be the end of the world for her.

It was past ten one Saturday evening when Adele walked inside the house and saw the light from the upstairs bathroom brightening the darkened hallway. Her father's store was now closed for the day and usually she'd hear the television set and her father swearing at something he disagreed with on whatever program he was watching that evening. Now she heard someone retching in the bathroom. At first she thought it was her mother, but then she saw Samira walk across the hallway and gently push open the bathroom door. "Are you all right, Youssef?" she asked.

Adele stood quietly at the front entrance and listened for his reply.

"Let me be. Go back to bed, Samira," Youssef said, his voice raspy.

"You're not okay if you're resting your head on the rim of the toilet," Samira said, concerned. "Let me help."

"How can you help me? Are you going to vomit for me?"

Adele hung up her coat then walked into the kitchen, where she grabbed a glass and filled it with water from the tap. She walked down the hallway and up the stairs until she was standing next to her mother. "Here," she said, handing the glass to Samira.

"Drink some water," Samira said.

Youssef turned his head, his eyes red and sweat dripping down his forehead, "Leave me alone! Can't I be sick without you both harassing me?"

"We're only concerned, Babba," Adele said. "It's only been a few weeks since the last time you were ill and now you've gotten the stomach flu again."

"Shut up!" Youssef shouted, before hurling into the toilet.

"God, Babba, you don't have to be so mean. We're only trying to help you." Adele stepped away.

Youssef lifted his head, wiped his mouth with the back of his right hand and mumbled, "Wait, Adele ... I'm ... I'm sorry."

But Adele had already crept into her bedroom, closing the door softly behind her.

The next morning, Adele packed the last of the customer's

groceries in a paper bag and handed it to him. Her father had not gotten out of bed yet, still feeling unwell. Adele would have to miss her classes today and if her father didn't start feeling better, she would have to quit her job at the bookstore. Standing behind the counter, Adele stared at her father's small store. Youssef had not renovated the yellow store since the day he bought it some thirty years ago. He had painted it maybe three or four times and replaced some of the appliances, like the cooler and freezer, but the shelves were still the same, not metal like those in the more modern and new places, but wooden. The exterior was also unchanged. When Adele was a child, she had loved working in the store with her father. She'd dust and fill shelves and deliver groceries, but as she had got older, the store had become boring, and she didn't look forward to helping out. She was also embarrassed by her father's business and tried to hide the fact that she was the shopkeeper's daughter when she was in high school, which was only two blocks away from her father's store and where a lot of her classmates congregated for smokes or soft drinks and bags of chips. Deep down she knew she shouldn't have felt ashamed because it was her father's livelihood and it supported their family—this small space she now gazed at tenderly had helped them financially. And now her father was getting old and who'd run the place? Adele certainly couldn't.

In her daze, Adele hadn't noticed her father coming down the stairs and stepping into the store. His face was paler than usual and he appeared to have lost several pounds in less than forty-eight hours.

"How are you feeling, Babba?"

"Better."

Adele couldn't help but feel sympathy for her father as he stood across from her in his baggy trousers; the belt that held them up was worn and too large for his waist, making Youssef crop the end of the leather strap so it wouldn't be too long. She didn't understand why her father wore things until they were ragged; they weren't poor.

"You can go now, Adele," Youssef said, moving behind the counter, and lightly touching Adele's shoulders. "Thanks for opening the store."

"I can stay, Babba. You should rest."

"I've rested enough."

"Maybe you should go see the doctor."

"What for? So he can send me back home and prescribe rest and lots of fluids. It's just some kind of stomach bug. Don't worry. Go paint or whatever it is you do."

CHAPTER 17

IT HAD BEEN SNOWING SINCE MORNING and the streets were now covered. Adele looked out her bedroom window, watching pedestrians trudging through the snow, bundled. Several things had happened over the past weeks as the seasons changed. Youssef had been diagnosed with an ulcer and Adele had been accepted to the University of Toronto again, but this time in the Fine Arts program.

Now she stood in the bookshop across from Bertha.

"Well, it's time for you to leave this old dusty and crowded shop and head to an even dustier and crowded place called T.O. Are you sure you wouldn't prefer Montreal?" Bertha teased, hoping Adele would have moved to Bertha's birthplace.

"I love Montreal, Bertha, but fate has sent me to another big city. I must confess that I'm a little scared," Adele said.

"Completely normal, my dear. If you weren't nervous that would make you apathetic. But don't worry, you'll do very well in Toronto. It will be so good for you to live on your own."

Adele nodded and smiled.

"How are your parents taking it?"

"Not very well but they can't make me change my mind, not this time."

"They'll eventually accept your decision. Every parent usually does."

"I hope so. I want to still be connected to them. I can always visit on long weekends and holidays."

"Of course! Don't worry too much. It's hard for parents, you know, to let go, especially ones like yours who were brought up in a different country with strong ties to family. They don't want to lose their baby. But you have to convince them that you're not lost, only living somewhere else," Bertha said, gently patting Adele's arm.

"You're right. I have to let them know that," Adele sighed.

Back home, she quickly headed up the stairs to her bedroom. Her suitcases lay on the floor opened and half packed. She couldn't believe she was actually leaving. Tomorrow she'd be boarding an airplane and heading to Toronto and finally living the life she wanted. Over the past few months, she often wondered how she would tell her parents that it was time for her to live on her own and now she was leaving without her father's blessing. Squatting down on the floor, Adele gazed at her clothes neatly folded in the burgundy luggage and she remembered what her father had told her: *If you must leave, then leave, but don't think you can come back to my house. I only have three daughters now.* Knowing her father's antics, she didn't want to give in as she had done the last time. This was her time. And she knew this in her heart.

Getting up, she walked across the room and pulled out some more clothes from her drawers, moving with the confidence of someone who knew where she was heading and what she was going to do. But did she really? Her shoulders were straight and her fingers didn't tremble while placing the items in the baggage but she did feel a pull in her stomach, an uncertainty tearing the muscles under her ribs, and at first she thought they were just phantom pains but she knew it was something else. In spite of everything, she still wanted her father's approval, wanted him to come in her bedroom and say that he approved of her going away to school. But she'd have to wait an eternity and she didn't have the time. Tomorrow she'd be gone.

The next day, Adele stood nervously at the Ottawa Macdonald-Cartier International airport. Her sisters stood around her as well as her mother. Youssef had refused to see her off. "Be sure to call when you arrive," Rima said.

"You're going to be okay, Monkey," Mona whispered, leaning into Adele's ear. Adele softly touched her sister's face.

"Thanks, Mona," Adele said. "I'm still fairly stunned, you know. I can't believe I'm actually leaving."

"This is what you always wanted," Katrina said quietly.

Adele didn't reply. Instead, she looked at her sisters and felt her body grow numb at the prospect of not seeing them every day. She wondered how she would survive this separation, but this was what she had always wanted, as Katrina had just said. Billions of people did it every day, packed up and left their loved ones for jobs, schools, marriage, or whatever, and they survived, so Adele knew she would survive too.

"Do you think Babba will ever forgive me?" Adele asked.

The sisters stared at each other then their mother. Samira lifted up her hands and rested them on Adele's face. "Don't worry. Remember to eat and rest well, okay? I won't be there to cook for you."

Adele moved back, pushing her mother's hands away from her face. "I know." Even now, that's all that mattered to her mother, Adele thought.

Samira said nothing and stuffed her hands into the pockets of her coat. At that moment, the intercom came on and announced Adele's flight. She quickly embraced her sisters, then mother before boarding the plane. Not looking back once, she imagined her mother and sisters shaking their heads and criticizing her.

PART IV: 1992

CHAPTER 18

ADELE DREW THE STONE HOUSE of her father's childhood home with a coal pencil, sketching grape leaves climbing along the side boulders of the residence and, at the same time, remembering her introduction to Elias, how he had stood shyly in the front yard before joining the family for *maza*. And now, in Canada, working in a studio at the University of Toronto, Adele drew this memory. She was immersed in her art when a man entered the studio and began to set up a blank canvas on one of the easels. She hadn't heard him cross the room and was startled when he stood in front of her, his right hand stretched out to her in greeting. "Hello, I'm Scott."

Slightly irritated, Adele put down the pencil and looked up at the young man. His brilliant green eyes kept glancing at her drawing. He wore a red baseball cap, which he removed to reveal a mop of blond hair. His face was clean-shaven. She breathed in wisps of his aftershave and, when she looked across at him, she thought he was beautiful. The strong, square jaw reminded her of Elias, but he was an English-Canadian version. His complexion was pale and his eyelashes were light. He wore a loose, long-sleeved blue shirt over his khaki trousers and a beaded necklace, the kind sold at vendor stands in Kensington Market.

She held onto his hand longer than she would normally, but there was something soft in the way his warm palm stuck to hers. "I'm Adele."

"Nice to meet you," Scott said. He pointed to her sketch. "That drawing is very interesting. Is it a place in Europe? It looks so old. You don't look European, maybe Persian. Are you?"

The question caught her off-guard; she had no idea what to say. She wasn't used to his directness. "No, I'm Canadian."

"Really? With your thick black hair and big brown eyes, you look so ... so...."

Adele stood with her arms tightly folded across her chest, suddenly feeling awkward and embarrassed by his probing questions. "So what? Un-Canadian?"

"No," he paused, "I'm sorry. I didn't mean that. You just look so exotic, that's what I wanted to say. I'm sorry if I've just insulted you, that wasn't my intention."

"What was your intention then?"

"I think it would be nice if we went out for coffee."

"I don't drink coffee."

"Then tea or juice."

"I'm busy today."

"Maybe another time." Scott walked back to his knapsack, pulled out a sticky note and scribbled something on it before peeling it off and handing it to Adele. "Here's my number for next time."

That night, lying in bed, Adele thought about Scott. She wondered what it would feel like to lie next to him, her head on his chest, listening to the rise and fall of his breathing, her hands tracing his ribs, his flat belly, and then she also let her mind travel further below to a place she had not yet visited. His flaccid penis grew with her touch. At this moment, she let her hands move down her belly, cringing only slightly when she felt her scar, until her fingers were in her underwear, spreading open her lips and she imagined Scott entering her body gently and slowly, her hands on his back pulling him closer to her. A few minutes later, she moaned softly while her thighs trembled.

After, she closed her legs and turned on her side and slept as the moonlight spilled shadows on her bedroom walls.

The next morning, Scott sought out Adele, standing next to her in the art studio and offering to help her set up before their class.

"Thanks, but I'm fine," Adele said quietly, her cheeks turning red.

"Well, do you want to help me?" Scott laughed. He had a deep laugh, originating from his belly and when he laughed, he threw his head back slightly, blond curls bouncing.

"All right." Adele held the easel while Scott positioned the canvas on it, setting his paintbrushes and palette on the side table.

"Thank you, Adele."

"No problem."

The instructor walked into the room and began to teach the morning's lesson but Adele's eyes kept moving from her canvas to the young man beside her, who winked when he caught Adele taking a peek. She turned away quickly, and this time focused on the task at hand.

A couple of days passed and Adele held the yellow sticky note with Scott's number in the palm of her hand. A few times she had put it down and hid it in her desk drawer, between piles of other papers, and just as quickly as she had placed it there, she reached back in and pulled it out again. Now she stood in front of the telephone, the note in her hands, and felt light-headed at the thought of speaking with Scott. Taking a deep breath, she finally picked up the receiver and began to punch in the number. She was about to hang up on the fourth ring when someone answered.

"Hello," a deep voice said.

Unsure if it was Scott, Adele asked, "May I speak with Scott please?"

"Speaking."

"Hi, Scott, it's Adele," she said, her voice slightly shaky.

"Hi Adele. How's it going?"

"Good and you?"

"Pretty good now that I've finished the piece I was working on earlier today. I love painting but sometimes it can be so frustrating. Isn't it odd how what we love to do can also cause so much grief?"

"Like the way you can love and hate someone at the same time?" Adele asked.

"Yeah, that's true. Love can be complicated but I think people make it more difficult than it really has to be, don't you think?"

"I suppose." Adele cringed, wishing she could think of something more intelligent to add to the conversation.

"Do you have plans tonight?"

"Not really."

"Do you want some?"

"Some what?" Adele asked softly. She fidgeted, the floorboards creaking under her weight. She cringed again. She felt so awkward.

"Plans, of course!" Scott laughed. "I know this really cool Indian restaurant."

"I've never tried Indian food before."

"Really? Do you like spicy food?"

"Sometimes."

"Well, I'll go easy on you and choose mild dishes. Is it a date?"

Adele smiled wondering if Scott would laugh if he knew this was her very first date, but she didn't mention it; instead she agreed to meet him that night.

Later that evening in a small Indian restaurant, Scott told Adele about his family. His life was so different from hers: his mother was a psychologist and his father was a lawyer. He was an only child. He had grown up in the affluent part of the English district of Montreal, had attended private school then later McGill University where he studied law. But in his second year, he had decided to abandon his father's dream of him following in his footsteps.

Scott explained how he had moved to Toronto with a girlfriend and how their relationship ended after only a few months in the new city. The scent of curry engulfed them as a waiter in white and black served them steaming plates of curried chicken, samosas, and rice. It was a Monday night and the restaurant was quiet; there were only a few customers, so the evening felt intimate.

As they started digging into their meal, Scott suddenly seemed preoccupied. "What's wrong?" she asked gently.

He was silent for a moment, then said, "My father called with his monthly lecture." Scott rolled his eyes.

"What's that?"

"It's when my father bribes me with countless offers of European vacations and money if I return to law school."

"Those offers don't sound too bad to me," Adele said, laughing.

"I guess but it's the way he goes about it. He doesn't get it. I'm not into money like him. I don't need, or want, the six-figure income, the huge house, and cottage. Those things don't matter to me. I just wish he could accept my decision, accept me the way I am. What about my happiness? I'm his only child for God's sake."

She laid her fork on her plate, reached over to Scott and rested her hand on his.

He glanced down at her hand, then mustered a smile. "I'm sorry to be such a whiner especially on our first date."

"You're not a whiner and don't be sorry. It helps to talk."

"Now you sound like my Mom."

She raised her right eyebrow. "Is that a good thing?"

"Most definitely. One day we'll go visit my parents," he said very casually. "We'll make it a mini-vacation. A weekend in Montreal. What do you say?"

"I don't know," she said, her tone serious. But she broke into a smile, and quipped, "Your father may think I'm a bad influence, being an artist and all."

"And an Arab on top of that!"

Her eyes darkened. "What do you mean by that?" She pulled her hand away from Scott but he grasped it and brought it to his mouth. He kissed her knuckles.

"I'm sorry. Your heritage makes you unique. Eccentric..."

"Eccentric? I thought that's what my art made me!"

"Let's finish eating before the waiter kicks us out in favour of the boring TV show!" They glanced back and saw him hovering in the doorway between the kitchen and the restaurant. A small television was perched at the edge of the bar, and his eyes were darting back and forth.

Adele suddenly asked, "Do your parents dislike Arabs?"

"No, it's not that," Scott said, sitting back in his chair and crossing his arms over his chest. "It's just that they think..."

"What?"

"With everything going on in the Middle East, they think Arabs are hot-tempered."

"Yes, we're passionate people and what's so wrong with that?"

"Nothing, Adele. Can we change the subject?" he said in a low voice.

"I just don't understand why your parents wouldn't like a particular group of people simply because of what they see on the news. Have they ever been to Lebanon or anywhere else in the Middle East?"

"No."

"Do they even have Arab friends?"

"Adele, please, let's talk about something else."

"Do you dislike Arabs too?"

"I wouldn't be here with you if I did." Scott smiled and reached across to take Adele's hand. He then leaned in and kissed her on the mouth. She kissed him with the inexperience of a young teenager. "You're a great kisser, let yourself go," he murmured in between their open-mouthed kisses, encouraging her. They were oblivious of the waiter by the kitchen door.

"Hmm ... thanks," she softly laughed. Finally freeing herself, she exhaled deeply. "I suppose we should finish eating."

Scott nodded. They abandoned the silverware and picked up the remaining rice and bits of chicken with their fingers.

A few months passed and Adele's world began to make room for Scott. They talked and talked, wove their stories together, listened to each other's lives, shared laughs and the occasional bout of sadness. And now Adele was going to meet his parents for the first time.

When Adele crossed the cobblestone laneway, leading to the spacious front porch lined with huge pillars, she felt herself return to her childhood neighbourhood, to Mrs. Foster's big white house. She felt a pang of grief for her old friend, no longer in this world. She was buried next to her late husband and Adele wondered if they were at last reunited. Sometimes she missed her so much that Adele would suddenly be overwhelmed with a longing to see Mrs. Foster. Sometimes she would even leave her apartment, and head down the street to have a chat with her dear friend, and then remember Mrs. Foster wasn't alive, and she'd realize she herself was no longer in Ottawa, but in Toronto.

Now she stood in front of this similar-looking home and before she knew it, her eyes were filled with tears. Scott looked at her puzzled, raised his hand and rested it on her face. Adele lifted her hand, rested it on top of Scott's, and for a while they stood on the porch with their hands connected, then their lips.

Finally freeing herself from his embrace, she exhaled deeply. "I suppose we should go inside. What will the neighbours think? The Miller boy has lost his mind—he's dating a gypsy!"

Scott wrapped his arm around her, and pulled her close. She rested her head on his shoulder. "My sweet gypsy girl," he whispered. "I love you."

She didn't know what to say in return, so she did the only thing she could think of: she pulled away and stood in front of the large door, waiting for Scott to unlock it.

CHAPTER 19

THE WOMAN WHO MET THEM in the hallway introduced herself as Kathy Miller, Scott's mother. She wore a yellow cardigan sweater around her shoulders, the arms tied together, hanging over the V-neck of her powder pink blouse. Crisp cream-coloured dress pants fitted perfectly on her small legs. She had the appearance of someone who was about forty-five but Adele had learned from Scott beforehand that his mother was fifty-eight. Her dirty-blonde hair fell around her high-cheek boned face in layers. Her lips were covered with a neutral-coloured frost. And she wore the same expression of warmth that Adele loved in Scott's face. She looked nothing like what Adele had expected. In her naivety, she thought Scott's mother would be heavy-set like her own mother, with dark circles under her eyes, and puckering skin, furrows creasing her forehead as Samira did. The folds of Samira's flesh were chiselled with the old world whereas Mrs. Miller's skin was smooth, youthful. Adele wondered why her mother always looked so far into the distance rather than gazed at the present moment. Resentment surged through her.

"Hello, Adele," Mrs. Miller said warmly. It's so nice to finally meet you. I've heard so much about you from Scott."

She stretched out her hand and firmly shook the older woman's. "It's very nice to meet you, too. I hope Scott had only good things to say," she said, giving him a friendly shove.

"Of course!" he laughed. He then embraced his mother.

For a while, they stood clasped together, his mother's hands brushing his mop of curly hair. Adele wondered what it was like to be hugged so tightly by a parent. She imagined the sensation of her mother's body melting into hers, but she couldn't recall such a memory. Perhaps there were moments in her early childhood when her mother or father took her in their arms and hugged her tight. Now she folded and unfolded her arms, stood uncomfortably in the foyer while her boyfriend embraced his mother with such love, a love that was returned by small gestures: ruffling Scott's hair, stroking his face, and smiling widely at each other.

Mrs. Miller led them into the living room. Adele admired the long leather sofas and overstuffed armchairs. Several pieces of modern art were interspersed throughout the large room, which had a spectacular view of the river. The midday sun poured through the enormous bay window. This room was so different from the drab white walls of her parents' home where old Italian furniture, paintings of tacky flowers, and sagging brown velvet curtains hung; the Miller house was inviting and silent. Adele believed she could lose herself in the sereneness. She took a seat next to Scott on the tan couch, placing her hand on his thigh and leaning close to him. He lifted his arm and rested it lightly on her shoulder. She could never do this at her parents' house: affectionately touching her boyfriend would be inappropriate, dirty, disrespectful, *ayb*, she had learned in her upbringing. But now her body relaxed in the warmth of Scott's presence and the house he was raised in.

"Mrs. Miller, you have a lovely home," Adele finally said.

"Call me Kathy."

"Your house is really beautiful, Kathy."

"Thank you. I tried to make it as comfortable as possible. My husband and I have such busy lives that when we come home, we just want to relax or as the young say 'chill.'"

"Bravo, Mom. You're very hip for an old broad." Scott winked at Adele, then turned his smiling face towards his mother.

She got up, ruffled his hair once more and said, "Adele, see how my *petit garçon* insults his old *Maman*? No respect at all!"

Adele thought there was no way she could tease her parents in such a manner and she couldn't help feeling resentment for the parents she had been given. She turned to look at Scott and noticed he was eyeing her with concern, ridges forming on his forehead. He took her hand and squeezed it gently. "Are you all right?" he whispered.

"Yeah. Why wouldn't I be?" she said, more curtly than she had intended. She shifted her shoulders, and tried to peel away from Scott. But he wouldn't let her. He leaned close and kissed her on the mouth in front of his mother. Taken aback, she dragged a sleeve across her face. Adele glanced at Mrs. Miller, whose smile tightened, then turned into a full frown. Realizing her mistake, Adele turned her head to the window and watched a crow swoop against the surface of the river then flutter its black wings, leaving a spray of water in its wake.

"Come, let's have lunch. Your father went into the office this morning and called to say he'll be late, Scott. We should start without him."

"As usual. Nothing ever changes, does it, Mom?" Scott sighed.

"Give him a break, Scott. Let's have a good time. Can we do that?" Scott reluctantly nodded. Adele took Scott's hand and let him guide her into the dining room.

A big, burly man with brown hair, almost as dark as Adele's, rushed into the dining room just as they had started eating. "Sorry I'm late," he said loudly. Then he reached across and introduced himself to Adele. "Nice to meet you, Adele."

"Likewise," Adele answered, smiling.

Mr. Miller pointed out the large window. "Those damn crows seem to have settled in our backyard. Apparently, they can smell death." He faced his wife. "My dear, I guess you should read the obituaries and see if we know anyone," Mr. Miller said, pouring a large portion of mash potatoes into his dish, topping it off with gravy and, at the same time, scowling at the crows circling around the house. He turned and briefly looked at Adele. "My wife has a habit of checking the obits. I guess when you reach a certain age this is what old farts do!" He laughed and Adele mustered a laugh too. But she noticed that Scott and his mother remained silent.

"In some civilizations, crows are considered good luck," Scott piped up.

"That's crap," Mr. Miller scoffed.

"Why do you always have to be right, Dad?"

"Because I usually am," he laughed.

From the corner of her eye, Adele watched father and son bicker over something as mundane as crows. Ian Miller was nothing like his son. He had a well-trimmed beard, greying in some places, and a loud, abrupt voice. When he spoke, it felt like the chandelier above the dining room table was shaking, as though from the tremor of a small earthquake. He wore a long-sleeved white dress shirt and navy blue trousers, having just returned from the office even though it was a Saturday afternoon.

"I've been reading up on Buddhism and crows are often seen as protectors," Scott continued.

"So you're not Christian anymore?" Mr. Miller said scornfully. "Have you become a Buddhist? Are you now chanting and meditating on top of painting and forgetting that you have certain responsibilities in this life? I would've hoped you had come to your senses, that you would've dropped that useless art major and returned to law. You know you'll always have a job at my firm. How do you expect to support a family with an artist's salary?"

"Now how did we get from crows to Buddhism to my failure as a son?" Scott paused, then glanced at his mother. "Help me, Mom. You're the psychologist."

But she didn't say anything, just pushed the food on her plate. Adele thought of her mother and how she'd do the same thing. Maybe Samira and Mrs. Miller were not so different as Adele had originally thought.

Mr. Miller cleared his throat. "That's not what this is about. I'm worried about your future. I thought you said you had good news on this visit, so I assumed..."

"That's your problem, Dad. You're always assuming..." Scott's voice cracked and he stopped suddenly. Adele reached over and squeezed his hand.

Mr. Miller looked at Adele. "My apologies for this outburst, Adele. May I ask you something?" He rested his elbows on the table and clasped his large hands together. He didn't wait for her reply. "How do you put up with my son? He's so damn sensitive. Look at him." He now pointed at Scott. "He's on the verge of tears for God's sake."

She held onto Scott's clammy hand, wanted to steady the tremor in his body. But she looked away from his tense face and stared at Mr. Miller. "Scott is bright, kind, generous."

"Generous?" he scoffed. "With what money? My money, of course, because he doesn't have a penny to his name."

"He might not be a lawyer but at least he's a decent and creative man," she retaliated.

Mr. Miller pursed his lips and then what came out of his mouth, resounded on the colourful, pastel walls, "I thought your kind only looked at a man's wallet."

Adele made a sound that was half sob, half laugh. Then she turned and looked at Scott's mother, but Mrs. Miller eyed Adele dismissively, then quickly looked down at her plate once more. Letting go of Scott's hand, Adele pushed back her chair. It scraped the hardwood floor, but she didn't care whether she had left marks on the glossy finish. "Excuse me," she said, before grabbing her overnight bag from the hallway and leaving the house.

She stepped outside and sat on the wide steps of the porch, her elbows pressed on her knees, her head in her hands. Were all families fucked up? she wondered. Were all fathers flawed in some way or another? Was this a universal thing rather than a cultural one? A few minutes later, she heard the front door open, the sound of footsteps behind her and before she knew it, Scott had slid his body behind hers, wrapping his arms around her waist. She felt his breath on the nape of her neck, felt beads of wetness slithering around her collarbone. His heart throbbed so hard that she felt it against her back. She patted his arms and watched the neighbours across the street busying themselves with their lawns or expensive cars.

They left immediately. On the ride back to Toronto, they shared a comfortable silence. Adele lost herself to the green pastures and countless trees that flew along the roadside. As a child, she had enjoyed long family drives. Her father used to cajole them in the car, some of her sisters preferring to stay home and watch TV. Adele never needed coaxing. She was always the first one in the green Chevy, making certain she got a window seat. On these rides, she'd forget her father's yelling, if only for a few hours, and witness a gentler side to him. They'd cruise along the highway, sometimes stopping for ice cream or pastries at one of the small towns in the Ottawa Valley. Now she leaned her head back on the car seat and smiled at the beautiful memory of the family drives with her father. Turning her head to the side, she glanced at Scott and noted that the lines around his deep-set eyes were no longer strained. With her left hand, she stroked his face. She felt the muscles around his mouth lift into a smile. How she loved him, his gentle soul. For a while, she rested her hand on his cheek. His green eyes flitted from the road to her face. "You're beautiful," he suddenly said.

"Hmm ... so are you," she murmured, her eyes fixed on him. He looked so young in the light of dusk.

"Now you're making me blush," Scott laughed.

Adele finally dropped her hand, and rested it on his thigh.

"Pull over," she said, her voice firm.

"Why? Are you going to be sick?" His eyes looked concerned.

"Do I look ill?" she teased. Her cheeks were flushed and her eyes were wide and shining. She felt Scott's thigh tense beneath her palm. He quickly pulled to the curb of the road and turned off the ignition. Then, she opened the door and got out of the car. She walked to the trunk and motioned for Scott to open it. His eyes stared at her through the rear-view mirror, unsure of what to make of Adele's peculiar behaviour.

After a few seconds, she slammed the trunk shut and walked to the driver's side. She leaned on the edge of the window, a thick blanket in her hands. She planted a quick kiss on Scott's mouth. "Come on," she said, standing straight again. "Let's go for a walk."

"Now? Don't you want to head back home?"

"You ask a lot of questions, Mr. Miller. Perhaps you were meant to be a lawyer after all," she giggled.

Scott frowned. His hands clutched the steering wheel.

She quickly reached into the car and squeezed his shoulder. "I'm sorry. That wasn't funny."

"Not really," Scott agreed, but he opened the door and slid out of the car. "Wherever you lead, I will follow."

They followed a trail into a wooded area along the highway. Tufts of weeds tickled their ankles as they gingerly walked hand-in-hand, the blanket tucked under Adele's arm. As they ventured further away from the paved road and the occasional zooming vehicle, the terrain changed from deep bush into a lush, green pasture with sporadic white birch and pine trees. Freeing her hand from Scott's, Adele spread the blanket out and laid it down on the ground. The fleeting colours of dusk began to fade. The scent of pine needles and fresh grass floated in the air. She reached for Scott's hand and motioned for him to lie down on the blanket. She lowered herself on top of him and then began to undress him, then herself. Her embraces were so urgent because she knew if she took it slow, then she'd stop and think about what she was doing. She'd lose the nerve and succumb to her father's voice inside her head: *you must remain a virgin until marriage.* Now the only thing she heard was Scott's throated, rhythmic groans. The pain was excruciating yet pleasurable at the same time. The smell of sweat and earth engulfed her. She watched Scott's soft face tighten, his neck craning, his mouth straining. Her eyes were half-closed; she was moaning, too. Scott closed his eyes until he shuddered and Adele collapsed on top of his chest.

Then she loosened herself from him. Something warm was running down her thighs. She gasped in surprise when she saw the blood that had spilled into the folds of the blanket. And before she knew it, she was weeping. She turned to her side, pretended she did not hear Scott's words, "It's okay, Adele. What we did was okay. Don't feel bad about it." She pretended she did not feel his gentle strokes on her back, pretended nothing had happened between them, that they hadn't made love.

Adele waited until Scott fell asleep, and then she rose from the blanket. She stood in the open field. She turned and looked at Scott's face. The lines around his eyes relaxed as his chest rose up and down with each breath. He slept with his mouth slightly open. Bending down, she traced his thick eyebrows, the small bump on his nose. She rose again, stepped back, and felt suddenly alone even though Scott was only a few feet away. She folded her arms on her chest then fell to her knees. Bowing her head to the ground, she cried. She cried for the thing she had lost to the medical profession and now lost again when she slept with Scott, the thing her sisters had saved as they had been expected to, that they had given up in the appropriate Lebanese way. At this moment, she felt a failure and it was while her sobs echoed in the evening sky that she heard the faint but audible phrases she had grown up with: *Look at what you've done. You've made a mess of everything, as usual. You'll never amount to anything. You're no good for nothing*. With her forehead pressed on the earth, she listened carefully. The script was not new. She knew the words by heart, had memorized them long ago, etched them in the lobes of her brain.

A while later, she awoke with a swelling in her head. It felt like she had a hangover even though she hadn't consumed one ounce of liquor. She blinked a few times before she realized Scott was standing in front of her. He bent down and helped her up from the ground, wiping the dirt from her clothes. He said in a quiet voice, "How are you feeling?"

"All right," she mumbled, walking past him towards the spot they had made love for the first time. Kneeling beside the blanket, she eyed the dark stains atop the checkered pattern of the blanket; they had melted into the fibres. Without a moment's hesitation, she grasped the cloth between her fingers and flung it in the air, removing everything from it, crumbled pieces of soil, loose pebbles, slivers of grass blades, everything but the dried crimson spots. In a way, she had followed her sisters' lead. She had a wedding sheet of her own. Clenching her teeth, she began to fold it messily.

Scott turned the car onto Adele's street. Her apartment was in an artsy neighbourhood. Huge maple trees dotted the sidewalks of the narrow street, enclosing the heritage homes, many of which had been converted into apartment dwellings. On their drive back, Adele had tuned Scott out. He had made idle conversation and she had nodded politely while fixing her gaze outside the car window. When Scott parked next to the sidewalk, and began to remove the key from the ignition, Adele quickly touched his wrist and said, "Please, let's call it a day."

Scott looked at the clock on the dashboard. "But it's not even late. It's only nine o'clock. Let me make you dinner. We can eat and talk."

"I don't want to talk," she said, a polite smile on her downcast face. "You understand, don't you?"

There was a brief silence. "Not really," he said, suddenly sounding harsh. "So we made love. We've been dating for a few months now. It's perfectly natural for us to head in that direction. I would've been worried if we didn't. Why are you acting like such a baby? Sulking all the way home! When I first met you, you had said you weren't a 'traditional' Lebanese woman but you're certainly acting like one. Premarital sex is not a big deal." He sighed, leaned forward and rested his forehead on the steering wheel.

She interjected. "Maybe not for you. But I was taught to believe that a good Lebanese girl doesn't have sex until she's married."

Scott lifted his head up and faced Adele. He said in a cold tone, "You're a hypocrite then. Don't pretend to be something that you're not. Why did you have sex with me then?"

"I don't know. We can still be friends."

"Friends? Now you want to break up with me?" he said, his voice full of hurt. "I don't need another friend. I want a girlfriend, a girlfriend who is not hung up on her old cultural ways. A girlfriend who is mature enough to have a healthy adult relationship."

"What do you mean by 'healthy'? Sex?"

"Of course!" he said, laughing out loud. "Christ, it's a big part of a relationship!" he said, rubbing his forehead in frustration.

"Sex isn't everything," she retaliated.

"Emotional, physical, sexual—they all go hand-in-hand."

"I'm sorry you feel that way."

"Grow up, Adele."

"Where's this coming from? I was wrong about you. I thought you were gentle and caring," she said, tears filming her eyes.

"At least I'm honest about what I want. I slept with you because I love you. You can't even begin to understand the complexities of adult relations because you're too uptight with your old-fashioned upbringing. Are you Lebanese or Canadian? You can't be both. Choose one and truly live it, breathe it, embrace it."

"What the fuck do you know?" she said through clenched teeth. "You're white. You've lived your whole life in Canada. You've never had to struggle with a dual connection to different cultures. You've never had anyone glaring at you as you walk down the streets just because of your appearance. I was born and raised in Canada but some people think I should go back to my country. What country? Lebanon? This is the only home I have known, not some village in the Middle East. You don't know anything. I can't choose one and live it 'fully'. When people look at me, they don't ask if I'm Canadian. *Greek? Italian? Spanish?* That's what they ask. Fuck, they can't even get my nationality straight when they insult me. I've been called a wop so many times. You've never had anyone shout at you 'go back to your country, bitch!'"

Adele paused to catch her breath, remembering when she had been harassed by an older woman who screamed "Bitch! Return to your country. You don't belong here, dirty Arab!" The woman had also hurled a glass bottle at Adele, who had moved quickly to avoid the blow. Those cruel comments had hurt Adele, but not as much as the turned-away faces of those who had witnessed the attack. Not one person had asked her if she was all right as she walked away from the woman who had continued shouting vulgarities. Not one person had come to her defence. "You don't know anything about me or my culture!" Adele snapped again, her face reddening. Scott dropped his eyes. She jumped out of the car and slammed the door behind her.

CHAPTER 20

ADELE DID NOT GO OUT WITH SCOTT ANYMORE. He had begun a new relationship soon after they had stopped dating. She passed him in the corridors of the university, watching him hold onto his new girlfriend's waist, leaning close and kissing her on the mouth. Not stopping even when he raised his eyes and saw Adele a few feet away. She studied the woman beside Scott as closely as she dared. She had blonde hair like Scott's. But then Adele would turn her head, the muscles around her mouth tensing and her heart beating rapidly. She hurried past Scott and his new girlfriend, hurried past the rest of the students until she turned a corner and rested against the wall, her arms folded on her chest, her back cold from the concrete. She would stand there for a while, waiting for her anxiety to subside. With the end of her sleeve, she wiped away the tears that finally came. And she forced herself to remember that she had also hurt him.

Life returned to its usual pattern. Adele woke up early, showered, dressed, ate breakfast then hurried to her lectures and art studio. She studied and painted all of the time, only taking the occasional break to eat and to bathe. The solitary life she had before Scott encompassed her world again.

All this changed the morning Adele received a letter. When she pulled it out of her mailbox, she recognized Mona's careful, small script immediately. But instead of opening it, she tucked it between the pages of her sketchpad. Now, sitting in the

middle of her apartment with the sunlight pouring through the
large window, Adele ripped open the envelope. She unfolded
Mona's letter.

Dear Adele,

*I hope this letter finds you safe and well. It has been
so long since we last talked, last saw each other, that I
don't know where to begin. Why don't you come visit us
anymore? I know the last visit was horrible with Babba
cursing you, but you have to remember that's the way he
is. He didn't mean it when he said you were dead to him.
You know how he is. Come home, Adele. We miss you.*

*We just received some terrible news about Elias and
I wasn't sure if you wanted to know about it or not, but
then I thought you had a right to know. From what I heard,
Elias was beaten severely by his father for embarrassing
him with your fiasco fake elopement. He has become
withdrawn and silent, not speaking to anyone. They now
say he is a shepherd, living and sleeping in the fields, the
animals his only companions. His poor mother leaves him
food when his father isn't looking. Your fake elopement
was very scandalous! But I must say that Elias is certainly
a decent person because he took full responsibility, not
blaming you once and that's one of the reasons he was
beaten. I suppose his father thought he could beat it out
of him. Apparently, he endured several thrashings before
his father stopped: actually, before several villagers and
Elias's mother had to pull the stick out of his hand. Yet he
never let out that you had agreed to his plan. From what
we've heard, he will not speak of you to anyone. He does
not speak much at all.*

Adele lifted her head from the letter and looked out the
window. She stared past the maple trees and gazed at the sky.
In the clouds, she envisioned Elias, the gentle lines around his

eyes. She frowned, then flinched at the thought of his bruised face. Why did he return home? she wondered. But she couldn't judge him because she had initially returned home too. She shook her head and continued reading the letter:

It is all so sad. Elias seemed like such a nice man. I still believe you would have made a beautiful couple, but that's in the past, isn't it?

Babba's still angry with you for leaving. When you last visited, his temper exploded a thousand times over. Now Babba is calmer. It's weird but he just sort of learned to accept you're not here anymore. And you know what's more odd? He seems sad. He mopes around the store, neglecting the shelves until a customer complains because he's out of something. He seems very small, Adele. His shoulders slouch, his head hangs low. He has even lost that infamous potbelly! And you're not going to believe this. One day, I caught him behind the counter, staring vacantly out the store window and I asked him if he was okay and he turned around and said, "I haven't been a good father." My heart swelled as he spoke those words. I wanted to deny it, but I couldn't. I couldn't believe the pain in his face, too. He looked up at me and squinted as if he were in agony. A few minutes later, he turned and looked out the window again.

Oh, Adele, why have you stayed away so long? I know how hard Babba was on you when we were growing up. But we're still family. I know we betrayed you when we went to Lebanon. Please forgive us for that. We're still sisters. I won't lecture you because I know that's probably the last thing you need to hear. Please call me. I think it would be good for us to talk. Too many tears, too much time has passed since we last talked. Don't you think it's about time we learn to heal? You're the artist, after all. You know all about suffering and how it can eat you up. But

in all that suffering, there is hope. Ah, I haven't become
new age, only as wise as the wisest person (and bravest) I
have ever known — you! Call me, Monkey.
    Love, Mona

Adele stared at the phone for a while before she finally lifted
the receiver out of the cradle. With unsteady fingers, she dialled
Mona's phone number.

Weeks later, the phone calls turned into a visit. For two days,
Adele scrubbed down the walls and floor of her apartment,
tidied her paint cans and various sketchpads and papers, bought
fresh flowers to liven the lonely place she had made her home
for the past three years. Her sisters would be visiting her and
she wanted to make her small dwelling inviting and comfortable. For the first time since her departure from her family she
considered whether her decision to live a separate life from
them was a good one. She began to feel sorry for herself. As
she scrubbed the hardwood floor, she felt her body tense. She
moved forward, sponge firmly gripped in her hands, knees sore
and red from the friction of wood rubbing on skin. She wanted to pick up the phone, cancel the plans with her sisters, to
have time to think. But hadn't she had plenty of time to think?
For a moment she stopped and stared out the large window,
watching how the thin branches of a tree supported a squirrel.
The tiny creature jumped from twig to twig, its black, beady
eyes focused on reaching the trunk. She listened to the birds
singing and car doors slamming. Then a light rain began to
fall. She returned to the tedious task of making her reflection
flicker on the spotless floor. By the time her sisters arrived, the
lemon scent of the floor solution flooded the room.

"Oh my God, it's so good to see you again!" Mona said,
pulling Adele into her arms. She squeezed her so tight that
Adele nearly lost her balance, forcing Mona against the wall
near the hallway. Adele lost herself in the defined bones of

her sister's slender frame, one that had stayed about the same size, if not smaller, from the last time they had seen each other.

With the sun now pouring through the window, and the light rain vanishing, Adele felt a sudden warmth for the sisters she had not seen for so long. The doubt faded with every embrace, greeting each one with a hug, and a thousand missed "hellos," and "I love you." She breathed deeply, hugging each of her sisters until she had to finally free herself because her body surged with so much love that she thought she'd drown in tears if she didn't let go. Adele led them inside and then gave them a brief tour of the place she now called home.

The windowsill of her large window in her living room, as well as the oak bookshelf next to the couch, was filled with clay figurines of naked women and men that she had sculpted over the years in her art classes. The robust breasts and flaccid penises glimmered in the sunlight. They were fine pieces of art, Adele thought. But she noticed the expression on her sisters' faces when they looked at the figurines and then at each other. They furrowed their brows, pursed their lips, even looked at the floor, eyes cast down to avoid the finely-detailed testicles and chiselled pubic hair. But Adele didn't flinch or blush. She picked one of the sculptures and held it up to her sisters. "What do you think?" she asked, as she turned the sculpture around so that they could view it from all sides.

There was silence then Katrina finally answered, "You couldn't have painted some clothes on them?"

Adele laughed out loud. "That defeats the whole purpose of 'nude' modelling. The human body is a beautiful piece of art: a masterpiece. These sculptures," she said, placing the figure back on the shelf, "will always fall short of the genuine article."

"Okay," Katrina said quietly. "You've changed, Adele, since the last time we saw you. You're no longer sweet…"

"You mean 'innocent,' don't you? What you should really say is I'm not so much a victim, a puppet under Babba's control."

"Let's not bring that up. Let's have a pleasant time," Rima said, resting her hand on Katrina's shoulder.

"Rima's right," Mona said. She reached across and squeezed Adele's arm. "Please, let's not argue. We haven't seen each other in a long time. This isn't the time to bring up the past. Some things you can't change."

But Adele had changed. She wore makeup if she felt like it and she didn't shave her legs for a month if she was busy with her art. She no longer adhered to the strict rules of what it meant to be a good Lebanese woman. She had a new style. She wore scarves around her neck, dangled earrings and jade bangles, wore flower-printed, loose-fitting pants and East-Indian-style shirts. And she was no longer a virgin.

"Let's have fun," Mona said cheerfully, cupping Adele's cheeks with her hands. "Okay, Monkey?"

Adele couldn't help but smile at the family nickname. Others had tried calling her that when she had shared her pet name, but it didn't roll off their tongues in the same way as it did when her sisters used it.

"Does the Monkey want to visit the zoo?" Katrina teased, playfully nudging Adele's shoulders. Then Rima joined in, tickled Adele under the ribs.

Adele laughed, wrapping Rima's arms around her belly. She was the baby of the family again. Her heart told her she was still loved. And she walked out of the apartment with a smile on her lips, her sisters at her side.

They wandered for hours through hurrying crowds of downtown Toronto. They browsed in shop after shop, walked through Kensington Market, and rested on a bench by Lake Ontario, enjoying the warm sun on their faces. Adele sensed her sisters were relieved she had not brought up the topic of their strict upbringing again. But Adele wanted to talk to them about their childhood and had stopped herself from doing so several times. She wanted to tell them how she felt, how the painful memories would sometimes make it difficult to get out of bed, but she didn't know how to begin. Instead they talked about the lake, the shopping, and the latest gossip in the Ottawa Lebanese community. They ate falafel sandwiches bought from a vendor and drank warm soft drinks. When the sun began to set, they decided to head back to Adele's apartment. They walked quietly up the steps to her apartment door, their shared silence broken only by the sound of their footsteps and the classical music coming from her neighbour's stereo. When she had closed the door behind her sisters, Adele spoke. "I have to ask you something." She didn't address a particular sister, just let the question hang in the air, waiting for one of them to reply. "Has Babba really changed? Has he become kinder?"

Katrina stared at Rima. Rima stared at Mona. And Mona stared at them both. But no one's eyes fell on Adele's probing gaze. They avoided her and the now uncomfortable silence overshadowed the violet dusk that crawled on the musty walls, and the framed paintings and photographs that hung there.

"Who's this?" Rima remarked, pointing at a charcoal portrait of Scott. It was positioned on the wall closest to her bedroom. She had wanted to destroy it, but Adele couldn't bring herself to do it. She still cared about him even though he was no longer a part of her life. He was the only person she had ever been intimate with. Now in the sunset that filled her apartment, Adele glanced at the image, and replied. "That's Scott. I used to date him." She wanted to say, "we were lovers" but she bit her tongue. She knew her sisters would never understand. They were traditional, even in their choice of husbands.

"Used to date him?" Rima asked, raising her left eyebrow.

"Long story. We won't get into that now. Let's make dinner, drink a toast to our reunion." Adele walked into the kitchen and began chopping some parsley and tomatoes while her sisters set the small wooden table.

The second bottle of wine was half empty when Adele told them more about Scott. "I met him about four months ago. He's an artist too. It's like we were meant to be together but then things came crashing down ... more precisely, I came crashing down," she laughed, intoxicated by the wine.

Katrina frowned, then looked at Rima and Mona. Adele noticed the disapproval in the ridges on her forehead. "What do you mean?" Katrina asked, looking back at Adele.

She hesitated for a moment, fiddling with the near-empty bottle. "I had sex with him, and then everything changed. I was consumed with guilt about what I did. Our upbringing came back to haunt me, I guess."

"Well, you should feel guilty," Rima snapped. "Our parents didn't raise you to be a *sharmouta*."

Adele opened her mouth, closed it, then opened it again. "I'm not a whore. We were dating. It wasn't a one-night stand."

"My God, Adele, what were you thinking giving in to this guy, this Scott? Couldn't you have waited until you're married? We all did. Jeez, I thought you would've matured over the years but you're still the same disobedient child, always getting herself in over her head. Now you're not a virgin. What decent Lebanese guy would want you now?" Rima lectured.

Adele laughed sarcastically. "You sound exactly like Babba."

Rima ignored her, and looked away.

Then Mona spoke, picking up where her eldest sister left off. "You can be so pig-headed sometimes but what you did was *stupid*. How are you going to explain to your future husband about the lack of blood on your wedding night?"

Adele placed the wine bottle down on the coffee table, sighed and looked out the darkened window. The streets had grown silent over the evening and even the music from her neighbour's stereo had ceased. She had thought she would be safe with her sisters, and then they attacked her.

"How are you going to explain that, Ms. Know-it-all, huh?" Mona asked.

"I can always blame it on the doctor who gave me my first pelvic exam!"

Her sisters looked at each other, then lowered their heads as they remembered the experience Adele had endured years before. Adele turned on her heel and ran into the bathroom, slamming the door behind her. She sat on the toilet with her head in her hands and heard the shuffling of feet on the floor outside the bathroom door, the clattering of plates and glasses in the kitchen. But in a few minutes, these sounds were drowned out by her sobs.

On the way back to the living room, she felt sad and confused. Maybe it was the wine—she had never drunk so much wine—but no, it was the presence of her family, a past she had tried to disguise in the oil colours she mixed on her palette and then placed on the canvas. Her sisters were fast asleep on the foldout couch. Rima's arms were splayed across Mona and Katrina's chests. They looked comfortable together, Adele thought. In spite of their presence, she had never felt more alone. The darkness engulfed her as she crept past her sisters and walked into her bedroom, and crawled under the sheets of her bed.

She awoke in the morning to the cheerful song of the sparrows on the tree outside the window. Morning was her favourite time of day. She loved the fresh breath of the world blowing into her room, making her heart swell with a sense of connectedness. But when she remembered the previous night's argument with her sisters, she frowned. She got out of bed and listened to the rattle of pots and pans travelling from the kitchen down the hallway to the slightly open door of her bedroom.

She pulled on a robe and walked into the kitchen less than enthusiastically. "Good morning," she said, wiping her eyes of the restless sleep she had endured.

"Hello, Monkey," Mona said, smiling. "Look, we were

just talking about what happened last night and we want to apologize. You've always been a little eccentric..."

"You're an artist, after all," Katrina added in a light tone.

"Aren't all artists fucked up?" Rima said, laughing.

Mona continued, "Well ... we're sorry we upset you."

"You don't have to apol..."

"Yes, we do. It was shitty of us to gang up on you. I don't agree with what you did, but it's your life and well..." she stopped, then continued, "it's your life and..." She tried again but still couldn't finish her thought.

Adele was shocked and delighted. She suddenly realized that she wasn't dreaming: her sisters had opened their minds. They had changed. And maybe it wasn't hopeless to think that her father had done the same.

After that visit, the letters from Mona, with postscripts from Rima and Katrina, began to arrive more frequently. They wrote more intensely about their father, and reminisced about the good times in their childhood. One letter brought Adele back to a memory she would later transform on canvas. It read:

Dear Adele (a.k.a. Monkey),

I was driving towards the Experimental Farm on my way to the grocer's when I decided to take another route, so I turned on the narrow streets surrounding the farm. Do you remember those colossal trees that lined that area? Remember how Babba used to zig-zag the car on the deserted road and how we burst into laughter? As I was driving, I did the same thing and then a strange thing happened—instead of laughing, I burst into tears. I haven't cried like that since childhood. How odd that a happy memory brought such sadness. There were happy moments in our childhood, weren't there? I guess I was crying because there were so few. All the other stuff suffocated the good memories. Can the noose be loosened,

*can the chain of a swing help us soar, and keep us floating
rather than being confined by the rope around our necks?*

*On that joyful note, how are you? Have you finished
your latest painting yet?*

Love, Mona

Dear Adele,

*Thanks so much for the letter and photograph of
your work-in-progress. It's looking good. Mama and
Babba would be so proud of you. Really, they would. I
know you may disagree but think back to your Grade 8
graduation. I know the dreaded junior high school years
are the last thing you want to remember, but humour your
older sister for one moment. Grade 8 graduation: Principal
requests applause be held back until the entire class had
gathered their diplomas. Babba and Mama stand up and
clap so loud when they see you walking across the stage
to get yours. Their pride captured on a roll of film by our
neighbour. Ah, the angst of teenage years! But in spite of
your embarrassment, they were so proud of you. May I
show them the photograph of your art? I will understand if
your answer is no but think about this, if we hadn't had the
parents we had, hadn't had the childhood, though difficult
as it was, would you be the artist that you are today?*

*Ah, I sound so wise! Who'd have thought me—the
pretty one—would be so philosophical! Ha! Ha!*

Lots of love, Mona

*P.S. Rima and Katrina agree—you've become a wonderful
painter!*

Dear Adele,

*Babba and Mama pass on their good wishes to you
and want to thank you for letting them see your work-
in-progress. You should have seen Babba's face when he
saw the picture. A smile (now that's no small thing, as you*

know) appeared on his mouth. What's more extraordinary were the tears that came to his eyes! He said your art took him back home. The image of the olive grove and the young man gathering the year's harvest delivered him to his homeland again. I will always remember that look of pride on his face and only wished I had photographed it for you to see. Just take my word for it, Adele, you brought him to tears. Now that's a big accomplishment—to elicit emotion from your hardest critic (though, I believe he's becoming your biggest fan)! You should hear how he brags to all the customers about his artist daughter. I'm envious to say the least. After all, I thought I was the favourite! (just teasing)

Love, Mona

P.S. Do you think Babba and Mama can come visit? Rima and Katrina send their love too!

Dear Adele,

Something is wrong with Babba. At first, we thought it was just the flu but the vomiting is consistent after each meal and sometimes even on an empty stomach. The 24-48 hour flu bug shouldn't last over a month. Mama and Babba are sorry they can't make your art show but given his recent illness, it's not a good idea for him to travel. He's scheduled for various tests and we hope it's just an ulcer and nothing else. I'll see you next week for your opening. And hopefully I'll have good news about Babba's condition.

See you soon!

Love, Mona

CHAPTER 21

ADELE'S ART EXHIBITION WAS HELD in a converted ware-house-turned-art gallery. There were more people than she had anticipated. She nervously paced the backroom, peering over the ledge of the wall and staring at all the guests who stood with their hands on their hips, tilting their heads slightly in that deep-concentrated sort of way, gazing at her paintings, her creations. She jumped when she felt someone squeezing her shoulder. It was Mona, who leaned in close and kissed her on both cheeks. "Thanks for coming," Adele whispered. She glanced over Mona's shoulders, searching the room for Rima and Katrina but the other two sisters were not there.

"They couldn't make it." Mona reached out and clasped Adele's hands in her own. They were trembling badly. "Don't be nervous, Adele. Everyone loves your work. I heard glowing remarks when I walked across the room. And if they don't like it, then fuck them."

The sisters laughed and then joined the crowd admiring the paintings that recreated their past and their parents' homeland, and that evoked the smell of cedars, the bitter taste of olives, and the sweet, pinkish pulp of figs.

As they left the art gallery, raindrops began to fall and Mona suggested that they go into a church nearby, not so much to get out of the sudden downpour but to talk.

When they walked inside, the smell of incense floated in their nostrils. It was ironic that the closest church happened to be Orthodox. Adele made the sign of the cross and slid into the pew beside her sister. They sat on the bench, staring straight ahead at the altar and at the colourful icons of saints that lined the walls.

After a brief moment of silence, Mona said in a quiet voice, "We need to talk about Babba."

Adele studied her sister's face. The smile she had at the opening was now gone. Even the darkness from the clouds and low lights of the church couldn't hide the sadness in her eyes, her sunken cheeks. "Babba's very ill, Adele. I didn't want to bring it up at your opening earlier. It would be just like Babba to ruin your show," she laughed softly.

Adele didn't laugh. "What's wrong with him? The ulcer again?"

Mona shook her head, stared down at her hands on her lap. "It's more serious. He has stomach cancer. The tumour has advanced to the point that it's blocking the passage of food and that's why he's vomiting. He's lost so much weight. He doesn't look the same. The doctors say the prognosis isn't good."

"What does that mean?" Adele said, alarmed by the news.

"He's dying. They give him a few weeks, a month at the most. The cancer is very advanced, very aggressive."

"No," Adele said, "No, no," she said again, surprised by her breaking voice. Mona reached over, put her arm around Adele and pulled her close. Adele rested her head on Mona's shoulder.

"Come home, Adele," she whispered. "Come see Babba before…" Mona hesitated, wiping the tears from Adele's face. "Come." She lifted Adele's head. She then clasped her hands together. "Come. Let's pray."

With her heart throbbing in her chest, Adele lowered her head, joined her hands and prayed for a man she had once wished was dead.

A few days later, she paced the living room of her apartment waiting for Mona to finish packing. She began to worry. What if things hadn't changed? What if her father had remained the same? she wondered. She stopped pacing, stood still with her hands on her hips, stared outside; the sound of traffic began to float into the open window. Walking towards it, Adele leaned over and rested her hands on the windowsill. She spread her fingers and examined them as if the answer to her 'what if' questions rested in the lines of her knuckles. Suddenly she dropped her hands, swivelled and walked about the room. There had been a time, months ago, when she had imagined what it would be like to reunite with her father. She had devised various scenarios—him hugging her until she could no longer breathe, him slapping her until she was bruised or him being totally indifferent, walking about the house as if she had never left. She stood still and for a moment, she placed herself in her father's worn shoes, felt the soft leather on her feet, the warmth left from him. Then she rubbed her face, flung herself on the sofa and began to cry. He was dying. The old man was dying! She had to set aside her anxieties, her fears. When Mona had finally emerged, suitcases in hand, the tears from Adele's eyes had dissipated.

They hurried down the wooden stairs, the creaks echoing through the hallway. As they emerged from the old apartment house, a strong wind forced the suitcases in their hands to hit against their legs. The sisters quickened their pace, nearly slipping on the leaves still wet from the early morning downpour. When they reached Mona's car, Adele leaned on the passenger side and watched the wind hurl other passersby as if urging them towards their destinies. Adele winked at a little child, her tiny fingers entwined with her mother's. The girl shyly looked away, pulled on her mother's arm and hurried her pace. The mother looked up at Adele and smiled, then explained, "She's shy."

"I was the same way. Still am," Adele replied, light-heartedly. "Have a good day!"

"You too!" the little girl piped up. Then she tugged on her mother's sleeve again. "See, Mom, I'm not shy!"

Turning away, Adele stared at Mona. She opened the trunk and carefully placed the suitcases inside. Then she walked over to the driver's side. A smile rose from Adele's full lips. Her eyes twinkled. "What?" Mona asked, playfully flipping back her layered hair. "Did the damn wind blow my hair out of place?"

Adele shook her head. "No."

"Then why are you smiling so much?"

"I'm happy, that's all. I'm so glad we're sisters again."

"We were always sisters, Adele," Mona answered. "You just need to learn to pick up the phone more often. Better yet, get the internet. Email is the new form of letters." She chuckled.

"You know I hate computers," Adele grimaced.

"I know but you need to change that attitude."

"Do I have to?" she whined.

"Yes, my dear Monkey. Get with the times. We're no longer in the seventies."

Laughing, the sisters slid into the car.

CHAPTER 22

ADELE SLEPT THROUGH ALMOST THE ENTIRE five-hour drive to Ottawa. She awoke as Mona eased the car into the driveway beside her father's grocery store. She rubbed her eyes and looked up at the sign to the store: the letters of her father's name were chipped and the green paint was fading. Youssef's Grocery was now Ousse's rocery. Moving her hand along the yellow stucco of the shop, Adele felt the bumpiness she had memorized as a child all those times she had sat on the concrete stoop by the side of the door. Now when she pulled her hand away and examined it, crumbled stone stuck to her palm. For a while she stood still, studying the boarded-up store. Mona had mentioned that after Babba's illness, they had decided to close the shop for good. None of Adele's sisters or their husbands had use for the old corner store. A sadness overwhelmed Adele as she gazed at the emblem of her father's livelihood. This building was dying too.

Bits of memory flooded over her as she walked inside the house. She swore she could smell the strong scent of *ahweh* and allspice. Not much had changed over the years. She stood in the hallway for a few minutes, studying the cross that hung above the door. It was a bronze crucifix with Jesus' arms splayed and feet folded over each, knees slightly raised and off to the side. Then she looked at the brown velvet curtains covering the large window of the living room. Only some light managed to push through the curtains, illuminating the porcelain figurines her mother had bought from gift shops in Little Italy. Time had not altered the interior of the Azar house. Adele turned her head towards the doorway leading into the dining room and kitchen area. Her mother's voice rose in a high-pitched squeal, her footsteps hurrying on the hardwood floor. "Adele!" she shouted, wiping her hands on her apron. You're home! My *habibti* is home." Before Adele could open her mouth in reply, Samira pulled her close. Adele gently stroked her mother's back as they clung to each other. Then her mother's sobs began, shaking Adele so much that her legs grew weak and she thought she might fall to her knees. She hadn't expected this welcome, such warmth. When Samira finally let go, Adele looked at her mother. It had been a while since they had stood face-to-face, since she had heard her mother address her affectionately as *habibti*, or honey. Tenderness filled her heart. Samira's black hair was short and tinged with strands of grey; it also looked brittle. A few extra pounds rounded her high cheek-boned face and folds of skin now sagged around her cheeks and mouth. Her full lips were chapped and her palms cracked. Adele felt their sandpaper texture when Samira cupped her face and stroked her cheeks. "Too thin, *habibti*, too thin. Don't you eat in Toronto?"

Adele smiled weakly, resisting the urge to cry at the aged appearance of her mother. "The food doesn't add up to yours, Mama. Nothing can replace your wonderful cooking."

Samira beamed. "Are you hungry?" She took Adele by the hand and led her into the kitchen.

The table was full of food. Platters of *maza*—*taboulleh*, *hummus*, *kibbeh nayeh*, stuffed grape leaves—had been prepared and even a small glass bottle of *arak* sat on the table. Samira pulled out a chair then motioned for Adele to sit. Mona sat across from her. "Welcome home," Samira whispered.

Finally, the tears streamed down Adele's face. Samira stood across from her, wiped her face with the end of her apron.

"No tears. No tears, *habibti*. You eat your Mama's food. Eat, no more cry."

Adele nodded. She sat on the chair and let her mother dish out large portions onto her plate.

By the time Adele finished her meal, she was ready to go upstairs. She stared at the staircase and remembered all the times she had raced up these steps two at a time, whether in a fit of happiness or rage. Now she slowly ascended and listened to the creaky notes each one made. Midway, she stopped and looked down at the hardwood floor of the living room. She heard the voices of her sister and mother conversing in the kitchen. They had thought it was better for her to see her father alone. And she had agreed, but now with his bedroom only a couple feet away, she was not sure it had been wise to orchestrate this private meeting. After a moment of standing perfectly still, she thought she might faint, and tumble down the flight of stairs. But she brought her mind back to the present. Her father was dying. She couldn't hold off this difficult reunion, couldn't leave and return next week because he might not be around in a week. Taking a deep breath, she clasped the banister and pulled herself up and up, her feet seemingly taking over her shaky body. What could her father possibly do to her now? What could he possibly say to her? She was no longer a child; his words couldn't bring her to tears anymore.

It wasn't his words that made her eyes well up as she stood at the open door of her parents' bedroom. Mona had warned her but Adele hadn't expected her sister's description of their father's illness to be so accurate. When she looked across at him, tucked quietly under the thin sheets, she hadn't expected his potbelly to have vanished, his hipbones to be jutting under the covers, his body shrivelled and small like a child's. She hadn't expected the jaundice that had yellowed his pale skin. His sunken eyes were closed in a nap but as soon as Adele inched forward, the floorboards creaked, waking him up.

"Sorry Babba for startling you…"

"It's okay," he interrupted.

Adele sat on the edge of the bed and hesitated for a brief second before resting her hand on her father's fingers. She gently squeezed his hand; it had become smaller than hers. Tears fell from her eyes and landed on her father's slowly rising chest. She realized every breath was a struggle for him. For a while, they stared at each other without speaking. She searched his face for signs of the man who had called her so many hurtful things, but all she saw was an old person with sad and sunken eyes. He was looking at her tenderly, his mouth opening and closing as if he wanted to say something. But he remained silent.

Finally, in a cracked voice, he said, "Are you all right, *babba*? I know I haven't said this often and I'll always regret that…" he paused and looked past Adele's shoulders, then brought his gaze back to her face. "I love you. I always loved you. I just didn't know how to say it or show it. You're my beautiful daughter. You're worth more than a hundred boys put together. I should've been a better…"

This time it was Adele who stopped the words. She got up and rushed out of the bedroom. Leaning against the hallway wall, she slid down and sat crouched, clutching her belly. She rocked back and forth. She couldn't listen to the words she had so long yearned for when growing up. She glanced up and peered into the open door of his room. She watched her father weakly raise his hand to his eyes and drag his fingertips across darkened eyelids.

It was late in the night when Adele felt someone's hands on her shoulders, jostling her awake from her sleep. Samira then walked across the room and flicked on the light switch.

"Hurry, Adele," Samira said, her face pale. "It's your father."

Adele rubbed her eyes and immediately sat up. "What's wrong?"

Samira shook her head. "I don't know." She motioned with her hands. "Come quick."

Without her earlier hesitation, she ran out of her room and into her parents' bedroom. When she entered, her father was shivering under the sheets. She reached underneath the covers and began rubbing his legs and arms.

"I'm so cold. I can't stop shaking, Adele."

Adele rubbed harder in an attempt to warm his flesh.

"Warm now?" she asked in a quiet voice.

Youssef shook his head and spoke between chattering teeth. "No, no. Cold. I'm so cold. Help me." Adele slid under the covers beside her father and pulling the blankets tightly over them, while her mother watched, her hands covering her mouth. Adele wrapped her arms around him, pulling him close, letting her own body warm his. She held him so tight that she could smell his flesh; the scent of old age and unkempt hair. Slowly, the shaking stopped. Adele held tighter, only shifting slightly even when she felt the urine slide down her father's legs and onto the mattress, drenching her own pajamas. She didn't flinch. "I'm sorry," Youssef mumbled, "I'm so sorry." His face crumpled and he began to weep. He was the man of the house—a Lebanese man—and he couldn't even control the urine that trickled down his own legs and onto Adele's. Her chest tightened; she thought her heart might explode. When she looked at her mother she saw that her hands were now pressed together in prayer.

The next morning Adele awoke with the bright sun blinding her half-closed eyes. She blinked a few times before lifting her hand to cover her eyes from the light flowing through the large window of her parents' bedroom and filling the entire space. She looked at her father lying next to her, his face tired and weary. Slowly, she slid out of the bed, her body stiff and her pajamas crinkled with her father's urine, the odor permeating the air. She hadn't realized things would be this bad, that the man she had once fought constantly with would be reduced to a helpless infant. She had heard and read about cancer but hadn't realized how the disease robbed its victims of dignity—the vomiting, the shakes, the loss of bladder control. Now as she stood beside her parents' bed and gazed at her father, depleted and worn, she began to understand the devastating effects of the illness. She turned away from him and looked out the window again. The sky was a pale blue, and the clouds were tinged with gold. When her father began to stir, she moved closer to the bed.

"Good morning, *babba*," he said, smiling weakly. "I'm sorry about last night."

Adele raised up her hand. "No need to apologize."

"But I need to," he said, struggling to breathe. Each breath was shallow and sounded so painful that she wished she could help him by giving some of her own breath. He turned his head to face her, his white hair dishevelled on the pillowcase. "I wasn't a good father. I could've been better. I should've been better. Do you know how proud I am of you?" His voice began to break.

She smiled weakly.

"I'm so proud of you. You're a very clever girl. Smarter than me, smarter than the entire family. I don't know how such a smart girl came from me. Look at me," he said, lightly patting his chest. "I'm a peasant boy, a retired grocer..."

"Who supported an entire family," Adele added.

"I suppose," he sighed, "but I didn't support you in the way you needed."

Adele looked down at her hands.

Youssef cleared his throat. "I wasn't a good father. I yelled too much. I criticized too much and praised too little. I made your life miserable, so miserable that you had to run away. Why else would you have left?"

She shuffled her feet, and grasped his hands, hoping to comfort him.

"I don't want to be remembered as a bad father. I hope one day you'll remember the man that I have become. I hope you'll remember the good memories. We did have some good times, no? Adele, please don't remember all the junk I stuck in your brain. Please, will you do that for me?" He lifted his head off the pillow a little bit and looked directly in Adele's teary eyes. "Adele?"

Adele wanted to escape her father's sudden openness, but he would not let her go.

He pleaded, "Adele? Adele?"

She couldn't say anything.

"I can't make you forgive me," he said softly, "but I need you to know how sorry I am for all the pain I caused you."

Why had she spent so much time fighting with her father? she wondered. And now he wanted her to forgive him, to remember only good memories. Was that even possible? She needed to be alone, needed time to think. She excused herself and went down the stairs and into the kitchen, where she grabbed a container of allspice. Then she flew back up the stairs and entered the bathroom. She let the bathtub fill with water and, as the water rose, she sprinkled in the allspice. Returning to her parents' bedroom, she reached over to her father, slid her hands under his back, wrapped her arms around his frail body, and lifted him out of the bed. She struggled down the hallway, dragging him along the floor into the bathroom where she began to undress him. Her mother appeared at the door and said, "Let me help you, Adele."

Adele shook her head and said, "You're tired, Mama. Let me help while I'm here. Go rest for a bit. I'm okay."

"Thank you, *habibti*," Samira said as she turned and went back down the stairs.

Adele stared at the reflection in the mirror of the shrunken man across from her. His head was bowed, his hands covered his penis. She submerged him into the warm water, the smell of allspice mingling with the steam.

CHAPTER 23

THE STEAM OF THE BATH AND THE SCENT of allspice and jasmine soap rose around them. Adele focused on the tufts of grey at her father's temple. She didn't let her gaze fall below his waist. On her knees beside the tub, she ran a cloth along her father's back until he whispered, "Thank you, Adele." Sobs escaped his throat. "I know I should be a man and stop crying, but..."

Adele interjected. "It's all right, Babba."

He wiped his eyes, then nose. "I feel like a child again."

Adele bit her lower lip before scooping some water in a plastic container and slowly pouring it over her father's body.

For the next few weeks, Adele and her father settled in a routine. She'd help her mother by bathing her father, dressing him, and trying to feed him, though his stomach always refused food. Then Adele cleaned the remnants of the meal her mother had carefully prepared from a bucket beside the bed. Oftentimes, she simply sat at his bedside and listened to him tell her stories.

"I felt so disloyal to my heritage for abandoning my birth country, my mother. I should've stayed in Lebanon but now it's too late. I thought the only way I could preserve my culture was through my children. I wanted you to speak Arabic, eat our foods, learn our customs and traditions. I wanted you to embrace it fully—be fully Lebanese, not half. What kind of life did I have here?" He shuddered and sank further under the covers.

She had often wondered what it was like for her parents to have left their homeland for a country so new, so different. Were they as scared as she had been when she left her family? Now she knew. She gave her father a gentle smile and said, "You raised a family here. You did pretty well for someone who didn't know the language. You should feel proud. It was no small thing to pack up and leave and start fresh in a foreign country. You succeeded, Babba. You should feel proud."

Youssef frowned. "I was like my father."

"It's okay, Babba. It's okay."

"No, it's not." He shook his head, tears on his face too. "I made you feel less than what you really are—a kind, beautiful person."

"It's okay," she mumbled.

"It's that easy, Adele? Can you forgive so easily?"

No, she wanted to say, but she didn't. He was dying.

"You're an amazing daughter," he said in a low voice, barely audible.

She laid her head on his flattened belly and began to weep all over again. She felt her father's hand weakly smoothing her curls.

"Did you know that I had another sister, Adele?" Youssef said to Adele while she changed his socks.

"Besides Aunt Nabiha?"

"Imagine that! My sister Nabiha thinks she's the one and only sometimes, eh?" Youssef laughed until he began to retch. Adele quickly picked up the bucket beside his bed and held it under her father's mouth. Afterwards, she walked into the bathroom and emptied the vomit into the toilet then headed into her father's bedroom again.

They picked up the conversation as if nothing unusual had happened. "Aunt Nabiha means well, I suppose," Adele said.

"Well, my mother had another daughter before Nabiha was born. Her name was Hanan and she was a beautiful baby. My mother loved her dearly. But one day Hanan just stopped breathing. I remember poking her while she was in the crib and she wouldn't wake up, so I ran to my mother and when my mother picked her up, Hanan was a lifeless doll in her arms. I will always remember the anguished wails that came out of my Mama's mouth, such a sad song for my baby sister."

Adele slumped on the chair across from her father's bed. "I never heard about this." She looked down at her hands, rubbed them together, realizing she knew little about her father.

"I didn't tell anyone but your mother. I pushed it out of my memory but now my thoughts are turning to Hanan, that precious angel baby."

"Sito must have been devastated."

"Yes, she couldn't even attend Hanan's funeral. I had to carry her tiny body into the crypt. My aunts had wrapped Hanan in a white cloth as if she were being baptized. I had to carry her into the burial place because neither one of them would do it. I was afraid and I didn't want to do it either, but they said, *Youssef, you must be a man and carry your little sister to her final resting place. Don't look at the other bodies, just place her in an empty spot and come back out, okay?* I didn't want to but I had no choice. The crypt was so small and smelled of rot like the way vegetables do when you let them get too old. There was so much dust too. I thought I was going to be blinded by the haze, but I couldn't rub my eyes because I had Hanan in my arms. And as quickly as I entered, I found a place and left her next to a body that must have been there for several years because spiders were crawling on the old yellowed cloth. When I emerged outside, my aunts ran to me and hugged me tightly while kissing my cheeks. They kept telling me that I was a brave boy but I wasn't so brave, I had wet my pants. When my father saw the stain, he pulled me out of my aunts' embraces and slapped me across the face. *You're nothing but a kalb. Worse than a dog, because even a kalb knows how to raise his leg without pissing himself.* I remember running away to the river where I cleaned myself and wished it had been me that had died and not my sister Hanan."

Adele got up and stood in front of her father. "I'm sorry, Babba."

"Don't be, *babba.* We all have our hardships. These times make us stronger, don't they?"

"Do you really believe that?" Adele asked, her voice rising.

"I have to. How else can I explain why I treated you so badly?"

Breathing deeply, Adele left the room and headed downstairs; she needed a break.

Two days later, Adele sat on the edge of her father's bed and held a glass of water against his dry lips. He hadn't eaten much in several days but on this day, he requested a small glass of water. He took slow, forced sips, most of the water slipping down his chin. Adele's long fingers wiped his chin with efficiency. She had learned over the past weeks about the work of a nurse or caregiver. By the end of each day, she was exhausted and saddened. She'd crawl into her bed and fall into a deep sleep. Each morning she mustered the strength to get out of bed, shower, dress, eat breakfast, and begin the whole process of taking care of her ailing father once more. Where she found the courage, she didn't know, but every day she felt more determined to help her father die in a peaceful and dignified way.

She smiled as she held the glass against her father's thin, chapped lips and remembered all the times he had done so for her when she was too young to hold a glass by herself. There were good memories; they were just buried deeper in her mind, hidden by the negativity that sat at the top. Slowly, every day, the daily routine she had developed with her father helped each beautiful memory to ripen like the grapes on the

vines of the homemade trellis her father had built years ago
in their front yard for Samira's grape leaves.

Adele placed the glass on the bedside table then wiped the
leftover drops of saliva and water around her father's mouth.
His frail fingers reached up and encircled her wrist. "Thank
you," he said in a hoarse voice. When he dropped his hand,
Adele got up and sat on the chair across from his bed. With a
sinking heart, she contemplated her father's gaunt body. She
used to tease him about the roundness of his belly by saying,
"so when is the baby due?" She touched her wrist and felt the
coldness his flesh had left on her skin. His ankles were now
as thin as her wrists, she realized, staring at the shape of his
legs under the blanket. She watched the rapid rise of his chest.
Each breath was a struggle. Suddenly Youssef closed his eyes
and let his head fall back on the pillow. She moved closer and
gently stroked his face. Youssef opened his eyes again and
smiled weakly.

Adele finally spoke the words she had always wanted to say
but hadn't known how to, ashamed to show to this man who
had hurt her in so many ways, how much she needed him. "I
love you, Babba."

Youssef smiled again, his eyes shiny and wet. His breathing
became shallow and his eyes opened and closed as if fighting
an oncoming, urgent sleep. "I love you too. Remember that.
Remember how much I love you. Take care of your mother."
He paused, licked his lips.

Adele called out, turning her head in the direction of the
hallway, "Mama! Hurry! Come quick!"

Youssef smiled again. "You're a good daughter. Promise me
you'll remember me. Promise me ... remember me."

"You're my father. How can I ever forget you? We still have
time. Don't close your eyes, Babba. Stay awake," she said,
stroking his forehead, then resting her head on his chest. She
listened to his rapid heartbeat. "We still have so much to say,
so much ... stay," she pleaded.

Youssef grew silent. He closed his eyes, a small smile lifted his mouth.

Adele buried her face in his chest. She didn't hear her mother's quickening footsteps, only Samira's wailing.

CHAPTER 24

IN THE YEAR THAT HER FATHER DIED, Adele took a sabbatical from her studies and returned home to settle the paperwork and sale of the store her father had owned and operated for thirty years. She hadn't expected the property to sell so quickly, but a local developer had plans to convert the corner store and house she had grown up in into condominiums.

Adele stood outside and shuffled her boots through a pile of leaves that had blown in front of the yellow grocery store. Leaning against the exterior of the shop, dried bits of stucco sticking to her palms, she watched the movers take down the Coca-Cola sign with her father's name plastered in green letters. Its rusted hinges creaked in the cool autumn breeze. Shivering as the wind blew through her trench coat, she pulled the collar close to her neck. The men teetered on the steel ladders placed on each side of the rod that had supported her father's sign for the thirty years it had swayed in rainstorms, or stood perfectly still on humid summer days. Now it was as dead as the shopkeeper whose name was peeling and fading from its metal surface. Adele jumped when one of the worker's pliers fell from his grip and came crashing down on the asphalt. She picked up the tool and handed it back to the man.

She let herself sink onto the cement stoop beside the store. Her father was gone. His store was gone. The life she had known with him was gone. Shortly after his death, the initial shock and disbelief had transformed into the cold reality that he was really gone. She had slept restlessly for weeks after his death and it was only now that she could sleep through the night, rising only with the sun and not a full moon. The coldness of the stoop filtered through her trousers forcing her to get up and pace, listening to the opening and closing of the toolbox, the jangle of tool belts. She turned around in time to spot the sign being swallowed between the folds of a blue moving blanket, then buried in the mover's truck. Adele had arranged to store what was left of her childhood home in the basements of her sisters' houses.

After the moving truck left, Adele walked inside the house. She glanced at the naked walls, stripped of all the photographs and paintings. There was nothing left that spoke of her family's history. How could an entire lifetime be erased with the removal of a collection of artefacts? She thought of the many voices that used to blow through the hallways like a gentle breeze and sometimes a hurricane. She recalled the many times she had run up the stairs she was staring at this moment. She wondered whether her fingerprints would still be on the banister, whether her footprints were imprinted in the steps. Suddenly, she heard the floorboards in the hallway leading away from the kitchen heave. She looked across at her mother. Samira had lost several pounds since Youssef's death. Her dress hung off her body, which now seemed stooped and shrunken; the weight loss had made all her clothes ill-fitting, but Adele knew her mother couldn't bring herself to buy new ones.

"So everything is gone?" Samira asked, throwing her hands up in the air.

"Yes, Mama," Adele replied, noting the resigned, sad look on her mother's face.

"Will you change your mind?" Samira asked, mustering a smile. There was a strained hopefulness in her voice, a yearning for Adele to conform at last to the Lebanese way, to move back home with her, take care of her Mama.

Adele sadly shook her head. "I can't. I need to get back to Toronto. I have a life waiting for me there."

"You can have a life here again, *habibti*."

"No, that's not possible. I'm sorry, Mama," Adele said, her voice cracking.

"Anything is possible."

"Not that, Mama. I can't do it."

"You don't want to do it," Samira sighed. She sat down on the stairs. "You have always wanted to do things your own way. Why couldn't you be more like your sisters? They followed tradition. They listened to all I had to say. But you," she threw her hands up in the air again, letting them fall hard on her lap. "God rest his soul, but your Babba always said you were a little different. I tried to teach you all that I had been taught but you always struggled against everything I knew." She looked out the window next to the front door. Several leaves had blown up the steps, scraping against the concrete as if begging to come inside. Then a gush of wind scattered the leaves down the small street Adele had grown up on. Samira began to cry, her shoulders rising up and down until she bent forward. Kneeling in front of her mother, Adele stroked her head, smoothed the unruly greying curls.

Samira looked up at her, her eyes glassy and red. "I failed you as a mother."

Adele shook her head. "No you didn't, Mama. I just wanted my own life, not yours."

Samira took Adele's face in her hands and stroked it gently. She held her like that for a moment, before she finally let go, rose from the steps, and said, "Well, I don't want to live with your sisters and I can't live alone in this country. I should've learned the language but that's too late."

Adele stood up too and said, "No, it's not late. I can sign you up for ESL classes. I'll find you a nice apartment."

Samira shook her head. "Too late for that. This isn't my home anymore. It never was. I was always an outsider."

"What are you going to do?"

"Well, I guessed you wouldn't stay with me, so I made a few plans of my own with the help of your Aunt Nabiha. Before you go back to Toronto, will you do something for me?"

She nodded, leaned in close to her mother. Her throat tightened as she listened carefully to her mother's words.

They ate in silence that night on the living room floor. Adele had laid an old bed sheet in the middle of the room and placed the take-out Chinese food she had ordered for her and her mother on it. After a few bites, Adele pushed away her plate. She glanced across at Samira, lifting a sweet and sour chicken ball to her mouth, the red plum sauce sliding around the corners of her full lips. "Are you sure you want to do this, Mama?" Adele asked, her voice barely a whisper.

Samira stopped chewing, put her fork down. "This isn't home to me, Adele. Like Ottawa isn't your home anymore. Your sisters have their own families. They don't need me. Anyway, I can't live here without your father. He did everything for me."

Samira blinked rapidly but tears slipped out anyway. Adele tried not to blame her father for her mother's lack of the English language, her lack of sophistication when it came to functioning in this city. She pressed her teeth together and tried to stop the pressure she felt rising in her stomach, chest, and throat. He was dead. And it was too late for her mother to return to the first few months in Canada before she had met Youssef. Adele remembered how her mother had spoken fondly of the few ESL classes she had taken upon her arrival in Canada. Then she met Youssef and she relinquished her desire to learn English to babies, cooking, and housekeeping.

Samira quickly wiped her eyes then folded her hands on her lap. The wind thrashed the branches of the trees against the brick exterior of the house, making Adele look out the window. She watched autumn's urgent push for change. The empty room they sat in, feasting on their last dinner of egg rolls and chop suey in this abandoned house, was a sign of an ending and a beginning. Adele lifted her head and took a deep breath. The room smelled of Asian spices and dampness. She reached across and placed her hand on top of her mother's.

CHAPTER 25

WHEN THEY ARRIVED IN KFARMICHKI a couple of days later, Adele rested her hand on her mother's arm, squeezing it gently. Samira put her hand on hers and smiled. "It's good to be home. It's so good to be home." She knelt on the ground, clasped a handful of dry earth, rose and opened her clenched fist; the pebbles fell through her fingers, the wind picking them up and swirling them towards the low mountains bordering the village.

It had been years since anyone had inhabited the old stone house across the mountains. It had belonged to Samira's parents, both long dead now. Since her siblings had built their own homes in the village, the dwelling had been empty for a long time. But the red brick shingles of the roof still stood bright against the immense blue sky of the Bekaa Valley. The day before, Adele and Samira had removed the wooden planks from the windows and now golden rays entered the small house, awakening it after a slumber. They scrubbed the walls, floors, cupboards, tub and sinks; they made the old home liveable again. This was the second time Adele had visited her parents' homeland, but this trip didn't have the strain and deception of the first one. There was no secret betrothal for her. No extended family. Just her and Samira in an old, deserted house that now gleamed though it smelled of cleaning detergents from the ferocious scrub-down it had endured.

The following day, Adele poured coffee into a small cup. She held it to her lips, her mouth tensing, her eyes pinching at the bitter taste. Opening the front door, she walked out into the yard, and lay the cup on the ledge of the window. With her hands on her hips, she stared into the distance, admiring the glorious mountains and fields. The field directly in front of her was empty except for grazing sheep and a shepherd. The shepherd's staff bobbed up and down in rhythm to his staggered walk. Adele raised her right hand to her eyes, protecting herself from the rising sun. She squinted harder. The shepherd had a long, scraggily beard and a thin frame. Dishevelled hair fell around his face, some strands lightened by the sun, others a dark chestnut with streaks of silver. He wore a tattered tweed blazer with worn patches on the elbows. Adele lifted her hands to her mouth before she began to run into the field, the clean windows absorbing the dusty trail of her sprint.

"Elias!" she shouted midway, waving frantically. But the shepherd didn't look up. His eyes were fixed on his flock until Adele stood before him, out of breath and clutching his arms. "Elias! It's you. My God, I thought I'd never see you again." She pulled him into her body and embraced him. His arms stayed close to his sides as he eased himself back. Adele let him go. She gazed into the greenish-blue eyes she had admired years before. Now there was a vacant, glassy look in them— the look of defeat. "Elias," she repeated, "It's Adele. Do you remember me?"

He remained silent, the staff in his hand slowly shaking.

She then held his head between her hands, brought his face close to hers. "It's Adele. Remember how you helped me. You helped me." She began to sob. Letting go of his face, she turned and looked back at the house again, and saw the silhouette of her mother standing by the doorframe. She started to walk towards her mother when she felt a hand gently squeezing her shoulder, and heard her name. "Adele. Adele. Adele," Elias repeated over and over, his strained vocal chords learning to speak their first words since his long and self-imposed silence.

"I didn't think I'd see you again," Elias said, his voice cracking.

"I felt the same way. I often thought about you. Remembered how sweet and kind you were to me. How you helped me escape. You made life better for me."

He cleared his throat. "You did that on your own. I only got you out of here. You did the rest yourself."

Adele smiled at Elias, then turned towards the house. Her mother stood there with a basket of mint leaves in her hands. Adele began to cross the field, then turned and motioned for Elias to follow her. Moments later, they stood in front of Samira. "Mama, do you remember Elias?" Adele asked.

Samira nodded. "*Marhaba*, Elias." Then said to her daughter, "I'm heading to my brother's for the day. I'll see you in a few hours, okay." She kissed Adele on the forehead, then touched Elias on the shoulder, addressing him in a forced politeness, "It is good to see you again."

Elias nodded, then timidly looked at Adele who flashed him a kind smile.

Samira lifted her head in the direction of the sheep. "Don't forget your flock."

"No, Auntie, I won't forget," he said, his voice dropping a little.

Adele's eyes followed her mother, watching her walk down the dirt road to her uncle's house. Then she stared back at Elias. His eyelids were shut tight as if holding back the tears she had seen well up in them when her mother spoke to him. It wasn't fair. Elias hadn't done anything wrong. He wasn't to blame for her fleeing. Reaching across to his face, she put her hand on his cheek and stroked his scraggily beard.

"What happened, Elias?"

"I don't know," he croaked, trying to control the tremor in his tone.

"Why did you return? I thought you wanted to leave, to start fresh."

"I don't know." His chest rose up and down, his breathing ragged.

She touched the rough facial hair, entangling her fingers in its coarseness. She leaned in close to his left ear and whispered, "Let me help you." She let go of his beard and held her hand out to him.

And without saying a word, he accepted her warm palm and allowed her to guide him inside the house, down the hallway and into the bathroom.

CHAPTER 26

A DELE ASKED ELIAS IF SHE COULD HELP him bathe. At first, Elias looked away shyly but when Adele went to the clawfoot tub and filled it with bubbles and warm water, Adele heard Elias strip off his dirty clothes. When she heard Elias shuffle his feet across the floor, she turned so that he could slip into the tub without Adele catching a glimpse of his naked body. She wished she had some allspice to soothe Elias' rough, suntanned skin but there was none in the house so instead, she poured the water slowly over his head, the dirt sliding away and disappearing in the soapsuds of the jasmine shampoo she had massaged into his scalp with the tenderness of a lover and the compassion of a caregiver. She didn't stop kneading her fingers even when he wept in shame at the state of his body, the filth that layered his skin. After she rinsed his hair, she got up from her knees and grabbed the scissors and a razor blade from the medicine cabinet. She knelt beside the old tub again. Bit by bit, strand by strand, the hairs fell in the bubbles until the handsome face she had laid eyes on years ago reappeared. "Better. Now I can see you," she said, smiling.

Elias raised his hands to his face, brushed his fingers across his clean-shaven cheeks. Sobs escaped his throat once more. He wiped his eyes, then nose. "I'm sorry I'm acting like a baby."

Adele interjected. "It's all right. It's like you're meeting a long-lost relative after a lengthy separation."

"Yes," he agreed, still sniffling.

With the bar of soap, she lathered the cloth in her hands, then dropped it on his back. She scrubbed his flesh in circular motions, starting with his back, shoulders, then chest. When she guided the rag to his groin, Elias stopped her, gently holding her wrist. He sadly looked down. His limp penis floated in the fading bubbles.

"It's okay, Elias," she reassured. "I've seen…" she stopped, leaned in close to his face and said in a sexy voice, "and felt a penis before."

"You naughty girl," he laughed.

At first she had thought he might say that small but forceful word her father had always used but he didn't. *Ayb* was nowhere on his beautiful, full lips.

Proceeding with the bath, she rubbed his penis, had almost hoped it would rise if only a little bit but it remained flaccid. Elias didn't look at her face, but kept his gaze straight ahead. She knew he wanted to cry by the tension around his mouth, but instead he bit his lip.

Adele moved the rag between his legs, the absence of his testicles made her eyes water but the steam of the bath hid her sympathy, something she was thankful for because he didn't deserve to see the pity she suddenly felt. After a few quick movements, she finished cleaning his thighs, calves, then feet.

"All done," she said.

Elias lifted his hands from the water and flicked some drops on her face.

She wiped her forehead with the rolled sleeve of her shirt. "What was that for?"

"It's your turn!" He rested his elbows on the edge of the tub and reached for Adele, playfully trying to pull her into the water.

"No, no," she squirmed free. "Well, this is the thanks I get for helping."

He frowned in a teasing way. "I suppose I should feel grateful."

"Yeah," she laughed.

"You've given me back my handsome, sexy looks." Strands of wet hair fell around his face.

"Now I wouldn't go that far."

He cupped some water in his hands and threw it at her, wetting her hair and neck.

"Oh, that's it! No more Ms. Nice Girl!" She lunged at him, ducked his head back in the bath, then let go quickly. As he rose out of the water, forgetting his earlier timidness, he burst into laughter along with Adele. Then there was silence. Elias sat back in the tub and wiped the wet strands of curls from Adele's face, brushing them behind her ears.

"How long are you planning to stay, Adele?"

"A month or two until my mother gets settled. My mother will spend part of the time here and in Ottawa. I'll be back for the summers."

"Tell me about your life in Toronto," he whispered.

"It's great. I'm an artist. Toronto has been good to me. I have a lot of friends. I have a lot of independence—my own apartment, my own routine, my own life."

He looked sad for a moment, then smiled. "I'm happy for you." He placed his right hand on the edge of the tub.

She rested her fingers on his. Sunlight entered the small bathroom, making the haze of steam rising from the tub a yellowish-orange shade. "What about you? You once mentioned moving to France to become an Arabic literature professor."

"You remember that?"

Adele nodded.

He removed his hand from Adele's and folded his arms on his chest. "That was a long time ago. I can't do it now."

"You can do whatever you want. Do you really want to move to France?"

"I don't know," he said in a quiet voice. "I don't know what I want anymore."

She softened the lines around her eyes, then raised her hand and dabbed at the sweat beads above Elias's lips. She then pressed her palm into his cheek, wiping the tears streaking down his face. And she remembered the man who had helped construct the beginning of a free, yet now connected, life from her family. She said determinedly, "I think you'd make a wonderful professor."

"I often think about it, you know. My thoughts always turn to France."

"Okay, then, tomorrow we'll start making a plan for you. I'm here for two months so by the time I board a plane back to Canada, you'll be off to Paris." Adele winked then handed Elias a towel before she slipped out the door and stared out the kitchen window at the distant mountains, the gold sky. She opened the front door and stepped outside. She smiled, remembering her mom's race up the mountains with her brother, and Adele began to run.

ACKNOWLEDGEMENTS

Warmest thanks to my extraordinary editor Luciana Ricciutelli, my amazing publicist Renée Knapp, the talented cover designer Val Fullard, and the rest of the wonderful team at Inanna Publications for believing in my work and guiding this book into publication. I also want to thank my agent Morty Mint for his support, wisdom, and faith in my writing. Special thanks to the Humber School for Writers and Karen Connelly who mentored me many years ago and offered invaluable advice as I wrote this story. Thanks to Joanna Reid for reading an earlier version of the manuscript and for her enthusiasm and support. I want to express my appreciation to Dr. Lamees Al Ethari, Terri Favro, Shilpi Somaya Gowda, Anita Kushwaha, Debra Martens, Dimitri Nasrallah, and Ian Thomas Shaw for generously reading the manuscript and providing great endorsements. My deepest gratitude and love to my friends and family for always encouraging me in my writing life. And, finally, to my dear readers, thank you for holding this book in your hands and for journeying into Adele's world. Your support means the world to me.

Excerpts of this novel, or earlier versions of them, have appeared in *Writers4Peace*; *Maple Tree Literary Supplement* and *Paragon*.

Photo: Nora Nesrallah Haggar

Sonia Saikaley was born and raised in Ottawa, Canada, to a large Lebanese family. The daughter of a shopkeeper, she had access to all the treats she wanted. Her first book, *The Lebanese Dishwasher*, co-won the 2012 Ken Klonsky Novella Contest. Her first collection of poetry, *Turkish Delight, Montreal Winter*, was published in 2012 and a second collection, *A Samurai's Pink House*, was published in 2017 by Inanna Publications. She is currently working on a novel called *Jasmine Season on Hamra Street*. A graduate of the Humber School for Writers, she lives in her hometown of Ottawa.